"ONE OF THE BRIGHTEST NEW WRITERS TO COME ALONG IN YEARS."
Roger Zelazny

"KUDOS TO LINDSKOLD."
Starlog

Praise for
JANE LINDSKOLD's
CHANGER
A Novel of the Athanor

"A smart, funny, well-detailed romp of an adventure story that still finds room to address some serious concerns—a fabulous Romance in the best, and old, sense of the word . . . Simply put, I loved this book."
Charles de Lint, *Fantasy & Science Fiction*

"Plenty of surprises . . . a delightful multi-cultural mix."
Locus

"In *Changer*, Lindskold imbues the modern world with rich mythic resonance. If you love the urban fantasy novels of Charles de Lint or Emma Bull, here's an unusual, magical, and thoroughly entertaining new book to add to your shelves."
Terri Windling, author and World Fantasy Award-winning editor

"Before I read *Changer*, I thought the fantasy field had run out of fresh, original, and eminently readable takes on the 'immortals among us' theme. I was wrong."
David Weber, author of the *Honor Harrington* series

Other Books by
Jane Lindskold

BROTHER TO DRAGONS, COMPANION TO OWLS
MARKS OF OUR BROTHERS
THE PIPES OF ORPHEUS
SMOKE AND MIRRORS
WHEN THE GODS ARE SILENT
CHANGER

With Roger Zelazny

DONNERJACK
LORD DEMON

JANE LINDSKOLD

Legends Walking

A NOVEL

OF THE

ATHANOR

This is a work of fiction. Names, characters, places, and incidents either are the product of the author's imagination or are used fictitiously. Any resemblance to actual events, locales, organizations, or persons, living or dead, is entirely coincidental and beyond the intent of either the author or the publisher.

AVON BOOKS, INC.
1350 Avenue of the Americas
New York, New York 10019

Cover art by Gregory Bridges
Published by arrangement with the author
Library of Congress Catalog Card Number: 99-94998
ISBN: 0-380-78850-0
www.avonbooks.com/eos

First Avon Eos Printing: December 1999

AVON EOS TRADEMARK REG. U.S. PAT. OFF. AND IN OTHER COUNTRIES, MARCA REGISTRADA, HECHO EN U.S.A.

Printed in the U.S.A.

WCD 10 9 8 7 6 5 4 3 2 1

As ever, for Jim

The more you love your children the more care you should take to neglect them occasionally. The web of affection can be drawn too tight.

—D. Sutten

Life has its own scent. Contrary to common belief, there is nothing light or floral about it. Rather, it is akin to the yeasty scent of rising dough or the earthy richness of freshly turned soil.

Catching this scent one morning upon the wind blowing from the Sandia Mountains of New Mexico, the Changer knows that the change he has been considering is upon him. Without further hesitation, he barks.

His sharp-voiced summons is answered by the emergence of his daughter from beneath the gnarled juniper where she has been drowsing. Twigs and dried juniper foliage cling to her fur. She yawns and shakes, emitting a jaw-creaking whine.

When she is alert, Changer begins walking, setting his course downhill, out of this patch of autumn sunshine, ultimately out of the mountains. His daughter follows him without question, partly from trust, partly because she lacks the vocabulary to ask anything as simple as "Where are we going, Dad?"

¤◘¤

The baby weeps, his little brown face twisted tight but his eyes wide open as if he seeks to make sense of a universe that hurts so very much. His infant skin is thickly marked with swollen pustules, dark red and running against cocoa-colored skin.

His mother, a young woman just out of college, cradles him in her hands, gently lowering him into a basin of water in the hope of bringing down his fever. The water is tepid, but it seems to bring some comfort. The baby stops crying. After a moment, his mother realizes that he has stopped breathing as well. She screams.

The dull slap of bare feet on an earthen floor answers her cries. A shadow darkens the door to a bedroom now become a death chamber. Beyond the shadow can be heard the murmur of many voices, gossiping, conjecturing, a few raised to wail, but the shadow does not speak.

It crosses the room and in the light from the partially curtained window resolves into a large woman, full-breasted and mature, but lovely as a ripe yam is lovely. She lifts the infant's body from where his mother's hands still cradle it within the cooling water.

"He has been taken by this illness," the older woman says, "as are so many others."

"Oh, Oya, how I hate the King of Heaven!" the young woman sobs.

"So do I, Aduke," Oya answers, studying the girl quizzically. "I think the time has come to make him answer."

¤◘¤

Chris Kristofer opens the front door of the hacienda at Pendragon Estates to find a tall, lean man standing in the sandstone entryway. The man's black hair is long and loose. He wears nothing but a pair of red-nylon gym shorts, this despite the fact that the overcast November day is anything but warm.

"I want to use the telephone," the man says in a deep, gravelly voice.

The last time Chris had seen this man he had lacked an eye, but now he has two, both the same yellow as those of the young reddish gold coyote bitch sitting on her haunches beside him. Catching Chris's glance her way, the coyote thumps her tail in greeting.

Clearing his throat, Chris says, "Come right this way, sir. You're the Changer, right?"

"Yes."

The Changer doesn't seem inclined to say more, but when Chris started this job a month and a half before, he had been given a short list of people who were to be assisted without question. The Changer had topped this list. So now Chris leads the Changer into an empty seminar room and indicates the telephone.

"Is that all, sir?"

"Get me Frank MacDonald's number."

Chris pulls an electronic organizer from his pocket and scribbles a number on the pad by the phone.

"And tell Arthur I'm here."

"Yes, sir."

"And don't call me 'sir.' "

Chris exits without another word, noting as he does so that the young coyote has happily settled down to chew on the corner of an expensive handwoven rug.

"Arthur?" Chris enters the King's office after a polite tap at the door. "You have a guest."

The athanor who is once again using the name Arthur Pendragon looks up wearily from his computer screen and glowers at the human standing in the doorway. Chris Kristofer is an Anglo of average height and average build. His brown hair is neither too long, nor too short. His hazel-green eyes behind large wire-rimmed glasses are intelligent. There is nothing distasteful about his appearance, except that he is not the person whom Arthur wishes was there.

"Yes? Does this person have an appointment?"

Chris knows perfectly well that the King resents him. However, he also knows that keeping this job is a matter of life or death for him. Literally. He schools his voice to patience and answers:

"It's the Changer, Arthur."

"Oh!" Arthur's blue eyes widen. He stands, smoothing his neat, reddish gold beard in a thoughtful gesture. In that attitude, he no longer looks like a slightly overweight desk jockey. He looks like the king he has been in many lifetimes. "Ask the Changer if he will come to me here."

Chris hesitates. "Shahrazad is with him, sir."

Arthur remembers the young coyote with a fondness that is tinged by memory of the destruction she can create.

"I see. The day is too chilly for us to sit in the courtyard. Ask the Changer to come to the kitchen. He'll be hungry after his journey. Shapeshifters always are."

"Yes, sir."

Another thought strikes Arthur.

"Is the Changer wearing anything?"

"Gym shorts."

Arthur sighs. Doubtless the shorts are stolen. The Changer not only has no respect for personal property, he doesn't really acknowledge its existence.

"Chris, there are clothes that should fit the Changer in one of the ground-floor guest rooms. Ask him if he wants them."

"Right."

When Chris has left, Arthur recalls that the last time the Changer arrived unannounced on his doorstep, all sorts of trouble had ensued—trouble that had nearly meant the end of Arthur's reign. The trouble hadn't been the Changer's fault, but Arthur has never completely discarded the primitive superstitions that he had imbibed along with his mother's milk in ancient Sumer.

"It can't possibly be that bad again," he says to the empty air. But leaving his office he raps his knuckles against his desk. The gesture is comparatively modern—having originated in ancient Rome.

"Touch wood," he mutters.

¤◘¤

First their reservations had been lost. Then the plane had a flat tire that necessitated an overnight layover at some obscure airfield until a new tire could be flown in. After that, they had paid a small fortune in bribes—"dash" the Nigerians called it—before they could clear Customs. Then they had paid even more money to be taken to a small hotel run by friends of Anson, only to be told that the manager and his wife had cleared out a week before, leaving no forwarding address.

Fresh from the United States, from not only civilization but also from the privileged life of a wealthy man, Eddie Zagano is having the most fun he has had in years. He'd forgotten how much fun it could be to be irresponsible, not to be at anyone's beck and call, not to have it matter when he arrived somewhere or when he left.

True, he'd fidgeted a bit at first, but his traveling companion, Anson A. Kridd, had laughed at him so hard that Eddie had fallen into a sulk. He'd let Anson deal with everything. Then, when after a day or so no catastrophe occurred, he realized that Anson *could* deal with everything. After that, he had relaxed and enjoyed the ride.

"Your soul is taking color from your face, eh?" Anson says some days after they arrive in Lagos. "Not so much hurry-hurry, lots more taking the day as it comes."

Eddie nods. "Ifa alone knows the destiny the unborn soul has chosen, not me. Prayer might change my life, but worrying won't."

His speech is in flawless Yoruban, spoken with the accent of a native of Lagos, but Eddie is no more Yoruban at heart than he is naturally dark brown of skin, hair, and eye. Both his mastery of the language and his new appearance come courtesy of Arthur's staff wizard, Ian Lovern. These sorcerous alterations enable Eddie to pass as a citizen of Nigeria, born to the Yoruba people, and a resident of Lagos. The false papers he cobbled together from his complicated data bank back in New Mexico complete the trick.

To conceal his ignorance of Lagos, Eddie's cover story is that he has been studying for the last ten years in the United States and has only just come home. Since Lagos is as large as New York City and not an intimate family compound, he could memorize enough details to maintain his deception.

Anson A. Kridd (also known as Anansi the Spider, and by many other names, not all of them complimentary) needs no such elaborate cover. In this life he is registered as Anson A. Kridd and possesses dual citizenship in Nigeria and the United States. For this trip, he has cropped off the long dreadlocks he had worn until recently and colored his English with a heavy local accent, but otherwise he remains as before: long, thin, and wiry with only a small potbelly despite his voracious appetite.

For Eddie, who only recognizes the perpetual five o'clock shadow in the face that looks out from his reflection, Anson's constancy is the buoy he holds on to as he launches into the uncharted chaos of Lagos.

"So, what's next, boss?" he asks, as they come out of a shop where Anson has been interrogating the barber.

"I want to find my friends who are missing," Anson says, "and I begin to think I know where to find them. All the gossip says that they received a message from their home city, Monamona, and went there."

"Without leaving a forwarding address?" Eddie asks, the organized American in him surfacing. "And knowing that you were coming?"

"They must have had a reason," Anson answers, but he frowns as he says this. "Fortunately, I, too, have business in Monamona."

"You do?" Eddie says, almost indignant. "This is the first I have heard of it!"

Anson grins. "So, maybe I forget to mention it, eh? No matter what good Arthur think, I have a job and earn my living by it. That job is what will take us to Monamona."

"Oil," Eddie says. "Right?"

"Oil," Anson answers. "Come. I ask some more questions. Then we see how best we get to Monamona. Maybe we kill two birds with one stone and eat from a full pot."

"Do you ever think about anything except eating?" Eddie laughs, watching as his friend tosses a few *kobo* to a market woman in exchange for a bag of thick *chinchin.*

"Oh, yes," Anson answers, passing Eddie a couple of the

sweet fried dough balls. "Sometimes I think how I can fix it so that others can eat, too."

¤◙¤

Over bowls of lamb stew liberally seasoned with green chile, the Changer tells Arthur his plans. "I'm taking Shahrazad to Frank MacDonald's place in Colorado. I want her socialized."

Arthur cocks an eyebrow. "I thought the entire reason you hauled her back into the mountains was that you *didn't* want her socialized."

The Changer almost smiles. "Yes. I've discovered that I was wrong. She has a much more companionable nature than mine, but I can't have her running around with other coyotes. Until she gets bigger, they'd hurt her while jockeying for position."

"I thought you considered such punishment part of the natural course of things," Arthur gibes.

This time the Changer does smile. "I do. For coyotes. Shahrazad is athanor. She needs to learn that there is more to getting along with others than being able to beat them up."

Arthur relents. "I wish that more of our number had learned that lesson early in life."

"Indeed."

Shahrazad whines and places her paws on the counter at which Arthur and the Changer are seated. Her father hits her soundly on the nose and, when she has dropped back to the floor, rewards her with a chunk of lamb.

"I see that you're not above a bit of parental brutalizing," Arthur observes.

"I *am* her father."

"Do you have plans on how you're going to get to the OTQ Ranch with a coyote passenger?"

"I am open to suggestions."

"Very good. I'll put one of my pet humans on it. Bill, I think. Chris is already too busy."

"How are they working out?"

"The humans?" Arthur sighs. "Well enough. I just wish I

didn't need to rely on them so exclusively. It's a bloody nuisance that both members of my staff have taken off just now."

"I thought this would be a good time for you to be without a large staff," the Changer observes. "There won't be another Review for almost five years. The humans seemed intelligent enough when I met them."

"They are." Arthur's tone is grudging. "But I am accustomed to having Eddie on call. Where he is in Nigeria with Anson, he's lucky if he can get out a letter, much less a phone call or e-mail."

"And Vera is still with my brother and Amphitrite?"

"That's right. Plans for Atlantis are proceeding apace, but I can't hope to have her back full-time for months, maybe even for years."

"But you can still make arrangements for me to travel to Frank's place?"

"That I can," Arthur promises. "That is simple compared to some of the other requests I've had recently. The day I can't play travel agent is the day I turn in my crown."

¤▣¤

Further inquiries after his missing friends turn up nothing, so Anson leads the way to a bus station. As they walk through the herd of vehicles parked every which way on the packed dirt, Eddie pulls Anson to one side.

"Spider," he begins, only to be stopped when Anson lays a finger to his lip.

"Hsst, not here, my friend," Anson cautions. "That's a powerful name in this country."

"Anson," Eddie begins again, drawing on some of his legendary patience, "we aren't riding in one of those, are we?"

"I was thinking that we do ride in one," Anson replies, a twinkle in his dark brown eyes.

"But they're not safe!" Eddie gestures toward a typical bush taxi, a Peugeot 504 designed to carry eight and already loaded with twelve men and women, assorted infants and small children, bundles and duffel bags, produce, and a nanny goat. A cage of chickens is being lashed to the roof, along with more bundles.

"That one runs," Anson grins, shrugging.

"That one must have been bought during the oil boom of the mid-sixties," Eddie declares, "and I doubt that it's had its oil changed every three thousand miles much less a tune-up. Look at the tires! They're more patch than tread!"

"Quietly, quietly, my friend," Anson cautions, drawing Eddie back to where the maligned vehicle's owner will not hear him. "Your English is good, but still the driver may understand you."

"Let him!" Eddie declares, but he lowers his voice. "Anson, I've let you handle most of our expenses since we've gotten here, and I know you've been spending the *naira* pretty freely. If you can't afford to hire a private car, I'm willing. Hell, I'll *buy* us a car."

"You are kind," Anson says, "but I think not. I wish to go to Monamona without drawing too much attention to ourselves. A personal car—or even a private hired vehicle—will make much gossip. People will remember us as visitors with money."

"So?" Eddie replies, still somewhat frantic at the idea of trusting himself to one of the bush taxis. "That should make finding your friends easier: 'Here's a rich man. He pay much *naira*, much dash.' "

"Has it made finding them easier so far?" Anson counters. "It has not. Indeed, I think that some few who might have answered my questions have not precisely because we appear wealthy."

Eddie grumbles, "And no one in Monamona knows that you're wealthy?"

"I do most of my business in Lagos," Anson says, "not Monamona. Besides I could have lost my money. Fortunes come and go quickly in Nigeria. There is no FDIC to insure banks, no Better Business Bureau to issue warnings, very little reliable insurance. Money come, money go. That's one reason why family ties are so strong. You help them when times are good; they help you when times are bad."

"Enough lecture!" Eddie pleads. "I surrender. If you want

me to ride in a bush taxi, I'll ride in a bush taxi. When do we leave?"

Anson pats his friend on the arm. "I see if we can get a driver to promise to wait for us in the morning. More business comes from Monamona to Lagos than from Lagos to Monamona. So the bus might not be so crowded, and the driver might take a reservation."

"Wonderful."

"Hey, you've known worse in your life," Anson says, the phrase almost a proverb among the athanor.

"I know."

"And I promise you protection of the finest type," Anson says, mock solemn.

"Oh?"

Anson points to a figurine secured to the dashboard of the nearest bush taxi, waving his fingers to indicate the other vehicles, many of which bear some version of the same figure.

"What's that?" Eddie says, giving the figure—a powerfully built, dark-skinned African man—a closer look. "The African version of a plastic Jesus?"

"Oh, no, my friend," Anson assures him. "Much better than that."

"Tell me."

"It is a plastic Ogun—the Yoruban god of war and iron. In these modern days he has become the patron of lorry drivers as well. Don't you feel more safe?"

"Ogun!" Eddie swears. "Dakar Agadez. He still has worshipers here?"

"Oh, yes. The traditional religion is not quite gone. Many who call themselves Christian or Moslem become traditionalists in the bush—or when they need extra protection against witches and other dangers."

"Ogun."

"Yes. We travel under his protection."

"For whatever good that is," Eddie says, thinking of the athanor he had last seen drunk and brawling with his longtime rival.

"For whatever good," Anson agrees. He lowers his voice

to a whisper and places his lips near Eddie's ear. "And I share a secret with you."

"Yes?"

"I told you I had business?"

"Yes."

"Dakar is one of those with whom we do business." Anson straightens, pleased with himself. "So certainly we will arrive in Monamona safely."

Bill Irish—tall, slim, coffee-dark from his Jamaican father, lightened with cream by his American mother—taps his computer keyboard:

>> **Wanderer:** Arthur has a job for you. Transport of two, one vaguely illegal and somewhat messy. Contact Pendragon Productions, my address or phone. Bill.

Running his hands over his head, he tugs the end of his short ponytail to punctuate his reread, then sends the message.

"That should do it," he says to Chris. "The Wanderer makes his living moving questionable cargo. He sure did a good job transporting Lovern and his gear to the new academy."

Chris swivels around his desk chair, reads the message, and nods. "And getting Swansdown there when she flew in from Alaska. You know, I hadn't realized that transporting a coyote would be such a nuisance. It's a shame she can't shapeshift like her father."

"Or that her father won't drive himself," Bill adds.

"Would you really want him to?" Chris challenges.

Bill considers the feral ancient who, once more in the shape of a grey male coyote, is sleeping in the hacienda's central courtyard.

"No. Not really. He's spooky."

"Yeah."

"And he'd probably speed."

"I wonder if he can even drive," Chris says.

"He has a driver's license."

"Big deal. Arthur has a birth certificate stating that he was born in England about forty years ago. And Eddie—who was an Anglo when we met him—is now darker than you are and apparently African by birth."

Bill shivers slightly. "These athanor take a lot of getting used to . . ."

The ringing phone interrupts him. He reaches over and answers it.

"Pendragon Productions, Bill Irish speaking."

"Bill?" The voice on the other end is unfamiliar. "This is the Wanderer."

Bill sits up straight, his feet, which he had been about to park on the desk, hitting the floor with a thump.

"Wanderer?"

"That's right."

"We must have a bad connection," he hazards. "I didn't recognize your voice."

"Oh. Right."

A clicking sound, rather like a fingernail tapping something hard and plastic, follows, then the Wanderer speaks again.

"Is that better?"

Bill frowns. "Yes. I wonder what caused that?"

"Don't worry about it. What's the job?"

"The Changer and his daughter want to go out to Frank MacDonald's ranch."

"When?"

"Soon as you can leave."

"Anyone after them?"

"Not that I've heard. Of course, the Changer isn't exactly the type to volunteer information."

"No. Never has been. I'll charge double what I did for moving Lovern's gear. Half in favors, half in cash."

"That's quite a bit."

"I doubt that Shahrazad's exactly house-trained, and I live in my van. I want to be paid up front for the cleanup I'm going to have to do."

Bill, thinking of what he has seen since the pair's arrival, says, "I think Shahrazad's better behaved than she was at the

Review, but when you put it that way I don't think Arthur will quibble about the price."

"I'm up at the hot springs in Ojo Caliente," the Wanderer says. "If this isn't a rush job, I'll be there tomorrow morning. If there is, I can be there in about two and a half hours."

"I don't think waiting until tomorrow will be a problem."

"Great. See you in the morning."

"Thanks."

Bill hangs up the phone. "The Wanderer says he'll be here in the morning."

"I'll tell Arthur," Chris says. "I have some papers I need him to sign." He pauses in the doorway. "What was that fuss about at the beginning of the call?"

Frowning, Bill looks up at his friend. "The connection seemed perfectly clear, but at the beginning of the call I . . . you'll think I'm crazy . . . but I could have sworn that I was talking to a woman."

Ay, now I am in Arden: the more fool I; when I was at home, I was in a better place: but travellers must be content.

—SHAKESPEARE

"THE DRIVER," ANSON SAYS TO EDDIE, AS THE TWO MEN depart the bush taxi in Monamona and watch it speed off, throwing up clouds of dust in its wake, "charged three times the going rate, and said that he refused to stop here for longer than the time it would take to drop us off."

His announcement, even spoken as it had been in the calmest, most thoughtful of tones, destroys the feeling of contentment that had been clinging to Eddie since their departure from Lagos.

Despite his earlier dread, Eddie had enjoyed the trip north and west from Lagos. The Peugeot 504 had not been full. The only other passengers had been two men who had sat toward the front and chatted with the driver. This arrangement had left Anson and Eddie with five seats for themselves and their luggage, an unprecedented luxury that Eddie had enjoyed without question, choosing to believe that either Anson had successfully bribed the driver or that they were simply ahead of even the early-morning travelers.

Now, as he studies Anson's expression, all memories of the more pleasant aspects of the day's journey vanish, to be replaced by an unfocused but no less intense sensation of dread.

"The driver didn't want to stop here?" Eddie asks. "Did he say why?"

"He say there a great trouble in Monamona," Anson says, still calm. "That he don't want to stay too long."

"And you didn't think to mention this to me?" Eddie's tone is colder than he had intended.

"What could you do about it?" Anson says reasonably. "I couldn't do anything—what could you do? So I think I not worry you, let you enjoy the scenery, tell you what is what when we get here."

"Maybe I would have wanted to stay in Lagos."

"Alone? While I go into trouble?" Anson chuckles warmly. "I no think that, my friend."

Eddie frowns. "I would have liked to make my own choice."

"Okay. I give you the choice. You want to go to Lagos or you want to stay here and help me find my friends?" Anson shakes a long thin finger at him. "Remember, whatever trouble is here, I may end up in the middle of it. So, what do you do?"

For a moment, Eddie feels a surge of raw anger. Then he begins to laugh, realizing that Anson has just explained how he had concluded that Eddie would not leave his friend to venture on alone. When his laughter stills, Eddie says:

"I'll stay with you, Anson, but"—and Eddie shakes his finger in deliberate mimicry—"next time you no leave me in the dark. You tell me what I need to know, and I'll decide whether or not to worry."

"Ah, okay," Anson says, slightly aggrieved. "I was just trying to spare you."

"If you don't promise," Eddie says, "I'll never stop worrying."

"Eh?" For once, Anson looks confused.

"Yeah, if you don't promise to fill me in every step along the way, I'll be worrying the whole time about what you're not telling me."

A smile splits Anson's face, white teeth against dark skin.

"You have me," he says, laughing, "and my promise. Now, come, we go into the city and ask some questions."

¤◙¤

Chris has only just taken off his coat when he is summoned from his office by the sharp rapping of the front-door knocker.

There are times, he muses as he hurries down the hallway toward the cathedral-ceilinged entry foyer, that he might have been smarter to move into the hacienda as Arthur had suggested when he'd taken this job.

However, the ruler of the athanor is too demanding a boss. Chris knows that if he had been in residence, he would be expected to be on call twenty-four hours a day—much as his predecessor, Eddie Zagano had been. He isn't ready to surrender his autonomy to that extent. Neither, apparently, is Eddie.

Undoing the deceptively simple lock on the front door, Chris pulls it open as the knocking starts a second time.

"I'm here!" he says, a touch testily. "Hold your . . . !"

He stops in mid-phrase, for the person standing on the sandstone stoop is not the Wanderer, as he had expected, but a rather plain Anglo woman. Her dull black hair is cut short: blunt bangs over dark brows and darker eyes. Blue jeans, work boots, and quilted denim jacket do nothing for a figure that might politely be termed "average." Her button nose is cute, though, and her smile both witty and sly.

"Good morning, ma'am," Chris says, hoping that politeness will cover for his initial rudeness. "May I help you?"

"I'm here to get the Changer," the woman says in a pleasant, melodic voice. "I said I'd be here early this morning. Is he ready?"

Chris swallows his initial incredulity, remembering what Bill had said after yesterday's phone call, remembering, too, some of the things he has learned about the athanor since taking this job. He steps back and motions the woman inside.

"I just got here myself," he says apologetically, "and haven't had a chance to check who is where. Would you like to wait or come along to the kitchen for some breakfast?"

"I'll take breakfast," the woman says, shrugging out of her jacket, revealing a green-and-black flannel shirt underneath. "Do you know if Arthur's awake yet?"

"He should be," Chris says, taking her jacket and hanging it in a hall closet. "He may even be in the kitchen."

As he turns to lead the way, Chris is halted by a firm but gentle pat on his shoulder. Surprised, he looks back and finds the woman smiling up at him.

"Good recovery, Chris," she says. "Very good. Keep it up and you may convince even Arthur that there's some use for humans." She chuckles, and it's a warm, musical sound. "That's something many of us have been trying to tell him for a long, long time."

Later that morning, when the Wanderer is in conference with Arthur and the Changer, Chris tells Bill about his early-morning encounter.

"It's a good thing you told me about that phone call," he says, "or I might have made a complete ass of myself. I wonder if he—I mean 'she'—pulled the appearance switch just to jerk my chain?"

"Who knows?" Bill says. "I'm only sorry that class made me miss the show."

"Show!" Chris snorts. "I'd like to know if you would have done any better. No one bothered to tell me that the Wanderer is a cross-dresser!"

"I checked his/her file," Bill says. "The Wanderer—or the Vagrant as he/she is commonly known—is listed as a limited-ability shapeshifter—not a transvestite."

"Still," Chris grumps, "someone could have told us."

"I suspect that getting surprised is going to be par for the course for this job." Bill grins. "Remember how we both felt when we learned that 'Rob' Trapper was really 'Rebecca'—and a sasquatch to boot?"

"Stunned," Chris says, remembering and smiling despite his pique, "scared, and positive we didn't want to show any of it. I'll never forget."

"At least the Wanderer is one of the athanor who likes humans," Bill continues. "The ones I'm afraid of are those who think we're spies just waiting for our chance to reveal their big secret to the world."

Chris rises and paces; halting, he strikes a mock-solemn, stagy pose, miming as if reading from a sheaf of notes.

" 'Immortals Among Us,' " he pronounces in the tones of a television news anchor. " 'Myths and Monsters Real! Film at Eleven.' Damn it, Bill. We wouldn't live twenty-four hours if we told, no matter what kind of insurance we tried to take out."

"But the important thing is," Bill reminds him, "that we don't want to tell. Right?"

"Right," Chris says, slumping back in his chair. He wonders at the lack of conviction in his own voice.

¤◘¤

"Witches! I say that witches brought the illness that killed my baby!" weeps Aduke, still half-mad with grief and rage. Her infant had been buried that morning, wrapped in a cotton shroud dotted in red, black, and white. A deep cut had been made on the lobe of his right ear. "That baby wanted to live. He was no *àbikú*, longing for the other side!"

Oya, knowing that the mutilation of a corpse already ravaged by disease had been the last straw for the young mother, gathers the girl in her arms and hugs her to her ample breast, crooning as she does so.

"Easy, easy, little mother. We on the earth do not know what fate the soul chooses before birth, only Olodumare knows this, and he tells only Ifa. When you are stronger, we will go to the *babalawo* and have him cast the palm nuts for you. Then you will know how to name your next son."

Aduke sniffles something incoherent and Oya continues:

"Don't blame the old mothers for marking the boy before he was returned to the earth. They did it for love of you and love of him. If your next son is born with the same mark, then you will be warned and know to take precautions against those companions from the other side who try to lure him back to them."

Aduke raises her head. Her pretty face is smeared with tears, but she is no longer crying.

"I understand, Oya," she says meekly.

Oya is an odd woman. When first met, she introduces herself as Oya, adding no family name nor praise name. That the name she gives is that of one of the old Yoruban goddesses is quite interesting. That she gives the name not as part of the *àbíso* name given by her family, as would be common enough, but as if it is her own name is fascinating.

This adoption of a goddess's name would be impertinent except that the name fits Oya so very well. Some of the old people mutter that this woman who calls herself Oya is the goddess come among them in these bad times. No one, not even the chiefs or diviners (who between them claim to know the answer to every mystery) contradict this.

In this moment of intimacy, Aduke almost asks Oya who she is and where she lived before she came to Monamona a month or so before. The words are on her lips, but they shrivel into silence as she meets the older woman's knowing eyes. Instead she says:

"Oya, when can I consult the *babalawo*?"

"Not today," Oya says firmly. "We will wait until you are a little farther from death."

"But if there are witches!" Aduke protests.

"Shame, shame!" Oya tuts. "And you educated at the best schools and even the university in Ibadan. What would your professors and white friends think if they heard you talking about witches?"

"They might laugh," Aduke says defiantly, "but they have not had their baby taken by a disease that is supposed to be dead. They have not seen what walks the streets of Monamona or how we are bound into ourselves by a conspiracy of silence."

Oya chuckles softly, not in mockery, but a warm sound, like the clucking of a sitting hen.

"I forgot, little one, that you are not only an educated woman, you are the child born after twins. The gods have given you power and, it seems, they have given you wisdom as well. Very well, Aduke Idowu, we will go to the *babalawo* soon and inquire after witches and other such dangers."

"I am ready now," Aduke says, surging to her feet.

"Wait," Oya cautions. "If there are indeed witches attacking Monamona, then we must take precautions. Do you remember what you said when the boy had just died? You accused someone then, and not just a witch."

Aduke's eyes grow wide as she remembers. "I said that the King of Heaven had taken my son," she whispers.

"You are Idowu, the child born after twins," Oya says solemnly, "and Olodumare has let you chose a special destiny. Listen to yourself. There may indeed be witches in Monamona, but these may not be the usual witches. These witches may be in the service of a terrible god."

¤▣¤

Singing country western tunes, the Wanderer drives along the long, empty Colorado roads. They'd crossed onto Frank's land about ten minutes before, and she had phoned ahead to alert him of their imminent arrival.

She suspects that Saint Frank had not needed the warning. Jays and crows have been pacing the van, flapping alongside for a few yards, then wheeling off, cawing and screeching alarm to their fellows, one of whom will certainly relay the word to Frank. Old MacDonald owns miles of the surrounding territory in fact and still more (owned in theory by various government agencies) is under his unofficial administration.

The Changer rides beside her in the passenger seat, not complaining about her singing. She doesn't know if this is indifference or because he likes the sound. It's impossible to tell what goes on behind the impassive countenance he slips on when they're not actually chatting. The Wanderer has decided not to worry about it.

Shahrazad is asleep in a kennel cage in the back, the latter having been deemed necessary when she wouldn't obey her father's injunctions to stop dashing back and forth—sometimes jeopardizing the Wanderer's ability to see the road. The young coyote had cried for a while, then resigned herself to sleep.

"We're almost there," the Wanderer says. "Maybe ten minutes to the main gate, but we're already on OTQ Ranch land."

"What," the Changer asks, "does 'OTQ' stand for? I've always meant to ask."

The Wanderer chuckles. "Frank's official job is raising quarter horses. 'OTQ' stands for the 'Other Three Quarters'—as in, 'If they're a quarter horse, what's the other three quarters'?"

The Changer laughs, a thing that lights his otherwise neutral features and makes him handsome. The Wanderer feels a distinctly female awareness of him and wonders . . . Then she suppresses the desire. She's not at all certain she wants even a passing involvement with the Changer. Her own history is strange enough; she can't even begin to comprehend his.

She knows that some athanor believe that she herself (or more precisely her "his" side) is the source of the tales of the Wandering Jew. Others hint that she is the original for the story of Cain, sentenced by God to walk the Earth in permanent exile. The Wanderer neither acknowledges nor denies these rumors, taking pleasure from people's uncertainty.

Compared to the Changer, however, she is just a child. Some say that he is the oldest of them all. Certainly, she cannot remember a time when legends of the protean shapeshifter had not been told wherever the athanor gathered. The same uncertainty she delights in evoking in others keeps her from getting too comfortable with him.

She wonders if he knows. Something in the sardonic expression that flickers across his features as he turns to look at the jay now pacing them makes her think that he quite possibly does.

Eddie and Anson walk into downtown Monamona from the bus station. Superficially, the city is nearly as busy as Lagos. Goods are hawked in the street. Food, clothing, electronics, shoes, plastic jewelry, photographs: The offered wares are a strange mixture of useful items and cheap trash—much of it stamped "Made in Taiwan."

Quickly enough, though, they see that things are not all

right. Numerous shop fronts are closed and locked. Idlers cluster on street corners, not dancing or singing to pass the time, as had been common in Lagos, but absorbed in intense conversation that quiets as they pass and then picks up again.

They spend the first night in a cheap hotel where the owner inspects them carefully before agreeing to give them a room. Now, as the sun rises on another hot, dusty day, they breakfast in their rooms while Anson outlines their plan of action.

"The hotel keeper, he will keep our bags for a fee."

"And rob us blind," says Eddie, who had not liked the sly-looking fellow at all.

"No, he won't do that," Anson says. "I have locks and locks to protect them, eh?"

Eddie nods, understanding. "Where do we go from here? Do your friends have family here?"

"They do, but first I want to go to the local god's shrines. We will hear gossip there, and someone may have left me a message."

Monamona is not as large as Lagos or Ibadan, not so revered as Ife or Oyo, but it is large enough and revered enough to be home to all the many aspects of modern Yorubaland. So Eddie and Anson make their way through streets bordered by modern concrete high-rises, breathing air contaminated with automobile exhaust, hearing confused fragments of the latest musical sensations, all the while heading toward a place whose ultimate root is in the oldest traditions of the Yoruba people—the place where the traditional gods are enshrined within a grove of wind-battered baobab trees.

"The Yoruba people have always been city people," Anson explains, as they thread their way through the crowded streets. "Even before the British came, they preferred to live in cities and villages."

"I thought they were farmers," Eddie says.

"They were that, yes," Anson agrees, "but the farms were outside of the towns, in land cleared from the bush. Only hunters (who most people think are touched by strange influences) stay in the bush overnight."

"So the farmers went out to farm during the day and came home to their houses at night?"

"That's right." Anson has acquired some fried yam strips from a chop bar and is chewing on them complacently as they walk along. "Families lived in compounds—a man and his wives and children; sometimes several generations lived so. The precise arrangement depended on how wealthy the family was—and how dominating the father."

"Some things never change." Eddie chuckles, snagging a strip of yam for himself. He lacks the shapechanger's demanding metabolism, but the sweet, almost granular, yam's flesh is tasty.

"Too true," Anson agrees. "When the family had its own compound, each had its own shrines. Sometimes a town had shrines, too, especially for cults or secret societies. When the Yoruba moved into the modern cities, there had to be changes. A family shrine doesn't fit too well in an already crowded high-rise apartment.

"Moreover, many of the families are—a least in name—Christian or, more rarely among the Yoruba, Moslem. I think, too, there was a desire on the part of those who held to the traditional ways to make a public display, like that of their competitors. So here in Monamona, we have the Grove of the Gods."

"And you hope to learn something there?"

"Oh, yes. When trouble comes to call even atheists decide there is no harm done in burning some incense or making an offering, eh? Those more in touch with traditional ways will be holding *sàarà* for their friends."

Eddie nods. His magically installed vocabulary defines *sàarà* as an offering to the gods, a sort of shared feast. Beyond that, he is ignorant, but he trusts that if the time comes for him to take part in such a ritual banquet, someone will teach their poor Americanized guest how to mind his manners.

The Grove of the Gods is as busy as Anson had predicted, so Eddie's last trepidation, that they would be easily noticed strangers, fades away.

The Grove is divided into two sections. The outer area is an unfenced cluster of baobab trees under which old men drowse or play *ayo* or watch the little children who dash hither and yon.

A few are carving wood, and Eddie recalls that the Yoruba are considered masters of this art. In the old days they had made everything from intricately carved doors and house posts to ceremonial staffs and wands. Today their work is more likely to find its way into the hands of tourists, a sad commentary on both Nigeria's economic and spiritual health.

"Many Yoruba creation myths," Anson explains in a soft voice, "say that when Olodumare commanded Obatala to create the Earth, the first thing created was a baobab tree. Thus these trees have remained sacred. The center of a traditional town would often be beneath their shade. Here, then, is an attempt to recreate that village closeness. Public festivals, dances and such, would be held here."

He shrugs. "We, however, must go down that path."

Eddie looks to where Anson has gestured. A trail traveled by serious-looking men and women, many in their best clothes, leads through remarkably thick scrub growth. At its end, he can just glimpse an ornate iron fence.

"That's where the shrines are?" he asks.

"Yes." Anson nods. "Later I will come out here and listen to the elders' gossip. Most of what they say will be useless, but perhaps one *àgabàlagbà* will have more than dust between his ears."

In silence, they pass through the iron gates. Within, unlike the tree-shadowed area without, is a roughly circular open space. There are no formal temples here. Instead, intricately carved wooden statues, each at least twice life-size, are set about the perimeter. Before each is an altar.

Though Eddie had been born Enkidu the Wildman in ancient Sumer, had served in the courts of both pharaohs and medieval kings, he cannot escape the sensation that this place is old—though by strict count it is certainly younger than he is. Yet a persistent aura of antiquity, of primal desires and fears, clings to the shrines and to the rituals carried out among them.

Obediently following Anson and mimicking his gestures of respect, Eddie tries to identify to which deity each shrine is dedicated. He recognizes enough to feel certain that Anson is right. The Yoruban people of Monamona are turning to their gods for assistance in this time of crisis—whatever the crisis may be.

Osanyin, the Master of Herbalism, has obviously received many sacrifices, as has Olodumare, a deity often conflated by missionaries with the Christian god. Eddie grins to see that his fellow athanor, Ogun, has ample offerings spread before his ornate shrine.

Interestingly, Oya, a goddess his magically installed vocabulary/reference notes is associated with storm winds and the River Niger, has received as many appeals as either Osanyin or Olodumare. This seems odd, for although she is multifaceted Oya is not particularly associated with healing. Perhaps, he thinks, this is a turning to the mother figure in a time of crisis, or perhaps since this is the *harmattan* season, when the dry winds blow strong, the residents are playing it safe.

Eddie is still musing on this when he notices that Anson is squatted alongside a makeshift shrine so heavily covered with offerings that Eddie cannot tell to whom it is dedicated. Coming to join Anson, Eddie realizes that this shrine lacks the dominating statue. All it holds is a crude clay figure of a seated man sitting on a chunk of rough laterite. The figure's surface is embedded with cowrie shells so that his skin seems pitted.

Clearly this shrine was erected in some haste.

"I don't suppose that this one is for you," he teases Anson. "Isn't the shrine to Eshu a piece of laterite?"

"Household shrines, yes," Anson replies abstractedly. "Here Eshu has a shrine like those of the other gods."

His voice low, his tones measured and without any trace of his usual humor, Anson continues, "This shrine is to Shopona, the God of Smallpox. In modern times, Nigerian government has made his worship illegal. They feared that priests might actually be spreading the disease. You see, the priests of Shopona's cult would claim for themselves the goods of those who died of the disease."

"Nice job if you can get it," Eddie says.

Anson remains serious. "The government may have been

right to forbid worship of Shopona, but here is a shrine to the King of Heaven, decked with offerings."

Eddie frowns. "But I thought that smallpox had been wiped out. I'm certain that I read a World Health Organization report to that effect in the early 1980s."

"Apparently that is not so," Anson says, straightening, "for all that I have seen since we have come here indicates that smallpox is precisely what the people of Monamona fear."

¤▣¤

Long, thick brown lashes are the first thing anyone ever notices about Frank MacDonald; afterward one feels his calm, soulful presence, like that of a saint in a Renaissance painting. Average in height, weathered and muscled from a long life spent mostly out of doors, Frank stoops a little as if under the great burden he bears, though that burden is self-assumed and welcome.

At the main gate of the OTQ Ranch, Frank meets the van. He is dressed for riding, a Stetson atop his long brown hair. Waving to them, he leans down from the saddle of his black quarter-horse mare to unlatch the gate before waving them through.

"Hello, folks. Have a good drive?"

"Easy," the Wanderer answers as if she has not been driving for the better part of two days.

The Changer nods agreement. "Had to lock the pup up, though. She hasn't enjoyed the trip at all."

"Why not let her out?" Frank suggests, locking the gate. "She can't get off of my land from here. Once she runs herself tired, I'll have a couple of the jackalopes chase her up to the house."

"Good idea," the Changer says, "but she's grown quite a bit. Sure the jackalopes can keep up with her?"

"They can."

The Changer asks no further questions. What Frank MacDonald doesn't know about the capacities of animals—natural and otherwise—he has the wisdom to ask.

Once the young coyote is nothing more than a ruddy golden streak disappearing into the near distance, they drive up to the ranch house. It is set well back from the public roads, back even from those private roads a trespasser might venture upon. Built of local fieldstone and shingled with cedar, it blends into the landscape, as do the surprising number of outbuildings: the barns, sheds, coops, and stables that house a portion of the reason this isolated ranch exists.

The Other Three Quarters Ranch may be listed on the Colorado tax rolls as a horse farm raising fine blood quarter horses, but in reality the OTQ Ranch is a haven for what might be the least fortunate of all the athanor: the athanor animals. These, gifted with long life but with no greater intelligence than is the wont for their species (though many survivors learn cunning), are the least fit to adapt to an increasingly human-dominated world.

The OTQ Ranch is also a haven for some of the athanor who, though not strictly animals, closely resemble them. Among them are unicorns, jackalopes, griffins, hydra, and cockatrice: creatures who survive in a world where their kind has become myth.

These athanor for whom Frank has made himself guardian are the "other three quarters" for which the ranch is named.

When they arrive at the house, Frank dismounts, pulls off the blanket which had been the mare's only trappings, and sends her off with a grateful slap on her shoulder.

"I'll groom you later," he promises, then turns to his guests. "What did you think of her?"

"Pretty," the Wanderer says, sliding open the side door of the van to haul out the luggage. "Looks like good stock."

"Yeah," Frank says, a satisfied smile on his face. "You'd never recognize her for a unicorn, would you? She's wearing one of Lovern's new illusion disguises."

The Wanderer makes astonished noises; the Changer grins slightly.

"I knew what she was by her scent," he admits, "but no human would."

"But her scent isn't right?" Frank asks, concerned. "I wonder if I should complain to Lovern?"

"I wouldn't," the Changer says. "Humans don't use their sense of smell, and smelling like a unicorn may protect her from those predators who have learned to respect a unicorn's horn."

"True," Frank admits.

He leads them into a stone-flagged great room, offers them seats, and comes back bearing a tray laden with a variety of drinks and snacks.

"This is just to hold you until dinner," he says. "Changer, will you eat vegetarian?"

"Yes. Shahrazad shouldn't though. She's still growing."

"Don't worry. Either she can hunt, or I can feed her from the freezer."

"Let her hunt, then."

"You let hunting go on here?" the Wanderer asks, accepting a cup of hot cinnamon-laced apple juice and gathering up a handful of butter cookies. "You've never served me nothing but cheese and stuff like that. I thought it was policy."

"I did ask if you minded eating vegetarian the first time you came," Frank reminds her.

"Yeah."

"I must allow hunting," Frank continues. "Many of my charges must eat meat. However, I prefer not to do so, though I keep a store for the carnivores against lean times."

"Frozen?" the Wanderer asks.

"And some live," Frank admits. "Mostly rodents for those birds and reptiles who will only eat live food. I try not to talk with them, and, fortunately, your average white mouse doesn't have much to say."

"Speaking of rodents"—the Changer's body language is now subtly alert—"there were two rodents given into your custody last September. Are they still here?"

Frank's expression is guarded. "If they were, they would be as much my guests as you two are."

The Changer glances at the Wanderer, who nods. "We respect that," he says.

"They are here," Frank admits, "still a mouse and a ground squirrel. I keep them caged, in a locked room."

"Prisoners?" the Wanderer asks, almost sympathetic. Like many athanor, she has an antipathy to being kept enclosed.

"Not really," Frank explains. "These two are . . . incompetent, for lack of a better word. Now, after about six weeks in their current shapes, they are doing better."

"Incompetent?" the Wanderer asks.

"That's right." Frank sighs, poking the fire into a blaze as he continues to speak. "At first, they didn't know how to act as their shapes demanded—didn't know how to groom themselves or how to use their whiskers properly. Yet they didn't act like humans either."

"I have seen those shapeshifted by sorcery behave in a similar fashion," the Changer says, "but something of the human usually came through in the body language."

"This time the human didn't come through," Frank says. "The main thing motivating them seemed to be fear. They have adapted somewhat and, currently, there is little to separate them from the rest of the rodent kingdom."

"But you keep them locked up," the Wanderer prompts.

"Their passivity could be a trick," Frank answers. "Remember, not long ago, Louhi and the Head were among the two most potent sorcerers the athanor possessed."

The Wanderer raises a hand, remembering too well the pain of the Disharmony Dance.

"Hey, I'm not saying you should take any chances!"

"I don't plan to," Frank assures her.

"Have you spoken with them?" the Changer asks.

"I have tried, but even in the best of times a mouse or ground squirrel doesn't have much to say." Frank grins. "Talking to the animals is often highly overrated."

His grin fades. "Neither of them discusses anything but what one would expect from a somewhat retarded rodent. Food. Water. Shelter. They express fear or hunger, can identify a cat or a hawk. The female—Louhi the Mouse—does not appear to have come into heat. I haven't offered the Head a mate."

"Don't," the Wanderer advises. "He gave me the creeps."

"Yes," Frank admits as if it is a failing, "me too."

A silence falls as they remember a human head grown by sorcery to be a wizard's tool, a tool that had turned against its maker and had nearly destroyed them all.

"And has anyone heard from Sven?" the Changer asks into the silence. "He may have escaped that night."

Frank shrugs. "I haven't heard anything, and I'm certain he hasn't come here. My tenants would know. I trust them to miss nothing smaller than a mouse."

"Sven's a rat," the Wanderer says with a coughing laugh. "Literally, as well as figuratively."

"If he's even alive at all," Frank agrees. "The Cats of Egypt hunted on the night he escaped, not to mention several hawks, eagles, and owls, and a few human-form as well. There was great slaughter that night, but whether Sven was one of the rats slain down in the bosque is open to question."

"Has anyone tried scrying for him?" the Wanderer asks.

"I know that Lovern did," Frank replies. "Lil as well. No one has found him, but that doesn't mean he is dead. Sven has had wards in place for a long time. They would have been crafted to survive shapeshifts."

The Changer frowns. "Once, upon Ragnarokk's battlefield, I thought that I had slain Loki. I was wrong. He is one I will not believe dead until I see the body—and maybe not even then."

What though youth gave us love and roses,
Age still leaves us friends and wine.

—THOMAS MOORE

"SHAHRAZAD," SAYS FRANK MACDONALD, STANDING ON the patio outside of his house, "I want to introduce you to the two athanor who are going to be your chaperons during your stay here at the Other Three Quarters Ranch."

He speaks calmly, in English, and the young coyote seems to understand him perfectly. The Changer and the Wanderer, watching from the shelter of the kitchen, trade glances.

"If you're going to ask me if she understands him," the Changer says sotto voce, "I can't say. She is only my daughter. I do not know her limitations. That is one of the reasons why I have brought her here."

"Well, everyone does say that Frank can talk to the animals." The Wanderer giggles. "I guess the real question is do they listen?"

Frank motions forth two jackalope from the shelter of the brush, where they have been waiting. They resemble jackrabbits except for the antlers, similar to those of an antelope, that sprout from between their long ears. Larger than the cute "bunny rabbits" with which most humans are familiar, long-limbed and lean, they are colored (as Shahrazad herself is) to blend into the brownish golds that dominate the landscape, even in the height of summer.

"This," Frank continues, indicating the buck, "is Great Trimmer of the Tall Greens. This is his mate, Singer to the Moon of the Sweetest, Most Ancient of Songs."

The doe, whose antlers are slightly shorter than her mate's, rises on her hind legs to inspect Shahrazad. From the rapid wiggling of her nose, she seems to find the young coyote wanting. Looking up at Frank, she lets her ears drop limp.

Frank, swallowing a chuckle at a joke only he among the human-form understand, continues his introductions. "Since their names are rather long, they permit me to call them 'Hip' and 'Hop.' You may do likewise."

"I think," the Wanderer says softly to the Changer, "that she intends to call them 'Lunch' and 'Dinner.' "

Certainly Shahrazad's expression, her red tongue lapping out to lick her muzzle, is in keeping with the Wanderer's assessment.

"She has met jackalopes before," the Changer says, "during the Lustrum Review and again at the later September meeting. However, she has grown a great deal, even in the six weeks or so that have passed since the latter meeting, and she has become quite cocky. She may have forgotten what she learned of them before, or she may simply believe that she now exceeds her puppy limitations."

"And you're going to leave her to find out on her own."

"That is correct. Frank knows that I want her both tested and taught. If he chooses as his intermediaries two athanor herbivores, I shall trust his judgment."

The Wanderer turns to study him. "Are you leaving her here, then, like sending her off to summer camp?"

"Autumn into winter camp," the Changer corrects. "Not immediately, no, but once she adjusts somewhat I will take a few jaunts. She has always been able to depend on me. I want her to learn to rely on herself as well."

"Necessary," the Wanderer says, "although not always pleasant for the child."

"Nor for the parent," the Changer says. "I am closer to this little one than I have been to any of my get for a long, long time, but I do her no favors if I am overprotective."

"She is athanor," the Wanderer says. "The Harmony Dance proved that. Is she anything more? Did she inherit any of your other gifts?"

"I don't know," the Changer says, "and I don't really know how to find out. She may simply be an immortal coyote."

"That's not bad," the Wanderer says, thinking of the various athanor animals she has known over the years.

"No," the Changer agrees. "Sometimes, being a coyote is a very fine thing indeed."

Introductions completed, Shahrazad tears away from the house, daring her "chaperons" to keep up with her. She knows that, whatever she thinks of them, it would be bad manners to eat Frank's friends in front of him. In any case, there is so much that she wants to see and smell.

The evening before, when she had arrived, she had gotten the impression that all of this land was hers to roam. Today, with youthful enthusiasm, she plans not only to roam it, but to claim it as her domain. Here the air is cleaner than even in the forested reaches of the Sandia Mountains where she had lived with her father. There are no great roads, no low buzz of tires against asphalt, just space and grass and low trees and wonderful, heady smells.

Skipping the area immediately around the ranch house—it is far too lived in for her wild tastes—she lopes outward, away from the dirt road they had driven in on, away from the pastures where odd-smelling horses graze (raising their heads to study her as she runs by), out to grassy reaches that hint of rabbits and mice and other tasty things.

Shahrazad is so absorbed in her explorations that she doesn't notice the raven who soars above, joyriding on the winds. She forgets the jackalopes who trail her, stopping to graze when she slows. She forgets everything except the caution her father has schooled into her and her delight.

Mice, fat with grass seed, make a good lunch. Grasshoppers, slowing down as summer moves into winter, are easier to catch, and fun, too. Springing into the air from a standstill to come down on a single point, like a ballet dancer on her toe, wears her out after a while, and Shahrazad drowses on a sun-warmed rock. When she awakens, she doesn't realize that her nearly invisible guides have steered her back toward the house until she crosses her own trail.

By then, evening is falling and the lights of the ranch house and the memory of how warm a fire can be and how her father's strong fingers feel when they rub her neck and shoulders lure her back to domesticated ground. Unlike a wild coyote, human houses hold no special terror for her, especially one where her father is dwelling. Shahrazad spent much of her young life within the walls of Arthur Pendragon's hacienda. Houses can mean food and the pleasant drone of human conversation to lull her to sleep.

Her pace increases as she draws closer, picking up her feet in something like a trot, her head held high, her bushy tail in a line straight behind her. Hearing conversation from the outbuildings, she turns that way as the one voice that means home draws her in.

In a large horse barn, Frank MacDonald, assisted by the Changer and the Wanderer, is doling out grain and hay to the eager residents, mostly horses with a small intermingling of unicorns. This is Shahrazad's first close encounter with one of the creatures she had mentally tabled as "odd" horses, and she halts as a unicorn turns to face her.

As in most artistic depictions, the mare's coat is a pale, bluish white. She is small, hardly larger than a pony, with a build delicate enough to make the daintiest Arabian look chunky. Her slim legs end in feathered hocks over cloven hooves.

Although the unicorn's mane is a fall of snowy silk, her tail is like a lion's (or a donkey's), tufted only on the end. China blue eyes beneath a spiraling nacreous horn study the young coyote with unblinking interest, and the unicorn's beard waggles as she chews a stray bit of hay.

Frank, apparently, hears more than chewing, for he says aloud: "Yes, that's right, Pearl, this is the Changer's daughter, Shahrazad. Shahrazad, this is Pearl, the senior unicorn of our community here."

Shahrazad backs off a step, her bushy tail low, not at all certain that she likes this horse with a sword on its brow.

She knows what swords are: Eddie and Arthur have several, and she had watched them fence before her father had taken her back into the mountains. It does not seems fair that an herbivore should be so well equipped to defend itself. Her experience with deer has been limited (and jackalopes still do not count in her assessment), so perhaps her shock is greater than it might otherwise have been.

"Pearl," Frank says, returning to tearing flakes off the hay bales, "was born in France—or what is France today—about the time that the Romans were expanding that direction. It's a wonder she survived, but . . . Well, that's a story for another day."

Shahrazad sidles to where she can press herself against her father's legs, very carefully avoiding Pearl and her sword.

"I don't think"—the Changer chuckles—"that you've convinced Shahrazad that the unicorn is friendly."

"Good," Frank says. "She may just survive her visit here."

A muffled stamping on the sawdust-covered floor of an open box stall draws his attention.

"I'm sorry," Frank says, glancing over. "I have been remiss in my introductions. Shahrazad, the husky fellow glowering at me from the stall at the end of the row is Sun. He's Pearl's current favorite, originally from the Harz Mountains. Along with a dragon who was killed in the fourteenth century, he made life hell for the residents of the area. They called him the Golden Warrior, and kings offered enormous fortunes and lofty titles to the one who would capture him. Needless to say, no one ever managed the trick."

"Husky" seems an understatement when used to describe the unicorn who steps forth to acknowledge this introduction. Easily seventeen hands at the shoulder, deep-chested and muscular, the unicorn stallion seems wrought from molten gold. His coat is a glowing palomino, but where a palomino might have white points or a pale mane, Sun's mane and tail are the same brilliant gold. Even the horn that spirals from his forehead is metallic gold, and the irises of his golden eyes seem pupilless.

Shahrazad simultaneously backs away and clings more closely to the shelter of her father's legs, a course of action that bumps her into the horse in the stall behind her. Panicked, she crumples, rolling onto her back in a plea for mercy, even before her slitted eyes and flared nostrils bring her the information that this creature is just a horse. Then she collapses in embarrassment, certain that she can hear piping laughter from the jackalopes, who have followed her into the stable, and snickering from the cats lounging in the rafters.

Frank MacDonald's easy tones penetrate her shame: "The gelding at whose hooves you are reclining, my dear, is an old friend of the Wanderer's. In fact, the Wanderer is responsible for Tugger not accidentally giving away the athanor secret to his owners."

Shahrazad rolls onto her feet, trying (and failing) to give the impression that her wilderness-honed reflexes rather than fear had dictated her surrender before the dapple gray plow horse who now studies her with his mild brown eyes.

The Wanderer pours grain into a horse's feed bin and takes up the story: "Back in the mid–eighteen hundreds, I had a tinker's route up through New England. That was in a male incarnation, of course. In Massachusetts I always stayed with a particular farming family, descendants of a French mercenary and a local Boston girl. They'd done well for themselves, mostly through hard work and perseverance, but as the years went on they started giving more and more credit for their luck to the fact that one of their plow horses never had an off day.

"When some sickness wiped out a quarter of the horses in the area and ruined about half of the survivors, Tugger didn't even sniffle. The worst that ever happened to him was a bout with colic and—funny thing—he seemed to understand what had made him sick. I think it was an overindulgence in clover."

"Apples," Frank corrects in response to a "brr-hmm-pph" from Tugger.

"Apples, then. He stayed away from them afterward." The Wanderer leans back against a partition, her eyes half-closed as she remembers. "Tugger was smart, too. Learned how to draw a plow real steady, and would stop as soon as the blade hit something that had to be grubbed out by hand. Though he wasn't pretty—sorry fellow, but you're not a carriage horse—the Beaumonts got so fond of him they'd tie ribbons in his mane and have him pull the family to church on Sundays. Mistress Beaumont swore he liked the hymn singing.

"All this was fine at first. Tugger had been bought at a public market, and the fellow selling him had been a shady type who hadn't been too certain about his age. From his teeth, they'd figured him for a young horse, though. The thing was, Shahrazad, Tugger stayed a young horse—a horse in his prime. At first the family just regretted that he'd been cut so they couldn't breed him. After a while, when the children who had ridden him were starting to have children of their own, some folks started to comment on this horse that didn't age.

"The Beaumonts weren't stupid, and they were fond of Tugger. They stopped bringing him to church, saying that he was too old for that sort of work, but they couldn't bear not to use him for the spring plowing. By then he was so savvy he could plow twice what any other horse could do. And people noticed.

"Now, Massachusetts was past its days of witch burning—or so it claimed—but it was still pretty nervous about things that weren't normal. The Beaumonts were torn. On the one hand, they didn't like the way their neighbors were looking at them and shying from them when they met at the market or in church. They didn't like the whispers that followed them either, or the fact that no one was coming to court their two younger daughters, even though they were as pretty as any girls in the land.

"On the other hand, Tugger was their luck. They felt that deep down inside. They couldn't just sell him, and they certainly couldn't send him to the knacker, but it was beginning to look like they couldn't keep him either.

"Well, I'd been watching this situation develop, and I suspected that Tugger was like me, but that, being a horse, he didn't have the smarts to hide it."

This brings an indignant snort from the dapple grey gelding, which Frank refuses to translate.

The Wanderer grins and continues: "Now, I had a lucky charm that I'd bought from a wisewoman who lived in the region that's now Bangladesh. I knew it was lucky, but it was small enough to fit in a small box or be hidden somewhere in a house where no one could see it. Privately, I spoke with Madame Beaumont and offered to buy Tugger, saying that I'd throw in this lucky charm and that she should hide it away, but that she should let no one, not even her own children or husband, know of it until her death.

"We haggled for a while, then she haggled with her husband, but the long and short of it was that I bought Tugger. When we were out of that area, I rechristened him 'Bob,' dyed his coat a nice dull brown, taught him to walk with a bit of a limp so that no one would covet him. Under different names and different colors, Tugger pulled my wagons for the next fifty some years. We moved our route out of the Beaumonts' area soon after, as I was living out the usefulness of that identity. When cars started coming into use, I put Tugger out to pasture, first on my own nickel and later with Frank."

During the story, which she heard mostly as the comforting rise and fall of human voices, Shahrazad has forgotten her embarrassment. Sitting on her haunches, she scratches busily behind one ear, examining Tugger and trying to decide whether he is as interesting as the Wanderer and Frank apparently think. She decides to take the matter on advisement, wondering with a great deal more intensity what might be for dinner.

"What," says the Changer, his gravelly voice breaking the comfortable background music of equine chewing, "ever happened to the Beaumont family?"

"As I said, the charm I traded to Mistress Beaumont was a real one," the Wanderer says, "for the family had been good to me from her grandfather's day forward. When she died, she passed on the word of the charm to her son, who had taken over the farm by then. He passed on the information to his daughter, but she dismissed it as the ravings of fever. Still, her family did well as long as they stayed on the farm.

"When she was getting on, the decision was made to parcel up the land and share out the profits among her children. I lost touch with them around then. A few years later the house was torn down, and the charm lost. I was traveling at the time and didn't hear until it was too late to save it. A subdivision stands there now. I think they call it Lucky Acres, but I doubt that it's any luckier than any other piece of land."

The conversation shifts then to lucky pieces, protective enchantments, and the like. Shahrazad drifts behind the human-form as they finish feeding the OTQ residents, absorbing nothing much from their conversation, mostly hoping that they will not forget that a few mice are nowhere near enough dinner for a growing coyote.

Loverboy >> Hey! Hey! We have the word!:) Lil's agreed and Tommy'll be playing in our area. Who wants to go to the show?

Monk >> Sounds like a plan. Can we get a discount on tickets? Those arena shows aren't cheap!

Demetrios >> More importantly, will the disguise charms be ready in time? We've only seen sample tokens, and the one I was sent was flawed. Made me look like a goat—not a human!

Loverboy >> Who cares about disguises? We fared fair at the Fair! Let's sally forth in pants and boots. I want to go dancing with the toots!

Rebecca >> Georgios, when did you take up rhyme? Demetrios is right. We need to find out when the charms will be ready. I'll e-mail my aunt. She's down from Alaska and is helping Lovern at his Academy.

Monk >> OUR Academy. Lovern shouldn't be permitted to perceive the new Academy as his own personal kingdom. He is already arrogant enough, and his creation of the Head shows that he is not worthy of such power.

Rebecca >> Does it matter what we think about him?:(He's Arthur's wizard and in charge. Everyone's forgotten the Head. After what happened . . .

Demetrios >> I haven't forgotten it. Monk has a good point. Let's press to have our charms in time for Tommy's show. We lobbied back in September for the simple right to do things like go to a concert. Besides, if Lovern's busy filling our orders, he won't have time for more black-magical creations.

Monk >> I'll second your motion.

Demetrios >> I'll send Lovern a formal request that our charms be finished on time for the California show.

Loverboy >> I'll e-mail Tommy. He'll get us that discount and seats near the stage! It's gonna be great!:)

¤◙¤

Bill Irish, reviewing the latest from the theriomorphs chatroom, frowns and drums the desk top with the rubber eraser on the end of his pencil, a quirk that, unconsciously, he has picked up from Arthur.

The theriomorphs' site is no longer a strict secret, as it had been a few months before when the theriomorphs had been planning their rebellion against the policies of the Accord, but it is still shielded from all web-browsing programs, and the address is a closely guarded secret. Therefore, it remains used mainly by the theriomorphs, and they tend to forget that their discussions can be monitored.

Given that Rebecca Trapper had been his entry into the world of the athanor and was directly responsible for his current lucrative and fascinating job, Bill feels rather bad about spying on her, but that is Arthur's command.

Neither he nor Chris is to log in to the chatroom for discussion; instead they are to "ghost" the site, downloading the discussions every couple of days and reviewing the material for evidence of dissatisfaction or a return to rebellion.

Arthur may have come to understand the theriomorphs' point of view, even to sympathize with it somewhat, but that has not altered his awareness that of all the athanor the theriomorphs would find it easiest to reveal the presence of their kind to the world at large.

The works of a sorcerer might be dismissed as magicians' tricks *à la* Copperfield or Houdini, the claims of a human-form immortal as a scam, but if the sasquatches, fauns, or satyrs want to convince the human world that the weird and wonderful still exist, all they need do is walk down the street.

So Bill faithfully follows Arthur's orders and reviews the chatroom talk. Until today the discussions have been mild, even boring (once one dismisses the fact that the creatures typing away are real monsters). Today, though . . .

Bill thumps the pencil a few more times, saves his file, zaps a copy to Arthur's e-mail, and then goes to find his employer. He may be jumping the gun, but perhaps the King should know about this before it goes any farther.

¤◙¤

The bar is dark, though the day outside is sunny enough: sunny, hot, and windy. Inside, just enough light comes through the imperfectly sealed walls and open front door to give color to the decorations on the wall. These are posters mostly, advertisements for beers and wines. Smiling white people hold the long-stemmed glasses or elegantly shaped bottles, enjoying themselves on beaches or in elegantly furnished rooms the like of which most Nigerians will see only on television, if at all.

The bar's sole occupant, other than the bartender who stands in the doorway chatting with some of his cronies, grimaces at the posters and drinks a bit more of his warm beer. There had been a time when he didn't mind his beer warm, but fresh from America he does mind and resents being forced to sit here drinking warm beer. Perhaps palm wine would taste better. They had nothing like it in America, so his taste for it should not have been ruined.

"You!" he calls to the bartender, knowing that he is being rude but already too drunk to care. "Do you have palm wine?"

"I do," the man says affably, trading a soft-voiced comment with his buddies before coming inside and rooting around behind the bar. "You want a glass of it?"

"Do you have a bottle?"

"Of course."

"Give it to me."

The bartender insists on payment in advance, naming an outrageous amount in *naira*. The drinker knows that he is being overcharged but doesn't deign to barter, just slides the amount across the table, moving carefully to avoid knocking over the palisade of beer bottles that he has erected between himself and the world.

Seeing the money, the bartender hastens across the room, bringing the bottle of palm wine with him. He sets it down, then gathers up the money and stuffs it in his pocket.

"And pick up some of this mess."

"Right, boss." The bartender sounds respectful. He whistles, and a small boy dressed only in a pair of ragged trousers scampers in from the street.

"Pick these up and wash them," the bartender tells him, "and don't break any like last time."

"Yes, Pa." The boy starts gathering up the bottles.

"And when you're done, come to me." The bartender jingles the coins he has dropped into his pocket, and the boy's sullen expression vanishes.

"Yes, Pa!"

The customer hardly hears this conversation, is slightly more aware of the muted clinking of glass on glass as the boy carries away the bottles. He is busy studying the bottle of palm wine. It is clearly home-brewed—tapped would be a better description—for palm wine is tapped directly from the top of the tree.

In the old days it would have been stored in a keg or perhaps even a gourd. He should remember, but his head is too fuddled to be certain. All he is sure of is that palm wine did not always come packaged in a glass bottle that had once held something else—soda, he thinks or maybe grape wine—that it was not always closed with a makeshift stopper and sealed with candle wax.

He pours some of the palm wine into a glass that the bartender had brought him with his first beer and which he had ignored. Holding up the glass to one of the shafts of light that penetrate the slatted wooden walls of the bar, he studies the contents. The palm wine looks rather like dirty dishwater.

He sips. Maybe it's the beer numbing his tongue, but it tastes rather like dirty dishwater, too. Still, the warmth doesn't trouble him as it had with the beer. He continues drinking.

He had arrived in Monamona a few hours before and had

checked into the hotel under the name Ogunkeye, an *àbíso* name meaning roughly "The god Ogun has gathered honor." It was one of many cultic names referring to the god Ogun: Ogunlola, Ogunrinde, others. In the old days they had been given to the child by a wise man, a *babalawo*. Today, if they are used at all, they are most frequently used in the same fashion as a first name is among the Europeans.

The hotel keeper had expected him to supply a surname, and in a fit of insanity the man had told him "Hunter Smith." The fellow hadn't even blinked.

"Ogunkeye Hunter Smith," he had repeated, writing it down in his ledger.

Remembering, the man drinks more palm wine.

"I might as well have told him Dakar Agadez for all it meant to him," he mutters into the glass. "Dakar Agadez."

Caught in memories new and those awakened by the taste of the palm wine against his tongue, he does not notice that two men, one thin, one stocky, have walked up to his table. Then the stocky one speaks:

"I've been meaning to ask you," he says, pulling out a chair and seating himself without waiting for an invitation, "how you came to use that name. Aren't both Dakar and Agadez the names of cities in this area?"

"But farther north," the thin man agrees and Dakar/Ogunkeye vaguely recognizes him as Anson A. Kridd, otherwise known as trouble and nuisance in a sometimes human form.

He growls something, realizes he is inarticulate, and begins again, addressing the stocky man.

"I was drunk," he says with careful enunciation. "I had been in trouble, and I needed a name. Fast. There was a map on the wall. So . . ."

He shrugs, somewhat shamefaced, aware that he is drunk again but too tired to get belligerent about it.

"I was drunk," he repeats.

"It happens," the stocky man says in a tone of voice that adds wordlessly, *"Far too frequently where you are concerned, don't you agree?"*

Dakar props his head on his hand. "Who th' hell are you?"

Anson A. Kridd chuckles. "Don't you recognize our kinsman? You stayed at his house until just a few weeks ago."

Dakar recognizes that he is being baited and simply glowers. It is the same glower that stares out of the faces of all those wood or iron or plastic figures glued onto the dashboards of automobiles and lorries racing along the streets outside. It is the glower of a god who does not like being made angry. Anson relents and lowers his voice, although this is hardly necessary since they are alone.

"It is my good friend, Eddie Zagano. He has come here to see Nigeria and to get away from his too-demanding overlord."

"He's black!" Dakar says, stating the obvious.

"Lovern's work. It is still Eddie."

Eddie's new face shows white teeth in a weirdly familiar grin. "Shall I whisper secrets from your file? Tell you what you asked for the last time you called Pendragon Productions? I can prove I am who I say . . ."

Dakar stops him with an abrupt gesture, reflecting that several days in the company of that obnoxious trickster has done nothing good for Eddie's manners.

"I believe you." He is about to offer them some of the palm wine, notices that the bottle is nearly empty, and frowns. He draws breath to shout for the bartender when Anson places a hand on his arm.

"I have an idea. Let's go and find something to eat. We need to lay the groundwork for our business and . . ." It is his turn to frown. "Some new troubles have developed that I must tell you about. Can you walk?"

"Of course"—Dakar surges to his feet—"I can."

He staggers a few steps, then pitches forward. There is a dull thud as he hits the packed-earth floor.

Eddie kneels and rolls Dakar over, finding him completely passed out. He shakes his head as he looks up at Anson.

"He can walk all right, just not very well."

¤◘¤

It's like binary, Aduke thinks as she watches the *babalawo* casting palm nuts for his client.

She and Oya have come to the Grove of the Gods, seeking answers to her many questions. Now they stand in the doorway to one of the diviner's shelters, watching the *babalawo* cast the palm nuts for another client.

The casting falls into a rhythm like a dance, though the Ifa diviner remains seated. First, he tosses the sixteen nuts between his hands. The rhythm is rapid, rather like ceremonial drumbeats. Thus, this stage is often called "beating" the nuts.

When the nuts have been beaten sufficiently, the *babalawo* attempts to pick from his left hand as many nuts as he can with his right hand. If one nut remains, he makes two marks in the smoothed wood dust held in the divining tray set on the mat before him. If two remain, he makes one mark. Any other end result—three nuts or no nuts, for example—calls for a repeat.

Then the *babalawo* gathers up the nuts and begins again until sixteen sets of marks have been drawn in the dust. It is a long process, sometimes made shorter by use of an *opele*, or divining chain. Oya, however, had insisted that they go to this diviner.

"The *orisha*," she had said seriously, "are said to listen more carefully to the fall of the palm nuts, than to that of the chain."

Aduke, who was beginning to hear her college-educated self arguing with her traditional self, had not resisted.

There are 256 possible figures that can be arrived at in either form of Ifa divination. Each is tied to a series of stories; the wiser the diviner, the more stories he knows. All the stories are held within the diviner's memory—though some scholars like her brother-in-law Kehinde have tried to record them. In the stories are the answers to any problem a client may bring.

So the elders say.

Yes, it's rather like binary, Aduke thinks, remembering that lecture on computer languages. *Binary is 1 0 1 0, open shut open shut. So much has been said about the abacus as an ancestor of the adding machine. Has anyone ever noticed that the Yoruba invented the computer?*

She sighs. So often she is like this, a woman of two worlds. In one world she is what the Yoruba sometimes call *onikaba*, a gown wearer, a westernized woman. This is the

Aduke who has been to the university, speaks and reads not only English but French and some German, knows history and dates, theories and theorems.

In the other world she is little better than an *aróso*, a wrapper wearer, like the women in the market when she was a child. This Aduke trembles at the stories of *àbikú* and dreads that her baby might have been one, that she is doomed to bear the same frivolous ancestor spirit back to earth again and again, suffering each time it dies. The *aróso* her looks upon the *babalawo* and his palm nuts with respect and awe, hoping he can show her the path her personal ancestor spirit chose for her before her birth, hoping that he can guide her to discover which god demands a sacrifice or what actions she must take to ensure that her next baby is born willing to dwell on the earth with her.

When her mind is torn like this, Aduke feels more like a twin than a single person. Certainly Taiwo, her husband, the firstborn of twins, does not seem to feel any such confusion. His university education sits easily on him; his only mention of the traditional ways is to make jokes about the old customs. Kehinde, his identical twin, is interested in the things Taiwo is not. He is forever listening to the old people's stories. At first he wrote them down, now he tapes them. Perhaps that is one of the powers of twins—to split a single destiny between two people and so move into life without confusion of purpose.

And who, she thinks to herself in amusement, *are you now? Are you the* aróso *believing that twins are born with greater power than other people or the modern student of psychology analyzing the quirks of the human psyche?*

"I don't know," she says aloud, and her companion, the strange woman Oya, turns to look inquiringly at her.

"What don't you know, Aduke?" she asks pleasantly.

"I . . ." Aduke certainly doesn't want to tell her thoughts here, not where the *babalawo* might hear and be insulted. But then, if he truly is a "father of secret things," as his title implies, might he know anyhow, might her lying block his ability to help her?

The two sides of her mind pull her in separate directions like a woman tugged by two small children (*like,* her westernized mind whispers, *the charioteer in Plato's story, pulled by the two horses, the unruly black and the patient white*).

Which is the unruly side? Aduke wonders desperately. Her black side seems the more patient one, willing to accept what happens and be guided by tradition and custom. It is her "white" side, the one that has been exposed to the contradictions offered in her European-influenced education, that seems unruly.

Belatedly, she realizes that Oya is studying her, still waiting for an answer.

"I can't say," Aduke answers lamely, choosing neither to lie nor to enlighten.

She wonders if Oya might understand her confusion. The older woman seems completely comfortable with traditional ways, yet Aduke heard her speaking to a tourist a few days ago, speaking perfect English and using modern idiom. There is definitely more to her than first impressions would suggest.

"I am," Aduke says aloud, in complete honesty, "very tired. My breasts ache with milk I cannot give my child. My heart hurts, and I am sick of the heat and the wind."

"Don't ever feel sick from the wind," Oya says. "The wind is a woman's friend, the storm power that remained hers when Shango took the thunder and lightning. Sickness comes when the wind stops blowing in fresh air."

"It is an ill wind that blows no one good," Aduke quotes with a smile. Only after she says this does she remember the old Yoruban story. It had not been just any woman who had possessed the wind. It had been Oya.

The *babalawo* is ready for her now. He greets her, welcoming her to sit on the ground in front of him. She does so, placing a few *naira* on his mat as Oya has coached her. Even as she moves, she recites the appropriate greetings for a young woman to an older man, for a supplicant to a priest.

The Ifa diviner is an old man, and what hair he has is sparse and white. His costume is the traditional long robe of striped cotton, bright and clean except where it has trailed in the dirt. Clearly his family treasures him. Kehinde would treasure him, too, as a repository of nearly lost stories.

When the old man smiles at her, he shows more gum than

teeth. When he speaks, slight whistles and lisps slip out where the teeth should be, but Aduke understands him without too much difficulty.

"Daughter, what do you wish to know of yourself?"

"I had a baby," she says, and despite the fact that she has rehearsed these words over and over in her mind her voice cracks, "a son, still nursing. He was taken by"—she drops her voice low, leaning forward so only the father of secrets will hear her—"the Owner of Hot Water."

She feels hot water falling on her hands and bare arms and realizes that she is crying. Letting the tears fall, she continues:

"Baba, why did my son die? Do I have an enemy? Is he *àbikú*? What can I do to keep my future children, if I am blessed with them, alive and safe? Will I have other children?"

Aduke stops, realizing that she has departed from her prepared speech. She swallows hard. Somehow she is leaking all over: tears from her eyes, milk from her breasts, words from her mouth. Whatever happened to the Aduke she thought she knew?

Another question, she scolds herself. *Be silent and listen.*

The *babalawo* seems to know that she has collected herself.

"It is easiest," he says with a gentle smile, "if we begin with one question. The stories may give you the answers you need at once, but if not, you can ask more questions."

Aduke nods. "Yes, Baba."

"What is it you want to know?"

Aduke reiterates her first question. "Why did my son die? I know the simple answer. There was an illness, but . . ."

She stops in mid-word. That had been the *aróso* speaking, prating about simple answers and illnesses. In a moment she would have been talking about bacterial infections, vaccinations, disease vectors. Why ask if she knows the answers?

"I'm sorry, Baba," she says repentantly. "My question is 'Why did my son die?' "

The *babalawo* smiles and nods. Then he taps a bell against his divining tray to get the god Ifa's attention. When this is done, he scoops his sixteen palm nuts, polished with frequent use, from the carved wooden cup made specifically to hold them. This cup is particularly beautiful. A man on horseback surrounded by his entourage is carved around the stem of the cup. The cup itself is over their heads, like a ceremonial umbrella.

Normally, Aduke would have admired the artistry. Today, she is too nervous.

While he casts the nuts, Aduke feels her thoughts wandering again. She lets them go, feeling them blown on a wind she rides.

Ifa divination is not the only form of traditional divination she might have chosen. There are many simpler forms: casting four cowries or four kola nuts; water gazing, and trance utterances. Some Yoruba use forms of divination taken from other cultures, like Islamic sand cutting or even reading tarot cards or casting dice.

Initially, she had been drawn to a form of divination similar to the casting of the palm nuts. In this form, sixteen cowries are cast instead. The way they fall onto a wicker basket indicates the verses to be recited, just as in Ifa divination the combination of ones and twos indicates what verses are to be recited.

What had attracted Aduke to this form, even though it was less complex and thus (to her westernized way of seeing things) could offer her a less precise answer, was that in the divination with sixteen cowries, the diviner might be a woman. *Babalawo* are always men.

Aduke had thought that confiding her grief to a woman would be easier and that a woman might be more sympathetic and so give her better advice.

Oya had dissuaded her from this course of action.

"Cowrie divination is good in its place," she had said, "very good, but it has one weakness that Ifa divination does not. All Ifa diviners take their learning from Orunmila, who has been given this wisdom directly from his father Olodumare. Since it is Olodumare from whom the ancestral soul requests his new destiny, the chain of knowledge is simple and direct. Olodumare to Orunmila to the *babalawo*.

"However," she had continued, her voice growing soft yet

more firm, "the chain of knowledge is not so simple in the divination with sixteen cowries. Depending on which deity the diviner is consecrated to, the verses differ slightly."

Aduke had protested. "But one of the *orisha* to whom the sixteen cowries divination is given is your own namesake, Oya. Another is Shango, who is the patron of this city. Yet another is Eshu, for whom each household keeps a shrine. Perhaps the personal *orisha* will intercede more closely with his diviner, and so the knowledge will be more precise. Certainly Olodumare cannot be expected to keep track of every destiny he grants!"

Oya had frowned sternly at her. "You sound like a lawyer or a medieval Christian invoking a patron saint! Since you are so wise, tell me, who are all the *orisha* who employ the sixteen cowries in their personal cults?"

Aduke had blushed. "I can't remember precisely. There are several. The ones I already mentioned: Oshun, Yewa . . . There are others, but I would need to look them up in Kehinde's notes."

"I will spare you the trouble," Oya had said coldly. "In some areas the cult of Shopona uses the divination by sixteen cowries. Now tell me, wisewoman, who is the one *orisha* of the many, of the over four hundred named deities, who is the only one whose worship has been banned by the government?"

Aduke had not been brave enough to use the terrible god's name. "The King of the World."

"The same King of the World who left his mark on your baby?" Oya asks mockingly.

"The same." Aduke's answer was in a whisper.

"And will his worshipers announce their alliance publicly?"

"No, ma'am."

"No, that is so." Oya's tones had softened. "Now, young mother, let me tell you my thinking. If I had been raised and trained in the cult of an outlawed *orisha*, I would not want to waste all the training I had been given, especially since that training serves my patron as well as me. Remember the saying, 'A boy learns to divine in poverty. When he knows Ifa he becomes wealthy.' So this diviner has been poor, and is going to be denied the chance for wealth. Do you think he—or she—will think this fair?"

"No, ma'am."

"So what does this diviner trained in the cult of an outlawed deity do? Tell me. You are wise."

Aduke had straightened and given the answer she knew Oya expected. "Go out and do the work for which he—or she—has been trained but say that you are from another cult, perhaps that of Eshu, for Eshu is a difficult god for any mere human to predict."

"Good girl!" Oya had seemed genuinely pleased. "I hadn't thought of the Eshu connection. Good! Now do you see why I want you to go to a *babalawo*? One cowrie diviner might pass as belonging to the cult of another—the verses do not differ greatly, and how they do is mostly in emphasis. An Ifa diviner, however, must know many more verses, for there are many more combinations open to him. There a substitution could not be carried off."

"I understand, Oya, and I will do as you say." Aduke, warmed by Oya's praise of her insight forgives the older woman for making her feel like a child again. "But I had hoped to speak to a woman. This is a woman's matter."

Oya had reached and stroked Aduke's hair. "Is it, child? Then you haven't looked to your husband since the baby fell ill. Still, since you wish a woman to consult, I will accompany you. My patron *orisha* would request no less of me."

Afterward, Aduke has trouble remembering precisely what had happened. The *babalawo* had finished casting his palm nuts, checked his divining tray to see what series of stories were indicated, then had begun reciting them. Her role was to listen and then to select which story out of the many applied to her situation.

Before they had come, Aduke had been worried that none of the stories would apply or that all of them would seem to apply. However, in the dreamlike state in which she listens to the *babalawo* speak, these concerns recede. However, the *babalawo* seems reluctant to give her advice.

"This story is very old," he says in a quavering voice, "and even my teacher was uncertain of its meaning. Certainly, many *orisha* are involved in your troubles, daughter."

"Which *orisha*, Baba?"

"Many."

And that is all he will say. In a break with precedent, he accepts only a small offering for his labors. Usually, he would tell her what sacrifices to make based on the verse selected. His reward would be determined by the verse as well.

"In the next house of Ifa," he says, "is a *babalawo* who uses the divining chain. Since the chain is quick to talk, you can ask more questions and find out more precisely what you are to do."

Perhaps if Oya had not been with her, Aduke would have cut her losses then and gone home. Under the older woman's watchful gaze, she cannot retreat. As the new diviner's chain begins to fall (the sixteen shells along its length land either up or down, so indicating the appropriate verse), she falls again into a dreamlike state in which she asks her questions and hears the answers.

In the end, the news is not encouraging. Of the five types of good fortune, only one is indicated with any certainty: money. Defeat of enemies and long life are possibilities. However, the good fortune Aduke desires most of all—children—is not indicated.

"At this time, daughter," the *babalawo* comforts her. "Perhaps when your troubles are ended, then the *orisha* will grant you children. Certainly Olodumare would be a cruel god to send you children with such evils on the horizon."

He shudders as he says this, and Aduke can only agree. Of the five types of bad fortune, the *opele* had indicated that four loomed over her: loss, conflict, illness, and death. Aduke hasn't the heart to have him refine his predictions, to learn, for example, if the death predicted is her own or that of someone close to her.

The *babalawo* seems eager to have her leave—and no wonder. If his predictions are correct, Aduke and those closest to her are specially singled out for the attention of powerful evil forces. Aduke rises, says the appropriate things, and lets Oya lead her from the crowd.

"Did you hear?" she asks.

"I heard," Oya says grimly. "First we make the prescribed sacrifices. Then we start preparing for this conflict. At least the divination showed that you have luck in one way."

"What!" Aduke looks at her in astonishment. "Never has there been so much doom predicted for a single family! The *babalawo* was nearly as white as an Englishman before he finished speaking."

"Ifa is sometimes called a 'white god,' " Oya says reassuringly. "This may be a good sign."

"What is the luck we have?" Aduke demands.

Oya chuckles. "Nowhere in all his verses did the *babalawo* predict that want of money would be among the evils you would face. That's a good thing, because all those sacrifices we gotta make are going to cost a bundle!"

Allzu Klug ist dumm.
(Too clever is stupid.)
—GERMAN PROVERB

"ARTHUR'S SURE IN ONE HELL OF A MOOD TODAY," BILL comments to Chris as they settle into their office one morning. "I just brought him a summary of some stock information he'd asked me to look up, and he was barely civil. Didn't even thank me for the work I did upgrading his Internet access. I'm beginning to understand why Camelot fell."

Taking off his glasses, Chris rubs his eyes, musing that there are times when he wishes he drank coffee. He'd been up late the night before covering a concert at Tingly Coliseum for the *Journal*. No matter how well his new job pays, he doesn't want to cut his ties to his former employers—and when the editor had requested that he cover the show she'd added backstage passes and choice seats.

"It's nice to feel wanted," he says aloud. "Arthur has forgotten how to deal with employees rather than vassals."

"Guess so," Bill says. He scans his e-mail, looking for a message from Lovern. Nothing. "Have you heard from Lovern?"

"No. Just a list of supplies he wants purchased and driven out there. It's quite eclectic: two bolts of midnight blue satin, matching thread and the like, a case of sandalwood incense, six dozen pure beeswax candles, a whole list of different herbs, polymer clay, and forty pounds of small quartz crystals."

Chris grimaces. "Most of this I can find, but where the hell am I going to find forty pounds of quartz crystals? I could clean out every head shop and 'mystic' supply place in town without finding half that much—and they'll cost a bundle. Lovern forgets that his Academy doesn't have an unlimited budget."

"Try Southwest Minerals and Gems," Bill offers, "down by the Fairgrounds. They've got just about every type of rock there is—finished and unfinished. You know, you should ask Lovern why he wants the crystals. If he needs them to make jewelry or amulets, that same store sells both finished findings and molds."

"Thanks." Chris scribbles a note. "That reminds me. The Smith is arriving in a couple of days to brief Arthur on progress with Atlantis. Then he's going out to the Academy. If I get most of this stuff together before then, it can go out with him and save us a trip."

"Don't forget the groceries," Bill reminds.

"I won't. I've already got a trip to the wholesaler planned. They must love us. The Cats of Egypt refuse to eat cat food now that they're on the staff there. They want lightly grilled chicken and lamb or fresh fish."

"What did Frank feed them?"

"Cat food. Apparently, they earned their keep mousing around the grounds out at his ranch."

"I don't suppose he could talk with them for us?"

"We could try." Chris shrugs. "But they do have a point. Lovern insists on his perks. Why shouldn't they?"

"True."

They work for a few minutes, silent but for fingers on keyboards or the rustling of paper. Then Bill sighs.

"Here's another message from Rebecca Trapper asking if their request for disguise amulets has been approved. I guess I'd better nag Lovern again."

"Ask him about findings, would you?"

"Righto."

The intercom buzzes, then emits Arthur's irritable voice:

"Bill, come down to my office. My computer has frozen up."

"On my way."

Heading out the door, Bill turns and grins at Chris.

"I bet Eddie's sure glad that he's not here."

"Yeah. Bet he's really enjoying his vacation."

"Yeah."

The buzzer sounds again. Bill dashes out the door. Chris reflects for a moment, wondering what it must be like to be immortal, rich, and even magical. Probably solves most problems you don't create for yourself, he decides, and you have a long time to work out even those problems.

Then he turns back to his work.

¤◙¤

Those are faces in the rocks, Shahrazad is certain of that now. Not so much faces as *Eyes*. And not very friendly Eyes either—muddy grey undershot with a green light. She hunkers down in the long grass, wishing her father was with her, almost scared enough to wish that Hip and Hop weren't down in the vale below.

Almost. Although for a coyote only six months or so old Shahrazad has seen some tough times—starting with the murder of her mother and littermates when she was just a few weeks of age and progressing to her being kidnapped and held hostage when she was only slightly older, Shahrazad possesses a coyote's resilience in full. When the Eyes do nothing but stare at her, she decides that maybe staring is all that they *can* do. With that resolution her courage returns.

Raising herself from the grass, the young coyote circles to where she can take a scent on the wind. The Eyes move, their gaze following her. There is a glint of something the color of bone—fangs? She cannot tell for certain. Then the wind shifts and a scent, hot and rank, is momentarily carried to her.

There is something vaguely reptilian about the scent, something, too, of spoiled meat, poison, and musk. Instinctively, her hackles rise. This is something to fear, something to avoid, but she has learned this too late. The Eyes are emerging from their shadows and the whiteness beneath them *is* fangs: fangs set in flat, reptilian heads on long, snaky necks.

Shahrazad wheels to flee. Tail no longer in line with her body, but firmly clamped to her backside, she runs. There is a noise behind her, many feet crushing grass and small plants. When the wind shifts, the scent of the Eyes is mixed with that of broken sage.

The sun behind both her and her pursuers sends shadows to loom over her. These obliterate her own running shadow, an omen of doom.

Then comes a screeching cry, shrill, meant to paralyze the hearer. Had her running legs not possessed a mind of their own, Shahrazad might have frozen in place and fallen to her pursuer, but her legs are smarter than her brain. They have realized that the sound comes not from behind her, but from in front of her, in front and a little to the right.

Her legs adjust her course away from this new threat even as her strange not-quite-coyote soul takes hope. Hasn't she seen her father take the form of both owl and eagle? Certainly this is he, come to her rescue. Had she not been so terrified, she might have experienced a moment's pity for her pursuers, for the Changer is the most wonderful, most terrible, most terrifying creature in Shahrazad's universe.

She gallops on, down into the vale where she can see the antlers of Great Trimmer of the Tall Greens visible over the tall grass. Singer to the Moon is hurrying to intercept her, loping with the blinding speed Shahrazad had come to expect from these lepus kin.

A few breaths ago, Shahrazad would have been embarrassingly glad to see the jackalopes. Now, confident that her father has come to her aid, she moves toward them more as familiar points in the sea of grass rather than as allies. From behind her the screeching has sounded again, the cry of an eagle attacking, but louder than any eagle she has ever seen.

Changer.

He will rescue her, and when he has done so he will punish the jackalopes for not keeping her in better care.

(Conveniently, she forgets that she had deliberately left her chaperons behind).

She remembers hearing of her sire's wrath when the Changer had learned she had been stolen from Arthur's house. The memories are mixed in with images of a cruel woman, a fire-headed man, a Head that spoke though without a body, her father weakened and lacking an eye.

These are uncomfortable thoughts, and she pushes them away. The tromping of pursuing feet through the grass has stopped. The rank smell of the Eyes is fading. Neither Hip nor Hop show any undue fear, though both sit up on their haunches in what Shahrazad has learned is their guarded stance: ears high, antlers slightly forward.

When she has passed Hip and drawn abreast of Hop, Shahrazad slows, trotting in a circle to check what is behind her. There is no sign of the Eyes, but what she does see is so amazing that her tired legs give out beneath her and she plops down to check if her nose will confirm what her eyes have seen.

Eagle. Big eagle, just as her ears had led her to expect but . . .

Shahrazad whines slightly, vocalizing her puzzlement. Mixed in with the scent of the eagle is that of a cat. A big cat, like the pumas she and the Changer have occasionally crossed paths with in the wild. A big *female* puma. This, then, is not her father. The Changer takes many shapes, but all of them are male.

The creature with the eagle-puma scent flaps her wings in the direction whence the Eyes had come. Her posture is arrogant, as if daring the Eyes to return, but knowing that they will not have the courage. After holding this pose long enough that Shahrazad's racing heartbeat slows, the eagle-puma turns her attention to the trio watching from the rear.

Now Shahrazad gets a better look at her savior and, no longer assured that it is her father, she feels a new rush of fear. In the wild, one predator often steals prey from another, either after—or before—the kill. Perhaps the eagle-puma has chased away the Eyes for that purpose. Might not the jackalopes (mere herbivores that they are) be standing not in watchfulness, but paralyzed by the screeching cry as she herself had nearly been?

Shahrazad begins to back away, hoping the eagle-puma will be content with the two jackalopes, only to be halted by a soft, unmistakable titter of laughter from Hip and Hop. Shame mingles with residual fear, freezing her as terror alone could not. She sneaks a glance away from the eagle-puma toward her chaperons.

The jackalopes have relaxed their vigilance. Their ears are relaxed, their antlers no longer ready to impale. Hop is sitting, thumping behind one ear with a big foot, as casual as if they are all gathered before Frank MacDonald's fireplace listening to the chatter of the human-form.

Terror departs, leaving only embarrassment and hot indignation. It is smart to flee from something bigger than oneself, especially when that something smells like two of the greatest hunters on land or in air. Coyotes know when to run, know when to fight.

Shahrazad considers shaking the jackalopes' laughter from her ears and trotting off in a fit of pique. Curiosity keeps her in place, curiosity and a sense of gratitude toward the eagle-puma that had saved her—not to eat her—but for no other reason than that she wanted to do so.

Pretending not to hear the jackalopes' laughter, Shahrazad takes a few hesitant steps toward the eagle-puma; then, when she does not warn her off, Shahrazad brings herself within the creature's range.

The eagle-puma is neatly divided, golden brown eagle to the fore, golden brown puma to the rear. The only crossover between the sections is that the eagle head possesses small, alert ears, slightly rounded at the tips like those of a puma.

As Shahrazad approaches, the eagle-puma turns her head to keep the young coyote in sight, her scent and mien watchful but not threatening. When the coyote has had opportunity to make a full inspection, the eagle-puma flutters her wings and paces majestically away. She does not fly, but her stride is long. In a few moments, she is lost to sight within the sun-dappled boulders.

Shahrazad cocks her head, then barks a sharp note—a coyote friend-to-friend sound—after the vanished creature. Then she follows the jackalopes away from where the Eyes may still watch from the shadows of the rocks. Her fear is forgotten, replaced by something that mingles attraction and awe.

In the near distance, a large black raven launches into the air, riding air warmed by autumn sunlight, bright eyes watching from afar.

¤◙¤

"Witchy lady, I've got the coolest idea."

Tommy Thunderburst ambles into his manager's office. The newest, greatest sensation in the rock/pop world smells slightly of wine and weed, but his usual loose-limbed gait is unimpaired and his long golden brown hair is clean.

Lil Prima assesses his condition without conscious thought. She has been Tommy's companion for a long time now. Her role is a bit less than keeper, as she will not stop him when he begins to slide, yet a bit more than casual observer, as it is in her best interest to make the eventual crash as interesting as possible.

Now, as she tucks a lock of artificially blond hair behind one ear, the woman who claims responsibility for the fall of Adam notes that Tommy has gotten on top of the despair that had seized him when he had learned how Sven Trout and his cohorts had perverted one of his songs. No doubt the fact that Tommy has been actively preparing for his first concert tour of this incarnation has helped.

In between auditioning backup musicians and planning the choreography and costumes, Tommy has been immersed in new composition, churning out songs whose themes gradually shifted from despair and disillusionment to a resolution to face and—if necessary—obliterate those who oppose him.

Lil freely admits to herself that she has encouraged him in this course of action, even to the point of authorizing the recording of a new album although Tommy's debut album is still strong on the charts.

"What's your cool idea?" she asks in a voice that suggests, even without effort on her part, that the idea doubtless involves something intensely sexual.

Tommy shakes his lion's mane slightly. Centuries of hearing that voice have not immunized him to Lil's charm, but he has other, greater passions. In the grip of one of these—as he is now—he simply charges on.

"The new album. We'll call it *Pan.* That means 'all' in some language . . ."

"Greek," Lil says dryly. "Your natal tongue."

"Cool. I knew it was from somewhere. Anyhow, Pan means 'all' in Greek, but it means something you cook with in English, right?"

"So I've heard," says Lil, who has not cooked a meal for herself since the invention of servants, takeout, and microwaves.

"Right. Something that gets real hot." Tommy grins. He's getting ready to reveal his big surprise. "And it's also one of the old gods—the Great God Pan."

"I believe I met him," Lil answers. She had indeed met the athanor who then had been called Pan and had drained even his legendary goatish lust.

"Right. He's dead now."

"Shot by an enraged husband," Lil recalls.

"But there are others who look pretty much like he did—the fauns and satyrs."

"Lots of them are his descendants. He was prepotent, which is more than any of them can say, and he'd fuck anything that moved and a quite a few things that usually didn't."

"I want them," Tommy says.

"Slow down, lover. Who do you want?"

"I want the fauns and satyrs—at least some of them—to be in my stage show for the concert. It's a great idea. They've got music in their souls—they won't need much training—and no one will have seen anything like them."

"They certainly won't have," Lil murmurs, thinking of the satyrs' aggressively jutting phalli, of the infectious charm inherent in the fauns' dancing.

"Fauns and satyrs are the original party animals," Tommy continues happily. "We'll release *Pan* right before the first show so even the critics will get the connection. What do you think?"

Lil thinks of the fact that more and more single-act arena shows are failing to sell out, of her worry that even with her magical assistance Tommy will fail to be a sensation in this age of video. So much of his charisma doesn't translate electronically.

And she thinks of King Arthur and how he will react when he learns that his worst nightmare is about to come true.

"I love it," she purrs. "Let me get on it right away."

Tommy moves to her side, lifts her from her desk chair, and embraces her, lifting her right off her feet, as happy as a child who has been given a present.

"You love it?" he asks, disbelieving.

"I do," she answers. "The arrangements will be interesting . . . I can't wait to hear what Arthur will say."

Tommy smiles, innocent of the ramifications of his plan, caught up in the image of what an utterly fantastic concert this will be.

"Tell him he can have complimentary tickets," he says. "Ringside seats. He won't miss a moment of the show."

¤◙¤

The sacrifices and ceremonies have been completed and Aduke finds, somewhat to her surprise, that she feels better—more focused, more at peace.

Taiwo, her husband, had driven out from Lagos, where he is confidential assistant to some important businessman, to attend the events, but now he has departed again.

Kehinde, his twin, had also been present. Aduke wonders if anyone other than she had realized that the scholar had concealed a tape recorder in his pocket. He'd really been quite clever at changing the miniature cassettes, but she'd caught him at it.

She hadn't given him away. In their very different ways, both of the twins are fighting for the survival of modern Nigeria. Taiwo works toward its economic future. Kehinde preserves the foundation of the past. Besides, Taiwo would never have forgiven her. She knows without jealousy that her husband's twin is the single most important person in his life.

Now the apartment is comparatively quiet. Most of the women have gone to the market, taking with them the noisy brood of children. Aduke had remained behind in order to write some letters for her mother and to deal with some confusing official correspondence. That completed, she paces restlessly, pausing at the door to the bedroom that during the day changes from a nursery to Kehinde's study.

Within, her brother-in-law is busy transcribing one of his tapes, rewinding and replaying each section as he laboriously scribes not only the words, but the tonal marks without which so many Yoruban words would blend into each other. Easing the door open a crack, Aduke watches him, head bent over a yellow legal pad, pencil resting loosely against the web between thumb and forefinger as he listens to the tape, his lips moving as he sounds out a possible spelling for one of the *babalawo*'s archaic terms.

Someday he hopes to have a computer, but not only would purchase of even a primitive PC put a strain on the family's finances, the electric power in Monamona is unpredictable at best. Kehinde would need a computer with battery backup. He might as well wish for the moon.

A faint wind touches Aduke's cheek. Turning away from her watch post, she discovers that Oya has come in. Yetunde's year-old infant is strapped to the older woman's back, sound asleep, and her arms are full of bundles.

"Aduke, come and help me with these. Your sister asked me to bring them by so that she could stay in the market. Business is better today."

Aduke hastens to relieve Oya of her burden, gently closing the nursery door so that Kehinde will not be disturbed.

"My brother is writing," she explains. "He gets so little quiet time."

"Life is noisy," Oya says with a shrug. "If he cannot work with the noise, then he should learn."

"But the crying of the babies, the squabbles of the little children and the women." Aduke gestures vaguely to indicate the entire extended family that lives crowded into the apartment as they once would have lived in a more spacious compound. "He is preserving our history for future generations. It is important work."

"What is the future," Oya says sensibly, "if it isn't noisy babies and chattering women?"

"The future is something else," Aduke says, stowing away a package of crayfish and trying to find words to articulate the concept as she had learned it in the university. "It is something beyond individual people—the sum of promise of what is to come."

"Bosh!" Oya says gustily. "You've been speaking too much English. Remember, in the language of the Yoruba, the future is only separated from the past and the present by what you do with it. It is not some vague thing made up of nebulous people who must be humored or inspired. The ancestral soul is always reborn."

Aduke considers this as she continues putting the groceries away, folding up bags and wrappings to be used at another time.

Oya does have a point—at least about languages. In Yoruban, past and present are not as sharply delineated as they are in English or the other European languages she has learned. Literally, time *is* what you do with it, not what you say it is: "He put on a hat" rather than "He was wearing a hat."

She wonders where the past had been before the English had arrived to explain it to them. Had it existed at all, a thing unseen but solidly real—like the Himalayan Mountains or the Continental Divide—or was it more like etiquette and table manners, things belonging to each culture and real only within that culture?

Aduke frowns, shaking her head to banish such useless meditations.

"I have been wondering," she says, automatically starting preparations for dinner now that groceries have arrived, "if I should move back to Lagos to live with Taiwo."

"Why?" Oya asks. "I thought you didn't like Lagos. I thought you wanted to be here with your mother and sisters and their children."

"That was when," Aduke takes a deep breath, "I was raising a baby of my own. I didn't want my son to grow up with only his mother and father for family."

"And so, what has changed? Don't you want a child anymore?"

"I . . . don't know," Aduke says, knowing full well that she does want a baby, very much, but faithfully articulating the confusion that her *aróso* self has been raising within her.

Oya looks sympathetic. "Are you afraid of being hurt again? That you are indeed doomed to bear a child born to die? The sacrifices did not seem to indicate that such was your fate."

That would be the easy answer. Say "Yes, that is what I fear." Let warm, comforting, maternal Oya talk that fear away—because it is a real one.

Yet, that answer would not be completely honest, and now, in the rare moment when the only competition for her attention is the faint drone of Kehinde's recorder from behind the closed door, Aduke finds she wants to speak her thoughts.

"I was thinking that perhaps I am wasting my talents being a mother. Taiwo could use me at his side. I could be a great help to him."

"True." Oya looks at her sagely, even while adjusting the sleeping infant on her back and shifting coarse meal through a bit of screen to remove the grit and gravel. "You could. Are you unhappy with the role of mother?"

"I am not a mother!" Aduke says desperately. "My son is dead. I am just a . . ."

"Mother. These little ones"—Oya shrugs toward the baby on her back—"don't care whose womb bore them. They care about having a warm back to sleep against and arms to rock them and, yes, voices to scold them when they are out of line."

"Maybe."

"Hm." Oya chops up some peppers. "How many wives did your father have?"

Despite herself, Aduke is shocked. Hasn't Oya been an intimate of the household long enough to know that her father had been a superior person, so fully modern that he had believed in education for both men and women?

"One," she answers stiffly. "My father was a government official, not some bush chief."

"Sometimes," Oya says, ignoring Aduke's pique, "it seems

to me that everyone's father has been a government official. Nigeria has certainly had enough governments these last fifty years. That may explain it."

"What?" Aduke is confused.

"Why you don't understand that being a mother is more than wombing a child. You had only one mother yourself."

Aduke snorts, but Oya continues as if she hasn't heard.

"Listen to me, Aduke. If you stay here with your sisters, you will be a mother to all of these little ones, and when your next child is born he will have many mothers and many brothers and sisters. Isn't that why you came here when he was born?"

Aduke nods, realizing that beneath all her westernized talk of "support systems" and "extended family units" what she had really wanted—wanted so much that she had agreed to live apart from a beloved husband—was many mothers and many brothers and sisters for her little boy.

"A lot of good it did him," she mutters.

"Nonsense," Oya says briskly. "Now you are being obstinate. Your son had many to watch over him during his short life. If you had been in Lagos, he would have had you and maybe some nurses. That's all.

"As I see it, the worst thing about modern education is that it stops many good women from doing what they wish—just as the old ways stopped women from being other than wives and mothers. There is room for both ways. If you wish to raise babies, do so! Anyone can have a job. Only a woman can have a child."

"But can't any woman bear a child?" Aduke asks timidly.

"Can any?" Oya looks suddenly sad, then wields her chopper with even greater force. "Not everyone is so lucky. Fewer still are fortunate enough to have the gift of being good mothers."

"But I can read and write and program a computer," Aduke says, perversely playing devil's advocate against herself. "I can speak English as well as an Englishwoman and some French as well. I know geography and mathematics and science."

"So? Is there any reason a mother cannot do these things?"

"But should I do what any breeding animal can do when

I can do so much more? Don't I owe the nation use of my education?"

Oya shakes her head. "You are thinking like a silly girl, not like a woman who has borne a child and suffered his loss. Your education means that you have more to give your children—or to your nieces and nephews if you persist in splitting the family up into little parts. With your example, your sons and daughters will learn to read and write. They will learn hygiene and nutrition, and, when they are older, to understand why the jobs that men like Kehinde and Taiwo do are as important as driving a lorry or hunting in the bush."

Aduke laughs, knowing full well how glamorous a child would think either of the latter occupations.

"I shall take your advice under full consideration," she promises. She was about to say more when the door bursts open and her sister Yetunde runs in, a horde of weeping or shouting children surging in with her like foam on a wave.

"Lost! Lost! We are lost!" Yetunde wails dramatically. Before she had given her attention to marketing and raising children, Yetunde had been famed as a singer and performer. Clearly those days are filling her lungs now.

"What are you saying?" Aduke says, automatically gathering two of the weeping toddlers onto her knees and patting them quiet. "How are we lost?"

"The owner of this building," Yetunde continues, as dramatically as before, "he is speaking to our mother even now, but I have heard enough. News of what the *babalawo* said has come to his ears. He claims to have prayed over the matter at length but in the end he says that he can do no less out of thoughtfulness to his tenants, and so we are lost!"

Oya looks at Yetunde sharply, but her expression is free of the rising panic that Aduke feels claiming her.

"Speak clearly, you silly woman! What has the landlord said?"

"He says it is not for him alone, but that other tenants have come to him. That they will leave if he does not do it."

Oya raises her hand as if to slap Yetunde and the other woman hastens to clarify:

"He does not believe that the evil the *babalawo* has predicted will follow our family has been averted by the sacrifices. Neither, apparently, do our neighbors. Despite eating our food and drinking our beer and wine, they have threatened to move if we are not evicted."

"Oh." Aduke can't think of anything more intelligent to say.

"And no one else will take us in!" her sister continues. "They won't dare, for then *their* tenants will protest. We will sleep on the streets as the minions of the King of the World flutter through the darkness and breathe fever into our nostrils!"

From the back of the apartment, the nursery door flings open, hitting the wall with such force that the children fall silent as one.

"Can't anyone give me even a few hours of peace in which to write?" Kehinde shouts angrily. "What is going on here?"

Aduke replies with a calm that amazes even herself.

"It seems, brother, that we have been evicted."

The children begin to cry again. Bending to comfort one, Aduke takes a peculiar satisfaction in seeing that her educated and sophisticated brother-in-law looks like little more than a child himself.

It seems as though I had not drunk from the cup of wisdom but had fallen into it.
—SØREN KIERKEGAARD

SOBERING UP DAKAR AGADEZ PROVES TO BE MORE OF A job than Eddie and Anson had bargained for. The morning after they carried him from the bar, he awakens with such a hangover that Anson carefully measures out just enough palm wine to take the edge off Dakar's headache.

Later, when he and Eddie leave to talk with one of the street children Anson had paid to find news of his missing friends, Dakar locates the rest of the palm wine and drinks it. After that, they are careful not to leave any alcoholic beverages in the hotel room.

They thought they had taken all of Dakar's money, too, but apparently he had stashed a few *naira*. When Eddie and Anson return from tracking down the useless lead they find Dakar out cold, reefed about with beer bottles. After that, Eddie stays with him and Anson goes out alone.

Dakar is no great companion. At first he is nearly unconscious. When the hangover claims him, he huddles on one of the beds, his face to the wall, whining whenever even the slightest amount of light is shown. Eddie humors him, curtaining off the bed with a sheet and reading local newspapers near the window where a small amount of light penetrates the closed Venetian blinds.

What he reads is no great comfort. Apparently, some government official has declared a news blackout regarding the smallpox epidemic, but the evidence of its effects is there in the length of the obituary columns, notices of shop closings, and advertisements for patent medicines. However, disturbing as the news is, it is preferable to Dakar's company, especially when, after two days, he quits sulking and starts fuming.

Eyes ruddy as old coals gleam demoniacally against the deep blue-black of his skin when Dakar emerges from behind the makeshift curtain. His huge fists are clenched: massive bludgeons of meat and bone anchored at the end of arms muscled not from working out in a gym but from swinging a hammer in war or in peace. Naked except for a pair of khaki shorts badly in need of a wash and mend, Dakar looks like what many have called him, a god forged of black iron and polished with oil.

Folding his paper and leaning back in his chair, Eddie is glad that he and Anson had anticipated this reluctant resurrection and had taken steps to prevent Dakar's departure.

Dakar glowers at Eddie. "I'm going out."

"If you say so," Eddie says, a small teasing note lurking beneath his level tone.

"I am, and you're not going to stop me, little man."

Eddie is hardly a "little man" by most estimations. Although not strikingly tall, his natural build is thick and solid, almost blocky. Since the Yoruba are also a solidly built people on the whole, he had not needed to trade his preferred shape when designing his disguise. Moreover, Eddie has been a warrior from his earliest years—for so long that it takes more than taunts to fire his blood.

"Go then," Eddie says to the glowering god, and leans back in his chair to watch the fun.

Somewhat unsteady on his feet, Dakar goes over to the door. He wiggles the knob to see if it is locked. It is.

"Give me the key, or I shall twist the lock out of the door."

Eddie digs the key from his pocket and tosses it to Dakar.

"That would be a pity," he says. "Good locks aren't easy to buy these days."

With some effort, as if he is still seeing double, Dakar fits the key into the lock and turns it. There is a click as the mechanism releases, but when Dakar tries to pull the door open it won't budge.

Sweat streaming down his face—the temperature is in the nineties although the dry-season humidity is barely above fifty percent—Dakar pulls again. The door remains not only closed but immovable. Dakar tugs, the cables of muscle in his back standing out in high relief. He applies enough force to lift a bull out of a mud wallow, to raise a truck off a flat tire, but the door does not move.

He stomps around to face Eddie and the Summerian-born athanor shrugs.

"Maybe it swelled shut in the heat?"

Dakar actually considers this for a moment before realizing that he is being twitted. Then he smashes his fist against the door panel. The force of that blow should have shattered even the solid, well-seasoned hardwood. Instead, there is a dull thud followed by the snapping of teeth meeting as the force of the blow communicates itself up Dakar's arm with sufficient energy to force his head back.

Angry now, Dakar tries to pull his hand back for another strike, only to find that his fist remains stuck to the door.

"Africa has its 'Nansi stories, doesn't it?" Eddie asks conversationally. "Some of the same ones that found their way to America as the tales of Brer Rabbit and Brer Fox. I think Caribbean folklore has them, too, or am I mistaken?"

His fist still adhering to the door panel, Dakar turns his red gaze on Eddie.

"Spider."

"Yep. He didn't want you leaving before he had a chance to talk with you, so he sealed the door with webbing and left a bit to hold you."

"How dare he!"

"He's only thinking about your well-being," Eddie replies. "You were in pretty bad shape when we met up with you."

For a moment, the anger fades and is replaced by sorrow.

"I found death in the streets and my shrine covered with prayers I couldn't answer."

"So you got drunk."

Eddie's evident scorn reawakens Dakar's rage. With a tremendous effort, he wrenches his hand free from the door.

"I'll go out the window if I must!" he roars.

This is not a contingency either Eddie or Anson had anticipated. Rising to his feet, Eddie moves to intercept Dakar.

"We're five stories off the ground, you ass!"

Dakar roars inarticulately and charges.

Eddie has little choice but to intervene. Even an athanor can be killed by a five-story fall. Dakar may have some trick of which Eddie is not aware, but Eddie isn't going to gamble. Right now, the African athanor seems enraged enough to jump out a window without considering the consequences.

All of this flashes through Eddie's mind in the space of time it takes for Dakar to roar his challenge and lumber forward. Unimpeded by his thoughts, Eddie lifts the small table on which he had been resting his newspaper and flings it into Dakar's gut.

Dakar fails to block and bends in half, his breath knocked from him. Unfortunately, he recovers before Eddie can do more than take a few steps toward him. Now Eddie must dodge as the same table comes toward him. He does so, and there is the sound of breaking glass as the window behind him shatters.

"Damn!" Eddie curses under his breath. Then he does what might seem foolish to those who do not know him. He charges directly at Dakar and wraps his arms around the larger man's waist.

Dakar is taller than Eddie by as much as five inches. However, in build they are alike, though again Dakar both outmasses Eddie and is in better training.

Eddie, however, is very old. When civilization was young he had come forth from the wilds to challenge and later befriend a king called Gilgamesh—known also as the Wrestler. Arthur might have left those days behind him, but something of the Wildman lurks behind Eddie's reasoned exterior. Indeed, one of the bonds he shares with Anson is a passion for professional wrestling.

Moreover, Eddie has never ceased to study hand-to-hand combat. He views himself as Arthur's bodyguard, and in modern days he cannot always carry a weapon.

Dakar breaks from Eddie's hold. Then he swings his fists with such force that more than one missed blow (for Eddie wisely chooses to dodge rather than block) leaves a hole in the wall. Running with sweat, he begins to pant, but his fervor is undiminished.

From outside the door they hear shouting. Eddie, dodging blows and landing an occasional one himself, all the while keeping himself between Dakar and the broken window, manages to shout an answer to the queries.

"No, no. We don't need help. Everything is"—he dodges a fist and slows Dakar with a kick to one kneecap—"under control. My brother has had too much to drink, and the wine demons are chasing him."

Eddie hopes his explanation fits the local mythology. He doesn't really have time to look things up.

"The window? Oh, we'll pay to repair the window!"

His words remind Dakar of that potential exit. Eddie curses himself and flings a heavy leather-bound chair at Dakar. There is more shouting from without.

"Yes, yes! And the table."

Dakar hefts the leather-bound chair in preparation for a throw, but its smooth upholstery slips against his sweat-slick skin, and he drops it on one foot. His howl of pain seems to intimidate the interrogators, or maybe they have been satisfied by Eddie's answers, for the hubbub without falls silent, and Eddie is able to concentrate on Dakar.

Taking full and unfair advantage of Dakar's smashed foot, Eddie knocks him down. He stands with a foot on the other man's broad chest and takes a pointed poke at the injured member.

Dakar growls but seems almost grateful for an excuse to stop struggling. He doesn't surrender, however, and it is in this pose that Anson finds them when he dashes in a few minutes later.

"I was only a few blocks away when the table came out the window," he explains, shutting out the curious onlookers who have followed him up, "but I gotta fight through the crowds downstairs. You are lucky that the manager is greedy. He doesn't want to share the dash we gotta pay him with the local police or right now you'd both be on your way to prison."

"I'm already a prisoner," Dakar rumbles, but the fight has gone out of him. "Let me sit up."

Eddie does so, keeping a wary eye on him, but Dakar only leans against a wall and shields his eyes from the sunlight pouring through the damaged window.

Shaking his head, Eddie goes over to the window and pulls in the curtain that had been carried out along with the table, making the room somewhat darker.

"Thanks," Dakar says. Then, after a moment's thoughtful reflection, "I could really use a drink. Anything. Cola. Tea. Even water."

Eddie brings water and Dakar accepts it. While he sips, he studies Anson.

"You're too quiet, Spider. You should be joking with me, teasing me about being beaten by a smaller man—or by a bottle—but instead you sit there with your face long and your big mouth closed. What is wrong?"

Anson looks out from wherever his private meditations had carried him.

"I think I must stop looking for Adam and Teresa," he says after a long pause. "Today I finally found the house where someone told me they were staying. I was certain that I would find them there. Instead, I found an empty house. Inside I found this."

He holds up a small metal badge, the type of bright gewgaw with which the local constabulary is wont to reward its rank and file.

"By now," he continues, "they are either dead or imprisoned. If I continue to look for them too publicly, I can only do them harm."

"You're not going to give up!" Eddie protests.

"No," Anson says, "but I must move quietly, and I must accumulate favors so that important people will be forced to do my bidding. That means"—and here he turns a hard gaze on Dakar—"that we must get to business."

Dakar nods slowly. "You'll have to remind me what we

are doing. I remember it has to do with selling oil, but the fine points . . ."—he shrugs—"have escaped me."

"Very well," Anson says. "I will brief you, but let me tell you now that my interest in making this work has just gone up a thousandfold. If you cause me trouble, you can forget any deals we have made; you can forget that this is your birthland."

Dakar frowns, momentarily angry, then sees the depth of the ancient eyes that face him.

"I understand," he mumbles.

"Very good," Anson says. "The first and most important thing we need to do is collect Katsuhiro Oba. He is scheduled to arrive in Lagos three days from now."

"What!" Dakar surges to his feet, forgetting his smashed foot before it sends him sinking back to the floor.

"That's right," Anson says. He grins at Eddie, some of his usual good humor returning. "To make this work, Dakar is going to need to make nice to one of his oldest rivals."

¤◘¤

"And so," the Smith concludes, "that's the story with Atlantis. Production is moving on nicely, but it will be a while before non–water breathers can use it as a refuge without personal charms or a whole lot of diving gear."

"Then Vera is running the operation well?" asks Arthur.

"To perfection." The Smith grins. "What I can't get used to is seeing her as a mermaid, fishy tail and all."

"And all . . ." Arthur clears his throat. "Vera did say something about her human form being impractical. All Duppy Jonah could offer her was a loan on a selkie pelt, but she insisted she needed hands to work and a mouth to talk. I suppose I should have realized that she would opt for mermaid form, but Lovern said nothing about what he had done for her. How does she look?"

"Sexy," the Smith says bluntly, "which is quite a surprise given this is Vera, our perennial virgin."

Recalling the chaste woman who had dwelt in his hacienda for the past several years, Arthur finds himself agreeing. Although she had changed her appearance many times over the many centuries of her life, Vera had always opted for an appearance that was attractive, but in a distant sort of way. To imagine her as a mermaid—a sexy mermaid . . .

"Is she . . ." Arthur clears his throat and begins again. "In what fashion is she attired?"

"Do you mean, 'Is she going topless?' " the Smith prompts.

"Well, after a manner of speaking, yes."

This time Arthur does blush. Several marriages and other less formal liaisons have not removed a certain inability to understand what motivates women. Dealing with them had been easier when he was young and women could be captured as prizes. Later, when courtship entered the picture, he had taken refuge in politically arranged marriages whenever possible. He'd always been comfortable with Vera precisely because her very public commitment to maintaining her virginity had made her something other than a woman—just a person with bumps in odd places.

The Smith knows all of this, of course, and so he chuckles, enjoying Arthur's discomfort for a moment more.

"Actually, she's not," he says at last. "She's wearing a bikini top. I think she ordered a whole bunch of them from some swimsuit catalog. I don't know if she realizes it, but some of them are pretty alluring. Even Amphitrite of the sweet bare breasts wears one from time to time. Now that's a lady who knows a little bit of concealment can be sexier than . . ."

"Amphitrite," Arthur interrupts stiffly, "is the Queen of the Sea and a powerful person. I don't think we should be discussing her in this fashion."

"Oh," the Smith says breezily. "She wouldn't mind."

"But her husband might," Arthur continues. "Duppy Jonah is very possessive of his wife."

"Well," the Smith concedes. "That's true enough."

He leans back in his chair, stretching his legs out in front of him. One is noticeably shorter than the other. Bending, he begins to rub it.

"Sorry," he says, glancing up, "but all that moisture really got to my leg. It hurts like the dickens."

"Aspirin?" Arthur offers. "Or something else?"

"I have some pills that Garrett gave me," the Smith replies, "but I'd appreciate something to wash them down with."

Arthur nods. "What will it be?"

"Orange juice. Garrett says the vitamin C helps me absorb some of the nutrients."

"So it's more than just a pain pill?" Arthur says when he returns with the glass of juice.

"Therapy." The Smith accepts the juice and downs his pill. "After all these centuries of abuse, the bone is really starting to deteriorate. It may be time for a permanent shapeshift."

"I've often wondered why you didn't have one before," Arthur says. "You certainly can afford to pay a mage for the spell."

The Smith shrugs. "Vanity, I guess. Someone like me . . ." He gestures to his brawny build, to his homely but distinctive features, "shouldn't give in to cosmetic surgery. It would be like velvet and lace on an ape. Anyhow, the limp goes with the myth, you know?"

Arthur does know and smiles. "I guess you could have the shapeshift mend the damage but not relengthen the leg."

"Nope." The Smith shakes his head. "That would be vanity of another sort. I'm planning to find out from Lovern when he'll have time to get around to designing a spell that can mend the leg but leave the rest of me alone. All my magic's in my smithing, or I'd do it myself. I'd considered constructing a prosthetic limb, but I don't work well with plastics, and a metal leg would just be too heavy."

"And set off every metal detector in the world," Arthur adds.

"That too," the Smith agrees.

"Pressure Lovern," Arthur advises, "if he is reluctant to give you a straight answer. The Academy isn't even set up yet, and the demands for the promised disguise amulets have been unceasing. My poor wizard is threatening to rechristen the place 'The Factory.' "

The Smith chuckles. Like most athanor, he hasn't minded seeing Lovern taken down a peg or two. Lovern had been too inclined to look down upon even his peers.

A knock sounds on Arthur's office door.

"Come."

Bill Irish enters, his eyes bright with suppressed excitement.

"Yes, Bill?"

"Morning, Bill," says the Smith. Like the Wanderer, he approves of the integration of humans into the King's household.

Bill flashes a smile at the Smith but, knowing that Arthur is a stickler for precedence, keeps his words for the King.

"I was just reviewing the messages that came in, and there was one I didn't think you should wait to see. I realized you wouldn't be working . . . I mean, have your computer on since you were in conference with the Smith, so I printed out a copy and brought it directly to you."

Arthur puts out a hand. "Was it sent to my private e-mail or to Pendragon Productions?"

"Pendragon Productions, of course." Bill rolls his eyes, though only the Smith notices. "We aren't to read your private mail."

The Smith swallows a chuckle. Trust Arthur trying to catch his new help usurping privileges that only Eddie could claim.

"Good news," he asks, "or bad?"

Bill answers, "Well, a little of both."

Arthur chooses that moment to erupt. He waves the slip of paper at Bill: "And how, young man, could you consider this good news?"

Unconsciously, Bill straightens like a solider on parade.

"Well, sir, you had been worried . . ."

"I am never worried!"

"Concerned, then, sir, concerned about how Lovern and his colleagues would find time to create all the disguise amulets in time for the concert. This does take off some of the pressure, doesn't it, sir?"

Arthur growls something rude and thrusts the slip of paper at the Smith.

"Read this."

Then, to Bill, "You may go now. Don't mention this to anyone except Chris."

"Yes, sir!"

Bill slips out, clearly grateful to get away.
The Smith, meanwhile, is reading the message:

ARTHUR—

TOMMY AND I WANTED YOU TO BE THE FIRST TO KNOW ABOUT OUR PLANS FOR PROMOTING HIS LATEST ALBUM, *PAN*. TOMMY HAD THE VERY CLEVER IDEA OF USING SOME OF THE FAUNS AND SATYRS AS BACKUP SINGERS AND DANCERS IN HIS STAGE SHOW. AS THEY WON'T NEED COSTUMES, THE SAVINGS TO US WILL BE CONSIDERABLE. THE VERY IMPENETRABILITY OF THEIR "STAGE ATTIRE" WILL BRING US HOSTS OF FREE PUBLICITY. I WOULDN'T BE SURPRISED IF WE HAVE SELLOUTS FOR EVERY STOP ON OUR TOUR.

NEEDLESS TO SAY, OUR OFFER IS JUST WHAT THE THERIOMORPHS HAVE BEEN REQUESTING. THEY'LL HAVE A CHANCE TO GO OUT IN PUBLIC, MINGLE WITH THE HUMAN RACE, AND SHOW THAT NON-HUMANFORM HAVE THEIR PLACE ON EARTH, TOO. WE PLAN TO BRING OUR OFFER TO THEIR ATTENTION THIS AFTERNOON. AT LEAST AT FIRST, WE'LL STAY WITH THOSE WHO ARE RESIDENTS OF THE UNITED STATES SO THERE WON'T BE A PROBLEM WITH PASSPORTS AND SUCH.

HOPE YOU'RE AS EXCITED ABOUT THIS IDEA AS WE ARE.

LOVE AND HUGS—

LIL

"Well," the Smith says thoughtfully, "Lil does have a tempting offer here. Some of the shyer ones might not take it, but lots of them will."

"Especially the satyrs," Arthur agrees gloomily. "Can you excuse me? I'd better get on this right away."

"Can I help?"

Arthur sighs. "Sure. Contact Jonathan Wong in Boston and fill him in for me. Tell him I need to know if there is any way we can invoke the Accord to block this."

"Right." The Smith leaves, heading for one of the conference rooms where there is both a computer and a phone.

Arthur picks up his phone and punches a number.

"*Prima!* Gallery," says a silky female voice.

"Lil," Arthur says, "this is your king. We need to talk."

¤▣¤

Arriving in Lagos, Katsuhiro Oba permits an eager, smiling porter to take his bag but carries his sword case himself.

The latter piece of luggage has been ensorcelled so that no Customs official will ever consider it worth inspecting. He had paid heavily for that enchantment when he had made his first venture outside of modern Japan and considers it well worth the expense to have it renewed periodically.

Now, feeling smug, he strides through the airport, sensing rather than seeing the crowds part before him. He may be Japanese, but no one will ever call him a "little Nip." Always tall for a Japanese, as the centuries have passed he has made certain to remain just a bit taller than the average. Most athanor haven't bothered with such adjustments, with the result that all but the shapeshifters are beginning to be smaller than the average. He wonders at their lack of self-respect.

However, they are not Japanese, a thing he has always remained, even when his Asian feature have made him stand out. He still wonders that Anson had even dared suggest that he, born Susano, the Swift Impetuous Male, god of storm and thunder, could disguise himself as an African! He snorts through his nose, kindling his indignation. The porter carrying his luggage mentally halves the amount he plans to charge for his services and forsakes any hope of dash.

Such suggestions had been the reason Katsuhiro had decided to arrive in Lagos a few days before he is expected. He will look around, ask some questions, become acclimated.

As he goes through Customs (where officials, usually confident in their corruption, take a closer look at the aggressive tilt of his bearded face and decide that he is not the one to bother), changes yen into *naira*, and confirms his hotel reservations, Katsuhiro never ceases smiling like a cat with a mouse securely between his paws.

Once outside in the sweltering November heat (in Japan the weather had been placid and mild), he sends the now-trembling porter for a cab. If his hotel's air-conditioning is not working, he decides, he will move to one whose does. The porter is jogging back, pointing to a cab that is freeing itself from the milling chaos of traffic, when a man's voice, low but authoritative, speaks just behind him.

"Mr. Oba, welcome to Lagos."

Katsuhiro does not wheel, does not do anything dramatic, but the more skilled of his students would recognize that the man who has addressed him is now in mortal danger.

"Yes?" Katsuhiro says, the word short and clipped.

"I am here to meet you on behalf of people who hope to do business with you." The speaker's accent is Nigerian.

For a moment Katsuhiro is crestfallen, believing that Anson has anticipated his little joke. This emotion vanishes when something small, cylindrical, and hard pokes into his upper back.

The porter comes trotting up, smiling: "This is your lucky day, mister. My own brother is driving a cab. He will take you into Lagos fast and safe and so cheap . . ."

His words dribble off into silence as he realizes that Katsuhiro has company.

"Go, boy," says the man holding the gun.

If Katsuhiro had not been certain that the danger was real, the expression on his porter's face as he suddenly flees into the crowd without even waiting for payment would have been warning enough.

That he could disarm the gunman, Katsuhiro is certain. That he could do so without harm coming to one of the people in the airport crowd is less certain. He has never been one to take war to civilians, so he replies mildly:

"Meeting with those who wish to do business would be interesting. I am here with business in mind."

"Very wise. We have a limousine just a few meters down the curb to your right. If you will walk in that direction, I will make certain that your bag is taken after you."

Katsuhiro turns his head slightly.

"I see the limousine," he says, and walks.

None of the dark-featured and sweating throng who enviously watch him slip into the air-conditioned car realize that he has just saved their lives.

¤◘¤

Shahrazad had expected the jackalopes to tell Frank about the eagle-puma and the Eyes, but one day passes and then two and nothing is said about it. The puppy decides that either the events had not been as important as she had thought or that Frank knows already. She stops vaguely dreading an encounter with him, keeps clear of the rocks where she had seen the Eyes, and falls into something of a routine.

The autumn days are slipping into winter now, sometimes overcast, sometimes, when the sun is out, warm and golden.

Because the sun's heat makes such a difference to her comfort, Shahrazad falls into a diurnal pattern. She rises near dawn (which isn't so early now as it had been, something of a puzzle for her, as are the shorter evenings) and slips out one of the many door flaps to hunt for breakfast.

The Changer, she has discovered, will not let her go hungry, but he no longer brings her interesting food. If she does not hunt, her meal is hard, dry dog kibbles. Since she is forbidden table scraps, and knocking over the trash can is a major crime, she chooses to hunt.

Even in this, there are rules. Her presence in the barnyard upsets the quarter horses and domestic fowl. Their alarm inevitably brings either a unicorn, Tugger the horse, or sometimes, most embarrassingly of all, one of the athanor barnyard cats.

These are entities distinct from the Cats of Egypt, the sand-colored magical cabal who had attended the Lustrum Review and who are now—so she has gathered—residing with Lovern, making it possible (according to the cats who remain) for him to have any chance at all of getting his magical Academy up and running.

The king of the barnyard cats is a great golden tomcat

called Stinky Joe. Most of Joe's time seems to be spent asleep, sometimes curled on a horse blanket, sometimes rolled on his back in the straw as if he is trying to tan away a white spot on his stomach. However, he has a disconcerting talent for finding Shahrazad in the wrong and jumping squarely onto the center of her back.

Even with her heavy winter coat, his claws hurt. Joe's yowling brings his cohorts and whatever other athanor are in the vicinity. Just a couple such encounters had been enough to convince Shahrazad to stay away from the barnyard unless she is in the company of Frank MacDonald.

She notices that the Changer also makes the horses uneasy, even when he is in human form and takes comfort in the fact that he is apparently perceivable as a coyote even when he is not shaped like one.

Shahrazad's favorite hunting ground—at least for breakfast—becomes the pastures. Feed from the horses' mangers and water from the tanks attracts all manner of mice and small birds. Since the horses are regularly rotated, there is always a pasture not in use. Farther out, there are rabbit runs. Her jackalope escort never seems to care if she hunts their apparent kin, so she usually begins there, knowing that if she fails, mice are easier prey. As a last resort there are always kibbles.

After breakfast, sometimes she returns to the house, sometimes she ranges out to explore more of her domain. The Wanderer has departed, wandering presumably, and the Changer is often busy assisting Frank with some chore that goes more smoothly with two sets of hands.

Still, almost every day her father finds time to play with her, sometimes running with her, other times demonstrating a fine point of hunting. The three athanor dogs who reside with Frank occasionally deign to play with her, but she prefers being alone (or almost alone, for Hip and Hop follow her everywhere). The ranchlands are nothing new to the dogs, but to her they are a great adventure.

Even with all of this to fill her time, there is one ritual that Shahrazad never fails to perform. The time of day at which she performs it varies, but never the routine itself.

When both Frank and her father are busy elsewhere,

Shahrazad sneaks into the ranch house. The jackalopes consider their duty done once she is back in the barnyard, so she is perfectly alone.

Walking as softly as she can, the young coyote makes her way down a corridor that leads to a back section of the house. Here there is a thick door made from wide boards painted white. Behind it is a room that—she has found from investigating without—has no windows and no other door.

Shahrazad has never been in this room. The few times she had tried to slip in after Frank he has shooed her back. Still, she knows that something very important, something intimately associated with her, is behind that door.

So each day she sneaks to the door, stands on her hind legs, and tries to push it open. It never opens, but every day Shahrazad returns and tries once more.

If the young coyote could talk, she might try to explain the attraction of this door to her father or to Frank, but she cannot talk human; nor does the coyote language have the concepts she would need. Therefore, she cannot tell either the Changer or Frank how each night she dreams about this door and how in her dreams she pushes it open and lets out what lives inside.

Evil is a hill, everyone gets his own and speaks about someone else's.

—African proverb

In the end, the family sleeps on the street that first night, and the night after that. When Aduke's sister Yetunde calms down, she remembers that there is a place where the market women who come from outside of Monamona camp. These, of course, are those women who do not have family to take them in or friends to shelter them.

"Just like us," Aduke says briskly. "That would be perfect. Iya Taiwo, can you finish preparing dinner—perhaps with one of my sisters' help? There is no need for us to go hungry. The landlord must give us time to pack. Perhaps we should insist on waiting until morning to leave."

Taiwo's mother accepts the paring knife that Aduke proffers.

"Send me Koko and she and I will finish dinner. Aduke, I do not think we should wait to leave until morning. I saw the eyes of our neighbors. Some were afraid, some were just greedy. If we stay, the one will stir up the others, and we may be chased away with nothing."

Yetunde begins to lament again at this. Aduke thrusts a basket of laundry into her arms.

"Yetunde, start making bundles of clothing and smaller

goods. Get some of the older children to help—work will steady them."

Nodding, Yetunde starts giving orders, her hysteria vanishing. Aduke permits herself a smile; she knows her sister well. She is only weak when unfocused; focused she might well be the best of them all. It had been a pity she had chosen to marry so young and not to finish school.

Next, Aduke snags one of the older nieces by the arm.

"Fasina, your job will be taking care of those children too small to help with the packing. Don't worry about the infants. They can stay with their mothers."

The girl, eleven or twelve and, by the old way of seeing things, almost a woman, nods seriously. She gathers up a half dozen or so children and herds them into the hallway outside of the apartment. Within a few minutes, she has them singing alphabet and counting songs, their fear, at least, forgotten.

Now that something like order is restored, Aduke stands, finger flattening her nose (how, when she was younger, had she longed for that nose to be thin and narrow like that of an Englishwoman or even a Hausa!) as she plans. She feels the warmth of a human close by and finds Kehinde beside her.

"What are your orders for me, sister?" he asks, his tone playful but respect in his eyes.

Here, then, is a modern man! Aduke thinks in surprise. Even her father would not have asked a woman for direction in a crisis. With a pang, she wishes that Taiwo were here. He would not ask for direction. He would take over, and she could go join the women making bundles and fussing quietly in the other rooms.

She shakes the thought away as if it is a fly. Taiwo is not here, and she should be grateful that Kehinde is modern enough to work with a woman. Trying to speak with proper respect and yet keep certainty in her bearing, Aduke addresses him, her voice low, for she doesn't want the other women to hear what she must say.

"We cannot take the furniture with us, brother. Yet if we leave it, the worst of our neighbors will steal it. We also must contact our sisters' husbands so they will know where we are."

Kehinde nods. He works as a private tutor and as a letter writer, so is often at home. Yetunde's husband drives a lorry. He won't be easy to find. Then there is Koko, Taiwo and Kehinde's sister, and her husband. Taiwo, of course, must be notified by letter or perhaps by telephone.

"The furniture must come first," Kehinde states, "as that can be stolen. Let us go together and speak with the landlord. Between us, we can play on his guilt and his greed and get something like a fair price."

Aduke nods. Crossing to where the old mother is efficiently transforming the groceries into a meal, she tells her where they are going. Malomo reaches and pats her on the cheek.

"It was a lucky day for me when my son Taiwo brought you into the family, Aduke. You and Yetunde are good daughters to this household."

Feeling her face warm, Aduke gives the older woman a quick embrace and hurries outside, stepping over the gathering of little children and down the stairs to the landlord's apartment. Behind her, she hears Kehinde's tread, firm and measured, counterpoint to the piping voices of the children as they sing a traditional song that Kehinde had taught them.

This, she realizes, is what Oya meant when she talked of being a mother, even without a child of her body. Only with that thought does Aduke realize that sometime in the chaos following Yetunde's announcement Oya had vanished.

Over and over again during the day and two nights that they spend in the open Aduke has reason to be grateful that this is the dry season. Although the weather is hot and the *harmattan* winds stinging, they do not have to sleep wet and slog through mud.

The lack of rain does make it more difficult for them to get fresh water. Aduke spends much of her spare time fetching water from a public pump and then boiling it over the portable gas stove they had used for cooking in the apartment. Her insistence on boiled water brings mockery from market women camping nearby, but Aduke closes her ears and takes comfort when not one of the children falls ill.

On the morning after the second night spent out of doors, Oya reappears just after the rest of the family has departed, most for the market. Kehinde has gone, he says, to tutor someone in English. Aduke keeps her doubts to herself. She suspects that he will find a quiet corner in a bar where for a few *kobo* spent on drinks he can have peace and quiet.

Oya sails up, her traditional wrapper billowing in the wind, just as Aduke is decanting her first batch of boiled water into containers emptied by breakfast preparations.

"*E karo, e karo*. Good morning, good morning, Aduke Idowu," Oya says as breezily as if she had not vanished without explanation just when the family had met with a terrible crisis. "I see you are doing well."

"Well enough," Aduke answers without offering the traditional greetings and inquiries in return. She knows that she is being rude, but she can't help it. Oya's defection had hurt her more deeply than her mere reappearance can mend.

"And your mother and sisters and children?"

"Well enough."

"And their husbands?"

"Fine. When we see them."

"Ah, then if everything is so fine, you will not be interested in some news that I have for you."

Reluctantly, Aduke looks up from her decanting. In any case, she needs to set another pot of water to boil.

"News?" she asks, motioning Oya to a seat on one of the pillows she and her niece had beaten clean earlier that morning. "Will you have some tea?"

"Since you are boiling water and it won't be an inconvenience," Oya says, "I will be honored to take tea with you."

Aduke feels her face growing hot. She is glad that she is so dark that her blush does not show. That had been something for which to pity the female European tourists. When they had visited the college campus and the men had hooted comments about their clothing and their figures, they might have held their heads high and pretended not to hear, but their own skins played traitor.

"There is some *gari foto* left from breakfast," Aduke says, by way of an apology. "It is still fresh, and my husband's mother outdid herself in the preparation."

"Then she is well," Oya says.

Aduke surrenders to protocol. While the water boils and the tea is brewed she supplies information about the health and well-being of her extended family.

Oya nods and blows on her tea to cool it. From a fold of her wrapper she produces a package of wrapped sweets.

"I brought these for the children, but a few will not be missed, and they will go well with our tea."

Knowing herself forgiven, Aduke accepts a sweet. It is after the northern style, honey and sesame seeds formed into a solid little square that needs the tea to warm it for chewing.

"You said you had news," she asks, her question now polite interest, not intrusiveness.

"Although you are doing very well here," Oya says, gesturing to the tidy camp, "I thought that you would be interested in having more permanent quarters once more."

"We are," Aduke says, trying not to seem too eager.

"The place is not a proper apartment building, nor yet a house," Oya says, "but it does have running water and is wired for electricity."

"The rent?" Aduke says hesitantly. "We cannot pay much."

"The rent would be reasonable." Now Oya hesitates, as if it is her time to feel awkward. "You see, the place has a reputation for . . ."

She stops, drinks tea, chews her sweet, so manifestly uncomfortable that Aduke finds it easy to be patient. At last Oya recommences, her voice so soft that Aduke must lean forward to hear her.

". . . for being haunted."

¤▣¤

Later, Katsuhiro longingly remembered that ride in the limousine as the last time for several days that he was cool.

Without wasting words on explanations, his captors drive him into Lagos, transfer him to a van, and then drive the van a long distance over very bad roads. As the van has no windows, Katsuhiro has no idea even what direction they are headed.

Escape proves impossible. In the limousine two guns are always kept pointed at him—three when the man in charge frisks him, taking his money, jewelry, watch, and pocketknife.

The back of the van proves to be completely empty. There is not even a bench or chair that he could cannibalize into a weapon—not that he needs one, but even a club could be useful. Only the fact that the floor is thickly carpeted saves him from a formidable bruising when the roads become rough. Even so, he is far from comfortable.

No guard is placed in the back with him, nor is one necessary. The doors of the van are key-locked and then padlocked on the outside. Katsuhiro hears the lock click shut.

There is no communicating window or panel to the driver's compartment. The walls, floor, and ceiling are triply reinforced, probably to stop bullets, but the layering of metal over metal ends his slim hope that he might burst out a weak seam.

And his own distinctive appearance is the final bond that holds him. Even if he escaped, for how long could he avoid recapture? A tall Japanese man on Nigerian streets would stand out like a chrysanthemum blossom against a wash of early snow. Moreover, he is reluctant to depart without his sword.

Katsuhiro had arrived in the Lagos air terminal around midday. When he is unloaded from the van inside a cavernous garage the glimpse he catches of the sky outside tells him that it is night. Guns reappear here and, fully respecting the harm they could do him, Katsuhiro permits his captors to escort him into a building adjoining the garage.

Although he maintains a calm, unconcerned attitude ("inscrutable" was doubtless how it would be described when his captors gave their report), Katsuhiro is fast losing hope. The slim hope that he was indeed being taken to visit some businessman—albeit one with an overdose of paranoia—begins to beat its wings for a fast escape when he is ushered down a flight of steps and taken into an area that smells of dungeon.

The odor is a mixture of common enough elements: damp, mold, urine, human sweat, dust. There is a tang of blood, too, and of vomit, feces, and tears. Katsuhiro had scented its like hundreds of times before, but only rarely has he been a prisoner. Now, as he is herded into a cell that seems pitch-dark after the light in the corridors, hope flees.

Like most athanor, Katsuhiro has an ingrained fear of being imprisoned. In a prison, under close daily observation, his secret may be revealed. This, added to his perfectly human terror, makes it difficult for him not to fling himself against the closing door or to assault his captors, no matter the end result.

Only many centuries of study in war and tactics reins in Katsuhiro's panic. Thus far he has not been beaten; he has not been tortured. He has no doubt that if he angers his captors one or both of these things will quickly follow. Injury would reduce his chances for escape—not to mention hurting a lot.

So, no matter how he feels, Katsuhiro puts a good face on his situation and even manages a small bow before the door closes, sealing him in darkness.

Eventually, he learns two things. First, the darkness is not absolute. A small window high in the exterior wall admits both fresh air and a hint of something that cannot be called light but is at least lesser darkness. Second, he realizes that he is not alone.

A shape, just visible as a blackness against greater blackness, is humped on the floor. Katsuhiro might not have seen it if it had not moved and might have believed he was hallucinating if it had not spoken. It has a male voice, deep yet cracked as if something in it is broken. What it mutters is unintelligible.

"What?" says Katsuhiro, keeping his voice low, for he is certain there is a guard in the hallway. "What did you say?"

The voice speaks again, this time in English so heavily accented that Katsuhiro wonders if he is being mocked. When he sorts the words out from their peculiar pronunciations and grammatical order, they prove to be: "A say, 'Who are you?' "

"Katsuhiro Oba, a prisoner."

There is a dry, cracked chuckle. "Na, so we all. A no tink you p'liceman."

"True." Katsuhiro swallows hard. "Have you been here long?"

"Dey trow me . . ." The cracked voice stops and resumes in English that, while still heavily accented is at least more recognizable. "They throw me in this cell for so long dat I tink they forgot me, except that sometimes they remember to feed me."

"Sometimes?"

"Na, most day A tink." Again the pause. "For a while I try to keep count by the daylight, but now I don't see so good. I see lights when it dark, dark when it light. Tha las' beatin' broke sometin' in my head."

Katsuhiro makes a sympathetic noise. "Maybe I can help you when it's daylight."

"You doctor?" The man sounds impressed.

"I know something of medicine." And so he should after all the battlefields on which he has served. "But I need light."

"So do we all."

Katsuhiro starts to ask the man why they have imprisoned him, then bites back the question. The man trusts him, at least somewhat, so far. If he starts asking personal questions, though, then the man might think he's a stooge sent in by the authorities. He decides on a safer question.

"Do you know where we are?"

"Monamona, A tink. Dat's p'lice get me. We no go ooo far then."

Katsuhiro grunts acknowledgment. Monamona is the city where he and Anson were to do business. That his kidnapping is connected somehow to that business seems a reasonable assumption. He puzzles for a while, chewing the bit of beard below his lower lip. Eventually, he falls asleep.

When he awakes, pale daylight is just visible through the narrow window above. After the night's blackness, it seems like a floodlight, though he can barely make out the color of his shirt.

His cellmate proves to be a lean, moonfaced African, asleep on his side on the packed-earth floor, his knees drawn up to his chest, his head pillowed on his arm. The man's face and shoulders show evidence of a terrible beating: black blood has scabbed tight in some places; in others the wounds swell with infection or run with pus.

Flies crawl over the man so freely that for a moment Katsuhiro thinks he has passed in the night. Then the ribs rise and slowly fall.

Leaving the man to whatever peace he can get from sleep, Katsuhiro inspects his cell. An open bucket that has not been emptied in some days is the only latrine. The furnishings consist of the ragged blanket on which his cellmate lies and a plastic bucket partially filled with warm, flyblown water. A closed slot in the door near the floor shows how food is delivered. A peephole, just wide enough for a pair of eyes, is set higher in the door.

"Lovely," Katsuhiro mutters, and takes inventory of himself. He is rested though stiff, hungry but not distractingly so, and thirsty. Drinking the water in the bucket will almost certainly make him sick, so he schools himself to resist thirst as long as possible.

His possessions consist of a now-soiled business jacket and trousers, matching loafers, shirt, socks, and underwear. His captors had taken his belt and tie along with his obvious weapons and money. Turning out his pockets, Katsuhiro finds a small box of aspirin, a handkerchief, a couple of business cards, and three small cubes of gum.

Two of these he substitutes for the lunch and dinner he has missed, reserving the third against need. The cool tranquillity of the mint soothes him as he hunkers down again and waits, though whether in anticipation or in dread he is not completely certain.

Loverboy >> I'm going to be a star! :) !! The babes will love me best by far! I'll wave out of my limo car!! And take 'em drinking at the nearest bar!!—Hey, what do you think of that? Aren't those the greatest song lyrics?

Demetrios >> Yeah, greatest . . . Georgios . . . Shouldn't you think more carefully about the implications of this offer?

Rebecca >> Those lyrics aren't great. But this offer. Wow! I don't know whether to be envious or terrified.

Loverboy >> Tommy's offer is all I can think about. Ever since I got his call . . . I thought it was going to be about the tickets. Then I find out it's to be in the show. Whoa! Hey, another rhyme. Whoa—Show. Maybe I'm setting my sights too low. Maybe I should ask Lil to manage me. Heh. Heh . . . Oh, what a babe she is! I'd like to manage her. ;)

Hunk >> I'm worried about the audition. What should I wear? Will Tommy want us to sing or dance? I haven't danced in public in years.

Stud >> And what about our day jobs? Should we keep them if we get in the show? I telecommute—I guess most of us who have "real world" jobs do—do we burn those bridges?

Loverboy >> Don't worry about it, dudes! We'll be rich and famous. Haven't you read *Rolling Stone* and *People*? Rock stars don't have day jobs.

Stud >> Are you sure? What about the term "starving artist"? It's gotta have a source.

Loverboy >> That's for the failures, bro. We're going straight to the top. Check out Tommy's web site—his first album hit gold. Rumor is that *Pan* is gonna ship gold—or maybe platinum.

Hunk >> But do we see any of that? I don't think so . . .

Stud >> Good point. We need to make certain to read the fine print on the contracts. I wonder how much Jonathan Wong charges for legal work?

Demetrios >> I can't believe the lot of you!! My only relief is that at least there are no fauns echoing your foolishness!

Rebecca >> Yeah! Don't you realize that this isn't about contracts and auditions?

Hunk >> I think Jonathan would be reasonable. I did a job for a client of his a while ago and he said he'd owe me one.

Loverboy >> Of course this is about contracts and auditions! Don't think the fauns aren't interested. They're just quieter 'cause you're such a dictator. Isn't this what we've been fighting for—a chance to do more than hide? Demetrios may be happy with his tree farm, but I want more and so do my buddies! I'm the speaker for my three roommates here. Stud and Hunk have their own communities.

Stud >> Yeah!

Hunk >> Not all of us would get in the show, of course. That's why there are auditions.

Loverboy >> True. I'll get in, I'm sure. I'm the best-looking of the lot.

Rebecca >> Listen to us! I've phoned Chris Kristofer and, though he won't speak out of turn, he did let on that Arthur isn't happy about this whole thing. The King's not convinced it's a good idea. He's probably trying to stop Lil and Tommy through some permutation of the Accord.

Hunk >> Who says you're the best-looking? You're bowlegged, and your hair is greasy!

Stud >> "Loverboy" indeed . . . Are you telling us something? Maybe about boys . . .

Demetrios >> Forget it, Rebecca. They aren't listening. It'll cost more, but I'll phone you. Maybe we can figure out what the theriomorph position should be on this issue.

Loverboy >> You limp-pricked jerks! You know who got the most looks from the girls when we were at the Fair!

Rebecca >> Right. This is degenerating.

Hunk >> They were only looking 'cause they couldn't believe how ugly you are!

Stud >> I'm the best-looking. Me!

Loverboy >> Oh, yeah! Says who?

"Fine!" Anson says, for once truly angry. "Don't be part of it! I wanted you in for several reasons, not the least of which is that if you're not with us, you'll get insulted and start queering the whole deal."

"So," growls Dakar, "you just want me in to keep me from giving you trouble. Why should I do what you want? Why should I let you use my birthland in this way?"

Anson shakes a long finger at him. "That's another reason I wanted you in. This is your birthland. Dis contri, you contri. This land is your land."

"Well it isn't your land!" Dakar bellows. "Your stories come from farther north."

"How," Anson says impatiently, "do you know where my story begins? I am far older than you, pup. I could be your father for all you know. Maybe you should show some respect, eh? Omo to baba, like, na?"

"You're not my father!"

"Grandfather, then? Great-grandfather? Great-great-grandfather? Maybe I should forbid you to call me by name and insist that you call me ancestor!"

"I don't have to listen to this!"

"So, go." Anson turns pointedly away. "Go. Fall down. Get drunk. Fuck prostitutes. Maybe breed a bastard or two if there is living seed in those pendulous balls. You are a nit to me, a thing I brush off my sleeve."

Eddie, who has been listening to this argument or versions thereof for the last thirty-six or so hours, decides that once again it is time for him to intervene.

"You two!" He laughs and rubs the stubble on his cheeks. "You two are good as a play."

They both glare at him, still ignoring each other. Eddie faces Anson, then Dakar.

"Anson has a plan," Eddie continues, "a good one not just for Nigeria, but for all of Africa. He knows, though, that to make it work there must be foreign connections, foreign capital that can be trusted."

"Trusted," Dakar grumbles. "Katsuhiro Oba cannot be trusted. He is impetuous, impulsive, mean-spirited, a bully, a cheat, and a liar."

"And an athanor," Eddie says, "so he knows that the long-term picture is important. In the twentieth century, we cannot ignore that the economy is global."

"Fuck global," Dakar retorts, predictably.

"Yeah. Das right. Tink big, big man," Anson replies, still not looking at him, his attention apparently absorbed by a half-melted chocolate bar.

"Oh, shut up, both of you!" Eddie yells. "Listen, Dakar, you've been mourning that you can do nothing for the people who heap offerings on your shrines. Here you have a chance to do something that will help them, and you sit on your hands!"

Dakar frowns, then nods a curt invitation for Eddie to continue.

Aware that this small victory could vanish in another tantrum, Eddie goes on, "It's a simple enough plan. Nigeria could be the single richest African nation because of the vast amounts of petroleum it possesses. But what happens? The money gets spent on crazy projects like the capital city at Abuja or on modern improvements that aren't maintained and so become so much junk. Or the money simply gets embezzled by government officials who have ten cars and gold fixtures on their toilets."

Eddie pauses for breath. He isn't saying anything that hasn't been said before, but his litany is giving the combatants a chance to stay put, to not walk out on each other because they are being polite to him. After drinking some mineral water from a sealed bottle (thus far he has managed to avoid all but mild gastrointestinal distress by such cautions), Eddie waves his hand in a gesture he had seen a marketplace orator using.

"So Anson comes up with a plan."

"A spider's web," Dakar mutters, "sticky and full of dead bugs."

Eddie ignores him. "We make a deal with a market that desperately needs petroleum products. Japan is perfect. It has a first-world economy and currently imports an overwhelming amount of its petroleum—which it depends on not only for modern conveniences, but also for the very industries that maintain its first-world standing."

Anson says, "That's true. They have some coal in Hokkaido and Kyushu, but production peaked in 1941. As with lumber, Japan prefers to import rather than diminish its own resources."

"So," Eddie says brightly, as if there had not been an interruption. "Japan would love a sweetheart deal for Nigerian oil, but local politicians don't have the connections or are too swayed by dash, by OPEC politics, by tribal concerns. The *sarimen* in their neat suits aren't going to be impressed by some African wearing too much gold braid on his uniform and insisting on being addressed with a string of titles he has stolen, not earned."

Dakar says, "The Japanese are the most bigoted people on this earth."

Eddie shrugs. "They're island-born. What can you expect? We can use that insular attitude to our advantage. We athanor are an island in our own way. Katsuhiro Oba may be Japanese, but he is also athanor. He can see that a stable inflow of hard currency will help keep Nigeria from becoming the dupe of whatever foreign power wants to play games."

"Ah, Biafra," Anson says, invoking in two words the civil war that had nearly destroyed the burgeoning nation in the early 1960s.

During the Biafran War, backing by foreign powers had turned what was basically a traditional tribal conflict into a war responsible for thousands of deaths. Only the rising demand for oil had saved the reunited nation, but the boom economy had collapsed in the early eighties when the demand for oil decreased once more.

"So," Eddie continues, "we make a private deal with Japanese investors who must work through Katsuhiro. Nigeria's interests will be directed by athanor who care not only about Nigeria, but about the continent as a whole."

Dakar actually looks at Anson, signaling that he at least will not stomp out without further provocation. Anson does not make any overt gestures of reconciliation, but when he next reaches for his soda he turns as if by accident so that all three men are facing each other.

Heartened, Eddie continues: "Now, we cannot completely bypass the Nigerian government. That would be impossible, but here in Monamona there is a government official who is also athanor. As you know, he has agreed to work with us on this."

He stops, ostensibly to reach for his mineral water, in reality to see if Dakar will explode again. Shango's role had been almost as much of a problem for him as Katsuhiro's had been. Dakar keeps his peace, and Eddie swallows a grin along with his water. This is actually going to work!

"So, we meet with Shango—he's calling himself Percy Omomomo these days—tomorrow morning. Then, while you keep an eye on him, Anson and I go to Lagos and get Katsuhiro."

Pause again. No eruption. Dakar only grumbles:

"Shango is another outsider. I was the first king of Ife!"

Eddie ignores this and goes on. "What do you think? Shall we at least give this a try?"

Dakar nods. Anson nods. Eddie sighs.

Some vacation this is turning out to be! He realizes with a guilty start that he hasn't called Arthur or checked his e-mail in several days. Never mind, no need to ruin Arthur's day with this. Let him at least enjoy quiet routine and peace.

¤◙¤

As a precaution against being followed by witch-hunting neighbors, Aduke's family had moved mainly after dark. Therefore, it is not until the next day that Aduke realizes how very different their new home is from the apartment they had left.

She had sensed the cavernous vastness of the building's lower story when they had entered. She had heard the echoes of their feet and seen how the beams of their electric torches were swallowed before they touched a wall. In the upper story, the light had come mostly from a few low-wattage yellow bulbs set in cages high on the walls in the corridors, enough to guide them, but not enough to reveal detail.

Now, awakening on a floor mat in the room where she had bedded down with several nervous children, Aduke looks around in mingled awe and appreciation. The room is easily thirty feet on each side, larger than two rooms from their apartment combined. Two large casement windows admit light and air. They even have screens, a luxury she hadn't dared hope for.

The walls are papered with brightly colored diagrams which, after studying them for a while, Aduke decides are instructions for assembling something, though for the life of her she cannot decide what it is. Perhaps part of the instructions are missing or perhaps the person reading them was presumed to understand some essential point that has not been included.

Gently moving the sleeping toddler who has his head pillowed on her lower leg, Aduke rises and goes to explore further.

Entering the main corridor, she finds three other large square rooms like the one in which she had awakened. These four rooms are separated from each other in one direction by the main corridor, in the other by a shorter corridor. At one end of this short corridor there is an indoor washroom and at the other is the largest closet Aduke has ever seen.

At one end of the main corridor there is a staircase going down, presumably the same one they had mounted the night before. After the landing, it extends up to another story. At the other end of the hallway is a large bright room from which comes the scent of coffee. Deciding that exploration can wait until she finds out who else is awake, Aduke trots toward the coffee.

The room she enters is as long as the entire building and about thirty feet wide. At one end a makeshift kitchen has been set up. Oya sits at a long table talking softly with Taiwo's mother.

"We can keep goats downstairs," the mother is saying, "and some chickens, too. I have missed such things. Is there any place we might plant a garden?"

"Quite possibly out back," Oya answers, then she hears Aduke enter. "Good morning, Aduke Idowu."

"*E karo.* Good morning, Oya. Good morning, Iya Taiwo." Aduke twirls, relishing the feeling of open space around her. "What a wonderful place this is!"

Oya smiles. "I am glad you like it. It was once a factory for the assembly of widgets for a Belgian firm. Downstairs is what was the garage and warehouse. This floor held some of the workrooms. This"—she gestures broadly with one arm—"was the cafeteria and rest area so that the workers would not have to go outside during the rainy season."

"Very thoughtful," the old mother says.

"For both them and their workers," Oya agrees. "The widget, I understand, would have been harmed by too much dirt. That is why there are large washrooms both near the workrooms and at the other end of this room. The Belgians wanted their laborers clean."

The mother shrugs. "Good for us, though."

"And what's upstairs?" Aduke asks, crossing to the coffeepot. She pours herself some in a plain white-ceramic mug that has words written in some language rather like French on the outside.

Oya looks stern. "That is off-limits. As I was telling your mother, strange things have happened in this building. These same strange things chased the Belgians away. I have consulted a *babalawo* and the indications are that the source of the disturbance is located on the upper floor. No one but me is to go there. I can set some charms to prevent the ghosts from harming you, but these must not be disturbed."

"Oh!" Aduke gasps softly, uncertain whether to be frightened or amused. Her good mood at finding herself in this well-lit, open place is such that she decides not to question Oya's ruling.

"I will warn the children," the old mother says, "and tell them that they are never to go upstairs."

"Good," Oya says. "And I will get a lock for it and keep the key."

"We are fortunate," Aduke says, to show that she also supports the edict, "that this factory has such a strange reputation. Without that, it would certainly be in use, if not as a factory, then as an apartment building."

"True," Taiwo's mother agrees. "Oya says that the rent is just about what we were paying for the apartment. Water and electricity are included."

Aduke smiles. "That's wonderful! Maybe the *orisha* did accept our offerings, and now our luck is changing."

Later, after the children have been fed, washed, and sent to play in the empty warehouse below, Aduke helps set up housekeeping. One room is to be the sleeping room for the children. Another is set up as sleeping areas for those who are without partners, with curtains between sections. The remaining two rooms are given to Yetunde and her husband and Koko and hers.

"There will be new babies soon enough," Taiwo's mother cackles happily. "That follows as the rains will follow the winds."

Aduke feels a sudden pang, wondering how with Taiwo in Lagos will she ever start another baby. The old mother sees her expression and pats her gently on the arm.

"I think that we do not want our married couples to get too fond of having so much space for themselves," she says. "In the daytime, one room can be a workroom for those who need quiet, like Kehinde or you when you are writing to the government for us. The other will be a schoolroom for the older children. The little ones will take their lessons in the nursery."

Aduke nods agreement, though such care seems hardly necessary. Surely there is space and to spare.

Looking around the open room, she feels a weight of gloom lift from her for the first time since her son died. Certainly the *babalawo* had been wrong. The family cannot be cursed. Or perhaps the gods have accepted the many sacrifices, and this relocation is their first gift.

Either way, Aduke is certain that things are improving for the better. She smiles and goes to write Taiwo about their good fortune.

¤◘¤

They let Katsuhiro Oba rot in his cell for an entire day before they bring him out into the light again.

Sitting on the damp dirt floor does nothing good for his suit, nor has the enforced waiting done anything good for his temper. His captors' infantile belief that forbidding him food will break him makes him furious. Like most athanor, Katsuhiro possesses a high metabolism, but he is no shapeshifter, dependent on regular meals. Only reminding himself that getting out of his cell is the least part of escaping keeps Katsuhiro from breaking down the door.

With the arrogance of a trained samurai, he has no doubt that he could overwhelm the guards. He fantasizes plans of escape until, if the opportunity presents itself, he will be ready to take advantage of it. Then he slips into meditations of forgetfulness.

Thus the hours pass. His cellmate awakens occasionally. During one of these periods of wakefulness, Katsuhiro washes his wounds, binding the worst—a terrible slash across the forehead—with cloth torn from his own dress shirt.

He tells himself that he does so from boredom or that the man is a source of information. In reality, he does it from pity—and to retain some feeling that he is in control.

When he hears the bolt on the cell door shoot back, Katsuhiro gets to his feet. His pride will not let him play the role of defeated and frightened prisoner, even though it might be to his advantage.

Three men wait for him without, all armed with handguns of impressive size, all wearing khaki trousers bloused into boots and clean white shirts. The outfit has something of the uniform about its cut, but is not overtly so.

One grunts a command, and Katsuhiro steps forward without a backward glance at his cellmate, though he hears the other man whimper. No wonder. Katsuhiro has seen the bruises on the man's sides, bruises that correspond quite neatly with the rounded toes of the guards' boots.

Nodding to the men as if they are his escort rather than guards, Katsuhiro walks briskly down the corridor in the direction from which he had come the day before. The guards are so startled that they actually let him go about ten paces before two hasten after him, leaving the third to relock the cell.

Fools, Katsuhiro thinks. *I could have been away in that time.*

In his heart of hearts, he is not certain that this is true, but it comforts him to think so, and in playing the role he becomes it. By the time he has been taken to an office on the second story of the prison building, he is as coolly confident as if he were about to conduct a class at his *dojo*.

Apparently following orders, his guards say nothing to him as they move through the corridors, but when they bring him into the office, the chief of the three reports to the man seated behind a solid American-style executive's desk.

"No problem with him, Chief," he says. "He came as quiet as a lamb. Maybe these Japanese are crazy. He acts like this is a normal way to treat a visiting businessman."

The man behind the desk replies, "Perhaps he is. They say his kind commit suicide at the smallest slight. If that isn't madness, what is? Leave us now. Set two armed guards at my door. Send someone down to question his cellmate. I want to know everything they talked about."

"Yes, sir!"

As they are speaking Yoruban, the Africans have every reason to believe that Katsuhiro will understand nothing of their conversation; nor does Katsuhiro give them any reason to believe otherwise.

The truth is that he learned to speak Yoruban many years ago when first his rivalry with Ogun, now Dakar Agadez, blossomed. He had learned that nothing drove Ogun into an uncontrollable rage faster than being taunted in his natal tongue by his adversary. It amused Susano to speculate on Ogun's ancestry, sexual habits, and hygienic practices in fluent Yoruban, complete with colloquial slang phrases and insults, then watch the results. The fact that Dakar had only learned to speak Japanese poorly and so couldn't respond in kind only made the exercise sweeter.

Now, Katsuhiro schools his expression to polite neutrality, a faint smile, such as an embarrassed *sariman* might wear, on his lips, and waits to be addressed in a language he can claim to understand.

After the guards depart, his host studies him without rising from his chair, as if reviewing a cadet or a naughty child. Katsuhiro returns the gaze with the same embarrassed smile, all the while fuming beneath his unthreatening exterior. At last, the man speaks in good English, marked, however, with the vaguely British intonations of the native Nigerian.

"So, you are Katsuhiro Oba."

Katsuhiro gives a brief bow, hardly more than a movement of his head. It signals acknowledgment of himself, rather than respect to the other. He doubts the Nigerian has studied enough Japanese etiquette to be aware of the slight, but it makes him feel better.

"You may call me Chief General Doctor Regis," the man says.

Katsuhiro doesn't respond, not even to sneer at this typically African accumulation of titles. He is studying this Chief General Doctor Regis, trying to decide what it is about the man that makes his skin crawl.

Regis is not a tall man, nor particularly threatening physically. His skin is not as dark as that of many of his countrymen, indicating an admixture of white blood—perhaps as much as half. His close-cropped hair is kinky, shaded that peculiar ocher-red often found in mulattoes. Skin and hair color are the only indications of his white parent. Otherwise, his nose is flat, his lips broad, and his eyes brown. These latter are bloodshot, though whether naturally or from exhaustion Katsuhiro cannot be certain.

When Regis rolls his desk chair back slightly, perhaps a nervous gesture, perhaps to return Katsuhiro's gaze with the minimum of effort, Katsuhiro sees that he is clad Western-style in shirt, tie, and tailored trousers. Instead of a suit jacket, he wears a white lab coat.

"You are very calm, Mr. Oba," Regis says. "Do you realize that you are in great danger to your life?"

Katsuhiro lets his nervous *sariman* smile broaden a touch but says nothing more. Regis seems nonplussed but not really angry. He touches a buzzer beneath his desk and in a moment a woman's voice speaks over the intercom.

"Yes, Chief General Doctor, sir!"

"Ice water. And a sandwich. Ham and cheese." Regis speaks slowly, as if dispensing great wisdom.

"Immediately, sir!"

Regis says nothing more and within thirty seconds (Katsuhiro counts them to distract himself from the involuntary salivation that even the mention of food had triggered) a pretty young Nigerian woman bustles into the office carrying a tray.

She wears a bright red dress with a short skirt that shows off good legs. Her hair has been straightened and arrayed in an elaborate coiffure that spills curls down from the top of her head. When she sets the tray on Regis's desk, his hand slides possessively along the curve of her bottom.

Watching without appearing to do so, Katsuhiro sees the woman's lips stiffen, but she does not protest. Clearly this attention is not welcome, nor is it unexpected, but she does not care to protest.

"That will be all, Teresa," Regis says, squeezing her bottom so hard that she cannot conceal a flinch of pain. "For now."

Teresa exits and Regis studies the tray. His office is but poorly air-conditioned and the ice water in the pitcher sweats droplets of water that bead down the sides.

Katsuhiro's mouth, despite the salivation triggered by the sight and scent of the food, feels as dry as cotton. He could easily knock this man unconscious and then satisfy his hunger and thirst. Yet he stands there, bland and obedient.

In a few minutes, as Katsuhiro had expected, Regis begins his meal, savoring each bite, smacking his lips after each long swallow of water, setting the sandwich aside from time to time as if he is finished, then starting to eat again. It is an elegant, terrible torture. Katsuhiro appreciates the man's skill even as he hates him more and more with every passing moment.

When at last the sandwich is eaten and the pitcher emptied, Regis returns his attention to Katsuhiro.

"You're a strange one, Mr. Oba," he says conversationally. "Most people would have protested when they were kidnapped. You accepted it quite quietly. Are you involved in something to which you would rather not draw attention?"

Katsuhiro shakes his head.

"You say not," Regis continues. "Still, it's a captivating thought. I have had my men search your clothing and your luggage. Perhaps a more thorough search is in order . . . one that delves into the body cavities."

He draws the last words out syllable by syllable, smiling all the while.

"That would please some of the guards quite a bit. They would enjoy the . . . probing."

Katsuhiro says nothing. He no longer trusts his temper. Chief General Doctor Regis is one of the more annoying mortals he has met in his long life. He would like to separate him into component pieces—and he need not have his sword to do so.

So lost is he in this pleasant fantasy that he misses part of what Regis says next:

". . . is true. I am interested in speaking with you about business, perhaps the very business that brought you here in the first place."

Regis focuses his bloodshot gaze on Katsuhiro, hoping doubtless for some expression of surprise. Katsuhiro chooses to disappoint him. He smiles blandly and imagines the mulatto's right arm resting on the desk in front of him, even as it is now, but no longer attached at the shoulder.

"I know your business," Regis says, "and I think it is a

very good plan, indeed, with one small exception. I would prefer that my friends and I be your Nigerian contacts rather than the group you intended to work with. That is simple enough, isn't it? You will still do your business, still make your money, but you will work with me."

"When the sky falls and the oceans all freeze," Katsuhiro says conversationally, "when the sun goes dark and the moon returns to the arms of her mother. That is when I will work with you."

Regis leans back in his chair and begins to laugh. It is an unpleasant laugh, merciless and humorless, yet somehow artificial. It sounds as if Regis has taken a tutorial on such laughter with the villains of every movie serial and television series ever written.

"So you *can* speak! I was beginning to wonder if we had taken the wrong man." He grows suddenly serious. "You speak big words, Mr. Oba, but I think I can convince you to think otherwise."

Katsuhiro, now that his tongue is loosed, cannot make it grow still again:

"If you think that torturing me as you did that poor wretch in my cell will change my mind, you are quite wrong. You cannot change my mind in that fashion."

"It might be interesting to try," Regis says. His tone is clinical.

Despite the heat of his own anger Katsuhiro feels his blood chill. Regis means what he says. Torture interests him.

"Perhaps I will try it," Regis muses, "just for experiment's sake. However, I would prefer you unmarked. Wounds you could show would be wounds you could turn to evidence against me. Still, I promise you most sincerely, I have the means of changing your mind. Don't force me to use it."

Katsuhiro clamps his lips shut on the insult that rises to them. Regis presses his intercom button.

"Teresa, send in the guards. My interview with Mr. Oba has ended." He returns his attention to Katsuhiro. "I mean what I say, Mr. Oba. Most sincerely."

The guards knock crisply, then enter.

"Take Mr. Oba back to his cell. He is to have clean water but no food."

The guards salute and take Katsuhiro in custody. They are marching him out the door when Chief General Doctor Regis's voice comes after them:

"And Mr. Oba, I suggest that you talk with that 'poor wretch' who shares your cell. Once you hear his story you might feel far less sympathetic toward him."

The laugh again, then, "Yes. Far less."

Our chief want in life is somebody who will make us do what we can.

—RALPH WALDO EMERSON

SHAHRAZAD IS PLEASED WITH HERSELF. SHE'S RANGED farther from the ranch house than ever before, and there's a fascinating canine scent on the wind. The jackalopes are nervous, too, and as far as she is concerned that's a bonus.

The young coyote trots a bit faster, eager to find the source of this smell—this despite the fact that her hackles stand on end whenever she gets a good strong whiff. For now, curiosity is outweighing prudence and instinct. She wants to know what are these creatures who smell like coyotes, yet not quite like coyotes, but not like dogs either. She trusts in her young strength and in her father to keep her safe.

She heads up a grassy rise toward a copse of trees that offers far more shelter than the surrounding grasslands. Deer are there, deer and elk, as well as rabbits, squirrels, and hosts of smaller rodents. A jay scolds her from a nearby evergreen.

Eyeing it as if to say: "You talk big, but if I had wings, you wouldn't talk like that to me!" Shahrazad takes a fresh scent.

There, in among the trees. Several of them. Male and female and young.

Intensely social, as her father had learned to his dismay,

Shahrazad wags her tail at the thought of playmates, contradicting the argument raised by her hackles.

Nose low to the ground, Shahrazad is heading into the trees when Hip, the male jackalope, interposes himself between her and her goal. Shahrazad growls, her hackles raised deliberately now, not from instinct, and shows her fangs.

Hip interposes his antlers and Hop, coming around Shahrazad's right side, prods the young coyote gently but firmly, clearly meaning to turn her back.

Shahrazad growls. What do they think they are doing? Isn't this *her* new domain? Isn't she the Changer's daughter, with the privileges that her father's power has won for her?

The two jackalopes don't seem impressed by her growl, nor does the jay who shouts raucous insults at her.

Shahrazad growls again, snapping at Hip, not really intending to bite him, just to remind him that she is larger and far more dangerous than he.

Her reward is a solid jab from his antler prongs. Though lacking the weight of a true antelope, the jackalope has strong hind legs and lots of practice in warding back importunate predators. Hip's aim is sure, and Shahrazad yelps in surprise.

However, she is no longer the little pup who piddled at every frightening thing. She is a mighty hunter, one who has killed scores of rabbits. Nothing that so resembles her natural prey is going to push her around—not even if it has points on its head!

Shahrazad backs a few steps, as if retreating. When the jackalopes drop from their haunches to all fours, she leaps.

The motion combines the hop she has perfected for mousing—a sudden jerk up into the air from all four paws at once—combined with a surge forward. Shahrazad clears the recumbent jackalopes so narrowly that Hop's antlers brush the long fur on her belly. The jackalopes wail for her to stop, an eerie noise, but Shahrazad is past them and running for the trees.

She expects to hear them thumping after her, but they do not. Only the jay flies behind her, scolding her vigorously.

For a moment, Shahrazad feels her aloneness, almost feels betrayed by the lepus kin. Then she brightens, her tail coming up and eyes searching the shadows under the trees for the source of the interesting scent. They must be near now. The scent that had been stale is fresh now. Shahrazad smells one, two, more: male and female both. The scent is odd, canine but mixed with something else.

Shahrazad is trying to place the other element when a massive canine steps from the shadows to confront her. There is no word in Shahrazad's vocabulary for "wolf" and yet something within her hindbrain's catalog mates scent with image. Instinct tells the young coyote that before her is a creature that, for all its apparent likeness to her, may be kin but is not kind.

Shahrazad crouches, trying to seem small, already beginning to back toward the open field. Then she stops backing. Too late she realizes that the wolves are all around her: grown wolves with pelts of dark grey, black, and dirty white. They outweigh her by a body and a half, would outweigh even her father, who is large for a coyote.

Frightened and afraid to surrender—because she does not believe that these creatures would accept her surrender but would take advantage of bared belly and exposed throat—Shahrazad crouches low and growls warning that she will not die easily.

For all her bravado, she has but one hope: that her father is somewhere near and will help her.

Although she cannot tear her gaze from the big alpha male stalking closer and closer, one ear flicks from side to side, waiting for the sound of her father's voice or of his footsteps, hoping in some strange corner of her mind that he will have the sense to take the shape of something larger than a coyote.

Rescue comes in an unexpected form, even as it had on the day of the Eyes. There is a drumming of hooves on the turf and Pearl and Sun, the senior unicorns of Frank's herd, come bursting into the grove where Shahrazad crouches in the midst of the circle of wolves. The jackalopes run with them, darting between the wolves until they stand flanking Shahrazad.

The wolves back away from the unicorns; most vanish into the forest. A few remain, including the big male who had been about to punish the young coyote for her temerity.

Growling far more ferociously than Shahrazad could do on her best day, he faces Sun. Sun lowers his golden horn and paws the turf, impressing Shahrazad with his terrible fury. Perhaps she has underrated these herbivores.

She has the sense that there is more than mere posturing going on here, but she has not yet learned any but the most basic (and usually most painful) forms of communication with the other residents of the OTQ.

After more growls and more pawing of the turf, punctuated by shrill imprecations from the jay, the wolves draw back. Her rescuers herd her from the forest as if she were little more than a mouse, but Shahrazad doesn't dare voice her indignation beneath the watchful arc of the two unicorns' sharp horns.

Instead, once she is safely out in the open, she lopes as fast as she can back to the ranch. She finds her father, human-form, helping Frank do something inexplicable with fresh-cut wood and tools. Trotting up to him, bristling with excitement and resentment, she squats next to him and lets loose a stream of rich, reeking yellow piss.

"Damn!" the Changer yells furiously.

He surges into the air in an almost involuntary shapeshift, turning himself into a jay remarkably like the one who had scolded her at the forest's edge.

Then he returns to human form, safely away from the puddle of urine. With a strength that one would not expect in his lean body, he scoops his daughter up by the scruff of her neck.

Too late, Shahrazad realizes that she has overstepped the limits of what her father will permit. She whimpers repentantly, but her whining does not stop him from cuffing her soundly. Dropping her to the ground, the Changer sends her off in disgrace with a last solid wallop.

"I am going," he says to Frank, his voice more gravelly than usual, "to have to do something about her."

¤◘¤

Katsuhiro never gets off the plane at Lagos airport.

After Anson pays some heavy bribes to a clerk with a

superior attitude, he and Eddie discover that the Japanese had arrived two days before, gone through Customs, and then, to all intents and purposes, vanished.

Katsuhiro had not arrived at the hotel where they had made him reservations nor had he checked in to any of the hotels that cater to foreign travelers. None of the taxi drivers would admit to having him as a passenger; none of the porters would admit to having carried his luggage.

Eddie and Anson spend the better part of Katsuhiro's scheduled day of arrival and the morning of the day after searching for him. Before they depart for Monamona, Anson promises substantial rewards to some shifty men in a darkened room if they can locate the tall, bearded Asian.

"I am praying," Anson says to Eddie, no trace of irony in his voice, "that Susano simply let his impulsiveness carry him into Monamona early."

"The same way it carried him into Nigeria two days ahead of schedule." Eddie nods, then frowns. "That would be nice, but I don't think it's likely. If that was the case, someone should remember him: a lorry driver, a hotel keeper, a car dealer, a porter."

"Yeah."

"And think of the trouble we had leaving Monamona. The quarantine for smallpox is getting tighter. If you hadn't known how much dash to pay and we hadn't been able to prove we'd been vaccinated, we would have never gotten out. I have trouble believing that Katsuhiro would have been as smooth."

"Keep cheering me up, friend," Anson says glumly, dipping his free hand into a bag of cookies. "My life can use brightness, eh?"

Eddie doesn't laugh. "I'm being practical. In case you hadn't noticed, things are getting out of control."

"I had noticed."

"Any thoughts about what we do next?"

Anson licks cookie crumbs off of his fingers. "One, we look for Katsuhiro or any rumor of him in Monamona. Two, we go ahead and have our first meeting with Shango. He and Dakar will argue anyhow. They don't need Katsuhiro present to do that."

"True." Eddie manages a small chuckle. "You certainly have chosen a contentious group."

"Are any of us not contentious?" Anson says. "I think not. Those of us who have survived a lifetime or two have a strong sense of our own worth and of our own territory. Humans go to war over countries established by people they never knew. Our people—we often established the country, eh?"

"And view those who come into it as interlopers," Eddie agrees, "even if they have been there for centuries. I really think that's why so many of us have emigrated to America—there aren't so many old rivalries."

"Not *so* many"—Anson shakes his head—"but some. Now, whether or not it is true, Dakar has come to identify with the tales that say he was the one who opened the way into Yorubaland for the gods and those who came after them. The first kings of the first city are supposed to be his descendants. Shango's lineage is old, but not that old. Besides, there are stories that Ogun's wife left him for Shango."

"Really?"

"True as can be. Her name was Oya. She is called 'The wife who is fiercer than her husband,' so I don't know why warlike Ogun still resents her moving on, but he does."

"Was she a real person?"

Anson shakes his head. "I doubt it, but you know how we athanor can be. Look at good Arthur. He never did half of what legend has attributed to the noble King of England, but now he expects to be treated as if he did it all and more besides. Our once and current king."

"He did a great deal," Eddie says, automatically resenting a slight to his ruler and close friend. "Much of what he really did has been forgotten. No wonder he clings to the legends."

"Maybe." Anson shrugs.

Eddie suddenly feels guilty. "I haven't checked in with him for too long. I should e-mail him at least. Do you want me to tell him about Katsuhiro?"

"Not yet. Let us look for him a while longer."

When they are back in their hotel, Eddie finds that both electricity and phone service are working. Since it is late, he has no trouble getting an international connection and downloads his e-mail. He is astonished by the number of messages waiting for him. By the time they have all been transferred, that astonishment has turned to concern.

Many of the messages are repetitions of an urgent request that Eddie call or at least e-mail. Arthur has not gotten over a primitive belief that many and louder requests will get action faster than one.

At last Arthur's messages begin to offer details, and Eddie quickly grasps the import of Lil and Tommy's plan to use the fauns and satyrs in their stage show.

His first reaction is a mirror of Arthur's. There is a good chance that such publicity will at least lead to the discovery that the fauns and satyrs are real. At the very worst, the athanor as a community may be exposed.

Much of Eddie's attention and energy for the last fifteen hundred years—as human society became less tolerant of multiple gods and multiple ways of viewing strange happenings—has been spent misdirecting attention from the athanor. Especially during the last two hundred years, ever since science won out over magic as the means of explaining odd events, the athanor have taken care not to draw attention to themselves. Now a rock star and his less-than-scrupulous manager plan to risk all of this for a flamboyant stage show.

Eddie's fingers are racing across his computer keyboard, drafting a reply to Arthur, suggesting strategies to counter, even hinting that he might be available for recall, when he suddenly recalls present events.

His fingers grow still and he stares at the wall of his hotel room. How much does any of this really matter?

During the last week and more he has been forced to face how much of the world still lives. He has seen people drinking water that in America wouldn't be given to a pet, children gaunt from malnutrition, and smallpox (which he had believed forever banished) rearing its head once more. In the newspapers he has read the statistics on the spread of AIDS in Africa—a plague that has hit Nigeria very hard because of its lingering tradition of male privilege and polygamous marriages.

An undercurrent to his and Anson's searches both for Anson's friends and for Katsuhiro has been their acceptance that human rights are very delicate things indeed, that all it takes is a few unscrupulous people in power to undermine all the rhetoric and make it no more meaningful than a child's nursery song.

Eddie's hands slip from the keyboard and he rereads the words that he has written as if they had been typed by a stranger. After a moment, he erases that message and types another:

> ARTHUR—SORRY THAT THINGS ARE LESS THAN PEACEFUL THERE. DON'T WORRY. MOST AMERICANS DON'T BELIEVE ANYTHING THE ENTERTAINMENT INDUSTRY DOES, EVEN IF THEY EXPERIENCE IT WITH THEIR OWN FIVE SENSES. GO SEE THE SHOW YOURSELF IF YOU WANT PROOF. JUST TRY TO KEEP THEM FROM TOURING INTERNATIONALLY SINCE CUSTOMS COULD BE A PROBLEM. BUSY HERE. TOO MUCH TO TELL NOW. I'LL TRY TO BE BETTER ABOUT KEEPING IN TOUCH.
>
> EDDIE.

After reviewing the message, Eddie sends it. He doesn't doubt that Arthur is going to be unhappy when he gets it. After a moment he types another message:

> CHRIS AND BILL—MY APOLOGIES, BUT THE KING IS GOING TO BE A BIT PISSY FOR THE NEXT COUPLE OF DAYS. OR MORE THAN HE HAS BEEN. I APPEND A MESSAGE I JUST SENT HIM BY WAY OF EXPLANATION. WEATHER THE STORM. I'M AUTHORIZING MY BANKER TO PUT A BONUS DIRECTLY IN YOUR ACCOUNTS. THANKS.
>
> EDDIE.

Once that message is sent, Eddie links to his bank accounts, arranges for the promised bonus, then arranges for more money to be sent to him in Nigeria. He suspects he's going to need it before this is over.

Gazing into his computer screen, he mulls over who else he might contact. Vera is probably getting a less intense version of Arthur's barrage, so Eddie sends her a brief message encouraging her to stay at work on Atlantis, no matter how much Arthur whines:

> IF THINGS DO GO SOUTH, (he continues) THAT REFUGE WILL BE WORTH FAR MORE THAN ANY SOOTHING YOU CAN GIVE TO ARTHUR'S FRACTURED PRIDE. ARTHUR ENVISIONED THAT ALL ATHANOR WOULD WANT TO FOLLOW HIS CONSERVATIVE PATH TOWARD EDUCATING HUMAN CULTURE ABOUT OUR EXISTENCE. NOW HE KNOWS HE'S WRONG. WHEN HE ADJUSTS, HE'LL BE AT HIS BEST AGAIN. HE'LL ADJUST FASTER WITH A MINIMUM OF HAND-HOLDING. TRUST ME. I APPEND A COPY OF THE MESSAGE I SENT HIM, SO YOU'LL UNDERSTAND WHY HE'S IN A FOUL MOOD.
>
> EDDIE.

This sent, he drafts a nearly identical message to Jonathan Wong, the athanor to whom Arthur is certain to turn for legal counsel. Feeling that he's covered all the bases, Eddie logs off.

When he tucks the computer into its case, he has a feeling that he won't be using it very often over the next few days. Problems here promise to need more immediate solutions—ones that will waste blood and sweat, not electrons.

¤◙¤

Katsuhiro does not get his cellmate talking all at once, but sharing the drinking water that has been liberally supplied for him, treating his wounds, and sympathizing with his misery finally gets the other man to open up.

The man's name is Adam. He is a Christian, a member of one of the ecstatic religious sects that blend African religious practices with Christian doctrine. It was after his return from a church service that he had been kidnapped.

"My wife and I," Adam says, speaking carefully in his

stilted schoolroom English, "come back to our hotel. We go into our rooms and there are men waiting for us. Men w' guns. They tell us that they want to know about some guests who are coming."

"Wait," Katsuhiro says. "You said, 'your hotel.' "

"Yes, yes," Adam says. "My wife and I, we have a hotel. Not so big but very comfortable. Even some air-conditioning and a backup generator for electricity."

"Ah." Katsuhiro has a bad feeling he knows where this is going, but he needs all the information he can get. "Please, continue."

"I tell them this is privileged information, but after they hit me a few times I show them the register." Adam frowns. "They not find what they want der. I can tell this. So then I know what they want."

Adam's voice drops, becoming so soft that Katsuhiro must bend his head to hear him.

"There is a man. Strange one. African, very wealthy, but I have no idea where his money come from. When I was at school, he made friends with my father. Later, when I want to start the hotel, he give me a loan. This man have called me some weeks before and say he need to get some rooms at my hotel and that he will need me to do a favor for him, too.

"I say 'Of course' because this man is my benefactor. He tells me that he not want that he staying there told to anyone. I say 'Of course'—he is a rich man. He not need beggars to follow him. He tell me that a foreign businessman will be coming, too. That he will need special food, special drink. My benefactor say 'I give you money for this. You order it.' I say 'Of course.' "

Adam pauses for breath. Katsuhiro hands him a plastic cup partially filled with clean, though warm, water.

"Drink," he orders. Then, "Your benefactor—what is his name?"

With the stiff motion of the totally blind, Adam holds out the empty cup so that Katsuhiro can take it.

"That is one thing they want to know," he says sadly. "I try not to tell them, even when they beat me. But then they take me to their big boss."

Adam shudders, his command of English slipping. "When I tink that the last ting I see is dat man's ugly face, I am sick. Dat man beat me more. I say nothing. Maybe he know that I hurt too much, 'cause den he say to me, 'Adam, you got a pretty wife.' I get real sick then, 'cause I have been thinking dat dey leave her at the hotel.

"The boss man say, 'Adam, you got a pretty wife. It be real bad if something happened to her.' I say, 'If you not hurt Teresa, I tell you everything.' So he promises, and I tell him. I tell him that my benefactor is Anson A. Kridd. I tell him that he have a big-shot Japanese man coming."

Adam falls silent for so long that Katsuhiro must prompt him.

"Anything else?"

"Then the boss man laugh at me. He pick up a gun and I tink he gonna shoot me dead, but he jus' spit into my face and say 'Good nigger boy.' Then he say to two guards, 'Tie him in a chair. I want him to watch me fuck his wife.' "

Adam is weeping now, tears trailing from his blind eyes. Katsuhiro reaches out, though normally he shies from physical contact with any but his most intimate associates, and puts an arm around him.

"He make me watch w' a gun to my head. Den when he done, he kick Teresa to the floor and pick up a gun again. He come and lean into my face, 'She's not bad for a nigger bitch. I think I'll keep her for a while.' "

Adam is talking fast now, forgetting to keep his voice low.

"I don't know, maybe Jesus give me the strength, maybe Ogun, but I get so mad that I forget I'm all beaten up. I go at him, even with the chair tied to my backside and my arms all bound. I hit him in the belly with my head and he falls and I fall on top of him. I try to bite him or crush him. Then the guards pull me off.

"The boss man he stands up w' the gun and I tink he gonna shoot me but he jus' hit me in the face w' it. That's the last I see. His face in a snarl like the devil incarnate. Then I not see nothing anymore, nothing but dese lights in my head."

Katsuhiro offers Adam more water and while Adam drinks he says:

"I promise that man will die if I make it out of here."

Adam smiles and shakes his head. "You no get out."

"Maybe." Katsuhiro will not share more of his budding plans with the broken man beside him.

"You tink Teresa still alive?"

Katsuhiro considers whether or not to tell Adam the truth. If Adam learns that she is alive, his captors have a hold over him, yet ignorance is its own torture. Regis had made certain that Katsuhiro saw the girl . . . why?

Adam speaks again. "If she is alive, she's in hell. I tink dey might make her whore by threatening to hurt me more."

Katsuhiro grunts noncommittally.

"The preacher say dat it wrong to kill yourself, dat you go to hell, but if you livin' is hurting somebody else, den is it so bad to kill yourself?"

"In my country," Katsuhiro says, "it is not wrong to kill yourself if you do so from honor, not from fear."

Adam sighs. "I been tinkin' I know who you mus' be. You talk English w' an accent like I been hearing in the movies. Tell me, Oba, is you Anson's friend, the Japanese businessman?"

"Yes."

"Den you mus' hate me, 'cause I why the boss man know you comin'."

"I don't hate you."

"Thanks."

They sit in silence for a long while, long enough that Katsuhiro decides that Adam must have fallen asleep. He occupies himself thinking of revenge, counting the booted feet that pass the narrow window above, trying to estimate his chances for escape. Then Adam's voice breaks the silence.

"I not know if I could kill myself. I have nothing to do it w'. Maybe I jus' starve. Dey not feed me for so long."

"Maybe." Katsuhiro is well aware how long it has been since he has eaten. His dreams the night before were haunted by that ham and cheese sandwich—and he doesn't even *like* cheese.

"I not tink I could not eat if they give me even a yam full of worms." Adam sighs. "Or stale bread w' mold. My stomach forget what hungry is, but my brain won't stop."

"Yeah," Katsuhiro pats him. "I know."

"Oba," Adam's tone is solemn now, "I want to ask you a favor."

"Ask."

"Kill me."

¤◙¤

"The trouble is," the Changer says to Frank MacDonald as they sit over dinner the day after Shahrazad's encounter with the wolves, "Shahrazad expects me to be there to rescue her."

The coyote puppy, sides rounded from her own dinner, thumps her tail sleepily from where she drowses on a rag rug in front of a blazing fire. She has learned not to mind that she must share the space with assorted cats, dogs, and jackalopes, or that the perpetually miserable clouded leopard gets the cushion closest to the blaze where he can dream of the warm rain forests that were once his home.

"Yes." Frank twirls some fettucini around his fork. "Her faith in you in unshaken, despite the fact that you haven't been the one to rescue her from her last two escapades."

"I was lucky," the Changer says, "that I found the griffin the first time or I might have had to intervene. The second time, Hip and Hop had already warned the unicorns where Shahrazad was heading."

"Would you have interfered if they hadn't shown up in time?"

"I'm afraid so," the Changer admits.

"Then Shahrazad is right to count on you."

"I've wondered if somehow she knows when I am near, even if I haven't given any indication."

"Some of the animals, the dogs in particular," Frank says, "claim that you have a distinctive scent that underlies whatever form you take. Could Shahrazad be scenting that?"

"Possibly, though I have taken care to be downwind of her whenever possible."

"More fettucini?"

"Please." The Changer heaps his plate high, then adds extra cheese sauce from a tureen that stands warming over a small candle. "How long have you had wolves here?"

"Since I founded the ranch. They have real problems, problems on a par with those faced by creatures like the griffin or unicorns."

"Worse in a way," the Changer says. "Humans fear them—even the humans who claim to love them—and they know wolves exist."

"Right." Frank sips red wine. "Ranchers are smart to fear wolf predation, don't get me wrong. A wolf pack coordinates in killing its prey, making it a threat to creatures far larger than any one wolf."

"I," the Changer says reminiscently, "have been a wolf."

"Yes, I'm certain you have," Frank says. "You have been most things. My wolf pack has special problems."

"I smelled them," the Changer says. "Man-wolves."

"Yes," Frank sighs. "Werewolves. They aren't very effective shapechangers. Their human form is primitive: bipedal but so heavily furred and with such a gross distortion of the facial features that a satyr has an easier time blending into modern society."

"I don't recall," the Changer says mildly, "a time when werewolves ever blended very easily."

"No," Frank agrees. "They don't really. They're not a whole lot smarter than your average wolf, and in human form they're rather short-tempered. They do make extraordinarily good wolves, though. The extra intelligence helps there. That's why some of them survived the Middle Ages."

"There was an aboriginal werewolf population in North America, wasn't there?"

"Yes. Unfortunately, even their athanor resistance to disease didn't stop them from falling to the same illnesses that devastated the Native Americans. And not even an athanor can resist a bullet to the heart or a cut throat."

"So your pack here?"

"Is part-European, part-American. I've heard that there is another community in Alaska. There may be another in Siberia. I'm not certain."

"Are they cross-fertile with wolves?"

"Varies from werewolf to werewolf, much as with most athanor. Lupé, the pack leader—the one who was ready to kill Shahrazad—does better than most, but most of his pups are just wolves."

"Athanor wolves?"

"Not many. Not for several years."

"Still his get has added to Harmony."

"Yes."

They finish the fettucini in silence, then Frank goes to the kitchen and returns with a pecan pie and a carafe of coffee.

"Dessert?"

"Of course. You know how shapeshifters are." The Changer smiles, and Frank colors.

"Yes, that I do."

He cuts them both large wedges of pie, tastes his, then continues:

"I rely on the werewolves to help me with many of the chores around here. They can't feed the horses or muck out stalls—the horses get too scared. But they can build fences or do repair work on the buildings. Just for safety's sake, I don't pasture any of the horses near the wolves' hunting grounds. The werewolves have a pretty good idea of what they should and should not hunt."

"And they have lots of experience hiding their tracks," the Changer says. "So they protect the normal wolves."

"Right. The deal has worked so far, but the wolf pack has grown larger than I like. I need to keep the athanor here, but I'm trying to find somewhere I can export some of the spares."

"Alaska?"

"Probably. The yeti would help them while they acclimated. The trouble is, a biologist would realize that they weren't from the local strain. That might raise some awkward questions. I might try Siberia instead. The former Soviet Union is such a mess that no one is going to be studying wolves for a while."

"A great, wide world," the Changer says, "and yet it keeps getting smaller."

"I know. Where are you thinking of going next?"

"Can Shahrazad stay here?"

"If she does, I'll do my best to protect her, but if she

doesn't learn to stay away from werewolves and hydra, there isn't much I can do."

"She wants friends," the Changer says. "You don't have coyotes on OTQ grounds, though, do you?"

"Not many, not for long." Frank shrugs. "Wolves don't like coyotes, and most coyotes have the sense to stay away from wolves."

"Shahrazad is still a bit of a snob when it comes to cats and dogs," the Changer admits, "and, though she won't say so, she's scared of the unicorns."

Frank nods. "That shows intelligence. There are some foxes who might play with her. Maybe I can get her to realize that even grass-eaters can be interesting."

"If anyone can do it," the Changer says, again with a smile that says more than his words, "I think it will be you."

Frank ignores the innuendo. "So where will you go? Back to Arthur's?"

"I don't think so. From what you have told me, he is facing another crisis. Besides, I'm not one for cities."

Frank frowns. "I'd prefer if you were somewhere I could contact you if Shahrazad did get into trouble, not out in virgin wilderness."

"Why don't I go visit my brother?"

"Duppy Jonah? That's not a bad idea. He's had telephone for quite a while. I think that Vera has been working on some way to get him and Amphitrite on-line."

"I can fly to the Gulf and swim from there," the Changer says. "Atlantis is being constructed in warmer waters."

"That would work then," Frank agrees. "You couldn't get here immediately, but I could reach you if I needed an opinion."

The Changer glances over to where Shahrazad is sound asleep, apparently unaware of the black-and-white long-haired cat that has curled up beside her.

"I'll explain things to her in the morning," he says. "She must understand that I will not be here to save her from herself."

Frank nods. "You're not going to enjoy that, are you?"

"No, but it must be done."

We are in bondage to the law in order that we might be free.

—Cicero

PREPARED BY EDDIE'S MESSAGE TO TREAT THEIR EMPLOYER as if he is part–temperamental two-year-old and part–mad dog, Chris and Bill are surprised by how courteously Arthur summons them to his office a few hours after they receive Eddie's message.

Entering the chief executive's office with barely concealed trepidation, they expect anything from a lecture on how useless they are or a diatribe about Eddie's disloyalty. Instead, Arthur stands politely when they enter and gestures to the good chairs he keeps for guests.

"Please," he says, his British accent courtly, "have a seat. May I offer you some refreshments?"

"Water," Bill manages, "would be nice."

Chris nods agreement.

Once they are settled with tall crystal goblets of iced water, Arthur resumes his seat behind his desk and clears his throat. It's about then that both humans realize that they are neither about to be fired nor lectured.

"You both are aware," Arthur says, "of the difficulty that has arisen regarding Tommy Thunderburst's plan to use fauns and satyrs in his stage show."

They nod.

"I realized earlier this morning that I have not been consulting you as I should have. After all, we are dealing with a question of how humans will react to the presence of something they believe mythical. Certainly, as you are human, you are the best people to advise me."

Chris clears his throat, remembering what Eddie had said to Arthur in the letter he had appended to their own. Eddie had hit the nail on the head. How best to reinforce his argument without letting the King know that they are in collusion?

"Well, sir," he says, pushing his glasses straight on the bridge of his nose, "the fact is that ever since television was introduced, humans have been conditioned to distrust the evidence of their eyes. We know that most of what we see is a trick—whether it's beautiful women on some soap opera or monsters on some SF special. They look real, but we know that they're not."

Arthur nods encouragement, so Bill picks up the thread.

"Back when the movie *King Kong* was first shown in the theaters," he says, "they say that women fainted and even went into labor prematurely. Today, most people laugh at how fake that big ape looks, but they still scream when some computer-generated dinosaur clomps across the scream."

"And," Chris adds, "even while they're doing it, there's this little voice in the back of their minds wondering whether these dinosaurs are going to look as fake as the original King Kong in a couple years."

Arthur nods again, pours himself a little more Earl Grey tea from the elegant teapot resting on the corner of his desk, and sips.

"So what you are saying is that even if the audience members at Tommy's show see, hear, and even smell a satyr, they won't believe that they're seeing anything other than a particularly well-done special effect."

Chris smiles encouragingly. "That's the long and short of it. I think that even if some starstruck fan shook hands with a faun, all she'd think is 'How cool,' then wonder how they did the makeup so well that it didn't show up close."

"You know," Bill adds, "that handshaking could be the

most dangerous part of the whole thing. When I was a kid, my folks took me to see Santa Claus. I tried to pull off his beard 'cause I'd heard from some kids at school that Santa was all a fake."

Arthur raises his eyebrows. "And what happened?"

"Santa screamed," Bill says, laughing. "He may have been a fake, but the beard was real."

Arthur chuckles. "I have never gone to see Santa at Christmas, but I did meet Saint Nicholas once in passing. That is the problem with me. I *know* that so many things from legend are not myths. This makes it hard for me to believe that creatures as intelligent as humans could be fooled."

"Thanks," Chris says dryly, "for the vote of confidence regarding intelligence, but the truth of the matter is that most people going out to a concert will have turned their brains off."

"Chemically," Bill adds, "in many cases. At the last concert I attended you could get high just from the smoke drifting around. The stadium was technically 'dry,' but some of the kids were really clever at sneaking in stuff to drink."

"And the officials just let this happen?" Arthur asks, amazed. "But there are laws!"

"Your athanor are pretty law-abiding," Bill says, "no matter what you think from time to time."

"Much for us all rests," Arthur says stiffly, "on maintaining both the Accord and Harmony."

"So we have seen," Chris assures him. "But most Americans have a shaky idea of just why a society abides by laws. I was a reporter, I know. Americans may have learned about the social contract in civics class, but most view laws as inconveniences—until they want to sue someone else for breaking them."

"And taxes," Bill puts in, "are looked at as an abuse and an indignity, but people still want someone to fix the potholes, maintain the parks, and pick up the trash without bothering them about it."

"Yes." Arthur actually smiles. "I have seen that response often enough in the kingdoms I have ruled. So, as you analyze the situation, most humans will *not* believe that they are seeing real fauns and satyrs."

"That's right," Chris says. "And of those who do believe, most will be unwilling to break that illusion. They *want* to believe in myth and magic."

"Until," Arthur says grimly, "it comes true. Then the witch-hunts start."

"We're not arguing with that," Bill agrees. "Anyhow, I hung around with Georgios when he was out here this past September, and I'm not certain that human society is ready for him in large doses."

Arthur looks relieved to find that they, at least, are not challenging his policy of cautious interaction. "Then what do you suggest?"

"Let them do the show," Chris says, "but suggest some safeguards."

Arthur starts taking notes on his computer. He nods for Chris to go on.

"First," Chris says, suddenly feeling the enormous responsibility of counseling a king, "suggest that Lil and Tommy play coy about just how they've managed this stunt. That will both increase the interest and assure most people that it's all a scam.

"Two, have the fauns and satyrs wear at least some stage makeup. That way if someone takes pictures with a telephoto lens they'll see the makeup and think that it's all just FX."

Arthur chuckles. "Clever. Anything else?"

Bill nods. "Yeah. Suggest that the more rambunctious characters don't give interviews. I don't trust Georgios, good buddy that he is, not to drop his pants and show off his endowments."

"Good point," Arthur says. "I have seen him do just that in a time long past. The woman, however, was not impressed. She was horrified."

"And," Chris says, "if some theriomorph insists on giving an interview, suggest that they be misleading—something like the 'real beard' thing that Bill mentioned before."

"You mean, actually invite an interviewer to pull a beard?" Arthur says, his fingers flying over the keys.

"Something like that. We can work out the details if the need arises."

Arthur looks up from rereading what he has just typed.

"I can hardly believe," he says, "that I am going to condone this madness. It is contrary to everything I have worked toward for the last several centuries."

Bill laughs. "Well, it's not like they gave you much choice."

"No," Arthur says solemnly, "and that will remain a difficulty. I can make suggestions as to their course of action, but I cannot command."

"Why not," Chris suggests, "get your own man in their camp? Or at least your own faun?"

"Who?"

"I was reviewing the theriomorph chatroom this morning," Chris responds. "Demetrios Stangos has been offered a job managing the theriomorphs. He's thinking about turning it down, but if you can get him to take it, I'm sure he'll work with you."

"Brilliant!" Arthur exclaims. "You both have been a great deal of help. I will call Demetrios at once. Now, return to your duties. I'll be certain to tell you what results from our discussion."

Chris glances at the clock. "It's getting near lunchtime. Eddie told me to make certain you don't forget to eat."

Arthur pats his waist. "I can certainly afford to miss a meal or two."

"Still," Chris says over his shoulder, as he and Bill depart, "I'll bring in a sandwich."

He doesn't know if Arthur has heard him. The King, the glow of battle in his eyes, has picked up the phone and is punching in a number.

They meet with Shango in great secrecy, a thing that surprises Anson quite a bit, for Monamona is Shango's city, even to its name, which means lightning in Yoruban.

Here Shango has ruled from behind the scenes for more than twenty-five years. He has managed at least one successful change of identity in that time and amassed considerable wealth. That he should insist on a private meeting is incredible.

Incredible or not, he insists. After a great flurry of minor illusions, skulking in doorways, and entering via side entrances, they arrive at a private residence.

Following instructions smuggled to them by a street urchin, they go to a room on the second floor. Therein, they find Shango waiting for them. He is alone, seated in a comfortable chair with empty chairs drawn up in a rough circle. The room is hot, for the curtains are all drawn and there is no air-conditioning. The slow action of electric fans keeps the room from becoming completely stifling.

"I warn you," Eddie tells Shango, while Anson and Dakar search for hidden guards, recording devices, or other evidence of skulduggery, "that I have left messages where they will be found if I do not report back to disable them within a preordained period of time."

Shango, a long-necked man with smile lines about his eyes and mouth, smooths the drape of his hand-printed *dansiki*, adjusts the bracelets on his arms, and tries hard to look cheerful.

"I believe you, Wild Man, Knight of the Round Table, Great Ancient of our people. I hope that you believe me in turn when I tell you that I intend no harm, no threat to any of you. Indeed, my insistence on meeting in this fashion is my first and best attempt at keeping you safe."

"The place seems clean," Dakar says, dropping into one of three empty chairs that are arranged near Shango's. "Seems the pansy has played fair with us—a shame, I was looking forward to messing up his pretty hair."

Shango touches his Michael Jacksonesque array of curls.

"I am a dandy," he says, neither his temper nor his locks the least disarrayed, "not a pansy. Ask my wives and children if you doubt my virility, though I wonder why you are so interested. What does it say about you?"

"And a good evening to you both." Anson interrupts the byplay. "Shango, we are here. Why this secrecy? When you and I first discussed this meeting, we agreed to meet at your office with the appropriate officials. Are you reneging on our preliminary agreement?"

"No, but things have changed since we made our plans."

"Changed." Anson frowns. "I can believe that."

"I have met with difficulties."

"And so have we."

"And I believe that I may not be able to fulfill my part of the bargain."

Shango rises from his chair in a sudden burst of energy that recalls the lightning that he wields. He brings out an ice chest containing chilled drinks and drops it into the middle of the circle formed by their chairs.

"My hospitality is not the most elegant, but the drinks are cold and individually sealed."

Anson leans down and pulls out a cola from among the ice cubes. He pops it open, continuing his interrogation while Eddie and Dakar get their own drinks.

"Shango, why do you believe that you may not be able to fulfill your part of the bargain?"

"Because . . ." Shango falls silent for so long that Dakar, who had shown remarkable patience when he discovered that all the drinks were nonalcoholic, growls. "Because I am afraid."

This is the last thing that anyone who knows the debonair African athanor would have expected him to say. Bluster is more his style, or charm, or, failing that, a surge of temper that might rival Ogun's. Never would they expect him to admit to feeling fear.

Anson asks carefully. "Of what are you afraid?"

"Of the King of the World."

Eddie clears his throat inquiringly.

"He means," Dakar says, his voice soft, like a child talking about a bogeyman, "Shopona, the God of Smallpox."

"We have seen signs of his presence," Anson admits, "but what does this have to do with our plans to sell Nigerian oil to the Japanese?"

Shango fingers a heavy gold hoop hanging from one of his earlobes.

"Shopona came to me—or I should say, a man claiming to be Shopona came to me. He had heard rumors, he said, from underlings in the city government, rumors that I was setting up a great investment plan. He wanted to be involved. Naturally, I told him that I had no idea what he was talking about."

"Naturally," Dakar prompts mildly. Mention of the smallpox has reminded him of the petitions crowding his shrine, of how little he can do for those who appeal—however misguidedly—to him for aid. Here is news of a real enemy. Hearing it, he becomes as patient as any good hunter must be if he hopes to take his prey.

"Modern medicine had taken his kingdom from the King of Heaven," Shango continues, "or so I believed."

"Me, too," Eddie says. "That's been bothering me ever since Anson and I saw the signs. I'm certain that the World Health Organization announced the defeat of smallpox in the 1980s. I don't think they even vaccinate babies for it anymore."

"So this man—he called himself Regis—said, but he said that he had the means of starting an epidemic. His family, it seems, had long been worshipers of Shopona and had preserved infectious matter against the King's defeat. If I continued to refuse him, Regis said he would begin an epidemic right here in Monamona and many would die."

Shango shrugs. "I thought him insane. You would have, too, this ugly reddish-haired man, half-white, half-black, and the worst of both worlds. He spoke as if he was educated, but as if he knew the old religion, too. Yet when I scoffed at his claims, he did what he had threatened. Now his altars are buried beneath sacrifices, and people die."

Anson crushes his empty soda can between his fingers. "Is he one of us—an athanor?"

"I don't think so," Shango replies. "If he is, he is well disguised, for I do not recall meeting him."

"I wish we had a wizard here who could tell us," Anson says, "so that we would know if the Accord protects him."

"The Accord is not designed to protect those who do such things!" Dakar protests.

"No," Eddie agrees, speaking as the voice of Arthur, upholder of that very Accord, "but it does give any athanor the right to a trial in front of his or her peers."

"Fuck trials!" Dakar growls.

"In this case," Eddie says, "all my sympathies are with you. Let's hope that we don't find out that this King of Heaven is athanor."

Shango nods. "I agree, but I do not know of anyone local who has the talent to tell who is and who is not athanor."

"Maybe," Anson says, "we can bring someone in—if it comes to that."

"I think it must come to that," Shango says. "I cannot calmly sit here and discuss oil deals while my city is ravaged. I think only the vaccinations given in the late 1960s have kept the disease from spreading more widely."

"That is quite possible," Anson says. "And I didn't think you could just sit."

"Nor can I," Dakar states.

"Nor," says Eddie with a deliberate pause, "can I."

"Nor can I," Anson admits. "I simply did not wish to force any of you into a dangerous course of action."

"Then we are agreed," Shango asks eagerly, "to destroy this Regis?"

"Definitely," Anson says. "That will be our first order of business, eh?"

"But what will," Shango looks about, as if realizing for the first time that Katsuhiro is not occupying the chair prepared for him, "our Japanese colleague think?"

Anson spreads his hands wide. "Remember how I told you that we had difficulties, too? That is our difficulty. Katsuhiro Oba has been kidnapped."

Shango frowns. "Kidnapped? Are you certain?"

"Certain. He vanished from the Lagos airport. We found no trace of him after that. Do you have any idea what might have happened?"

"I do not think I ever mentioned him to my associates by name, only that I might have found a foreign investor," Shango says. "I am certain I did not mention him, for the Japanese connection was to be our great secret. However, I did mention *you* a time or two. There seemed no harm in that since we have done small business before."

Anson purses his lips thoughtfully. "Did you mention that I would be bringing that foreign investor?"

Closing his eyes to concentrate, Shango says woefully, "Yes, I believe that I did."

"Then an ambitious person could have learned of Katsuhiro through one of my associates." Anson's features crease in pain. "The hotelkeeper Adam and his wife, Teresa, are also missing. I told them to prepare for a Japanese guest. This cannot be a coincidence."

"No."

The four men sit in gloomy silence, then Shango again surges to his feet, his features suddenly lit by a vicious smile.

"If Regis has taken them, I know where he must be holding them." He turns off the room light and pulls back the curtain.

"There."

Shango points toward a blocky shape, just visible in the night.

"That is Regis's stronghold, a veritable fortress. It was constructed during the oil boom by one of General Yakubu Gowon's cronies. After Gowon was overthrown in 1975, the building was abandoned for being too associated with tainted policies. It has passed through various hands over the years, but now I happen to know it has a new owner: the King of Hot Water himself."

"Then," Dakar says, more excited by the prospect of warfare than by any deep feeling for his fellow athanor, "we must break in there, get Katsuhiro out, and kill this King."

Eddie shakes his head. "Regis has one disease at his command. What else might he have? We cannot do anything overt unless we are certain that we disable his defenses."

"Spoilsport!" Dakar snorts. Then he shakes his head, unable to forget those laden altars. "But this time you are right."

Anson nods agreement. "We all must concur on this. To be impulsive would be to condemn people far more fragile than ourselves to this Regis's vengeance."

"Even if we can't attack at once, we can begin scouting out his fortress," Shango insists. "Can any of you shift shape?"

Anson nods. "I have a few shapes and a few illusions, but none are terribly powerful or terribly resistant to harm. Still, they will give us an edge."

"Will you go tonight?"

"After we leave here," Anson promises, "but first we must depart with the same care that you directed we arrive, eh?"

"*Na*," Shango agrees, "we don't want to be defeated before we begin."

Impulsively, Dakar thrusts out one beefy black hand. Three other hands grasp his in a gesture of solidarity.

"That's right," Eddie says. "All for one and one for all!"

"And," Anson says with a return to his usual irreverent humor, "thus we shall make the King of Heaven fall!"

Shahrazad goes to sleep unhappy the night following her father's departure. She had thought herself forgiven for her trespass into the wolf pack's territory, but now she learns that her punishment is to be far worse than any beating. The Changer is going to leave her.

The Changer had taken her hunting that morning, had shown her a new trick for disguising her scent trail, had even shown her that a coyote could climb a tree, if the tree was slanted just a bit. That had amused her greatly.

It had been while they were up in a tree, their forepaws dangling to either side of the limb on which they rested, that he had explained that he was going away for a while.

He had told her that he was no longer angry with her for the encounter with the wolves, had told her that he was only leaving so that she would learn what to do when he would not be with her, but Shahrazad had known the truth.

Her father is so angry with her that he is abandoning her.

Shahrazad has memories of other times her father has left her, but those times she had always stayed with Arthur at his hacienda. Even there she had not been safe. She shudders her skin at the memory of being taken away, tied up to a tree in the darkness. Can that happen again?

The Changer must have known of her fears, but he has left her anyway, has winged off into the afternoon sunlight on dark raven's wings. Even Frank's reassurances that he will continue to care for her are not any comfort. After darkness falls without bringing the Changer back, Shahrazad goes out into one of the pastures and sings her sorrow to a starlit sky.

No one answers.

Noticing Pearl the unicorn listening, Shahrazad retreats inside the ranch house. The rug beneath the chair in which the Changer often sat when he talked with Frank still bears some of his scent. She curls up there, nose beneath her tail, and dreams.

Daylight: pale blue, cooler white, like light filtered through clouds, then cast on fresh snow. Shahrazad trots down the hallway toward the Door. As always it is closed.

After her routine attempt to open it, an attempt that fails as always before, she is about to turn away and return to her bed when a scent tantalizes her. She takes a deeper sniff, casting about to make certain of the source but finally she is certain.

The Changer! He is behind that door!

Whining high and eager, acting like a barely weaned pup who smells a meal, she scratches again at the door. It doesn't open.

She collapses onto her side, puts her nose near the crack beneath it, wuffs deep to draw in the air from the other side.

Yes! There, mingled with scents of pine boards, wool rug, Frank's boots, and various other common household scents is that of her father.

But there is something not quite right about it, an intermingling of blood. His blood! She has smelled this before, when he traded his eye for her safety. Has he done this thing again?

Furious and panicked, she digs at the carpet outside the door, flings her shoulder against the wood, leaps and falls back until she is battered and bruised. Still she strives to rescue her father—then he will forgive her and stay with her always.

She hears footsteps on the carpet, feels the vibrations of Frank MacDonald's approach, and stops her frantic attempts. He must not see her, must not know, or he will stop her!

She cringes, looking for a place to hide, but Frank is looking down at her now, bending to lift her by her scruff as if she was but the merest pup and he as tall as the ceiling.

"What's wrong, Shahrazad?" he booms. "What's wrong?"

"Shahrazad?"

The coyote trembles beneath the human hand laid upon her shoulders. Fearfully, she opens her eyes, for, contrary to what her memory is telling her, she is not suspended in the air, but still on the floor where she had fallen asleep.

Frank MacDonald kneels next to her, clad in a cat-hair-covered old bathrobe and dog-chewed slippers. His strong hand strokes gently along her spine.

"Bad dream, pup?" he commiserates in a soft voice. "We all have them, time to time."

He pats her, then scoops her up, not in an undignified fashion, but carefully, as she has seen him carry one of the house cats. She does not wonder that he can lift her so easily. In her mind, she is a frightened pup; he is the adult.

Still carrying her, Frank pads into the kitchen, where he warms her some bread and cheese. After she has eaten this—slowly, as if she is still in her dream, rather than in two quick gulps as would be her wont—he carries her into his bedroom.

He has a large bed. It is already occupied by assorted cats, the clouded leopard, and one of the dogs, but he finds room to set Shahrazad down before taking off his robe and slippers and sliding under the covers.

"There now," Frank says, reaching out and patting her again. "No need to have nightmares. You're among friends."

Shahrazad, meeting the sleepy gaze of a dark red tabby as yellow-eyed as her father, is comforted. She shoves her nose against Frank and drinks in his scent. He smells of human, of the soap with which he washed before bedtime, of the animals he tends, and, beneath it all, of something else.

Too tired to puzzle this out, Shahrazad embraces sleep. Tonight, she knows, there will be no more nightmares.

When I play with my cat, who knows whether I do not make her more sport than she makes me?

—MONTAIGNE

ONCE AGAIN, THE FILTHY CELL IS DARK. BY NOW, HOWever, Katsuhiro's eyes have become so well adjusted to the poor light that he hardly notices. His thoughts are on Adam.

They have talked only a little since Adam requested that Katsuhiro kill him. At first the Japanese had interpreted the African's silence as expressing fear or regret. Later, when the guard refilled his bucket, he had offered Adam more water.

Adam had almost refused to drink. That was when Katsuhiro had realized that Adam's silence was one of waiting. He would not press Katsuhiro further, but he was ready to die.

And what other choice does he have? Alive, he is a hostage against his wife's actions. Only by a miracle can he hope to escape Regis's prison and even if he did, only by another miracle would he recover from his injuries. Faced with the choice of an ignominious death or one with its own peculiar heroism, Adam has made his choice.

As Katsuhiro now perceives the situation, he himself has no more choice than does a sword in the hands of a skilled swordsman. He is the weapon by which Adam will meet the death he has already chosen.

He says nothing to Adam of his decision, only offers him water, listens when he wishes to talk, and waits for night to fall. From his experience during the preceding three days, he knows that the guards grow lazy once the prisoners have been fed their dinner.

Of course, neither he nor Adam is accorded this privilege, but the more base of the guards delight in teasing them with elaborate verbal descriptions of the delights that await their fellow prisoners. One guard, whose cruelty is a crude mimicry of Regis's own, even goes so far as to push a bowl of some delicious-smelling concoction just through the slot in the cell door.

Knowing that the bowl will be withdrawn as soon as he moves toward it, Katsuhiro refuses to even acknowledge its presence. Infuriated, the guard takes the bowl away, then sits outside the door sucking up the contents with elaborate moans of delight.

But when darkness falls, the guards grow tired of such games. They retire to an anteroom at the end of the hallway, near the base of the stairs. There they play cards or *ayo* or brag about their exploits. Hearing a particularly heated argument developing, Katsuhiro acts.

Rising to his feet in a single graceful movement, he pads noiselessly across the cell to where Adam lies. The African's snores, loud because of damage to his bruised—possibly broken—nose, reassure Katsuhiro that he is sound asleep.

After folding his suit jacket into a rectangular pad, Katsuhiro kneels next to the sleeping man and presses the fabric against his mouth and nose, holding it firmly but lightly so that Adam will not awaken before he suffocates.

This is not as noble a death as *seppuku*, but to Katsuhiro's way of seeing things, it is much the same. Adam, by making his choice to die rather than permit continued dishonor in his name, has already slashed his sword through his bowels. Katsuhiro with his folded jacket has assumed the role of the second whose quick follow-through with his own sword severs the dying man's head to permit him to die with ease and dignity.

In a minute or so, it is over. When Katsuhiro removes his jacket, Adam is dead. The fabric is slightly damp, probably soiled beyond recovery, so Katsuhiro lifts Adam's head and rests it on the folded jacket as on a pillow. The guards are fools. They will not look closely at the circumstances.

Then he rocks back on his heels and bows his head as if in prayer, though long ago he had lost the belief that there was anyone to pray to beyond himself.

In this attitude, he does not see the large spider that lowers itself by an invisible thread to examine the body. Nor does he notice the spider's tears.

¤◙¤

Morning in southwestern Colorado: A florid man with a bulbous nose and thick, scraggly brows sits in the passenger seat of a four-wheel-drive pickup truck. In the driver's seat is a man wearing the neat jeans and button-down shirt of a government employee dressed for a day in the field.

"This is the parcel, Wayne," the government man says. "It hasn't been grazed for years. There's water and not much traffic. You should be able to set your herds out without any of those environmental busybodies knowing a thing."

Wayne Watkins nods sagely, chewing on the inside of his lip. He's only half-listening to what the man is saying. The days of easy access to government lands, days he remembers so fondly, are over now. That is, the ease is over, but not the access, not for a man who knows which palms to grease.

"It isn't great," he mutters, turning his head slightly so that he can watch the government man without the man being able to read his expression—a task made easier by the tinted sunglasses he always wears, "and I suppose I'll have to deal with interlopers."

"Well, it is public land," the government man says defensively, "so there may be the occasional hiker or camper, but this isn't exactly prime territory. There aren't any facilities for miles. The closest private landowner is a horse rancher named Frank MacDonald."

"I remember reading about him," Wayne says, "in your report. Quarter horses, right? He's the one who had the permit for this land before I got it. God knows why. It certainly isn't prime horse land."

Wayne unfolds the map where the lands covered by his grazing permit are outlined in red. MacDonald's holdings are indicated by a wash of yellow highlighter.

"Yep. Hell of a lot of land for a horse ranch," he comments.

"I think MacDonald does some subsistence farming," the government man adds helpfully. "Mostly he keeps to himself."

"He likely to give me much trouble?" Wayne asks. "Like I just said, he *was* my competition for the permit."

"I doubt it. His associates speak of him as a mild-tempered man. If he protests, it will be through the bureaucracy."

"Not much good that'll do him," Wayne chuckles. "Right?"

The government man, remembering an unexpected bonus in his paycheck, smiles conspiratorially. "Right."

"Now," Wayne says, dismissing MacDonald and getting to the point, "these are public lands. What are the limits of my use?"

The government man gets officious. "Well, no permanent construction, of course. You can build holding pens, truck in tanks for water, even set up a shelter, as long as it all can be removed when your lease is over."

"Good. Anything else?"

"Try to keep impact on the environment to the minimum."

"Shit, man! I'm grazing cattle here!"

The government man simpers. "Well, needless to say, the environmental impact will be assessed in light of the use for which you contracted the land."

"Shit. You talk more than my mother-in-law. How about hunting?"

"Well, Wayne, try not to abuse the limits of the permit."

"How about varmints bothering my cattle? Coyotes and suchlike."

"I don't see any problem with that."

Wayne takes one more look out over the land. It isn't as good as some of the land he's used in the past, but it'll do. The cattle get their final fattening in a feedlot, anyhow.

"Okay. I'll sign the papers," he says, his tone indicating that he considers that he is doing the government a great favor. "Let's go where you can buy me lunch while I do it."

"Sounds good to me, Wayne," the government man says.

Wayne waves to the land as they bounce out over the rutted road. "I'll be seeing you—me and my cattle."

"*And,*" he subvocalizes, "*my rifle.*"

¤▣¤

It doesn't look anything at all like a magic academy. There are no lofty towers, no white marble veined in gold, no pennants snapping in the wind. It doesn't even look like the popular conception of a wizard's cottage—no cobblestone walls or mossy paths or elf-haunted grottos.

What it does look like is a cluster of squat adobe buildings set in a hollow at the end of a dirt road. The surrounding terrain is mostly covered with golden brown dry winter grass, accented by some tired-looking piñon and juniper. The scenery is lovely, though: views in one direction of the Jemez Mountains, in another of the Sangre de Cristos, both ranges topped with snow.

As he gets out of the Pendragon Productions' van and stretches, Arthur can understand why the hippies who had first built this place had overlooked the inconvenience of the location and the likelihood that they would never be able to make a living from the dry, rocky land. It is beautiful.

More importantly, though, for the needs of the Academy, the buildings are made of old-fashioned mud-brick adobe, not the modern sham: frame stucco. Thus, there is almost no iron or steel in the superstructure. The pipes are copper—a metal that does not interfere with magic as iron does—and floors are pegged together, not nailed.

That the place had been melting back into the earth had been one of the reasons they had been able to buy it and twenty acres of the land surrounding it for a reasonable price. The other reason was that the well had gone dry some twenty years before, driving away the last of the hippies when they grew tired of trucking in their water.

Swansdown the yeti had managed to get the well working

again. For appearances' sake, however, they still truck in a few big plastic tanks of water every week. No need to raise the property taxes.

Arthur dismisses such everyday concerns when the front door of the largest building creaks open. A lean, handsome man walks out, his silver hair and beard tossed by the wind.

"Arthur! I'm so glad to see you."

Ian Lovern, once known as Merlin, grasps Arthur's hand in his own. As he returns the handclasp, Arthur notices that though the mage's fingers are still as beringed as ever, the palm is rougher and more callused than it had been a month and a half before.

"And I'm glad to see you, Lovern. How are things?"

"Busy. Chaotic. Insane. Demanding. Maddening." Lovern sighs, rubs his clear blue eyes with one bony fist. "Swansdown has most of our small circle working on an amulet. I bowed out so I could speak with you privately."

"Is something wrong?"

"Come inside. It's nippy out here." Lovern leads the way through the ornately carved Mexican front door into a Talavera-tiled foyer lined with boots and overshoes in various sizes and a few odd shapes. From there he turns into a small room lined with bookshelves.

"My office," Lovern explains. "It isn't much, but at least most of my references are at hand."

Looking about the cramped room, rubbing his hands against the chill, Arthur recalls the spacious suite Lovern occupies when at Pendragon Estates and silently agrees that this cubbyhole isn't much.

He doesn't want to sound depreciating, though, so he words his reply carefully. "You've certainly got it fixed up so everything is in reach. Now, tell me what's bothering you."

"Resources."

"If you mean your last order," Arthur says, "there are more supplies in the van. Chris notes where he made substitutions and for what reasons. Is that the problem?"

"No," Lovern says. "My problem is—for lack of a better word—human resources. I simply don't have enough people to carry out even half of the requests for magecraft you've forwarded. Swansdown is talented, but her skills are more geared toward healing and creative curses, not magecraft. The same is true of many of the others. Alice Chun came to help for a few weeks, but she says that she has other things to do and refuses to become a permanent part of the Academy. You'd think a former queen would have a greater sense of responsibility."

Arthur nods. "You would think so, but she hasn't been a queen for centuries. These days, she's just a novelist."

Lovern sighs. "You know, at first, the work we did here was kind of fun. We worked up a disguise amulet for Frank MacDonald to use on the unicorns. It was a simple enough illusion—hide the horn, bulk up the frame, fluff out the tail, fill in the hooves.

"Then we designed the shapeshift for Vera. That was more complicated, but I felt my students were learning something, and we were becoming a team. Now it seems that every day we get more requests for some amulet or other. Worst of all, everyone seems to think that I *owe* some service to them."

"You did," Arthur reminds him gently, picking up a pencil and drumming it against the arm of his chair, "nearly get yourself thrown out of the Accord when the rest of the athanor learned about the Head."

That moment, when Sven Trout had confronted Lovern with the result of his—well, not exactly black but certainly at least dark grey—magical experimentation, had been one of the worst of many bad moments during the recent upheaval. Lovern looks momentarily angry at the reminder, then he sighs.

"Yes. I did. But that's over now. The Head is residing in a hamster cage on Frank's ranch, and I'm forced to cope without my most potent magical tool." Lovern points to a pile of handwritten notes on his desk. "I haven't even had time to finish transcribing my spells."

"Aren't you using the computer we sent you?"

"Yes, to do the final draft"—Lovern pulls at his neat beard—"but I can't compose sorcerous prose on a computer. I just can't!

"And," he continues sulkily, "I don't type very well."

Arthur swallows a smile. That Lovern had resisted learning to type when typewriters had been made of steel had been understandable, but the advent of computers made mostly of plastic had not changed his resistance. Only recently had the King learned why. Lovern had possessed something far better than a computer.

Back in the days remembered as Ragnarokk, Lovern had grown himself a second head. When he separated it from himself, this truncated homunculus had become his organic computer and a repository for all his spells.

Although Lovern had kept the Head hidden for millennia, Sven Trout—once known as Loki—had located it and seduced it from its allegiance to its maker. But their rebellion had ended in defeat and, just as the rebels were about to be led away for punishment, someone had changed them into rodents.

One, the red rat who was Sven, had managed to escape, was missing, and, by the optimistic, presumed dead. The other two—a white mouse who had been the sorceress Louhi, and a ground squirrel who had been the Head—were indeed living in cages at Frank MacDonald's Other Three Quarters Ranch.

"Did you ever learn," Arthur asks, "who turned the three rebels into rodents?"

Lovern shakes his head. "I haven't. We've tried, but we come up with nothing but dead ends. These days I know the personal signatures of the mages who were present to cast the spell as well as I know my own: Swansdown, Lil, Tommy, the Cats of Egypt."

"I thought you said the signature had vanished by the time we'd stopped the critters from escaping?" Arthur asks suspiciously.

"The immediate signature was gone." Lovern waves his hand in the air, leaving behind a glowing rainbow trail. "However, one can uncoil a spell and learn from it—especially one so powerful that it won't disintegrate under the pressure."

"I understand," Arthur says, and does.

"Currently," Lovern continues, "my belief is that the Head was responsible. That would explain why I didn't recognize the signature. It would also explain the choice of shapes. He wasn't very worldly."

"No," Arthur agrees and thinks: *You made certain of that, didn't you, old friend?*

"So, until given other data—and more time to consider the question—that's my answer."

"Thanks." Arthur clears his throat, uncomfortably aware that he's about to add to Lovern's burdens. "Have you been following the developments with Tommy Thunderburst's new *Pan* tour?"

"Enough," Lovern scowls. "Swansdown's niece, Rebecca Trapper, has called her aunt repeatedly for advice."

"Tommy doesn't want to recruit *her* now, too!" Arthur exclaims, panicked that such a development could have occurred without his knowing.

"No"—Lovern strokes his beard—"but Rebecca is very close to the fauns and satyrs—you know she was one of the ringleaders of their movement. She wanted her aunt's advice as to what course they should follow."

"Did Swansdown encourage them?" Arthur asks, curious despite himself.

"Not that I know. Of course, I don't know if she discouraged them either."

"Well, that's neither here nor there." Arthur clears his throat, drums a rapid tattoo with his pencil eraser, and charges in. "The latest development is that I have convinced the faun Demetrios Stangos to take the job Lil Prima offered him as manager of the fauns and satyrs."

"You convinced him to *join* them?"

"I can tell which way the wind blows. At least some of the satyrs were going to take the job no matter what I said. I've gotten to know Demetrios quite well. He's steady, reliable, and, unlike some of his fellows, not in favor of their surging into society all at once."

"He wouldn't be," Lovern agrees. "He's the one who has protected the dryads all these centuries. He knows the risks."

Arthur sniffs slightly at the mention of dryads. Something hardheaded and practical in him resists the idea of sentient trees, despite ample evidence of their existence.

"Demetrios agreed to take the job on the condition that"—

Arthur sighs—"that I add even more to your burdens, old friend. He insists, and I must agree, that he must have a way to *make* the theriomorphs appear human—at his will, not theirs."

"Does he have any idea how impossible that will be!" Lovern wails, his customary dignity vanishing for a moment beneath sheer panic. "Unwilling shapeshifts are among the hardest spells to work—even Math the Ancient could only work a couple, and those were on his kin."

"Louhi didn't seem to have any problem," Arthur says, deliberately pricking the tension between Lovern and the woman who has been his lover, enemy, and rival. "Or was that just part of Circe's myth?"

"No," Lovern agrees grudgingly. "She could do it. I never knew how—she wouldn't share *her* secrets. I wondered after a while if it wasn't an innate talent, closer to a unicorn's ability to neutralize poison than to a true spell."

"Ah." Arthur lets the matter rest. "But Demetrios doesn't want the power to shapeshift his charges, only to disguise them. Wouldn't that be easier?"

"It might be," Lovern concedes.

"Our problem is," Arthur explains, "that whether or not your crew here can make disguise amulets for the satyrs and fauns, some of those satyrs and probably a few fauns—the New England contingent is less influenced by Demetrios than are his California brethren—are going to be part of Tommy's stage show. My human advisors . . ."

Arthur pauses, well aware that Lovern considers Bill and Chris little more than useful errand boys, but the wizard says nothing.

"Chris and Bill assure me that during the show most of the audience will rationalize what they're seeing as special effects. Where we're in danger is between shows—especially—well, if the female element enters the picture."

Lovern cocks a brow, for beneath his reddish gold beard Arthur is blushing.

"You mean that fauns and satyrs are well-known for their fondness for sex."

"Well, yes."

"And that if some nubile groupie eager to have bragging

rights about a novel conquest flings herself at one of our theriomorphic brothers, he isn't likely to have the willpower to resist."

"That's it."

"Arthur"—Lovern chuckles, his tension easing for a moment—"for a man who has had as many wives and lovers as you have had—and especially given some of the tales that have survived about Gilgamesh—I am astonished to find you a bit of a prude."

"I'm not!" Arthur protests. "It's just the satyrs are so . . ."

"Earthy?" Lovern offers, still chuckling.

"That. And graphic. Georgios, the one who calls himself Loverboy, can imply more without resorting to obscenities (which Rebecca Trapper has ruled out-of-line in their chatroom), in more detail, than I ever imagined. I almost admire him. He's wasted as a computer programmer. He should be writing smut."

"I think he did," Lovern says, "back in the sixties, before pornographic videos replaced dirty books. However, to address your request . . . You want me to come up with some sort of 'instant illusion' that Demetrios can use if things get out of hand."

"Basically."

Lovern chews a fingernail. "And this on top of the illusion or shapechange amulets that several of the theriomorphs have requested so that they can attend the *Pan* concert."

"Right."

"And that in addition to the magics that Vera is requesting for Atlantis."

"I'm afraid so."

"And that on top of the routine magics I was doing before this—wards for your household and other sensitive areas, permanent shapeshifts for athanor whose identities must be changed, communication spells for those who are traveling where they will be out of contact, and the rest."

"That's it," Arthur agrees.

Lovern shakes his head. "The problem remains the same. We don't have the human resources."

A thin, somewhat nasal voice, interrupts Arthur's reply.

"And that way of thinking, Lovern, is and always has been your greatest weakness."

There is a dull thump, and a cat lands amid the papers on Lovern's desk. She is Purrarr, queen of the Cats of Egypt.

Sitting up straight and tall, tail wrapped to encircle neatly aligned paws, Purrarr is a perfect match for one of the many statues of the Egyptian goddess Bast, right down to the gold hoop in her right ear. Her sleek, short fur is a reddish tan ticked with black, similar to the coat of a purebred Abyssinian.

Fixing her greenish hazel gaze on Lovern, Purrarr repeats: "That way of thinking, Lovern, is and always has been your greatest weakness. You think of magic as a human thing, but it is a force far older than you hairless newcomers believe.

"Humans"—and now the cat shifts her attention to the King—"are so amusing that way."

Except for a slight tendency to lose her plosives, the cat's speech is quite clear, m's forming neatly despite the absence of lips.

I wonder, Arthur thinks, not for the first time, *if that is because we expect a cat to be able to say an "m"? After all, in how many languages does a cat say "meow" or some close variant?*

"What," Lovern says to Purrarr, "are you talking about? Right now, I have a yeti working with me and all of you cats. I'm not restricting my resources."

Purrarr looks smug, something that is not difficult for any cat and is innate in one of the Cats of Egypt.

"Oh, yes," she says. "You have been so generous letting us come here and help."

"Don't tease," Arthur pleads. "You were a good advisor to me when I was Amenhotep. Tell us what we're overlooking."

The cat licks the tip of her tail, toying with them as much as one of her mortal kin might play with a mouse.

"You know that I am very old," she says, drawing out the "r" so that "very" becomes "verrr-i."

"Yes," Arthur prompts. "You were in Egypt before my time."

"The Egyptians were onto something," Purrarr continues, "as were those traditions that linked a mage with a familiar animal. Both acknowledged the magic we handless ones have."

Lovern nods stiffly. He has never bothered with a familiar—although some might argue the Head served a similar purpose—and has already learned that this is a sore point with the Cats.

Purrarr fixes him with her unblinking hazel gaze before continuing, "What I'm saying is that old Stinky Joe back at Frank's ranch has more magic in the broken tip of his tail than do most of the human-form you've been testing for potential. Yet, even though you have been to the OTQ several times these past weeks, you have not tested even one of the animals."

Lovern glowers at her. "If the other cats have so much potential, why didn't you tell us?"

"Why didn't you test them?" Purrarr retorts. "They are as athanor as Arr-thurrrr or Eddie, who you did test. You only brrr-ought us here because we talk and so our magic cannot be ignored."

Opening his mouth to argue, Lovern snaps it shut with an audible pop, his blue eyes very cold.

"Why have you been holding out on us?" he says at last.

"Prree-cisely what we might have asked you," Purrarr says. "We think it is because we lack hands. What do you think?"

Arthur interrupts this professional bickering.

"Are you saying, Purrarr, that Frank's barnyard cats have the magic the Academy needs?"

"I am saying that it is possible."

"Like batteries?"

"Not quite, nor so easy to use." She washes her shoulder for a moment, then continues. "Some of the others thought I should not tell you this, but I overruled them. We, too, are athanor and would not see our nonfeline kin suffer in these modern days."

Purrarr jumps from Lovern's desk and stalks from the

room before either of the human-form thinks to stop her.

"Arrogant, isn't she?" the wizard says dryly.

Arthur chuckles. "She always has been. I forget, sometimes, that you were not with us in Egypt. I know that you read hieroglyphics, but do you speak the language?"

"Not well," Lovern admits.

"You may have mistaken 'Purrarr' for a cute kitty-cat name," Arthur continues, "but it is derived from 'per-aar,' her name in ancient Egypt—a name, mind you, that she was called by humans and cats alike."

Lovern looks confused.

"Per-aar," Arthur explains, taking mercy on his counselor, "can be translated as 'from the great house' or 'from the palace.' It made its way into modern English as 'pharaoh.' "

"Oh."

"Yes. That little puss is the last surviving Egyptian pharaoh and don't think she ever forgets it, not even for a moment."

"I won't," Lovern says. "Now that I know this, I think I can work with her. I have much experience getting what I want from kings."

Now it is Arthur's turn to look rueful.

"I know," he says. "I know."

For they have sown the wind, and they shall reap the whirlwind.

—OLD TESTAMENT, HOSEA, VIII, 7

THE GUARDS COME TO BRING KATSUHIRO OBA BEFORE Chief General Doctor Regis soon after first light. As before, he causes no difficulty. He notes they are marginally less alert than they had been on their previous trip. He suppresses a derisive snort—any guards he trained would have been more suspicious, not less, when faced with a prisoner's apparent docility.

Regis's office is empty when Katsuhiro is brought in, but the chief enters before Katsuhiro has time to do more than note the fact. He is brushing a few crumbs off his lapel and carries a cup of fresh, hot coffee.

Katsuhiro doesn't like coffee, but this morning the rich scent sets his traitor stomach growling. Regis's immaculate grooming makes him acutely aware of his own grubby condition. The unlimited supply of fresh water means that he has been able to splash his face and rinse his mouth, but he can do nothing about the ground-in dirt on his trousers or his torn shirt. Today, of course, his jacket is missing.

Regis takes his time getting comfortable at his desk. When he is settled, he motions for the guards to depart, then he nods at Katsuhiro in a businesslike fashion.

"I trust that you have been comfortable."

Katsuhiro fixes his gaze on a spot just above Regis's left shoulder. Any answer to such a question could have been turned against him, so no answer is best. Besides, he doesn't trust his prudence once he gives himself permission to speak. Best to wait until he has something constructive to say.

"I have summoned you here to learn if you have reconsidered my offer that we become partners in the venture that brought you here to Nigeria."

Katsuhiro's gaze remains fixed. He is very good at this technique, so good that occasional interrogators have turned to check what he is staring at, making themselves look quite foolish.

"Have you reconsidered my offer?" Regis asks. Then, when he gets no response even to this direct question, he opens his desk drawer and removes a large tan envelope. "During our last interview, I believe I mentioned that I had the means of convincing you to work with me. Since you persist in being stubborn, despite my courteous treatment of you, I believe I must continue my efforts at persuasion."

Opening the envelope, he pulls something out. When Katsuhiro's eyes do not move to look at it, Regis, with an odd burst of humor that makes Katsuhiro grudgingly respect him—a lesser man would have simply grown angry—holds a large photo up over his left shoulder where the image must meet Katsuhiro's unwavering gaze.

"You said something eloquent and dramatic about skies needing to grow dark and something else freezing before you would work with me," Regis continues pleasantly, "and I promised you that I had the means of convincing you."

Reluctantly, Katsuhiro permits his eyes to focus on the photograph. What he sees there is so disturbing, not so much in itself alone as in its implications, that he must force his racing thoughts to concentrate on what Regis is saying.

". . . short of crude torture, of course. One of the beauties of modern technology is that borders are crossed so easily, even those of an island nation. Don't you think this is true, Katsuhiro Oba-san?"

Katsuhiro chooses his words carefully. "This looks like a picture of an African with some disease."

Regis laughs, a truncated version of his movie-villain laugh.

"It is," he says pedantically, "a photograph of an African—a Yoruban Nigerian to be precise—with an advanced case of smallpox. He died from it right here in lovely Monamona two days after this photo was taken."

Katsuhiro feigns diffidence. "Photographs are easily faked. It no longer takes much knowledge, only the right technology. Japanese computer technology, of course, is some of the best in the world."

Smiling thinly, Regis returns the photograph to its envelope. "If that is how you feel, then showing you the other photos in this envelope would be useless. Perhaps we should move on to the tour."

Katsuhiro's heart pounds just a little faster. If Regis takes him outside of this prison he *will* escape, even if it means answering to King Arthur and the Accord for the creation of anomalies that threaten the secret of the athanor. He will go overland to Cameroon, which shares a common border with this part of Nigeria. He will find *some* way to disguise his Asian features, perhaps a head and face wrap such as some of the desert peoples farther north wear . . .

No trace of his feverish planning shows in his voice or on his face as he shrugs. "A photo will not convince me, Regis, that you have anything with which to threaten me."

Regis dips his head slightly, then pushes the intercom button. "Teresa, I want four guards, a set of ankle cuffs, and another of handcuffs, stat."

"Yes, Chief General Doctor Regis, sir."

Katsuhiro is pleased to hear this. Surely Regis wouldn't take such precautions if they were going to remain within his territory. Freedom seems to touch him in the hot blast of *harmattan* wind that comes through the partially opened window.

However, he quickly realizes that he has underestimated Regis's caution. Once his ankles are shackled and his wrists bound behind his back (two impediments he had long ago trained himself to escape), Regis motions for him to follow two guards from the office. A third guard follows Katsuhiro so closely that the muzzle of the gun trained on his back bumps into him every few steps. Regis brings up the rear with the fourth guard.

"To the hospital," Regis directs.

As they leave the building which contains both prison and offices, Katsuhiro notes that it is four stories high and solidly built, with small windows and heavy steel doors, more like a fortress or bunker than an office building.

They enter an open parade ground, walking slowly enough that Katsuhiro has an opportunity to note that they are within a large compound. The walls are topped with barbed wire, and armed guards stand within watch posts at various strategic points. A quick glance up confirms that there are more guards on the roof of the building they have just left. Since Katsuhiro did not hear Regis give orders for these guards to be posted, he must assume that this is standard procedure.

Once again, he ratchets up his estimate of Regis. He is cautious and apparently has a fair-sized group of followers. He might even be a worthy opponent.

After crossing the parade ground, they come to a long two-story building, probably once a barracks though the windows have been covered with thick shutters that are open only at the top to let in a modicum of air.

At Regis's command, the guard unlocks the door, then opens it just enough to admit one person.

A reek of sickness so strong that it is like something solid flows out. The stench blends sweat and blood, puss and vomit, the thick odor of uncleaned privies, spoiled food, and decomposing flesh. Moans of pain and suffering eddy out with the stench but, tellingly, there are no cries for help or mercy.

From his pocket, Regis pulls a surgical mask and dons it. Then he permits his guards—one at a time—to do the same.

"I fear we do not have enough to give you one, Oba-san," he says. "Tell me. Have you been vaccinated against smallpox?"

Katsuhiro nods stiffly. Garrett Kocchui, the athanor once known as Aesculapius, is a fanatic for preventative health care. Any vaccination, for any disease, no matter how obscure, is available to the athanor for a token fee.

Katsuhiro has never been one to rely solely on the

athanor's natural resistance to disease. To him that is as foolish as waiting to sharpen your sword until the eve of a battle—it is the enemy you don't know who will have your head.

"Interesting," Regis says. "So few people are anymore. I assure you, this is not the time to act tough. Viruses have no respect for character."

Katsuhiro merely waits. After a moment, Regis shrugs and motions for the guards to let Katsuhiro into the "hospital."

"Go in," Regis invites him. "We shall wait here. There is no danger of your escaping."

Only the fact that he has seen as bad or worse in his long centuries of life keeps Katsuhiro Oba from retching at what confronts him. This is not a hospital. It is an abattoir wherein the butcher's knife has been replaced by disease.

The long barracks is furnished with steel-framed bunk beds set close enough together that a heavyset man would be challenged to move between them. Forty or so beds line each wall. One or more victims are crowded onto each bunk. More of the dying and several who must be dead litter the floor, bodies contorted where they had fallen and lacked the strength to rise.

As far as Katsuhiro can tell, the only source of water is from a faucet set in the wall at the end of the room. A large trough is beneath it, but the water has been contaminated by two bloated bodies, almost certainly those of sufferers who had dragged themselves into the tank, desperate for the relief that the water would offer their sores, and then had died there.

From outside, Regis calmly explains the progression of smallpox.

"It starts with headaches, chills, and fever. Children may even have convulsions—and I should note that one of the prevalent strains of smallpox in Nigeria is particularly fond of children. The fatality rate can be as high as thirty percent, not counting those who are mutilated or blinded.

"On the second day the fever rises very high. The patient becomes delirious. The lucky ones fall into a coma. Then, miracle of miracles, on the third or fourth day, the victim begins to feel better."

Regis chuckles, as if finding this amusing. "Perhaps there is a little rash or a little hoarseness. That is all. Then the first sores appear in the mouth and throat. They burn terribly and spread rapidly, traveling over the upper arms and trunk, then moving onto the back, and finally to the legs.

"Like some strange fruit they ripen, beginning as red blotches that eventually become terrible pus-filled wounds each as much as a third of an inch in diameter."

Katsuhiro says in the calmest voice he can manage: "I see ample evidence of that stage here in your hospital. You didn't mention that the fever returns along with the eruptions."

Regis sounds admiring of Katsuhiro's poise. "Yes, it does. And the face swells, too. Many people die at this stage not from the smallpox, but from secondary infections."

Katsuhiro kneels by the closest victim as if wanting a closer look. Examining the man's pustules and feeling the heat of his fever against his hands, Katsuhiro becomes certain beyond whatever faint doubt his mind had been trying to retain against this horror, that the man is dying of smallpox. Under the cover of his examination, he crushes the man's windpipe.

Only his great strength permits him to do this without being detected by the guard watching from the doorway. Thus Katsuhiro gains the small comfort of knowing that, like Adam, this man will soon be beyond Regis's control.

Regis continues his narration: "Smallpox takes about two weeks to run its course. Another month passes before all the scabs drop off. Did you know that worshipers of the god Shopona once collected those scabs and kept them against future need? My grandfather kept something even better."

Rising, Katsuhiro turns toward the door and cocks an eyebrow at Regis, who is now peering in. "I did not know," he says calmly. "Just as I see now that you did not fake those photographs."

Regis is obviously impressed, despite himself. "No, I did not," he replies. "Shall we return to my office?"

"Perhaps it would be wise for me to shower," Katsuhiro says. "I would not wish to spread the contagion to any of your staff."

Regis considers. "My staff—those whom I value—have already been vaccinated. However, I do receive visitors in my office, and although smallpox is not as contagious as people once feared, why should I take a risk?"

He turns to one of the guards. "Take Oba-san to the showers and let him wash. Watch him at all times. Afterward, give him clean trousers and a shirt from stores, but no shoes, no belt, nothing he can turn to a weapon."

"Yes, sir!"

"Bring him to my office in fifteen minutes."

Katsuhiro's small hope that he might escape when he is permitted to undress for the showers is dashed. His guards cut his soiled suit from him with a razor, so that his cuffs need not be removed. Then he is herded into the shower stall. The water is not heated, but, after sitting in a metal tank in the Nigerian sun, it is not cold either.

He scrubs himself awkwardly with a bar of disinfectant soap. His guards stand just outside of his reach, their guns still pointed at him, and make rude comments in Yoruban about his anatomy. Only the fact that he has decided to conceal his knowledge of their language keeps him from retorting.

After his shower, Katsuhiro is given a small towel with which to wipe away most of the water, then marched naked across the compound. Only when he is once again safely within the prison building is he unchained, first his feet, then his hands, so that he can dress in the loose cotton trousers and tee shirt provided. Apparently, Regis has given orders that he need not be kept chained in this building, but as at least one of his four guards always holds a gun on him, Katsuhiro must bide his time.

In any case, he does not care to depart until he confirms exactly what pressure Regis is bringing to bear on him. Katsuhiro suspects, but hearing it from the man's own lips will tell him more about his opponent.

Regis is at his desk once more when Katsuhiro is escorted in. Tiny dewdrops of water on his curly reddish hair confirm that he has also taken the time to shower.

"More comfortable?" Regis says, politely, looking up from a handwritten report. "Good. Some interesting news came in while we were inspecting the hospital. Your cellmate Adam is dead."

Katsuhiro grunts something noncommittal.

"I was wondering," Regis continues, "if you had opportunity to speak with him about his role in your being here—and if that might be the reason he died just when he did. I had inspected his injuries the night before we put you in with him. I had no reason to suspect that he would not continue to live indefinitely—in pain, certainly—but at least until he starved to death."

Regis's bloodshot eyes study Katsuhiro intently. "Do you have anything to add—that perhaps in your just fury you killed him? I could understand that. Indeed, then we would have something in common."

Astonished for the first time since he met this strange man, Katsuhiro realizes that Regis has not even considered the possibility that Katsuhiro might have slain Adam out of pity. Vengeful murder he can believe in and even admire, but mercy never occurs to him.

Unwilling to say anything, Katsuhiro settles for a small lifting of one eyebrow and a slight smile. Regis seems to read great meaning into this, for he laughs and pours Katsuhiro a glass of ice water. Then he produces a small package of saltine crackers, which he tosses to his "guest."

"I see we are coming to understand each other," he says delightedly. "Now, what do you think of my persuasion? Will you work with me?"

Katsuhiro unwraps the sealed crackers slowly, though his mouth is watering so furiously that he must swallow before he can speak.

"English is not my first language," he says, pleased that he has always retained the singsong notes of his Japanese accent, though he has spoken English for some four hundred years. "I may have missed some subtlety. Perhaps you could clarify?"

Chief General Doctor Regis looks momentarily pleased, delighted to be appealed to as the specialist in English rather than being cast in the role of the benighted native. Already Katsuhiro has sensed that, despite his evident intelligence, Regis possesses in full the inferiority complex of a third-world citizen when confronted with someone from the first world.

Regis clears his throat. Katsuhiro begins consuming saltines and water, trying not to eat too quickly.

"Well, Oba-san, my proposal is simple and direct. You came here to Nigeria to negotiate for Nigerian oil."

"As a private citizen," Katsuhiro cautions, leaving his current cracker half-eaten in a display of self-control, "not as a representative of the Japanese government."

"I understand," Regis says in tones that say that he fully believes that Katsuhiro is a private businessman in name alone. "My proposal is that you continue your negotiations, not with the delegation set up by this Anson A. Kridd you were to meet, but with me and my associates. I am well connected to certain powerful people in the government."

Katsuhiro nods encouragingly, trying to decide whether he should finish all of the crackers or leave a few. He estimates that he has eaten ten. Twenty or so remain. Would he make his point if he ate fifteen more, or should he leave ten?

"These people," Regis continues, "have connections throughout the southern part of Nigeria. With the money that would come from a foreign oil deal, they would soon be influential throughout the country."

Katsuhiro nods, deciding reluctantly that he must leave ten crackers at least. He understands what Regis is implying. The government in Nigeria has changed hands many times since it gained independence from Great Britain in 1960. More times than not, the change of power has been by coup rather than by election. Regis has just told him that he and his allies will stage such a coup when they have financial—and perhaps other—backing from Japan.

"And," Katsuhiro says, setting the waxed paper with twelve crackers on the desk, "if I do not agree to do business with you but prefer to honor my previous commitments?"

The glow of amiable enthusiasm that had lit Regis's eyes fades into something cooler.

"Then what you saw in that hospital will happen to Japan. I know a dozen ways that I could sneak in the infection. True, there would be those who were vaccinated, but many who are not would die. Even the survivors would be horribly scarred."

"I understand," Katsuhiro says. "What is to keep you from doing this to Japan even after we have made our agreement?"

Regis looks surprised. "I want Japan for a market. An epidemic would not be in my interest. Moreover, I need you as a contact with the business interests there. If I sent the disease, you would have no incentive to work with me."

Katsuhiro nods and sips water. The crackers are digesting nicely. He can feel the first sugars sparking his hunger-dulled brain.

"Of course," Regis continues, "if you do not choose to work with me, I would probably try once more to convince you before sending my emissaries. Perhaps a stay in my hospital would make you aware of the fate to which you would be condemning the children of your country."

For a moment, Katsuhiro considers stalling further. If he spent even a few days in the hospital, he could put more of those wretched souls out of their misery, get the bodies out of the water tank, perhaps find a way to escape.

Reluctantly, for he suspects himself of cowardice, he puts that idea from him. Those men and women will die no matter what he does. There is no promise that he will be able to escape, or even to make their deaths easier. And Regis is just insane enough to decide that he doesn't need Katsuhiro after all. Then Katsuhiro would go through that hell for nothing.

At last, as if he has been calculating nothing more than his own personal advantage, Katsuhiro nods.

"Yes, Regis. I believe that I did not understand what you were proposing before. Shall we talk oil prices?"

Regis grins mockingly. "But I am surprised. The sky has not fallen, Oba-san, yet you will talk business with me!"

"Hasn't it now?" Katsuhiro says with a mildness he does not feel. "Hasn't it?"

¤▣¤

Swimming fish-form, the Changer enjoys the illusion of freedom from any responsibility more complicated than getting enough to eat. Since he can assume any form he desires, the question of getting enough to eat is moot. The only decision he needs to make is what form to take. Although he can be an herbivore as readily as a carnivore, he usually chooses the latter, though not for the reasons others might think.

A herbivore is ultimately prey, and the Changer has no desire to risk his life. As far as he knows, he is the oldest living thing on Earth—he and his brother, Duppy Jonah. Far from being bored with living, life continually offers him new challenges—the latest one being Shahrazad. It is not that he has never been a parent before, but there is something about this little coyote, something he has not even permitted himself to puzzle out in full. . . .

He suspects that he is reluctant to discover what is at the heart of his concern about Shahrazad because, like many parents throughout the ages, he doesn't want to know the whole truth.

So today he is a large fish with a big mouth and toxic spines. He swims through the warm salt water, thinking hard about nothing but what his next meal will be and almost succeeding.

When a seal comes, summoning him to Duppy Jonah's side, he chooses to be grateful rather than annoyed. Forgetfulness hadn't been working as well as he could have desired.

Dismissing the seal, the Changer shifts into a triton. The shape takes no real effort for he had been sea-born long ago. During the days when many athanor had gathered in the Mediterranean basin, he had often used this shape or one similar.

Having too long been dark-haired, he gives this shape hair the color of sun-burnished bronze and tints the scales of his broad fish tail to match. His beardless features are akin to those of the young athletes who posed for statues later set in the Acropolis, but his skin has a greenish tone beneath the tan. In all this crafting, only the color of his eyes does not change. These remain coyote yellow, though whether from choice or from forgetfulness there is no one present to ask.

All this takes less time than it would take a man to change his trousers. Then, with a beat of his tail and a matching motion of his muscular arms, the Changer is on his way. He swims rapidly, but his concentration is not so absolute that he fails to enjoy the pull of the water against the light webbing between his fingers or the tickling where his long hair streams over his shoulders and along his back.

Swimming has often been compared to flying. Having recently done both, the Changer is in a position to assess those similarities and differences, but, creature of the moment as he so often is, he doesn't. He just swims.

A taste of grit in the water is the first indication that he is drawing near his goal. This is followed by a rhythmic pinging sound. As his ears are shaped to assess underwater sounds, the Changer hears this without the muting or distortion a human would. It comes to him clearly, and so he is not surprised when he swims over the top of a ridge to see someone driving a metal wedge into a crevice in the rock. What does surprise him is who that person is.

Like him, her form is human above the waist, fish below. The scales of her tail are variegated, aquamarine near her waist, gradually darkening to shade into the midnight blue gauze of her fin. Her upper body is that of a healthy young female, the skin rosy rather than tan and untouched with green. Long blond hair, caught back in an intricate clasp of gold set with cabochon sapphires, floats about her like the fronds of a sea plant only slightly agitated by her labors.

The length and motion of her hair effectively masks the mermaid's breasts, and when she turns toward him, perhaps alerted by some small noise he has made, perhaps warned by the little fish that swim around her, the Changer sees with some disappointment that she is wearing a bikini top. Its light blue fabric doesn't completely conceal the full swell of her breasts or the shape of her nipples. Male that he is, he approves, then he is slightly embarrassed, for he realizes who this must be.

The Changer has known that Vera was dwelling beneath the sea with Duppy Jonah and Amphitrite, but he had not expected her to be wearing a mermaid's shape, nor to find her calmly splitting rocks, so at home in her alien form. In all his acquaintance with her, an acquaintance that stretches back to her earliest incarnation as Athena, he has never seen her as anything but human, nor has he seen her looking anything remotely as sexy as this. He wonders if Amphitrite, the Queen of the Sea and wife of his brother, had anything to do with this.

Evidently, Vera has been wearing her new shape long enough that she feels no shyness about her naked midriff or nearly bare breasts. When she turns and sees him, her face lights with the gladness of a friend meeting a friend.

"Changer? Is that you?" she calls, and her voice no longer holds the Athabascan accent that went with the Navajo form she wore as Vera Tso.

"It is," he confirms.

"Duppy Jonah said you were coming!"

"When did he tell you?" the Changer says, swimming into the hollow.

"A couple of days ago. He said that you needed a break from Shahrazad and were going to grace us with your presence."

The Changer grins. He has no doubt that his brother had said something very much like that. Duppy Jonah has long resigned himself to his brother's residence on land, but he has never quite forgiven him. The Changer realizes that his brother's complaint is somewhat justified. When the Changer settles into a shape, especially one of the animal ones he prefers, he also settles into a life natural to that shape. Thus, he can fall out of contact for years at a time.

"Where is my illustrious brother?" he asks, noting that Vera is wearing a two-tiered necklace of biwa pearls just slightly pinker than her skin. They look very good and keep reminding him of her newly apparent femininity. He wonders if the pearls are ensorceled to do precisely that, then reminds himself to be polite.

When he is in animal form, his urges are moderated by the seasons. Lately, however, he has spent too much time as a human, and there is no seasonal limit on human sexual urges—or on those of the triton, who is very human in such matters.

Vera seems unaware of his interest, and the Changer feels a flash of gratitude that Amphitrite isn't present. There would be no fooling *her*.

"Duppy Jonah and Amphitrite have been called away," Vera explains, "something to do with an athanor dolphin caught in a tuna net. I offered to go with them, but they said someone should be here to greet you."

Amphitrite's doing, the Changer thinks, remembering how the seal's summons had brought him to this place. Then he shakes his head to clear it of that thought. Surely it is only raging hormones. Amphitrite would respect her friend's perpetual virginity. Wouldn't she?

"Thank you," he says, "but I don't need to interrupt your work. I can go . . ."

"Don't," Vera says, then she colors. "I mean, I've been here for weeks and haven't really had anyone to show Atlantis to. The Smith was here for a while, but since he was working on the project, that isn't the same."

"Very well," the Changer says. "Show me."

"You know the reason for this project?" she asks, aware from past encounters that one never knows what the Changer will have thought important enough to remember.

"Yes," he says. "It is meant as a refuge for the athanor if human contact doesn't go well."

"Right." She guides him past where she had been working, toward a wider crevice. "The challenge was finding an area that was both stable and yet had geothermal energies that we could tap. Fortunately, Duppy Jonah . . ."

She goes on, talking about energy sources, masking measures, the difficulties inherent in making Atlantis airtight so that water-breathing magics would not be necessary.

The Changer listens, commenting appropriately, approving of the complexity of the design, far too aware that he is attracted to this woman. He's going to need to do something about that, perhaps change his shape to one less warm-blooded.

Yet he regrets the necessity, even as he resigns himself to it. He has been lonely, very lonely since Shahrazad's mother was killed. Here, he senses, could be an end to that loneliness. He wonders, as Vera's eyes—still grey though everything else about her has changed—sparkle with the pleasure of having someone to talk with, if his attentions would be completely unwelcome. . . .

Probably they would be, he decides reluctantly, for she has forsworn sexual relations, and he cannot imagine an intimate relationship without them.

Oh, well. If only she didn't look so lovely and keep smiling at him that way!

¤▣¤

Late in the morning of the fifth day since Aduke's family had moved to their refuge, Oya comes to where the younger woman has just finished writing a letter to Taiwo.

"Walk with me," Oya suggests after asking after all the family. "We can stop by the post office so you can mail that."

Aduke nods. Her sisters are tending their market stall. Taiwo's mother can watch the little children. Kehinde is shut in his private study, supposedly working. Cynically, Aduke wonders if he gets any more work done now that he has his much desired quiet. Certainly, she hasn't seen any difference.

In any case, she is very eager to spend more time with Oya. During the four days that they have lived under the same roof, the other woman's mystery has grown, not diminished.

Lying on her pallet in the room she shares with old Malomo and Kehinde, lulled by the sound of their breathing into almost forgetting her own aloneness, Aduke has heard strange sounds from the floor above. The little children, giggling nervously in their nursery, insist that ghosts are the source of those sounds, that theirs are the muted voices or the fragmented notes of disjointed music. Aduke is less certain, and she wonders what Oya might be doing all alone in the vastness of the third floor.

Once she had tried to bring up the matter with Taiwo's mother, but the older woman refuses to be curious about Oya. To her, Oya is someone sent by the ancestors to help her family in their time of need. If Oya isn't the goddess whose name she bears, then she is at least her representative.

Questioning her actions is pointless. Those touched by the *orisha* always did strange things, strange, that is, to those who do not understand their secrets. When one does understand, then those same actions become completely comprehensible.

So, since Aduke is left with no one she can talk to about Oya, the best thing she can do is spend more time with the woman who might or might not be an *orisha* and learn what she can about her.

After asking Malomo what errands need to be done, Aduke follows Oya down the factory stairs into the warehouse and then outside. They depart the building through a small door that opens into an unused side yard to avoid drawing attention to themselves. Some of their neighbors would not approve of people who live in a haunted building. For the same reason, they don't hang their laundry outside, but string it instead in the vast cafeteria-lounge that has become their common room.

Outside, the air is hot and, for Nigeria, dry. The humidity is perhaps fifty percent. Aduke has read about places where the humidity drops to as low as five percent. She finds that difficult to imagine. Air is, in its own way, a substantial element, felt in the *harmattan* wind, bearing the rains, and laden with odors suspended in latent moisture.

"I can't imagine a desert," Aduke says aloud. "It must be very strange."

Oya glances at her, but with the vast reserve of composure she maintains, like oil floating to the top of a soup kettle, she doesn't comment on the strangeness of Aduke's words, just responds as if it is all part of a long, ongoing conversation.

"It is different," she says. "There are weeks without rain, and the air is so dry that your lips crack and the top of your skin flakes away as if your body is returning to dust."

Aduke imitates Oya's composure, though she is surprised. In her colorful head wrap and bright print wrapper, her skin shining with oil and sweat, Oya seems an incarnation of West Africa. Imagining her elsewhere is as much of a challenge as imagining a desert.

Oya glances over at Aduke, her brown eyes laughing.

"I have," she says, "done some traveling in my misspent life."

They arrive at the post office, then go from there to drop

a package at the home of a friend of Malomo, from there to the market to deliver a note to Yetunde, then Oya turns their feet toward the shrines to the old gods.

Aduke walks with her, albeit somewhat unwillingly. As hard as she has tried, she has not been able to forget the ominous pronouncements of the *babalawo*, nor the fear she felt when they were evicted and it seemed as if those pronouncements were coming true. Lately, she has tried hard to believe that the *orisha* accepted their sacrifices, that the plate of dog was enough to feed Ogun, that Shango liked the chicken and the yam porridge, that Oshun is wearing the bracelet made from twisted brass wire, that Eshu has been happy with his combination plate made from small portions of everyone else's sacrifice, that . . .

She shakes her head, trying hard to put these crazy superstitions from her, but here in the Grove, surrounded by the altars and the desperate intensity of the people praying, dancing, singing, making offerings, kneeling in the dirt before the diviners, here it is hard to dismiss such faith as mere superstition.

Oya has gone over to the shrine to the *orisha* whose name she bears, her posture not that of a supplicant, but of a housewife checking her mail. The guardians of the shrines do not interrupt her as she fingers the offerings, not even when she unrolls the slips of paper on which petitions have been written and reads the contents. Aduke wonders if they, like Iya Taiwo, believe her specially blessed by the goddess.

Aduke occupies herself by wandering from shrine to shrine, shying away from Shopona's—hardly recognizable beneath its heaps of placating offerings—and from the shelter where the old *babalawo* is counseling a man with the first twistings of grey in his beard.

She is making her second round when Oya comes up to her.

"Thanks for waiting, little sister. Can I buy you something to eat?"

Aduke smiles. "I *am* getting hungry, and Iya Taiwo won't know to make lunch for us."

They go to a small restaurant, a quiet place, most of whose customers crowd by the bar where there is a small television set tuned to a British football game. Oya takes a table in a shady corner and, after they have placed their orders and the waitress has torn herself away from the television set long enough to bring them iced sodas, Oya looks at Aduke, seriousness in every line of her round face.

"I want your help," she says, "to raise a wind."

Aduke looks at her in astonishment, certain she has heard wrong. Then she laughs.

"A wind?" Outside the *harmattan* is pushing dust, paper, and bits of broken palm frond down the street. "We have wind and enough, surely!"

"Wind, yes," Oya says firmly, "but not enough. I want to raise a wind sufficient to seal Monamona from the world outside, to cut us off from the surrounding countryside."

Aduke decides to humor her. She had been wanting to learn more about Oya and incredible pronouncements seem to be as much a part of her as her motherly bearing and talent for cooking *fufu*.

"A wind to seal Monamona from the world," she repeats.

"Yes." Oya falls silent until the waitress sets down their plates of *moi-moi* and vegetables and returns to the bar. "If it were another time of the year, I might try to use the rains to make the roads impassible. However, this time of year it must be the wind, and that is a good thing."

Aduke hazards a guess, "Because the wind belongs to Oya as the lightning belongs to Shango?"

Oya smiles, pleased. "Yes. And don't forget, Oya stole a bit of the lightning from Shango. It isn't for nothing that she is called 'The wife who is more dangerous than her husband.' "

"You're serious," Aduke says. "You don't really think that you're Oya, do you?"

Oya shrugs. "Does it matter what I think? Shopona again marks the strong and slays the weak, yet the World Health Organization claims that he has been conquered."

Despite the educated *onikaba* mind-set that she has been trying to maintain, Aduke shudders when Oya so openly names the *orisha* who brings smallpox. Oya notices.

"You believe in him," she says. "Why not believe in Oya?"

"I don't believe in him," Aduke says, not quite truthfully, "but I do know that smallpox has returned to Monamona."

"And it will soon spread to other cities," Oya says firmly, "if it has not already."

"I know," Aduke says. "The city government has set up checkpoints, but some people will slip through. I wish we had a way to make everyone stay put until medicine can be brought."

Oya looks triumphant. "But we do! We must raise a wind to seal off the city."

"You mean that!" Aduke exclaims. "You really mean that!"

"I do," Oya says firmly, "with all my heart, but I cannot summon the wind alone. I need help. I trust you, Aduke, and I sense great potential in you. Will you help me?"

Aduke eats silently until her plate is empty. She should leave, but how can she avoid Oya when her family is living in Oya's house? She could phone Taiwo, but there is no guarantee that he would listen to her. He has been so busy lately, and so often away from his phone. She cannot speak with Iya Taiwo or her sisters. The husbands are useless. Kehinde would probably think Oya's words a wonderful folklore project, but otherwise nonsense.

Oya scrapes the last *moi-moi* from her plate and licks her fingers. Then she gazes at Aduke until Aduke must meet her eyes.

"Will you help me raise a wind?"

Aduke shrugs. Certainly nothing will come from this, but she owes Oya something for all her help.

"Why not?" she says. "After all, ill blows the wind that does no one good."

Oya smiles. "And even if our wind blows no good, it should trap the ill. Right?"

Aduke giggles, helpless in the face of such confident insanity. Outside the *harmattan* wind blows more strongly, as if with their very decision the wind has already begun to rise.

¤▣¤

Shahrazad's nightmares did not return the first night she slept on Frank's bed, nor the next, so the young coyote joins the motley group of animals that crowd around their guardian.

Oddly, once she is freed from the nightmare, the compulsion to open the forbidden door fades. The young coyote still trots by the door at least once a day to give it a quick sniff, but she feels no desire to push it open.

Without her father, always her first choice as a playmate, Shahrazad begins to make friends with the other animals on the ranch. She hasn't lost her respect for the unicorns and still gives Stinky Joe and his cohort a wide berth, but she stops trying to outrun the jackalopes.

To her delight, Hip and Hop prove to be lots of fun to play with. They are as fast or faster than she is when running, able to jump farther and dig faster. They lack her endurance, however, and if she is patient and clever, she can trap them.

She also discovers that they can't climb trees. She takes to creeping out of the ranch house early in the morning, climbing one of the trees that shelter the ranch house, then jumping down when her chaperons come looking for her.

Far from being resentful, the jackalopes teach her one of their games—an elaborate version of hide-and-seek in which she is required to track, locate, and then chase down one of the pair, despite whatever distractions the other might offer. When she gets too good at this, Hip and Hop recruit a few of their fellow jackalopes and an athanor jackrabbit or two to add to Shahrazad's confusion.

Shahrazad, in turn, recruits the help of a couple of the crows by leaving them a share of her kills. They take to following her about, cawing directions excitedly when her "prey" works a trade with another lepus or goes to earth.

Needing a four-footed partner as well, Shahrazad appeals to the dogs, but they are not as smart as she is, nor as interested in elaborate subterfuge. She finds an unlikely ally in the despondent clouded leopard. The Colorado November days are far colder than the cat likes, but it does join in the evening romps in the house—romps that leave furniture overturned and Frank resigned to putting anything breakable away in cabinets.

One sunny afternoon, after watching forlornly from the window, the clouded leopard moves outside to join them. After that, he disdains the cold, proving to Shahrazad that cats climb trees even better than coyotes.

Frank MacDonald, watching the games from where he is rebuilding (with the help of a couple of cautious werewolves) a fence line along where the ranchlands border public lands—a fence line he hadn't worried much about as long as the lands were leased to him—smiles. He'll need to call the Changer soon and let him know that his daughter is doing much better.

When hide-and-seek palls, Shahrazad finds other things to occupy her. There are still acres of ranchland to explore and new things to discover. More than once, she comes back to the ranch house whimpering for Frank to fix something—mostly stickers of one sort or another, for there are cactus and porcupine aplenty on the ranch and neither needs to be particularly clever to do her harm.

When the cattle are moved onto the lands adjoining the ranch, Shahrazad takes a great interest, although not because of the cattle. They are far too boring to be interesting playmates. However, their stolid travels stir up the little creatures in the grass.

Hip and Hop, who understand Frank's warnings far better than Shahrazad does, do their best to warn her away, but she persists in slipping across the fence line. A fence meant to keep horses in and cows out is no challenge at all to a coyote. In any case, nothing here smells dangerous in the fashion the Eyes or the wolves had smelled dangerous. Here are only herbivores, bigger than the horses, true, but lacking the unicorns' horns and the horses' comparative intelligence.

Frank MacDonald observes her actions with some concern until he notes that the cattle's owner has turned them out with minimal supervision.

This is typical cattle ranching, but something that Easterners, still seduced by the romantic vision of the cowboy as perpetuated by movies, never quite believe. How could anyone leave something as valuable as a cattle herd out without anyone to guard it from predators and rustlers?

Such is the common practice, though, with both cattle and

their stupider ovine kin. Then the rancher is free to blame his losses on predators, rather than on poor management, and to lobby for higher bounties and stronger poisons.

For now, though, this lazy cattle management means that Shahrazad should be fairly safe. Frank concentrates his energy on repeatedly warning her that humans can be dangerous, and on teaching her to take cover whenever a vehicle comes up the road.

Somewhere in Shahrazad's brain is the memory of when her littermates were gigged from their den and killed, so she is willing to believe that humans are dangerous. Hiding from a truck is rather like hide-and-seek, and so she takes to it with enthusiasm.

Frank hopes that this will be enough and worries that it will not. Still, like the Changer, he knows that a wild creature must learn caution or it will become less than it should be. He just prays that Shahrazad will learn the real value of caution before she learns the too-high price of carelessness.

True it is that politics makes strange bedfellows.

—Henry Timrod

Regis doesn't have Katsuhiro returned to his cell following their interview. Instead, the Japanese is taken to a small apartment, well-appointed by Nigerian standards in that it has its own private bathroom complete with a shower. There is also a double bed, a low dresser with mirror, a desk, and a fairly comfortable chair. After the cell, it looks like paradise.

The guards escort him to the door but do not follow him in. Nor do they make a big point of locking his door. Katsuhiro understands that he is still imprisoned and does not press the point by checking the lock. If it is not locked, there will most certainly be guards. Regis is playing cat and mouse with him, teasing him with the illusion of freedom as he had with the ham and cheese sandwich.

Katsuhiro's luggage—with the exception of his sword bag—has been set by the bed as if by a bellboy too polite to wait for a tip. Catching sight of his reflection in the mirror, Katsuhiro decides that another shower would be in order, followed by a change of clothes. Although his luggage has clearly been searched, his toiletries are still there. His razor is not.

After luxuriating with soap and fresh water, and scrubbing his teeth, Katsuhiro dresses in a clean pair of slacks and a light sports shirt, then awaits developments. With the exception of the delivery of a light lunch, followed by a late dinner, nothing happens.

Nothing happens the entire next day either. Katsuhiro watches out the window until he has memorized the patrol circuit of those guards he can see. He eats the meals that are delivered to him, even the cheese, aware that his athanor metabolism will have taken its toll for the days that he was forced to fast. And he waits.

Soon after he has finished showering on the morning of the second day in his apartment, Katsuhiro hears the door to his room being quietly unlocked. This is followed by a polite knocking.

"Come," he says.

The guard is one he now recognizes as a senior fellow referred to as Balogun, which means "war leader." This might be a title, but it could also be the man's surname. Many Yorubans have fallen away from their tribal naming customs, customs that could involve as many as four separate names, none of which is the equivalent of a "family name." Therefore, following the European fashion, many Yorubans have adopted a title once held by a family member in place of a surname.

Others, like his former cellmate, Adam, and his wife had taken Christian personal names or had been given them by Christian parents. Lately, Katsuhiro knew, the trend was reversing itself, at least to the extent of children being given a "Nigerian" name, but the reasons behind certain names are becoming lost just as irreversibly as many other old traditions.

When his guards escort him into Regis's office, the Chief General Doctor is already in conference with a handsome young Yoruban man. Katsuhiro makes as if to withdraw, but Regis gestures for him to take a seat.

"Mr. Oba, please meet my associate Taiwo. Taiwo is in the employ of a very influential businessman in Lagos and has been sent here to represent his boss in our discussions."

Katsuhiro shakes hands, not revealing that he has observed this Taiwo crossing the central courtyard several times over the day and a half he has spent in his new apartment. From the young man's familiarity with the place, Katsuhiro had the impression that Taiwo had been there for several days even then. However, if Regis wants him to believe that Taiwo is newly arrived from Lagos, so be it.

"I am pleased to meet you, Mr. Tai Wo," he says, deliberately making his accent a touch stronger to help the man feel superior to him.

" 'Taiwo,' " the young man corrects politely. "It is my first name. My surname is Fadaka."

"I most humbly apologize," Katsuhiro says. "To my ear, it had the sound of two words."

"No, just one," Taiwo says. "It means something like 'Test the World'—a traditional name for the firstborn of twins."

"I see." Katsuhiro bows again, grinning the nervous grin of a Japanese *sariman.* He knows he must not overdo it, but these Africans with their love for titles—look how quick this "Test the World" had been to make certain he would not be called by his first name—are as susceptible as any people to a show of respect.

"I am sorry that I have not been free to tend to you, Mr. Oba," Regis says. "There has been some pressing business that I alone could resolve."

His stare is so pointed and so cold that Katsuhiro wonders if he suspects the Japanese's role in Adam's death. Then the cold stare vanishes, and Regis is again the affable but commanding businessman.

"In a few minutes, the rest of our group will be joining us," Regis continues. "Then we can resolve our plans for this fine international trade."

An image flits through Katsuhiro's mind of an entire group of prisoners all permitted to wash and dress in nice suits to have their meeting, all in thrall to Regis's threat of biological warfare. The image vanishes as soon as Regis's associates troop into the office and take their seats.

The first is a fat, round, oily-skinned man dressed in a military uniform so covered with braid and decorations that he rattles when he moves. Regis introduces him as Supreme General Agutan.

The next man wears a hand-tailored suit, but the expensive

cloth and fine sewing are wasted on his stooped figure. He peers about in a nearsighted fashion that reminds Katsuhiro of a slinking rat. Even his thick glasses, perched on the end of a long nose, remind one of a rat. He is called Mr. Ekute.

The final member of the group proves to be Taiwo Fadaka. Regis is certainly keeping matters close, but then each of these men represents more than just himself.

This is one way that Africans and Japanese are more like each other than they are like the Europeans and Americans. No one is an individual. Every person is bound by family ties, business obligations, and friendships. John Donne may have needed to declare "No man is an island," but to a Japanese or an African, this is self-evident. Americans might have questioned the propriety of John Kennedy making his brother his attorney general; an African would be surprised if he didn't.

Katsuhiro swallows a sigh. Those bonds of familial loyalty are what hold him here, though for him family is not restricted to those few he can trace to his loins. All Japan is his to guard and watch over, so he sits in the office and listens to the four Nigerians jockey for position, learning all he can, storing the information away as a weapon for their own destruction.

He must have played the role of cooperative toady well, for when he returns to his room, Katsuhiro finds that he has a guest. It is young Teresa, Adam's wife—or rather Adam's widow—and from the way she is dressed Katsuhiro guesses that she does not yet know of her change in status.

Even in her secretary's costume, her figure had fired lust. Now, as she stands just inside his doorway, it is all he can do not to gape.

Teresa is clad in a filmy robe of snowy white lace that glows against her dark skin. Beneath this, the lines of her body are accented by a close-fitting pink-satin teddy cut low between her breasts and high on her thighs.

When Katsuhiro enters the room, Teresa rises, standing on light sandals with thin straps and high heels. They make her almost as tall as he, but the effect is enticing rather than intimidating. The elaborate curls of her hair are interwoven with pale pink ribbon and strands of faux pearls. She looks, Katsuhiro thinks, like a box of Valentine candy: vanilla cream over rich, sweet chocolate.

He bows to her, giving himself a moment to recover. When he straightens, the bland smile of a *sariman* is firmly in place.

"Good afternoon, Miss Teresa," he says. "Your beauty enhances my humble quarters."

Teresa's smile doesn't touch her eyes.

"I told Dr. Regis," she says, the words sounding rehearsed, "that I found you interesting. He thought then to reward us both with this opportunity to know each other better."

On one level, Katsuhiro wants very badly to know Teresa better, to find out if her skin is sweet, if her body is soft and firm beneath the layers of lace and satin. On another level, he does not want to betray the brief but intense friendship that he and Adam had forged in their dark cell.

This, however, is not what keeps him from taking the hand that Teresa holds out to him. Pride stops him. He has no wish to be Regis's dog, taking the scraps the Chief General Doctor throws him, no matter how tasty those scraps might be.

So Katsuhiro smiles his nervous *sariman* smile and walks to the desk. A pitcher of ice water is there, an unopened bottle of wine, and a box of candy.

"It is very hot in here," he says, pouring water. "May I offer you a drink?"

"Let me pour," Teresa says, gliding over to him, graceful despite those impossible shoes.

"Very well."

When she is beside him, Katsuhiro leans close as if to kiss the graceful curve of her throat. Teresa stiffens only a little.

"Are we," he whispers, his mouth close to her ear, his nostrils full of the light scent of her perfume mingled with the more enticing smell of her body, "being watched or taped?"

The scantiness of her attire makes quite certain that she is not wearing a body wire, but he cannot search the room without his suspicions becoming evident.

Teresa's dark eyes widen, and the hand holding the pitcher

trembles slightly, but she trusts him, prisoner to prisoner.

Setting down the pitcher, she puts her arms around him and nuzzles his beard.

"I brought nothing," she murmurs, "but we may be watched. Regis has peepholes all through this building."

Katsuhiro's hand wants to stroke her back, and he lets it, but keeps his touch light.

"Then we must conceal our talking," he whispers, "beneath such play. Can you bear it?"

Now he feels her shaking in his arms. It takes a moment before he realizes that what he feels is laughter, laughter on the edge of hysteria.

"Most of the pigs," she says softly, "to whom Regis has sent me, would have raped me by now. I can bear it."

"I still want that water," Katsuhiro says aloud. "Pour for me, Teresa, while I take off my jacket and tie."

She pours two glasses and sips a bit from her own. While Katsuhiro drinks, he considers his next move. Some sixth sense warns him that they are being watched, perhaps videotaped. Therefore, he must tell Teresa about Adam carefully, so that she will not reveal her grief.

"Come here, woman," he says, "and undress me."

She does so, while he makes a great play of unfastening her robe and rubbing her nipples. Part of him feels guilty for his arousal, part of him cynically observes that if he did not appear aroused, certainly this charade would be revealed for what it is.

Teresa finds excuses to put her ear near his mouth so that he can whisper to her, rubbing her body against his quite shamelessly. Katsuhiro approves of her courage, even as he fights down an impulse to forget his duty to Adam and use her as Regis intended.

"I have bad news," he whispers, spacing his words out, "or perhaps good. You must decide. Are you strong?"

She has him naked by now and reaches out and wraps her hand about his erection.

"Very strong," she says aloud, her tone playful, but her eyes full of anticipated sorrow. "Don't you wish to see me naked?"

"You tease me almost beyond endurance," he warns her,

making his reply a genuine warning. "I am only a man. Won't Regis be angry if I take you?"

"He let me come here," she says, "and I wish to have you in bed and . . ."

She reaches and undoes the bow at her throat that holds her robe closed. Then she lets it fall to her feet. After letting him feast his eyes on her body clad only in pink satin, she peels off the teddy, her moves practiced and easy.

"Come here," she says, holding out her hand. "Let us get to know each other better."

Katsuhiro understands Teresa's intention. Lying in bed, they can whisper more easily, and their muttered words will be taken for pillow talk. Still, he wonders how long his self-control can last if he is naked beside her. He hasn't had a woman since he left Japan, and abstinence is telling. Perhaps Teresa doesn't care if he takes her. He has at least played at lovemaking, rather than just raping her.

He lets her guide him into the bed. She reclines on her side, her head with its adornment of pearls and silk on the pillow. Katsuhiro expects her first whisper to be a plea for the promised information but what she says nearly chills his ardor.

"Do not enter me," she hisses, "for I am death."

Her hand caresses his back beneath the covers to convince any observer that she is doing her best to please him.

"What?" is his surprised reply.

"Regis," she shudders with hate, not with passion, "tells me this when he fucks me. He does it like a dog, from behind, and grunts into my ear—'You are dead! And you are living death!' "

She makes a shrill cry that a listener might take for passion, but Katsuhiro can see her eyes and the tears of rage that fill them.

"Touch me!" she says aloud. "Please, touch me!"

Katsuhiro strokes her buttocks, then, when she presses his hand there, between her legs. He is unsurprised, but perhaps a little hurt, to find her as dry as the *harmattan* wind.

He kisses her forehead by way of apology. Why should he have expected otherwise?

Teresa buries her face in his shoulder, moving as if excited by his touch, but her words are cool.

"I think Regis has AIDS and has given it to me. He delights in using me to pass the disease to his rivals. I would kill him, but . . ."

"Adam?"

She loses her poise, though only for a moment.

"You know him?"

"We shared a cell." Katsuhiro now knows he brings this brave, lovely woman only relief. "He is dead these three days."

"Oh!" Teresa sobs, disguising her cry as that of a woman in ecstasy. Perhaps she is, in her own way. "Oh, dear God!"

Then, when she has control of herself again, she whispers, "Are you certain?"

"Very. He told me he wanted to die, to free you from Regis."

"He knew?"

"Not about the . . . illness." Katsuhiro finds that his erection has diminished since Teresa told him her suspicion that she carries AIDS, and that he is very grateful he has no cuts on his hands and has not kissed her mouth more than lightly. "But I think Regis taunted him with this . . ."

He runs his hand across her body to indicate her unwilling prostitution.

"And Adam is dead," Teresa whispers, her eyes bright with unshed tears.

"By my hand," Katsuhiro says softly, remembering Adam's fear that suicide would send him to Hell, "so God will forgive him."

Teresa understands, for which he is grateful. Katsuhiro had dreaded her reaction when she learned that her new ally is also her husband's killer.

"As God will forgive me for killing Regis," she murmurs.

Katsuhiro holds Teresa close, loving her for her courage. She should have been born Japanese. Perhaps she had been in another life.

"Can you keep on being brave?" he asks. "We cannot kill Regis until he is disarmed. If he has given any of the smallpox virus to his allies or made provisions for his sudden death . . ."

Teresa nods. "Regis would find a way to continue making people suffer, even after he is dead. He is as full of hate as the ocean is with water."

"Then you will wait?"

"I will." Her whisper is so soft that he almost cannot hear it. "Now, forgive me for this, but Regis will check . . ."

To his surprise, she pulls him on top of her.

"Do not enter me," she whispers, "for I am death."

Then aloud she cries, as if given over to passion, "Finish it now! I cannot wait any longer."

Her hips move, thrusting against him. Very careful not to enter her, Katsuhiro does finish, spilling his semen between her thighs, his orgasm and his pleasure unfeigned.

"Stay a while," he says aloud when she sits up afterward.

"I cannot," she says, "but if we are good, perhaps Regis will let me visit again. May I use your bathroom to change my clothes? I don't want your escort to see me this way."

"Of course." He waits beneath the covers, his demeanor that of a man who has just been laid and is pleased with the world.

When Teresa emerges from the bathroom, dressed again in a short skirt and neat blouse, and gathers up her lingerie, he does not escort her to the door.

"I hope I will see you again," he says.

"I think that is likely." She smiles, and departs. Before the door closes, Katsuhiro hears his guards jeering and making provocative noises. He wonders if any of them has been favored with Teresa's attentions.

He does think it likely that she will be sent to him at least once more, for Regis will want to make certain that the AIDS has taken hold. Rising from the bed, Katsuhiro heads for the shower, worried that despite her promise Teresa will kill Regis and release his farewell gifts upon an innocent world.

Beneath her surface calm, she does not seem terribly sane; nor does he blame her mind for breaking.

¤◘¤

Rebecca >> So what's it like being part of a rock and roll star's entourage?

Demetrios >> More work than I'd ever imagined. Tommy and Lil are still doing auditions. I get custody of those who get the job. I also get to arrange for the failures to get home without causing a fuss. I'm still trying to decide what's worse.

Rebecca >> Loverboy got a part, didn't he?

Demetrios >> Yeah and . . . well . . . so did I.

Rebecca >> Wow! That's great! :)

Demetrios >> IS it? I'm not so sure. I never wanted to be in the limelight, but Tommy won't hear otherwise and . . . I always liked the guy, but I never realized how persuasive he could be. One moment I'm telling him why I need to be offstage where I can deal with trouble, the next moment he's asking me to listen to one song, just one. Then he's strumming the final chords, and I find myself agreeing. I still agree if I don't think hard about why I shouldn't.

Rebecca >> Sounds like he charmed you. Literally.

Demetrios >> I thought of that. Shame he doesn't have a better outlet for all that power than making music.

Rebecca >> Music makes the world go 'round—or is that love?

Demetrios >> I think it's gravity. So we're to have a mixed group: six fauns, six satyrs. Fortunately, Tommy has picked his backup musicians out of those so we don't need to have many humans on stage. That just leaves a few dancers, roadies, and the people who do technical stuff with lights and sound boards and all of that.

Rebecca >> Shame you can't use theriomorphs for that, too.

Demetrios >> Don't you DARE suggest that, Becky Trapper! I've got enough people to look after.

Rebecca >> Sorry. I just wish I could be part of the fun.

Demetrios >> I'm glad you're safe there in Oregon. It's good to know that when this goes to hell I'll have somewhere to run.

Rebecca >> Don't be so pessimistic! What happened to the faun I first met, the one who wanted to rock the boat and change the way the Accord treats theriomorphs?

Demetrios >> He's still here, just a bit wiser and a bit more aware of the complications.

Rebecca >> Aunt Swansdown says that Arthur has convinced Lovern to cook something up for you—something to do with illusions. She was giggling on the phone when she told me about it. They're calling it fairy dust.

Demetrios >> Fairy dust? I'd better make certain Georgios doesn't hear that. On the other hand, what better thing could I threaten him with? Or maybe . . . Does saltpeter really dull sexual urges?

Rebecca >> Demi! What a thought! You could ask Garrett.

Demetrios >> Maybe I should. Later, now. I've got to go wipe tears from the eyes of a faun who didn't make the cut.

Rebecca >> Later, pal.

Eddie is reading a local newspaper when a long-armed, skinny monkey climbs in through the window of the boardinghouse into which they'd moved after Dakar threw the chair out their hotel window. The monkey drops wearily to the floor, chattering weakly and pointing toward its mouth.

"Just a moment," Eddie says. He drops the paper on the floor and crosses to the adjoining room. "Dakar, Anson's back!"

Then he gets a bunch of bananas from a cupboard and brings them to the monkey. He has to peel the first one and feed it chunk by chunk to the exhausted creature. After the monkey finishes a couple more, there is a blur of color and where the monkey had been is the gangling human form of Anson A. Kridd.

Anson finishes the rest of the bananas just as Dakar Agadez comes in from the adjoining room. Dakar looks at him with surprising compassion and lifts him from the floor to the bed.

"Got to get your skinny, naked butt off the floor," Dakar says, by way of greeting. "Still hungry?"

"Starved, but here is my good Eddie, ministering to my needs. I am like the King, eh?"

Eddie sets a laden tray down on the bedside table.

"We've had it ready for hours. I was about to give up and order another one, no matter what the landlady would think."

Anson dips his fingers into some yam *amala* and nods his thanks. When he has licked his fingers clean of the soft, doughy stuff he says:

"I have found him again."

"Katsuhiro?" Eddie sounds excited.

Even Dakar's disdainful grunt is unconvincing. Anson had located Katsuhiro the very first night he had investigated the Regis compound, but when he had returned the next night to talk with him, Anson had found the cell empty except for the body of his friend Adam. Since then, he has returned to continue the search, pushing his reserves dangerously low.

"Why'd it take you so long?" Dakar says, pouring Anson a glass of sweet soda. "It shouldn't take long to find one Nip in a batch of darkies."

Anson nods. "It shouldn't, but my forms are not infinite. The compound is so well guarded that I could not go there as a human, except possibly disguised as one of their own staff. I was not willing to risk that until I had exhausted all other courses of action.

"Next I tried as a monkey, but a monkey is a daytime creature. In the daytime, the guards took great delight in shooting at me."

"I remember," Dakar grumbles, though it had been he who found the injured monkey when he had grown concerned that Anson had not returned, and he who had bandaged its wounds so well that Anson had been able to return to his search the next night.

"So I must be a spider, with a few switches to monkey or man when no one seems to be about." Anson shrugs, his energy and his good humor returning now that he has consumed some four thousand calories, including a tub of butter, eaten in spoonfuls. "No one sees a spider, but a spider is not so swift, eh?"

"*Na,*" Dakar agrees. "So where is the Nip? Is he still breathing?"

"Breathing," Anson agrees, "but looking very serious, far too serious for a man who has just had a lovely woman come and climb into his bed."

Eddie looks astonished, Dakar indignant. After laughing at their expressions, Anson continues his tale.

"Window by window I checked the big central command building. I started at the top, climbing there quickly as a monkey and praying not to feel the sting of a bullet, then as a spider I lowered myself by a thread, checking each window.

"When I come to one window, I feel great hope, for there is Katsuhiro, naked and erect, climbing into bed with a beautiful woman—a woman, too, who I recognize as Teresa, the wife of my friend Adam."

Eddie frowns. "Adam, who you swear you saw Katsuhiro murder three nights ago."

"Yes." Anson finishes a partially melted chocolate-nut bar. "That's right. Now, I have seen much lovemaking, done a lot too, in this long misspent life. I think now I am going to watch the old horizontal bop one more time and resign myself to waiting. Then I notice, though they are careful to conceal it, Teresa and Katsuhiro are talking far more than they are fucking.

"I wonder why they are so carefully hiding what they say, and, suspicious old coot that I am, I study the room until I see that, well hidden above a doorframe, is a video camera lens, situated so that it can record most of what goes on in the room. Evidently, our friend Susano has more audience than just me. Someone is making blue movies of his bedroom performance!"

Dakar guffaws rudely, but Eddie looks serious.

"So you couldn't very well go in and speak with him there, could you? I don't suppose you overheard what they were talking about?"

Anson looks cheerfully shamefaced. "I tried, very carefully, I tried, but I only caught a word or two."

"Couldn't you get close?"

"Eh! You know our impetuous Katsuhiro. Here he is, naked in bed with a woman and trying not to take advantage of her . . ."

"Tell me another lie!" Dakar laughs.

"No, seriously. They put on a good show, but I don't think . . ." Anson shrugs. "That is not important. What I am telling you is that I did not care to put my fragile spider body near where Katsuhiro might blot it out with a single blow of his hairy fist."

"Good point," Eddie concedes. "Have his captors hurt him?"

"Katsuhiro does not seem to have been tortured, but I think he has learned things he does not like. You remember the 'hospital' I told you about, eh?"

The two athanor nod. Neither is likely to forget Anson's account of the smallpox barracks.

"I think he must have been shown that—it would explain why he hasn't escaped. Perhaps his entire island nation is being held hostage against his good behavior."

Eddie rubs his head, tugging at the woolly hair as if just remembering how he has been transformed.

"What can we do then?"

"We must get Katsuhiro out," Anson says, "but we should communicate with him first to make certain that he will leave. Then we get him out, both him, I think, and Teresa."

"Then kill Regis," Dakar says, his eyes shining with joy at the thought of his revenge.

"Unless he is an athanor," Eddie hedges.

Dakar snarls something inarticulate, but does not argue.

Outside the boardinghouse window, the *harmattan* wind intensifies, wailing the grief and frustration none of them dare express. Eddie crosses and slams the window shut.

"Hell," he mutters, "even if he *is* an athanor."

¤◙¤

Stinky Joe refuses to leave the Other Three Quarters Ranch, when Lovern requests magical assistance, but a significant coterie—led by Tuxedo Ar, Stinky Joe's perpetual rival—departs in the Wanderer's van, eager for new horizons and a chance to show off in the company of the Cats of Egypt.

With their departure, something changes around the ranch, something the unicorns sense so that they pause more often in their grazing to sniff the winds, something the griffin feels and so intensifies her alertness, something that makes the hydra lurk in the back of their caves when they long to be out basking in the winter sun.

Frank MacDonald is not unaware of his companions' changed moods. Riding Tugger, since the former plow horse doesn't mind a saddle, he makes the rounds.

"What troubles you?" he asks the unicorns where they tremble in one of their hidden valleys.

Pearl shakes the pale whiteness of her mane as she tries to articulate a feeling. Her answer is not wholly verbal, but is constructed of foot stomps and ear twitches, of tail flips and snorts through her nose. Frank, however, hears it as if it were words—this is an old gift with him, so old that he is uncertain whether it is magic or experience.

"The air seems clearer," she begins, then shakes her head. "No. Not that. But like that. We feel less well hidden, as if a fog has lifted and we discover that we are in the midst of an open plain."

Frank nods. The unicorns can tell him nothing more. The griffin is more helpful, perhaps because she is a predator rather than an herbivore and so more accustomed to planning rather than reacting.

"Always," she says, nervously preening her wing feathers as a person might chew a fingernail, "since I have come to live under your care, there has been an aura about wherever we have made our home. Like a song or . . ."

"A fog?" Frank suggests. "That is what the unicorns said."

"A fog," the griffin considers, "perhaps. More to me like a song saying, 'Look over there, just to the side, not straight ahead.' "

She preens some more, clearly dissatisfied with her answer.

"Misdirection, then," Frank says, "rather than concealment."

"Yes." The griffin scratches the dirt with a fore claw. "I thought that you had created it, if I thought about it at all. Most of the time I didn't. You don't think about the sun in the daytime until an eclipse makes it vanish. I just know that when I first came to you it was the thing that made where you were feel so different from the rest of the world."

Tugger puts a word in then. "Frank, I think it has to do with the cats."

"The cats?"

The former plow horse nods. “Yes. I think the cats created it, maybe not deliberately, but maybe by the fact that there were so many of them here.”

Frank considers this. “You may have a point, Tugger. I started collecting cats a long time ago—in the Middle Ages when people started killing them as witches’ familiars. They were good animals to have around, able to feed themselves, able to hide quickly. . . . I wonder if their hiding was purely physical?”

Tugger snorts. “I don’t think so. Sneaky creatures, cats. Even the cats I like are sneaky.”

The griffin, who after all is part-lion and so part-cat, does not comment on the behavior of her distant kin, but something in how she ruffles the feathers on her neck suggests that she agrees with the plow horse.

Frank nods. “They are sneaky, but that’s how they’re created. They could no more change their nature than you could—nor would they want to do so.”

“They do keep down the rats and mice,” Tugger concedes.

“And maybe do more than that,” Frank says. He turns to the griffin. “Could you pass along a warning to be extra cautious?”

The griffin gapes her beak, distressed. “I should not fly. If the protection is reduced, I might be seen.”

Frank frowns. “You’re right. I’ll get the crows and ravens to pass the word.”

“I’ll tell the hydra,” the griffin says. “They are so stupid they might eat a crow rather than listen. They won’t dare try to eat me!”

“Good.” Frank settles into his saddle. “Tugger, take me to the barn. I need to talk with Stinky Joe.”

While Frank is conferring with the great golden tomcat, working through the cat’s natural secretiveness to confirm Tugger’s guess that the cats’ concentrated presence conferred a protection on their home (and coming to suspect that the cats themselves had been unaware of what they were doing), another resident of the OTQ Ranch is sensing that something has changed.

A haze that has blocked her best efforts to reach out is

lifting, a clarity of thought is returning. For the first time, she can touch minds that are not untethered and drifting in dreams. Most of those she touches are either too stupid to be of assistance or are dangerous, for they may recognize her for what she is—an intruder.

Still, there are possibilities here. Her whiskers twitch and her little pink nose quivers with excitement. She leaps onto her exercise wheel and runs.

The Wheel of Fortune turns. When those who are at the top fall, those who are at the bottom must rise.

No quiero el queso sino salir de la ratonera.
(*I don't want the cheese, I just want to get out of the trap.*)

—SPANISH PROVERB

"WHO," ADUKE SHOUTS TO OYA, AS THEY CARRY THEIR baskets from the market to the factory through the buffeting of the *harmattan*, "would ever think we want to raise a wind!"

She laughs as she says this, and her eyes are sparkling. Over the last two days, she has felt more alive than she would ever have believed possible when worry and fear over her baby's illness first touched her, followed by the smothering blanket of grief.

Each day has begun with a visit to Oya's floor of the factory building, a journey Aduke makes in stealth so that the little children will not become curious. There, while the day is still somewhat cool, Oya has been teaching her dance steps; the thick concrete floors have muffled their barefoot stomping.

In the afternoons they have scoured the markets for the appropriate ingredients to offer Oya of the Winds. Today they have succeeded in finding the last and most difficult item, a set of perfectly matched buffalo horns, polished smooth. These once probably belonged to some devout family's shrine or were set in an *egungun* mask. Now, remnants of a "pagan" past so many Yoruba are anxious to relinquish, they had been sold.

Oya had paid the first high price the seller had asked for them, explaining to Aduke that to bicker and barter their cost down to only a few *naira* would be to diminish their value as well as their price. Aduke actually understands this, a thing that amazes her. It is not that she has turned off her brain and become some unthinkingly superstitious village woman. Instead, she has embraced an entirely new way of thinking, one that makes her brain feel full of fire and her heart beat hotter.

She wishes that Taiwo would answer her letters and come to Monamona for a visit, but she wonders if her most recent letters have even left the city. Every evening Yetunde has been full of market tales about how few people are permitted into the city—and how even fewer are permitted to depart.

Most travelling merchants are being forced to sell their wares at cut rates to city government agents and then trudge away unsatisfied, but unable to protest. Certainly those low prices are not reaching the average citizen. The cost of food rises higher and higher each day, and that which can be bought is not good quality. Aduke wonders how long it will be before the poorer people begin to starve.

But with the *harmattan* wind blowing hot and dry, full of the breath of the goddess, she cannot worry for long. She and Oya will summon the wind. . . .

She almost stops in mid-step as the immensity of their plan touches her. They will summon a wind? How? How to speak with it? How to hold it?

Oya, ever sensitive to her moods, reaches out with the hand that is not holding her basket and touches Aduke's cheek.

"Tomorrow morning, on the rooftop, high above most of the buildings in the city, open to the eyes of the *orisha*, we will dance. Our gods know to look for us in the cities, for the Yoruba have always been city people, and Oya's wind is the element that comes into our homes, even uninvited. How can she miss us when we are calling to her?"

Aduke nods, holding on to Oya's promise as firmly as she is holding on to her basket. Tomorrow morning, with the dawn.

Padding barefoot, Aduke sneaks from the room she shares with Malomo and Kehinde about an hour before dawn. Neither mother nor son stirs. Licking her dry lips, Aduke finds her way through the familiar corridors in the dark.

Passing the open door of the nursery room, Aduke hears the soft breathing of the children, a few whistling snores, a murmur of sleep talk. Then she is up the stairs and into the haunted section of the factory.

She had been distinctly afraid the first time she had come here to meet with Oya, but Oya had reminded her that the Yoruba had no reason to fear the dead.

"We have always honored our ancestors, built them shrines and carved *egungun* masks so that they can dance among us as if alive. It is the Europeans who fear their dead—lock them away below the ground with heavy rocks over them, tell them to 'Rest in Peace' lest they return. Even Jesus Christ's followers were afraid when he came back among them.

"We welcome our ancestors, name our children—as your own sister Yetunde is named—to celebrate when the oracles tell us that a beloved ancestor has chosen to be born among us again. The Christians must rely on name saints to carry their petitions to God, but our own family members intercede for us in Heaven."

Aduke had frowned. "Then why did the factory need to be closed?"

"Because those who haunted it had not been treated correctly," Oya says matter-of-factly, "and the Belgian Christians would not permit any 'pagan' nonsense. I, however, have built a shrine, poured out libations, and tried to comfort these lost ones. They seem peaceful enough to me."

And to Aduke, as she opens the door into the top floor that predawn, it does seem as if the spirits in the factory are calm: calm and even welcoming. She dances a few measures of one of Oya's dances by way of greeting, then she hurries down the long corridor to where she can hear Oya arranging their supplies.

This level of the factory is laid out much like the one below, even to the bathrooms, but where the common room is are a series of offices. At the end of the office section is a smaller break room, meant exclusively for the bosses and office workers. At the other end is a stairway up to the roof.

Oya has opened the roof door, and Aduke sees that the sky has lost its stars and is turning that shade of deep grey that says dawn is not far away.

"There is hot coffee in the bosses' room," Oya says, "and some sweet rolls. Eat something, then help me carry things up."

Aduke obeys, knowing that if their plan goes according to schedule, she will not breakfast for several hours. There will be food—ample food, hot and cold, spiced and sweet, succulent and delicious—but this will be for the *orisha*, and most particularly for Oya.

Walking down the hall to get her breakfast, Aduke wonders for a moment about the wisdom of this, of offering food to insubstantial spirits when Famine is considering Monamona as potential real estate. Then she remembers the *babalawo*'s old stories. Eshu, the trickster god, punishes no crime with more severity than holding back offerings to the *orisha*. Of course, that could be because Eshu gets a cut from every offering . . .

Giggling at this thought, she goes back to where Oya is just coming down from the roof.

"What makes you laugh, little sister?"

"I was thinking that Eshu, at least, will enjoy our offering this morning, even if Oya cannot grant our petition."

The human Oya smiles mysteriously at her. "Remember, Eshu rewards the faithful. I am hoping we will gain his help from this offering, as well as the help of the wind."

Aduke nods, sets down her coffee and partially eaten sweet roll, and gathers up a bundle of colored fabric.

"We won't know until we dance. Let's get to it."

* * *

They dance around a standard arrayed with nine streamers in Oya's colors, three each: crimson, brown, and purple.

Life colors, Aduke thinks. *Blood wet and blood dry and blood seen running beneath the skin.*

Her skin is reddened, too, rubbed with a salve made from camwood so that the dark brown seems to glow in a permanent blush, the blood brought to the surface. Two of Oya's colors and the third runs beneath her skin.

The *harmattan* wind whips the streamers around, snapping them so that they point away from the wind's origin in the Sahara, then going wild again for a moment, rattling the windowpanes and stripping the top layer of the soil and flinging it into the air, into people's mouths, into eyes scoured red and raw.

Mysteriously, the things they have placed upon their altar to Oya are not disturbed by the wind. The cow-tail whisk, the two small swords, the bowls of food, the heap of little white cowrie shells that the Yoruba once used for money, a few old British shillings, the pile of Nigerian *naira.*

The *bata* drum that human Oya will beat from time to time, when appropriate to the dance, stands to one side of the altar. Sometimes, in some places, a man would beat the drum so that the women could dance unimpeded, but here on this rooftop there will be only Aduke and Oya, making their plea to the goddess.

Then, with the first glow of dawn, they begin.

Feet thumping, they chant praise songs to Oya, songs that tell of her greatest victories and her terrible powers. They sing how she stole lightning for Shango but kept some for herself, how she is a warrior to rival Ogun, a witch to be revered—and feared.

Most of all, they sing how she is in the wind, of the wind, more potent than thunder (which is only noise), more dangerous than lightning (which only strikes in one place). They sing and they dance until throats are dry and feet are sore. They sing and they dance until the dark grey sky takes on light, and the light, even in a sky hazy with *harmattan* dust, takes on color. They sing and they dance and, just as Aduke's secret heart is feeling doubt, a miracle occurs.

The miracle is carried in the wind, as it should be. At first,

Aduke believes that the low rumbling sound which penetrates her exhaustion is Oya beating the *bata* drum. Then she realizes that, though alike, this sound holds the beating of many drums, a thumping no one drum could make, no matter how skillful the drummer.

Like an old-fashioned train running hard, huffing and puffing, rumbling and grumbling, the sound rises in volume. It overwhelms the sound of the *bata* drum, overwhelms the sound of their singing so absolutely that Aduke must touch fingers to her throat and feel the vibrations to be certain that she has not fallen silent. The she sees something forming in the air directly over the rooftop.

Spinning, colorless, but visible, the whirlwind takes form from dust and air. It starts small enough to twirl like a top in a street magician's palm, but rapidly gains both mass and color. That color must come from the dust in the air, the light in the sky, but to Aduke's eyes, the whirlwind is tinted with Oya's colors: crimson and brown and purple.

As the whirlwind grows in size, the streamers on Oya's standard ignore the *harmattan* wind and reach upward and outward in a twisting dance of their own. The offerings on the altar, unmoved until now, begin to jump and hop, as if an invisible hand is touching them, lifting the lids on the dishes of food, examining the *akara*, the shea butter, the snails, the kola nuts, and all the rest.

Once, Aduke is certain she sees a mark like an invisible finger going through the orange mass of pounded yam: Oya sampling the food prepared for her.

The two women keep dancing, even in the face of the miracle, their song reminding the *orisha* of what they need:

"Oya, who has fanned fires, Oya who has been water, Oya who is wind, give us a wind to cloak us!"

Growing ever larger, the whirlwind rises, no longer a mere whirlwind, but a full-fledged tornado. Aduke can hear her own voice again, loud amid curious stillness, for the rising tornado has wrapped them within itself. The steady beating of the *harmattan* wind has ceased. And the tornado swells, growing larger.

"Oya who is wind, wrap a wind around our city, blow us a barrier like that between the world of the living and that

of the dead, that sacred barrier of which you are customs keeper."

From the altar, the offerings rise, spinning in the tornado's hold: the two swords which symbolize the lightning Oya stole from Shango, the whisk with which she beats the unfaithful, the buffalo horns now reddened with camwood salve, and, last of all, the food.

To Aduke's astonishment not one of the many bowls is upset. The lids stay in place as they float serenely into the sky. Lastly, Oya's standard with its nine colorful streamers rises, the streamers whipping about like the blades of a helicopter, snapping against the stiff wind.

The tornado grows and grows. Beneath its funnel cloud, all is still and silent, even the birds and little animals say nothing. Respecting this new law, Aduke and Oya whisper the praise songs, keeping them for the *orisha*'s ears alone.

Once dusty, the air now seems fresher, the light brighter as if the tornado has sucked all the dust, all the pollution, up into itself. Then as sudden as a thought, the tornado disperses, its cyclonic energy becoming a swirling wall about the city of Monamona, an opaque wall at the base, but becoming clearer as it rises, as the *orisha* takes mercy on her children and does not rob them of the sun's light.

Oya's altar is empty. Later they will learn that in the Grove of the Gods the shrine to Oya has also been emptied, as has every little household shrine dedicated to the goddess.

"We did it!" Aduke says, letting her feet stop dancing, her eyes round with disbelief.

"She did it," Oya corrects gently. "Oya did it."

¤■¤

"The phone's not working either," Eddie says, setting the receiver back in its cradle. "No phone, no radio, no television, no electricity, and now this odd windstorm. I wonder what will happen next?"

Anson turns from the window. "We will get electricity once more. Shango will see to that—it is his responsibility. Telephone," he shrugs. "Who can say, eh?"

Dakar Agadez reenters the room, waits impatiently for Anson to finish speaking. His posture is changed. No longer is he mournful Ogun, drunk as much with grief as with wine. He is Ogun the hunter, Ogun the guide, Ogun the soldier, back from reconnoitering the situation.

"It started at dawn," he reports. "I've been talking with some market women who were setting up their food stalls for the morning trade. Soon after false dawn, the *harmattan* lessened, then stilled. Then a terrible tornado spread until it split, becoming this wall.

"After I'd heard all the market women had to tell, I walked to the edge of the city, over to where one of the checkpoints is. Police Chief Otun Maluu was there with some of his men. I stood and watched while they tried various things, but the long and short of it is, no one can leave Monamona."

Anson chews his lower lip. "In many ways, that is a good thing. If no one can leave, then neither can Regis send out his diseases. Our enemy is somewhat neutralized, eh?"

"*Na*," Dakar agrees, and would say more but Eddie interrupts.

"Wait a second! Before we start congratulating ourselves on Regis being neutralized, I want to know, which one of you did this?"

Dakar looks at Anson, only to find Anson looking at him. There is a surprised pause that Anson breaks with hearty laughter.

"Neither you nor me, then," he says. "Shango, perhaps? This is his city."

As if to confirm his guess, at that moment the lights come on again.

"But how?" Eddie bulls on stubbornly. "How could he create a wind like this?"

Anson grins and flips his palms out in a gesture expressing ignorance. "Who knows? Magical spells have never been my strong point, just a few little tricks and illusions. Shango, though, has always been able to tap strong powers like the lightning."

Dakar shakes his massive head. "No. Shango has never had the wind. In myth, the lightning and thunder were Shango's. Oya had the wind."

"Oya?" Eddie says. "Anson, you mentioned her a few days

ago, didn't you? She was . . ." He remembers now and pauses in embarrassment, but it is too late to retreat, "married to both Shango and Ogun."

"Oya never existed," Anson insists quickly, before Dakar can retort, "at least not as the name of an athanor. She was just the remarkable focus of a conglomeration of incredible legends. Right, Dakar?"

Dakar shakes his head stubbornly. "Shango has never had the wind. The wind belongs to Oya."

A knock on the door sounds, then the doorknob turns, and a hooded and cloaked figure, bent nearly double at the waist, slips inside. Even before the door has shut behind it, Eddie has a gun in his hand.

Dakar is more direct. Reaching out a massive hand, he clamps the figure behind the neck and lifts. The motion is like a cat lifting a mouse and the intention apparently the same, but before Dakar can snap the intruder's neck, the hood falls back, revealing the curled locks and handsome features of Shango.

Dakar's fist opens and he drops the other athanor as he might have a viper. Shango catches himself before he hits the floor and looks up from a crouch, a rueful expression on his face.

"I should have called ahead," he says, "but the phones were not working, and I could not trust a messenger. Which one of you did this thing? And how could you take such a step without notifying me first?"

Three dark faces study him blankly, then Anson says slowly:

"So it wasn't you?"

"No!" Shango shakes his head. "Don't you know your Yoruban mythology? Oya has the wind, not Shango."

He frowns as he notices that none of the others are laughing at his joke.

"Oddly enough," Eddie explains, "we were just debating that issue. Dakar seems to have won the point."

Dakar bobs an ironic bow, but his gaze remains fastened on Shango as if sorry he hadn't snapped his neck.

"So," he rumbles, "if you did not do it, and we did not do it, then who did do it?"

"A neat question," Anson says, "and one we must answer without delay. Shango, who else of power resides in Monamona?"

"No one that I know," Shango says, rising from his crouch and going to sit on the edge of one of the beds. "There are a few athanor animals—a lizard, a couple of birds—but as far as I know, there are no other human-form athanor here except for ourselves."

"Could it be humans with magical power?" Eddie asks, for these are known, though such powers are far rarer among humans than among the athanor.

Shango shrugs. "There are some, mostly some market witches and diviners—maybe a street performer with a bit of magical charisma, but, as I said, no one of great power that I know."

"No one," Dakar says. "No one that you know. No one that I know. Anson?"

The Spider shakes his head.

"But," Dakar continues pedantically, "there must be someone, for someone has raised this wind."

"True enough," Shango says. "I had not started inquiries because I was certain that one of you was the cause, and I did not want anyone looking for you. Now . . ."

"Now," Eddie says firmly, "we must find who has caused this. He could be a potent ally—certainly he cannot be ignored. Normally, I'd start searching databases for an athanor who might fit the bill. The phone's down, though, so I can't link to the Pendragon Productions databases. I certainly didn't bring those files on vacation. Any thoughts on how we should proceed?"

"Asking questions," Anson says. "Dakar has made a good start. By now the marketplaces will be full of gossip. The places of worship will be packed, too."

"I can check with my government contacts," Shango says, "now that I know you are not responsible."

"Wait!" Anson warns. "Don't look too hard in that direction. If the wind worker is someone we can ally ourselves with, we don't want Regis to get wind of him—or her. If you must make some motion of looking for someone who raised a storm, do it badly. Wasn't your current identity educated abroad?"

Shango nods.

"Then talk like an educated man," Anson says. "Mock superstition. Use big words like meteorology, convection currents, thermodynamics, and atmospheric circulation. Make speeches. Meanwhile, we will do the looking."

Again Shango nods, but this time he is smiling.

"I can do that. It should be fun." He puts on a pompous expression and speaks through his nose. "I was educated at Oxford, sir, and I tell you this is merely a minor meteorological event, a thermoscopic shift, perhaps anticipating a pluviometric situation clashing with local restive air."

Eddie grins. "That doesn't make much sense, but it sounds great. Can you pull it off?"

Shango grins happily. "In my sleep. The only difficulty will be keeping from laughing where anyone can hear."

"Very good," Anson says, all but shoving Shango out the door. "Put up your hood and go. Leave us to find this weather worker."

"You will tell me what you find?" Shango asks, covering his head.

"We will."

When Shango is gone, Anson turns to the other two.

"Shall we seek news together or separately?"

"Separately," Dakar says. "We will cover more ground. We can meet here in a few hours."

Eddie nods agreement. He has been in Nigeria long enough now that he feels comfortable both with Monamona and with his new persona.

"I wish we had television," he says as he puts on his shoes. "I'd love to see what the world news is making of this."

"I doubt they've even noticed," Anson replies. "Who ever notices what happens in Africa? A tragedy involving a single child becomes news in the United States, but a famine that devastates thousands of African children is never mentioned."

Dakar agrees. "A few meteorologists are going to be damn puzzled, but I doubt anyone else will ever hear."

"Won't the Nigerian government ask for help?" Eddie asks.

"Help for what? Dealing with a windstorm?" Dakar guffaws. "They'd be afraid of getting laughed at. Besides, asking for help would be showing weakness, and the only reason for showing weakness is to get foreign-aid money.

"No, for a while at least, the Nigerian government will stand and wait and watch. Remember, even in Yorubaland, Monamona is not the first city in size or importance. It doesn't even have a college."

Eddie nods, remembering things that he has long chosen to store at the back of his memory.

"I guess you're right," he says. "That leaves it up to us."

"I'll take the market again," Dakar says.

Anson nods. "And I'll take the *orisha* shrines. Eddie, that leaves the churches and mosques for you."

"Good," Eddie grins. "In my life I've pretended to practice so many different religions that I can pass as a member of any and all."

"Meet here in three hours," Dakar orders, very much military Ogun.

Anson twinkles. "I'll bring lunch."

¤◘¤

In an office decorated in pure white, Lil Prima leans back in a chair upholstered in fine-grained leather and smiles at the man behind the desk.

Almost without volition, he smiles back, his teeth as white as his carpeting, his hair silvery. His suit is not white, but the precise shade dictated by the fashion of the moment, tailored by a shop that considers Armani one step from off the rack.

Normally, he considers himself the alpha-alpha in a world where men act far more ruthlessly than wolves. Today, however, he feels like he's back in third grade with Mrs. Grundy the Formidable glowering at him from across the desk. The problem is, he has no idea why.

Lil Prima is beautiful, but almost every woman he encounters in the entertainment industry is beautiful. Those who are not signal danger, for their lack of physical advantage means that they made it to where they are by ability alone—always a frightening prospect.

But Lil Prima is beautiful: golden hair, green eyes, a figure that makes every fashion model he's ever dated seem like a cardboard cutout. Her voice is spiced with a delicious hint of a French accent. She's wearing a dress with a skirt so short that he can't avoid staring at her perfect legs, opaque stockings, and a few highlights in expensive jewelry.

And when she smiles he has to glance at the notes he jotted before this meeting so he won't forget what he was talking about. Why should such a delicious number make him feel like a boy—or like a randy adolescent with his mind in his crotch?

Clearing his throat he says, "As I was saying, since Blind Lion has had to cancel . . ."

"A pity, that," Lil purrs, "about how the lead singer gets the laryngitis and the drummer falls and breaks his arm, no?"

"No." The man shakes his head. "I mean, yes, a great pity. However, what it means is that an entire string of concert dates just opened up."

"What would you like me to do for you?" Lil asks, green eyes pools in which he could drown.

The man bites his lip before his automatic response can come forth, a response that would have nothing at all to do with concert dates, and quite a lot to do with things more primal.

"I'd like you to arrange for Tommy Thunderburst's *Pan* tour to take the road a few weeks early. We'll find someone to fill in for his dates. Maybe Blind Lion will be ready by then."

"*Oui*," Lil answers, "maybe so. What will you give us if we do this great favor for you?"

The man blinks. He's not used to this. The Blind Lion tour is far more extensive, far higher profile than the *Pan* tour would have been, but this woman is acting as if she would be doing him a favor. For a single moment, he gets angry enough that he forgets her charm; then she smiles and her full lips pout just a little and he's wondering if she just might be free for lunch.

"Well," he says, "perhaps we can discuss what you need over lunch?" He names a restaurant so high-profile and so expensive that the waiting list for tables is months long. Lil actually pauses to consider.

"I might do that," she says, "but first, promise me that if I convince Tommy to take this earlier date, you will make certain arrangements for us."

"Arrangements?" he says, his hand already on the phone to tell his secretary to make certain his table is being held.

"*Oui*, for security. Tommy is a great *artiste* and we have some surprises that we do not wish . . . unveiled."

The way she pauses before the word "unveiled" sends images into the exec's mind, very distracting images.

"Unveiled?" he says, and his voice is a croak.

"Is that not the word?" she asks. "Revealed. Unmasked. Stripped naked. *Non*?"

"Right." The man presses down the intercom button. "Sarah, make certain my table is ready and have the limousine brought around."

Lil leans forward, preparatory to rising. "Then I have your promise?"

"My promise," he says, then, almost without volition, his hand strays to paper and pen. "Let me give it to you in writing."

Lil smiles. Males are so easy to manipulate. It's hardly worth the effort, but it's fun, too.

¤▣¤

Something is definitely up. Katsuhiro notices when the *harmattan* ceases to blow, but his first real proof of some major disturbance is when Regis fails to follow up on the previous day's meeting.

He had waited in solitude for a full day, his isolation broken only by the arrival of his meals. The guards who deliver his tray won't tell him anything, but he can tell by the wideness of their dark eyes and the nervousness of their motions that something has frightened them badly.

Midmorning the following day, young Taiwo Fadaka drops in for a chat. The young man is apparently as agitated as the guards, but he hides his feelings better. His urbane poise is marred, however, by the way he fidgets: pouring a glass of water, lighting a cigarette, shifting his seat in his chair. Despite this, Katsuhiro is happy for his company.

"Have you heard about the change in the weather?" Taiwo asks.

"I noticed that the winds have dropped," Katsuhiro replies. "Is this unusual?"

"Very, but they have not dropped," Taiwo's tones soften, like a professional storyteller drawing his audience in. "They have changed."

He pauses for effect, then says succinctly, "We are trapped by a wall of wind. The *babalawo* say that it is Oya's doing. The preachers call it the wrath of God. The imam say Allah is holding his breath. I call it damned inconvenient."

Taiwo's accent, Katsuhiro notes, becomes more British when he is distancing himself from local beliefs. The boy is scared, then, very scared. Katsuhiro pretends not to notice this, instead concentrating on learning as much as he can about the wall of wind. Within twenty minutes, he knows all that Taiwo can tell him.

"Damned inconvenient," Taiwo repeats, this time sounding as if he means it. "Just when business was getting nicely under way. I can't even get the stock-market reports."

"Yes, quite inconvenient," Katsuhiro agrees, but his meaning is quite different. As he sees it now, the inconvenience is all on Regis's side. As long as the wall of wind lasts, the Chief General Doctor cannot communicate with the outside world and as long as he cannot do that, Japan is safe from his threat.

There are too many uncertain elements for Katsuhiro to escape immediately, but he can begin to plan. Perhaps Teresa will be an ally, perhaps even this Taiwo can be turned to his use. If only he knew how long this wall of wind would last! If only Regis's guards were less trigger-happy!

Even with such uncertainties to plague him, for the first time since he has been taken captive, Katsuhiro feels himself again, free to act without worrying that his impulsiveness will cause the death of a nation.

"Yes," he repeats, "very inconvenient, indeed. Still, we

must resign ourselves to the turning of the Wheel. Would you care to pass the time with a few hands of cards?"

¤◙¤

The November Colorado air, even at midday, holds a crispness that speaks of winter rather than autumn. Still, the day is sunny enough that for hard work Wayne Watkins has stripped to the garishly striped shirtsleeves of an old Western shirt.

Along with the Mexican he has hired as foreman, he jounces about his newly hired land in a four-wheel-drive pickup truck. The foreman, Jesus Carlos Martinez, sits in the passenger seat, stolidly soaking up the jolts. He would have been the better one to drive, since he's been living out here for the past several days and has had a chance to learn the temper of the land, but he knows better than to argue with his boss.

So far, the arrangement between them suits them both fairly well. Wayne likes having power over those who work for him and, short of holding an inheritance over their heads, as he does with his kids, he's found that the best way to have power over his employees is to know something about them that they wouldn't want widely known.

Jesus Carlos Martinez is an illegal alien, a wetback as Wayne frequently reminds him. He has aged parents back in Mexico who rely on him for support, as well as a wife and three young children he dreams of bringing to the United States. This is a suitable whip for Wayne to hold over his head, a whip sharp enough that Jesus tolerates Wayne's crude humor and occasional incompetence. The paycheck is good and steady, and Jesus is saving for the day he can leave.

"How's the grazing, Hey?" Wayne asks. His fundamentalist Baptist upbringing cringes at the thought of calling a Mexican "Jesus," even when the name is pronounced "Heysoose." He'd tried "Carlos" or "Carl" but the dumb greaser hadn't seemed to know that was his name. He uses "Martinez" sometimes, but it doesn't crack the whip the same as calling a man by his first name when he's gotta call you "Mister."

"Not great, *señor.*" Jesus shrugs. "It is winter, you know."

"I know it's winter," Wayne grumbles. Then he brightens. "But it beats shit having the cows out here tearing up the government's land while my pastures recover."

Jesus remains discreetly silent. He might even agree, but he's learned from long experience that volunteering his opinion is a good way to invite a harangue.

"Anything you and your boys need out here?" Wayne asks. The question isn't from kindness. He's paying the three Mexicans to keep an eye on this herd and on four others he has out in this general area. Ever since unexpectedly severe winter storms a few years back wiped out several hundred head of cattle in southern New Mexico and northern Texas, the insurance companies had gotten snippy about paying off on cattle that they felt had not been properly overseen.

"Perhaps, *señor,* a couple of good horses." Martinez gestures at the hilly land with its arroyos and sudden drops. "There are places the truck cannot go easily."

"And you don't want to walk," Wayne grunts. "We'll see."

They've come up to the area where Wayne's government land borders on the Other Three Quarters Ranch. To Wayne's displeasure, since he'd counted on running his cattle all through the area, he sees that a new fence has been strung along the boundary.

"When'd that go up?"

"Almost as soon as we brought the cattle." Jesus waves his hands expressively. "It went up like magic. We were greatly surprised."

"Magic, eh?" Wayne grunts again. "Just good American technology, barbed wire and posts."

Seeing what looks like a potential weak point in the fence, he stops the truck and walks over, Jesus trailing politely behind. Wayne pulls experimentally at the wire, decides that it's set more securely than he had thought, and is about to retreat when he catches sight of something in a shady hollow amidst a cluster of rocks. There's snow there, just a little, left over from an early storm.

Stepping on the bottom strand of wire, and raising the middle, he climbs through the gap. Martinez, more respectful of property lines—other than those dividing nations—waits, lighting a cigarette from the crumpled pack in his shirt pocket.

Several steps take Wayne to the hollow. He crouches and inspects his find, feeling a sharp thrill of elation. It's a track, just a single track, but he's been a hunter since he was a boy of six and can read sign like a scholar reading Latin.

Wayne's certain what he's looking at is a canine track, but something about the shape makes him certain that it's not a dog track. It's too big to be a coyote track. That almost certainly makes it just one thing—wolf.

He puts his finger in the track, feeling its depth, guessing its age from the amount of blown snow and degree of icing. It isn't brand-new, must have been made a couple of days ago, but wolf! Here, on his own land, or what might has well be his own land. Wolf!

Thoughtfully, he creeps back through the fence, already making plans. There will be no trouble at all if he shoots a wolf on his own land. Even in those places where the bleeding-heart conservationists are trying to reintroduce wolves, provisions have been made to permit ranchers to protect their property.

"Come on, Hey," he says, walking briskly toward the truck. "We've got more land to inspect."

"*Sí, señor.*" Wayne is too excited to hear the hint of mockery in Jesus's voice, a nasal intonation like that of Pancho in the *Cisco Kid.* "I come."

"I'll even let you drive."

"*Gracias, señor.*"

Wayne hardly listens as Jesus reports on the condition of the surrounding land, of the herds wintering on them, of the availability of water. He only asks one question.

"Any problem with predators?"

"No, Mr. Watkins. On this land we have not even seen a coyote. On the other parcels, some few coyote, maybe some wild dogs, nothing else, not even a mountain lion."

"But nothing on this piece?"

"*No, señor.* We have seen nothing."

Wayne debates letting Jesus in on his secret, decides not to. It'd be just like a greaser to shoot the wolf before he does.

"Well, keep a careful eye out. I'm worried about those dogs you mentioned. Let me know if you see any tracks at all but don't"—Wayne turns a gimlet eye on his foreman—"don't shoot anything unless it's actually attacking the cow. Let me know first."

If Jesus thinks this odd, he doesn't say anything. Still, Wayne feels a need to clarify.

"If it's dogs, we don't want you shooting somebody's hunting dog out for a bit of fun. So don't shoot anything, unless you've let me get a look at it first."

This time Jesus barely, just barely, cocks an eyebrow, but his tone is as respectful as ever.

"*Sí, señor.* I understand. No shooting of anything, unless it is actually attacking the cows."

"Good." Wayne thinks that he'd better change the subject. "I've been musing over your request for horses. I've got some, but it occurs to me that just over the way is a horse ranch. Maybe MacDonald'd be glad to move some stock. I think when we're finished here, I'll just mosey over, introduce myself, and find out what might be for sale."

And maybe, he thinks, *just maybe I'll be able to get a line on this wolf.*

No one knows the story of tomorrow's dawn.

—AFRICAN PROVERB

"THE FUEL TRUCK JUST DROVE RIGHT PAST US." SWANSdown looks across the field toward the main road, puzzlement on her broad, pink, yeti features. "I don't understand. That's the third delivery truck to miss us this week."

"Third?" Lovern shuffles into the room, a cup of rewarmed, stale coffee crooked in his hand. "Really?"

"Really. UPS, Schwans, and now this."

"I didn't think the road was so badly marked."

"It isn't," Swansdown says. "I had the Raven of Enderby go down and check. The sign's as clear as daylight."

Lovern looks around for someone, anyone, he can send after the oil truck, realizing in shock that he is the only human-form in the place.

"I'll go after the truck," he says, trying hard not to sound put-upon, though that is precisely how he feels.

After that minor crisis is solved, he retires to his study, picks up the phone, and hits the first number on his speed dialer.

"Arthur," he says, when he has the King on the line, "I can't go on like this."

"Like what?"

"I am running out of staff, and the jobs keep pouring in. I need help, experienced help."

Arthur's sigh huffs through the receiver. "Who do you have there?"

"I have one yeti, cats, and a raven. In a few days I'll be down to the cats and the raven."

"That's all?" Arthur sounds surprised, and Lovern realizes that the King doesn't realize how attrition has decimated his staff.

"That's all. Frank MacDonald is on his ranch—leaving me at the mercy of the cats. Lil Prima and Tommy Thunderburst gave me a couple of weeks. Now they're back to making pop music."

"*Pan*," Arthur retorts mildly, "is getting very good reviews."

Lovern ignores him. "Swansdown has been here for weeks, but she needs to get home to her family. The weather up north is going to get impassible pretty soon—even for a yeti."

"And?"

"And! There is no 'and'—other than the cats and the Raven of Enderby, I've been on my own. The Head is a ground squirrel. Louhi is a mouse . . ."

Arthur interrupts. "Remember, my wizard, both of them have been ruled out of Accord. And even if they had not been, neither of them would have been likely to work with you in any case. You made rather firm enemies of them both."

"I'd take my chances with either of them—or both," the wizard says defiantly, "if I could get them here. I'd even take Loki Firebrand if I was certain he was still alive."

A long pause follows this, then Arthur says in the distinct tone of one who is changing the subject:

"There must be someone else who is magically adept. Oswaldo Barjak had talent—untrained but true talent. Surely there are others like him who would be grateful for the opportunity to work at your side."

"Barjak is dead," Lovern says bluntly. "One of the reasons he wasn't trained was that there are too few adepts remaining. The Accord's insistence on secrecy has put quite a damper on our recruiting those who are not athanor."

"Don't you start griping about that, too!" Arthur snaps. "Just answer my question. Is there anyone out there who might have some scrap of talent you can use? Name names. I'll handle the recruiting for you."

Lovern remembers he is speaking to a king and moderates his tone. He's made his point anyhow.

"Names. Let me think." He hums, deliberately mimicking "hold music." "All right. Here are a few: either of the sea monarchs—if you can get them."

"I doubt it. Give me someone more under my control."

"Anansi."

"He's in Nigeria. I'll see what I can do to get him back."

"Garrett."

"Tough to say. He views his medical work as more important than anything else."

"Tell him this would be saving lives—athanor lives."

"I'll try." The King doesn't sound confident. "Next?"

Reluctantly, Lovern switches to the distaff side. "Patti Lyn Asinbeau."

"Possible. If I can get her off Wall Street during a bull market—or is it a 'bear market'?—anyhow, during a market when the fighting's fierce. If I get Patti for you, you have to promise to deal with her temper."

"Get her. I'll try to remember that she needs to think she's in charge. Next: Alice Chun."

Arthur grunts. "That'll be harder. I've been trying to get in touch with her on other matters for a few weeks. Her agent keeps saying that she's working on her next book and can't be disturbed."

"Other matters?" Lovern sounds vaguely horrified that Arthur is concentrating on problems other than those associated with the Academy.

"Minor," Arthur soothes. "Anson said that I should get another woman in my cabinet. I thought that since Alice was once a reigning monarch, I should ask her first."

"Another woman? You already have Vera!"

"That's what I said, but Anson sees things differently, and I did ask for his advice. I'll try harder to find Alice. Anyone else?"

Lovern pulls at his beard with his teeth. "That's all I can think of, right now."

"Won't any of the theriomorphs do?"

"I hadn't thought," Lovern admits. "For so many of them, their magic is innate. Yes. The *tengu* might be a help—and since they have a human form, we won't need to hide them as we have Swansdown."

There's a faint thumping sound. Lovern knows that it's Arthur drumming on the desk with the eraser end of a pencil. The familiar sound warms him.

"Well, Lovern, if you think of anyone else, give me a call. Meanwhile, I'll get started with this list."

"Thanks. And please put out the word that this is not and can never be a factory to create magical amulets. We don't have the staff. If anyone wants to enter into an apprenticeship—that's different."

"Right." The King *has* been telling everyone this, but it hasn't stopped those so long imprisoned by their shapes from hoping. "Now go have a nice cup of tea and then get back to work."

"Yes, Your Majesty." After hanging up the phone, Lovern permits himself a few more minutes of self-pity. He'd never imagined that at this stage of his long and illustrious life he'd be facing such problems!

Sighing deeply, he rises from his desk and, ever attentive to royal commands, goes and makes his nice cup of tea.

¤▣¤

The room is windowless, but features two doors. One is a trapdoor in the ceiling that leads up to the private quarters of Chief General Doctor Regis. The second, set in a more traditional fashion in the wall, exits into the sewer tunnels beneath Monamona. This second door is invisible from the tunnels. Only those who know where it is can find it.

Currently, those number two: Regis and Percy Omomomo, Minister for Electricity in Monamona. They have met there, as they have met many times before, each seated in a straight-backed chair, each with arms resting on a small square table. Their only other furnishing is an electric lantern hung from a hook on the ceiling from where it casts sharp black angular shadows.

"I don't like this new development," Regis says. "It is inexplicable."

"Not to mention inconvenient," Omomomo agrees. "You have your business circle gathered and then this! Now, no telephone, no radio, no communication. Maybe you set your plague out too soon, *na*?"

"I don't think so," Regis says stubbornly. "How else was I to inspire the correct level of fear and obedience? That Japanese would not work with me without such coercion."

"Maybe true," says Omomomo, toying idly with one of his gold earrings. "Maybe not so true."

"It is true!" Regis insists. "This Katsuhiro Oba almost frightens me, he is so intense. It is like having a lion in a cage. As long as the bars are strong, he is held, but if a bar breaks . . ."

The doctor makes a gesture like the swiping of a paw, claws extended.

"But now he work w' you?"

"Unless he sees another alternative. Meanwhile the others will become restless. For now, they are enjoying a little holiday, with women and ample food. Give them a few days, though, and they will be wondering what coups might be happening while they play here."

Omomomo nods. "That is a problem. Not only in their imaginations, either. Remember what happened to General Yakubu Gowon?"

"Who hasn't heard the tale? How humiliating to find out that you have been deposed over the BBC while you are making great noises about your importance at an international conference!" Regis frowns, runs a hand through his reddish hair. "That is why I am keeping Katsuhiro locked up. The only one I have permitted to visit him is Taiwo Fadaka, who you have vouched for personally."

"Good." Percy Omomomo straightens his elegant shirt.

It is a mystery to Regis how the minister can come to him through the sewers and remain so elegant—a minor mystery, true, but it annoys him, for it reminds him that Omomomo, of all his tools, is the one least under his control.

Regis glowers. "What are you doing to fix this problem?"

"I have many men at work," Omomomo promises, "both those on the city payroll and secret informers of my own."

"But what can they do about the wind!"

"Maybe nothing about the wind, but much about controlling the situation. Already, most of the food coming in is in our hands. Meantime, I have men loyal to me at all the checkpoints surrounding the city. If the wind stops . . ."

"When the wind stops!"

"Very well. *When* the wind stops, we will be the first to know. They have radios, so as soon as there is no interference, I will be one of the first to know. You will be the second."

"But this wind!" Regis rises from the straight-backed chair and begins to pace. "Where did it come from? Could it be some new superweapon of one of the first-world powers?"

Omomomo shrugs. "I don't know. As I say, I am trying to learn." He looks at Regis, shrouding his gaze beneath hooded eyelids. "Some in the streets and the markets, they are saying that this is caused by the *orisha*."

"Nonsense!"

Omomomo chuckles. "You don't believe in gods?"

"No! I am a man of science!"

"But your men think you one of the *orisha*. They think you the King of Hot Water, the Ruler of the World."

"It has been a useful ploy, one that commands more obedience than any bribe or threat. That is all."

Regis doesn't think anything will be served by telling Omomomo that there are times he *does* think he is Shopona born on Earth. His mother's family had been members of Shopona's cult before it was banned by the government and continued to worship in secret.

Regis had imbibed the worship with his mother's milk . . . along with—he believes—the AIDS that will someday kill him. Before he dies, though, he will have his vengeance for that, for his mother's prostitution to the white man who abandoned them both. Shopona has promised him this in his dreams.

"Still," says Omomomo, rising gracefully and adjusting the beads around his neck until they fall just so, "watch your men carefully. You have played at being a god. If they think the other gods are rising against you, then maybe they not fear you so much. Then maybe you have trouble with more than your caged lion of a Japanese."

If Regis hears the threat beneath those silky words, he chooses not to respond.

"A good thing to remember," he replies with a curt nod. "As for you, if you find a way out of the city, contact me at once. We may be able to work this to our advantage. Becoming the heroes of Monamona may be the perfect stepping-stone to our larger plans, don't you forget that."

"I don't," says Omomomo. "Not ever. Why else do you think I work with you? Like you, I have plans for Nigeria. Great plans both for the nation and for myself."

¤◙¤

"It's been two days since the wind started," Dakar growls, pacing back and forth. "Two days and we haven't learned anything!"

Anson, sprawled on one of the beds, a plate of *moi-moi* resting on his belly, scoops up a helping of the bean pâté before answering.

"I don't know about that. We have learned a great deal, just not about the source of the wind."

At that moment, like an actor responding to his cue, Eddie bursts in, "I think I've got something!"

Dakar wheels, lightly for such a large man. "This had better not be a trick."

Eddie shakes his head. His dark face is shiny with sweat, lightly appliquéd with dust. He holds a scrap of paper in one hand.

"No, I leave the tricks to Anansi. This is just plain boring patience and a touch of luck." Crossing to a plastic pitcher filled with cold water, he pours himself a glass as he continues. "You know that my beat was the churches and temples."

The other two nod.

"I can't say I thought it was going to do much good, but today, coming out of a service at one of the Christian spinoffs . . . Aladura, I think, or was it . . ."

"Get on with it, man!" Dakar rumbles

"I am," Eddie says, unintimidated. "I've been to so many services that I can't keep them straight. Anyhow, as this Christian service was letting out, this old *babalawo* was coming down the street. He refused to give way for the minister, and a bit of a fracas broke out.

"Normally, people here are pretty tolerant, but nerves are strung tight now. Those who weren't brawling were arguing, and one argument caught my attention. A woman in Western clothes was arguing fiercely with a market woman in a traditional wrapper. The gist of it was the same old song."

Anson sighs, maybe because his *moi-moi* plate is empty. "One god or many, eh?"

"That's it. I wasn't paying much attention, but the wrapper wearer started insisting that the *orisha* did still have power, great power. Her clincher was that Oya herself is living in Monamona, and that this wind is her cloak protecting the city."

"Oya?" Dakar looks undecided whether to be furious or merely frustrated. "I told you. There is no Oya!"

Eddie merely shrugs. "This woman seemed pretty certain. I kept remembering the stories about Oya's altars being swept clean, too. So I followed the wrapper wearer to the market. As I had hoped, she told her story to her associates with a great deal of enthusiasm. I managed to insert myself into the audience and, when the woman was done—her name is Yetunde, by the way—I got her attention and, the long and short of it is . . ."

"The long," Dakar mutters.

"Is that I have an address for this Oya. I considered going on my own, then I thought that the two of you might want to join me."

Anson swings his long legs to the floor, setting the *moi-moi* plate reverently aside.

"I'm coming. You, Dakar?"

"There is no Oya," Dakar insists stubbornly. "This is just some woman with the same *àbíso* name. Still, going after her is better than sweating in this room."

* * *

When the three athanor arrive at the address on Eddie's sheet of paper, they are surprised to find it is a three-story factory in a comparatively deserted portion of the city. Eddie shrugs.

"This is the place," he says, checking his paper. "Yetunde said to knock at the side door."

Then, since this is his mission, his discovery, Eddie raps on the solid door, wondering if the sound will even carry within.

"Traditional family, at least," Anson says, indicating a chunk of laterite to one side of the door. "That is an altar to Eshu, the messenger between the *orisha* and their worshipers. He's the trickster god, too. I don't think the factory owners set the altar up."

Eddie grins, but whatever he had been about to say is stopped when the door swings open. A pretty young woman, probably in her early twenties, peeks out.

"Yes?" she says in Yoruba.

"We have come looking for Oya," Eddie says, stepping forward and extending a package of *akara*. "We were told she dwells here."

The young woman's eyes widen, but her expression does not seem as much astonished or unbelieving as thoughtful.

"Come inside," she says. "I will run up and learn if Oya will see you."

Eddie extends the *akara*, which has been wrapped, at Anson's insistence, in a red-and-purple scarf.

"Please take these to her," he says as he has been coached. "Her praise songs say that these are among her favorite foods."

The young woman's gaze becomes more neutral, but there is something else there as well—approval? hope?

She does not invite them upstairs, so the three athanor wait in a dimly lit lower area that almost certainly started life as a combination garage and warehouse. Now, apparently, it is being used as a play area for an indeterminate number of children.

Dakar, prowling around restlessly, grunts in satisfaction as he picks up a toy lorry that has been made from a large can with cut sections of plastic pipe for wheels. Solidly glued to the dashboard is a tiny black figure.

"Traditional indeed," he says, pleased. "Ogun is not forgotten here either."

The young woman comes hurrying down the steps at this moment. She stops halfway down.

"May I have your names?"

Eddie speaks for them all. "I am Eddie Ibatan. This is Anson A. Kridd, and this large man is Dakar Agadez."

They expect her to run back up the stairs to relay the information, but instead she smiles and motions for them to come after her.

"You are welcome here."

Exchanging puzzled glances, the three athanor mount the stairs. The young woman doesn't pause on the second floor, though there is ample evidence of habitation there, including the high-pitched drone of children reciting their lessons and the scent of brewing coffee. With another polite smile, she continues up to the top floor.

"This way," she says, leading them down a central corridor toward the room at the far end.

Committed now, they follow, firmly expecting to find someone they know waiting for them, though none of the men is certain who this will be. Still, who else would recognize their names?

Emerging into a well-lit conference room, they find an ample-figured Yoruban woman of perhaps forty seated at a table. She wears a traditional wrapper made from a cotton print fabric in shades of brown highlighted with red and purple. Her hair is covered in a head cloth of the same fabric. Ropes of beads are hung around her neck, and bracelets weigh down her wrists. The slight shine of oil on her broad lips shows that she has been sampling the *akara*.

She rises politely when they enter. The young woman draws back to stand by the doorway.

"Eshu, Ogun," the woman who must be Oya says, "I have been wondering when you would come."

Anson and Dakar are stunned to silence. Eddie cocks a brow. Though he is certain he has never seen this woman before, he thinks there is something familiar about her. Or is he fooling himself, because he had expected the familiar?

Oya smiles and continues speaking. "Thank you for the *akara*. That was thoughtful of you. Aduke, bring forth the refreshments we have prepared."

The young woman departs, coming back a few minutes later bearing a tray laden with small servings of various traditional foods and a large pot of some sort of meat stewed with tomatoes and chiles.

The meat, Eddie thinks, is probably dog, the traditional sacrifice to Ogun. The other foods doubtlessly represent the small portions of every sacrifice that is given to Eshu to convince him to carry messages to the appropriate *orisha.*

What impresses Eddie is that much of the food is hot, as if this Oya had expected them. He wonders if she had—that would indicate that she possessed precognition, a rare enough gift, even among the athanor. Of course, a microwave oven would turn the trick just as easily. Eddie hides a smile, feeling the same thrill that Bedivere had felt when a rival knight had tossed down his glove in challenge in the lists.

"Please be seated, enjoy this meal, small as it is," Oya says. "Aduke will bring drinks as soon as you are comfortable."

The three men sit, respecting the customs that insist that hospitality be observed before business is approached.

"Let me introduce my assistant," Oya says when the young woman comes back with an assortment of drinks ranging from iced water to palm wine. "This is Aduke Idowu, formerly a student at Ibadan University, now residing with her husband's family here in Monamona."

The young woman nods shyly in acknowledgment of their various greetings. Is it his imagination or is there a trace of puzzlement in the gaze she turns on Oya? Eddie doesn't think it is just his imagination. Interesting.

He expects Oya to send the human away, so they can discuss athanor business openly, but she stays through the meal.

"Now," Oya says, putting aside polite small talk as she licks the last of the *akara* from her fingers, "we should turn to business."

Dakar, who had been remarkably restrained with the palm

wine, blurts out, "Are you responsible for this wind that has sealed off the city?"

"The wind is Oya's," the woman says with a slight nod, "and it does her bidding."

"So you called it," Dakar pushes.

"I did."

"Why?"

"To foil the King of the World, of course. Why else?" she looks exasperated. "We cannot permit him to roam free, can we?"

"No," Anson says. "We cannot."

"Well, then," Oya says, her manner like that of a fussy housewife. "Now he cannot leave."

"Of course," Eddie says dryly, "neither can anyone else." More and more he is certain that he knows this woman, but he cannot quite fasten on who she might be.

"Should anyone want to leave?" Oya retorts. "Certainly not when a plague threatens. The wind will fall only when the King is defeated."

"That's blunt enough," Anson chuckles. "You know your mind, eh?"

"I know mine," says she, "but not yours."

"We came here to do business," Anson says. "Oil business."

Dakar rumbles like the prelude to an exploding volcano, but doesn't articulate further.

Anson flashes a grin. "We were delayed in our business when one of our number did not arrive on time. A foreign gentleman. We were seeking him when you called the wind. We are yet to be reunited with him."

"Yet to be reunited." Oya plays with this phrase for a moment, repeating it with the stress on different words, different syllables. First, Eddie is reminded of a ritual chant, then of a theatrical exercise. Finally, Oya repeats the phrase a final time. "*Yet* to be reunited. That sounds like you know where he is then. You only seek the reunion. What is keeping you, Eshu, Ogun, Eddie?"

"What would you say," Anson offers, "if I told you that he is a prisoner of the King of Hot Water?"

"I would say either I hope that he recovers quickly," Oya parries, "or that you recover him quickly."

Dakar brings a mallet-fist down on the table so hard that the glasses jump and water sloshes from the pitcher.

"There is no Oya!" he shouts. "I know! I am Ogun! Who are you, woman? Are you a witch?"

"I am Oya," she answers firmly. "Nor am I a *babalawo* to ask Ifa for answers."

Eddie leans forward, mopping up the spill with one hand, restraining Dakar with the other. Thus far he has been content to keep his peace, but Anson is having far too much fun fencing with this strange woman.

"Let's make a deal," he says quickly. "All of us have good reasons to oppose this King of Hot Water."

He glances at Aduke Idowu and the young woman nods, sharp and decisive, tears in her beautiful brown eyes. He sees her hand press to her abdomen and realizes that her arms should be filled with an infant.

"Since we have a common enemy," Eddie continues, "then we should work together. First of all, Oya, I think we three have been remiss."

"Oh?"

"Yes." He smiles at her, wishing for a moment that he was Arthur with his easy charisma, then glad that he is not, for Arthur never has worked well with women. "We haven't thanked you for raising the wind."

"Ah!" She smiles, delighted. "You haven't, have you? Are you thanking me, Eddie?"

"I am," he says, "most sincerely. We have been absorbed in the problem of our missing friend, but not so absorbed that we have not noticed the illness stalking Monamona's people. For all of us, I thank you for caging the King's hot breath."

"You are welcome," she replies, a twinkle in her eyes. For a moment, he almost knows her, then again she is Oya, masked behind this new persona. "Now that you men have thanked me, I will thank you. Until you three came to me, I had no idea that the King of Hot Water himself was dwelling in Monamona. I thought that perhaps some of his worshipers had come to spread his wrath."

"There is a man here," Anson says, "who calls himself Regis. He resides within the former military compound to the west of here. In searching for our missing friend, I have seen the touch of his breath. Whether this Regis is the King himself or only his highest priest, I cannot say, but his men believe him to be the *orisha* himself."

Aduke cries out, "Eshu, can't you punish him?"

Anson looks at the girl without mockery. "Eshu only punishes those who have not made the proper sacrifices to the gods. This Regis has made his sacrifices. I can act to help another, but I cannot act against him personally. Do you understand?"

Aduke nods stiffly. "It doesn't seem right, though."

"Still"—Anson shrugs—"what is good for one man is almost always evil for someone else. Two men cannot have the same wife; two women cannot have the same child. If I punished Regis for his good fortune simply because it is bad fortune for those he rules over, I would be forced to extend that rationale to everyone. Would that be fair?"

"No, sir," Aduke says softly. "Does that mean that he is beyond the power of the *orisha*?"

"Not at all, little daughter," Anson assures her. "When men get power, men become drunk on power and believe themselves greater than the gods. Even the *orisha* must make sacrifice, if only to their own heads. When this Regis forgets this, he will be in my power."

Listening to Anson speak, Eddie cannot decide whether his friend really believes what he is telling the girl. Certainly, Anson looks as if he believes what he is saying. His eyes are almost preternaturally wise, and his voice is without even a hint of laughter.

"Moreover," Anson continues, "Shopona has acted rashly in taking our friend captive, for Ogun is *ogun*. What I mean is, Ogun, the same man who sits there across the table from you drinking palm wine, was given his name by Olorun from the word for 'war' and the taking of prisoners opens one to the retaliation of war. Isn't that so, my friend?"

Both Aduke and Dakar nod, their motions perfectly matched, as if Anson has charmed them.

"Now," Anson says, "I think the time has come for us to

plan our war. Lady Oya, they call you the wife who is more terrible than the husband."

"That was said when Oya was compared to Shango," Oya chuckles. "I don't think I want to offend Ogun."

"I was never married to you, woman!" Dakar shouts.

"Maybe so, maybe not," she says lightly. "That is not the point. What I am saying is that war is not my strong point. True, I have the winds, and I have stolen some small amount of Shango's lightning, but war is a man's profession."

Eddie asks, "Are you in contact with Shango, then?"

"No," she answers. "I have not seen Shango since my arrival in Monamona. Nor have I sought him out. I did not approve of his letting illness run through a city that claims him as its patron."

"Shango is here, too?" Aduke says, her voice tight, as if her grasp on reality is slipping. "I don't understand! Are you all truly *orisha*?"

"We summoned the wind together, Aduke," Oya soothes her friend. "Trust me a bit longer."

"I don't understand!" Aduke repeats, but although her tones are still urgent, she no longer seems in danger of slipping into hysteria.

"Understanding," Anson says, "is highly overrated. Does it matter what names we use if we are agreed to stop the smallpox plague that is threatening your people?"

Aduke bites her lip, then says softly, "I suppose not."

"Then trust us," Anson urges.

"And will it be all right, then?"

"We sincerely hope so."

"Then I suppose I must trust you."

In Aduke's smile, Eddie thinks, *so brave yet intelligent, is everything worth fighting for, everything good about the human race. Blind faith would be easier to take, and not nearly as worthy.*

Tout s'en va, tout passe, l'eau coule, et le coeur oublie.
(*Everything vanishes, everything passes, water runs away, and the heart forgets.*)
—GUSTAVE FLAUBERT

THE BLIND LION TOUR HAD BEEN SET TO KICK OFF IN LAS Vegas, and so to the City of Slots and Neon is where they go. Georgios is beside himself with excitement.

By the time the auditions had ended, Tommy had selected twelve theriomorphs for his backup singers and dancers: six satyrs, one of whom is Georgios, and six fauns, one of whom is Demetrios.

Georgios—who has decided that "Loverboy" would look a lot better in the program book—has established himself as herd stallion. Dominating the smaller, shyer fauns had been pretty easy. (He chooses to overlook Demetrios for now.) The satyrs had proven a bit more difficult, but a few solid brawls and he had come out on top. Stud has even stopped complaining about his bitten right ear.

And on top Georgios is . . . or he wants to be . . . especially when he looks at their choreographer, strutting up and down the line in her leotard and tights. Mary Malone has the body of a nymph but the soul of a drill sergeant.

"All right, you guys!" she shouts. "Let's go through the steps for 'Heart Teaser' one more time."

Georgios sighs. He'd never realized how much work went into those dance sequences in the music videos he'd enjoyed watching on MTV. Obediently, he moves to the side of the stage, stopping on the red X that is his mark.

"Where the hell is Lil?" Mary demands.

She starts to say something else—being as intolerant of absenteeism as she is of a sloppy dance step—then swallows it. After all, Lil Prima is the one who signs the paychecks. If Tommy wants her to grace the stage show with her presence, that's their business. Mary's job is to make it work, even when Lil doesn't show for rehearsal.

"I'll walk through Lil's part," she decides aloud. "You 'satyrs'—Hunk, Stud—pay attention, damn it! Fauns, are you ready?"

Demetrios answers for the group clustered around a couple of green X's chalked on the practice floor to represent the primordial grove that the folks in stage design and lighting are still working overtime to complete.

"Wait a moment," he says with the precise diction of a schoolteacher. "Phoebus has something clogged in his pipe."

This is too much for the satyrs. Guffawing and making lewd gestures, they mime what they'd do with a clogged pipe. Standing over where Lil would begin her entrance, Mary Malone is visibly regretting the waiver of sexual harassment that she'd signed as part of her contract.

"We're ready now, Miss Malone," Demetrios calls politely.

"We're ready now . . ." Georgios mimics in a prissy voice.

"Shut up and ready on my signal!" Mary hollers. "One and a two, and music!"

A roadie starts the recording. Thunderous chords from bass and rhythm shake the air, followed two measures later by a wild riff from the drums.

"Now!"

Mary walks a diagonal line across the stage, not strolling as Lil has in the few rehearsals she's attended, but waving her arms and shouting directions to the dancers.

Georgios, corrected for the third time in as many measures, feels the music, even in recorded form, touching something primal within him.

It isn't right that she tease him like this! There's a heat in his head, a swelling in his groin. He thrusts from the hips, answering the music.

"Not yet!" the drill sergeant barks. "That's in the next measure, Loverboy! Why did I ever promise I could get you idiots ready for an early debut! Cut the music!"

When the music dies, so does some of Georgios's frantic lust, enough so that he notes the worry in Demetrios's eyes. Then Malone is yelling at them again, reciting their steps:

"Leer right, leer left, follow her with a shuffle step, then begin to follow more rapidly. Short steps. When Lil stops to look at Tommy—that's when the pelvic thrust comes in. Remember! You're miming out the lust that she's containing, that he's too absorbed in his music to feel. Got it?"

Georgios nods stiffly. He's got to get laid. If he doesn't get laid, he doesn't know what he'll do. For a wistful moment, he wishes that he were at home, where the mares are near. Then he remembers that there is a city out there full of women available for a price.

Absorbed in this fantasy, Georgios shuffles back to his mark. The cowboy boots he's wearing hurt his hooves, but he hardly feels the pain. When the roadie starts the recording again, Tommy's music enflames his imaginings as he begins to plan.

He'll take a couple of the other satyrs with him. They can sneak away from Demetrios's surveillance if they're careful. Then they'll take a cab to the nearest red-light district and buy a couple girls for a couple hours.

Nobody'll listen to a whore if she says that a couple of men hung like horses—and with horse hooves and tails—bought a few hours of her time. They won't be violating their promise to Arthur and Lil that they'd be prudent.

Georgios licks his lips, imagining each of the women he'll have in exquisite detail: buttocks, breasts, long legs, round thighs, ripe mouths. He's panting as the music comes to an end and not just from the exertion of the complicated routine.

"Perfect! Perfect!" shouts Mary Malone, her leotard damp

and transparent with sweat. "That's just perfect!"

Yeah, Georgios thinks. *It will be just perfect.*

¤◘¤

When Chris Kristofer enters his office, he finds a note from Arthur glowing on his terminal.

"Meeting. My office. As soon as you've checked your mail."

Obediently, Chris does check his mail, thinking as he reviews the messages and taps out a few routine responses, that Arthur has become much more considerate over the last week. Before the conference about Tommy Thunderburst's concert, the King would have ordered him and Bill to appear without delay, then complained when they didn't have the answers he wanted.

Over at the other side of the office, he can hear Bill chuckling about something.

"What's so funny?"

"Nothing much, just a cat joke the Wanderer tacked to the end of her last report. She's on her way to Tennessee to get away from the winter weather."

"Lucky her. Ready for the meeting?"

"Yeah. Wonder what impossible quest King Arthur has for us today?"

They find out as soon as they get settled in the King's office, and Arthur has offered them juice and pastries from a tray that he had prepared with his own hands.

"Yesterday, I spoke with Lovern," Arthur begins, "and learned how desperate are his staffing needs. I agreed to speak with several athanor for him. I need your help in locating a couple."

When the humans nod acknowledgment, and Chris readies paper and pen (having learned that such little gestures reassure Arthur that he's paying attention), the King continues:

"One is Alice Chun, the novelist. You may be familiar with her books. I've been trying to reach her for several weeks, but I can't get past her agent. Find her.

"I also need to speak with Anson. I've left messages for

Eddie, but I have no evidence that he's picking up his e-mail."

A week before this omission on Eddie's part would have been enough to set Arthur sulking, but now he accepts it as the way of things. Chris can't help but wonder what Eddie had said to his friend and liege to so alter Arthur's behavior.

"Try and find him. Their itinerary places them in the city of Monamona, but I don't have a hotel address. You may need to phone every place in the city asking for either Anson A. Kridd or Eddie Ibatan or possibly Dakar Agadez."

Bill raises his hand. "Are you certain they're using those names?"

"I've checked our files here," Arthur answers, "and there is no record of any of them getting extra identification papers for this trip. If those names don't work, I'll give you the name of my one local contact. I don't want to call on him too soon, since I don't know the details of Anson's business."

Chris nods, understanding such delicacies from his days with the newspaper. "The last thing you want to do is mess up Anson's deal just when you need a favor from him."

Arthur grins. "Precisely. Can you get started at once?"

The two humans nod, but, despite Arthur's reformed behavior, Chris feels he must caution the King not to get impatient.

"I'll start tracking down Anson, sir, but remember, this may take some time. Do you have any idea if they'd prefer the tourist hotels or go for more 'native' accommodations?"

"Anson was working on a business deal of some kind," Arthur replies, "so they should be avoiding the low-end places—bad for the image—especially in a place like Nigeria."

"Thanks. That gives me a starting point."

Bill says, "That leaves Alice Chun for me. I think I'll bypass her agent altogether and see if I can learn something from her editors. Do you know if she has a web page?"

Arthur blinks. "I didn't think to check."

"I will, then." Bill rubs his hands together briskly. "I'll see what I can get done before my class this afternoon."

"Thank you," Arthur says. "Meanwhile, I'll be speaking

with some of the others. I've also thought of several people to contact who were not on Lovern's list. I may need your help later to find some of them. They've been out of touch for a while."

He rises then, both to dismiss them and to see them to the door. "Again, thank you for your help on this matter."

As they are walking down to their office, Chris says to Bill, "You know, I think he's getting to trust us."

"Yeah," Bill grins. "Things are getting better all the time."

¤▣¤

Seated in the dining room at the Other Three Quarters Ranch, Wayne Watkins savors his beer and studies his host.

Technically this is his second visit to the ranch. His first had been immediately after discovering the wolf track the day before. At that time, he had found Frank MacDonald shoeing horses and unwilling to be interrupted. However, he had invited Wayne to return the following day.

Now, after giving him a tour of the quarter-horse stables and putting a couple of the horses through their paces, MacDonald had invited him to stay to lunch.

"I can't do anything fancy," he had said, "but I've got some fresh bread and a bean soup."

Wayne, eager to get a closer look at this place, would have accepted an invitation to eat peanut butter and jelly on stale bread.

"Thank you," he'd said. "Just let me call my foreman and tell him that I'm postponing our meeting a few hours."

Now he watches as MacDonald places a bowl of thick soup—he'd have called it a stew—in front of him. There's the promised bread and some cheese, too.

The odd thing is that no one else joins them for lunch. MacDonald has at least twenty horses on the place. Wayne had seen other livestock: cows, chickens, ducks, guinea pigs, some sheep and goats. There'd been gardens, too, bedded down for the winter except for some cold-weather crops like cabbage and kale, but pretty extensive. Far too extensive for one man to tend. Yet no one else comes to the table, and MacDonald mentions no other residents.

A couple of big dogs of uncertain persuasion—but neither of them large enough to have left the print he saw—lounge nearby. Wayne drops a piece of cheese on the floor, but, though the long-eared hound nearest to him looks hopeful, it doesn't dive for the treat.

"I don't give them table scraps," MacDonald explains, taking his seat. "Keeps them sharp."

"Good idea," Wayne agrees.

They eat for a time in relative silence, Wayne not wanting to push his business and MacDonald apparently absorbed in the simple act of eating. *He's an odd one*, Wayne decides. *Quiet even in his body language, but with a sense of being aware of everything around him.*

When a thud comes from the kitchen, MacDonald doesn't even turn his head. He just says "Cat" in a strong, stern voice, and in a moment a chubby red tabby cat comes slinking out of the kitchen.

"Can't train them," MacDonald says. "They've got too much sense of themselves."

"Like people," Wayne says, though he doesn't really believe it.

"Worse," MacDonald replies.

"You've got the horses well trained, though."

"Hardly need to train a quarter horse to herd. Harder to keep them from doing it, they love it so."

"Yeah. I've seen that." Wayne follows this reflection with a long, convoluted anecdote about a cow horse belonging to a friend of his. MacDonald listens with apparent interest, though he must have heard stories like it plenty of times.

"I'm interested in buying a couple of your horses," Wayne says, when he's finished his story and MacDonald has told one of his own, "to work the parcel right next door. You interested in selling?"

MacDonald considers. "Maybe. I'd need to meet the folks you plan to have riding them."

"I've got a couple greasers riding herd," Wayne says. "Foreman's a good man for a Mex. He's the one who said he'd like a horse or two. Land over there gets rough at points."

"I know."

Belatedly, Wayne remembers that the land in question had been leased by MacDonald before he'd pulled strings with the government and gotten the lease for himself. Mentally, he kicks himself, hoping he hasn't queered the deal.

MacDonald is studying him now, or maybe not him, maybe the wall behind him. In the shadowy room, it's hard to tell where those eyes are looking, the lashes are so long, like a girl's or a cow's.

"Good not to have trucks ripping up the land," Wayne flounders. "We're hauling in most of our feed, so there shouldn't be overgrazing."

"That's good." MacDonald smiles slightly. "Not much there to feed anything. I used it for a buffer."

Wayne nods. "I'm not surprised. You strike me as a man who appreciates room." He thinks of an opening to the matter that really interests him and charges ahead. "It's pretty wild out here. Ever have any predator trouble?"

"Not really," MacDonald says. "I keep a close eye on the horses, send out dogs with them, dogs or llamas. Coyotes don't get messed up with things that can fight back. They can outsmart most dogs, but llamas think differently. Coyotes don't know what to make of 'em."

"Ah." Wayne tries desperately to think of a way to introduce the question of wolves. "I haven't seen much sign of coyotes on my land."

"That's good."

For a moment, MacDonald seems more than reasonably relieved. Wayne wonders why, then decides that the horse rancher must have hunted them out of the area and is glad to know that they haven't come back in.

"You hunt?" he asks casually.

"Not for many, many years," MacDonald says. "Got bored with it. Didn't seem much of a match, person with gun against critter."

"Ah."

Wayne decides to leave that one alone. Something about the ranch house had been bothering him ever since he had come inside, and now he realizes what it is. Most ranch houses are decorated with trophies: hides or racks of antlers at least, sometimes even whole animals stuffed and mounted.

There's nothing of the sort in MacDonald's house, not even an antler lamp-stand or a bit of fur on a cushion. He wonders if MacDonald is a nature lover or an eco-nut. If so, he wouldn't tell Wayne even if there *were* wolves in the area.

As if embarrassed by his gaucheness, Wayne brings the conversation back to horses. They talk for a while, then go see the animals MacDonald might consider selling. In the end, they agree that Wayne will return the next day with Jesus.

They part friendly, but as soon as he's on the road out, Wayne is on the phone, making calls. He's got to find a way to lure MacDonald off his land, even if just for a day or two. Then, when the OTQ is without its master, he'll make a reconnaissance of his own.

¤▣¤

Outside the rain is falling, not the warm rains of spring, the rains that herald hanami, *the celebration of the cherry blossoms, but the colder rains of autumn. Katsuhiro has the* kozo-washi *panels on the sides of the large central room of his house open to welcome the coolness. The wind that darts playfully through the* fusama *and the* shoji *is very welcome.*

Silver falls the rain, slanting lines.

There is a poem there, but he is distracted from composition by the awareness that someone else shares the room with him. He turns his head, aware that his hair is gathered in the heavy samurai knot he has not worn for decades, indeed, centuries. His clothing is old-style, too. The sleeves of the kimono are heavy with the gold thread and silk of karaori *weaving.*

Turning his head shows him a large piece of fabric spread out upon the floor. Parts of it have been covered with a thick paste. He smells the starchy scent of the rice flour and rice bran that went into its making. With the tip of one finger, he touches the paste and finds it still wet.

Someone is decorating a cloth in the katazome *style. Yes. There is the stencil set in place, awaiting the next application of paste. The pattern is quite elaborate and he doesn't think it is one of the traditional designs: cranes or flowers. Brides once prepared futon covers in this fashion and put them in their hope chests. Now clothes dyed in the* katazome *style have become rare and collectible. Women have better things to do with their lives. Better?*

He wonders, but then, he would wonder. He isn't a woman. Their lives are not his life.

Curious, he rises so that he can see the pattern from above, gain a sense of what it depicts, though its ultimate subtlety won't be visible until the dyeing is complete and the paste cleared away. For a precious moment, he begins to understand what is depicted there and is filled with such wonder and fear that his blood runs hot.

He is too hot, but when he tries to undress, the long sleeves of his kimono twist about him, come to life, snakes seeking to strangle the life from him. He thrashes, tearing at the fabric with his fingertips, heat growing so that sweat dampens the bindings, making them cut the bare flesh beneath.

He cannot reach his sword . . . Where is his sword? He has lost it! Lost it! Something touches the side of his face . . .

Awakening is sudden, triggered by the knowledge that something *has* touched the side of his face, a realization carried to him by trained muscles, combat-honed reflexes that even nightmare cannot fool.

He is in bed within the room inside Regis's compound in the hot, damp, stifling city of Monamona. Winter coolness is a dream. The binding fabric of his dream kimono proves to be only sweaty sheets entangling his naked limbs. Revelation is lost with wakening. The one thing he is certain of is that he is not alone and that, as in his dream, his sword has been taken from him.

Moving slowly, he frees his limbs from their wrappings. In the hot, still air, he hears breathing. Someone is sitting in the chair near his writing table, pulled back into the shadows. Remembering that his room is monitored (though he wonders if Regis cares about him any longer, for he has not been called into the Chief General's presence for two days now) Katsuhiro is careful.

Sniffing the air, he tries to identify his caller by scent. Taiwo smells of Old Spice aftershave, rather than of sweat. Teresa wears perfume. Regis, despite his use of Western antiperspirants, has a sour smell all his own: salt, vinegar, and sickness in the bowels. Katsuhiro smells none of these scents from the silent figure in the darkness. Instead he smells sweetness, like baked goods, a hint of chocolate, banana pudding, peanut-oil-fried *akara*, donuts.

In the darkness, then, he smiles and whispers a single word, speaking old Mycenaean, a language dead for thousands of years, but once used as a trade tongue among the athanor.

"Spider?"

A soft laugh. "Awake now?"

"Yes."

"You found me."

"Yes."

"Do you want out?"

"I want Regis dead and my sword returned to me."

"Good goals. I share one, sympathize with the other. Do you want to be released?"

Katsuhiro remembers his dream, remembers his horror at being disarmed. Takes it as an omen.

"I cannot leave without my sword."

"Where is it?"

"I don't know."

"Ah." A long pause, then. "Do you have anything to eat?"

Without wasting words, Katsuhiro rises, goes to his dresser, where he has stored away from the omnipresent insects the least perishable parts of his dinner. He realizes that the only way Anansi could have come to him was in another shape and that the Spider's body makes greater demands on him than most.

"Some fruit. Some candy."

"Good." Munching noises, then. "Regis protects himself well. If I bring you weapons, will you assist us from within?"

"Yes. My sword . . ."

"I will look for it. Do you have any allies?"

"Maybe one. Teresa."

"Ah!" The sound is full of pain. "Poor child. We must rescue her, too."

Katsuhiro decides that now is not the time to tell Anson that rescue may be too late for Teresa.

"Get her to look for the sword."

"I will try. I have not seen her since the wind wall came. I have not seen Regis either. Did you call the wind?"

"No." Another long pause, this one clearly for thinking as the food is gone. "There is one called Oya who claims the honor."

"Oya?"

"That's all we know."

"And the wall?"

"Meant to keep the sickness in."

"Good."

"I must go, so I have some darkness for scouting. Next time, I will bring a weapon for you."

"A gun." (The Mycenaean lacks the word, so what Katsuhiro says is "A metal slug thrower.")

"Very well. Save me some food."

"I will."

"And look for the sword. Demand to see Regis. Be difficult. The more demands on his attention, the better."

"Yes."

"Good night."

"Good night."

Katsuhiro sees something depart via the open window, something far smaller than a man. A monkey, probably. For a long time, he stands by the window, listening for an alert, planning what he would do if there is, but there is no disturbance.

With the dawn, he returns to his bed, composing himself for a few hours sleep. A warrior is responsible for being well rested before entering into battle.

¤◘¤

The Changer had forgotten how relaxing the green underwater world could be, had forgotten because it has been millennia since he has lived there. True, he came here not long ago as guide and guard to Lovern, but then there was tension, a sense of looming crisis. Now he is living day to day, much like a fish or seal, much like he would when in animal form.

The Changer realizes that he is happy.

Guilt has never been something he has carried with him, so, although he misses Shahrazad, he does not feel bad about enjoying himself in her absence. Nor does he worry about her. He has left her in good keeping. If there is a problem, Frank will call him. No call. No problem.

Triton form suits him here. In it he can talk with Vera, who does not understand the bubbles and fin postures of fish talk, and who cannot interpret any but the broadest of scent words. It also makes him an ornament to his brother's court, a court that is flourishing with those gathered to build Atlantis.

There are far more sea-athanor than most of the land or island-born realize. Many of those late-born land folk think that merfolk are only a shapeshifted form of another creature, rather as selkies doff their skins and acquire a human form. Those older or more knowledgeable know that once there were communities of merfolk but think that they have gone the way of the dragons.

The truth is between these. Certainly, there are fewer merfolk now than there were when the seas were open and unfished. However, there are far more than just the selkies. Many, like Duppy Jonah, whom they honor as their ultimate sire, are shapeshifters. They spend much of their lives in one form, swimming with a pod of whales or a school of fish, but can take other forms. Most have learned the mermaid or triton form because hands are useful things, just as most have learned the octopus form because lacking bones can be useful, too.

Vera had certainly been surprised to learn of the merfolk's numbers, but grateful, too.

"I had thought," she tells the Changer one day, a week or so after his arrival, "that I would be trying to build Atlantis with my bare hands and what help I could import from above. Why is Duppy Jonah so secretive about the size of his kingdom?"

"My brother," says the Changer, backing water with his tail as he sets in place sections of what will be a corridor, "has not told me. However, I suspect that he and his people view their numbers as their own business and none at all of the land dwellers'. You are, you know, a minority on this Earth."

"I know," Vera says, the trace of impatience in her voice indicating to the Changer that he is far from the first to tell her this. "Eighty percent water, twenty percent land."

"I suppose," the Changer continues, deliberately baiting her, "that Duppy Jonah just figures that common sense would tell anyone that there must be a good number of folks living on something like three-quarters of the globe."

"Oh, you!" Vera grins at him, suddenly aware she is being teased and welcoming the joke.

She has certainly learned to relax, the Changer muses. *I wonder how much is due to Amphitrite's influence?*

"If the seafolk are so scornful of the land," Vera asks, sealing the sections he has set in place, "why would they be working so hard to build a refuge for the land people?"

"I never said they were scornful," the Changer says. "That's your twist on it. Some of them, you know, don't quite believe in the land. It's a fairy tale to them. Others do, but they are rather pitying of those who live there in the dry."

He pauses, noticing that once again Vera is making him more talkative than is his wont. Aware that she is waiting politely for him to continue, he finds words for concepts he hasn't bothered with for a long time.

"Others are rather fascinated with the idea of land folk coming among them. Commerce has tended to be the other way—seafolk finding ways to investigate the land. They like the idea of getting a chance to meet the land folk without leaving their own element."

"Like in a zoo?" Vera says, slightly repulsed.

"Consider it more like a . . ." the Changer gropes for the words, his distance from human affairs crippling him somewhat, "a home-court advantage."

Vera nods. "I understand. Amphitrite was certainly at a disadvantage when she came to Arthur's for the Review."

The Changer swims to where the prefabricated sections are stacked and, when he has brought one back, Vera has another question.

"Arthur," she says, "has e-mailed to ask if next time I'm home would I let Lovern test me for magical potential. Apparently, demand far outstrips the supply. Many of the athanor—the theriomorphs especially—are becoming impatient."

She pauses. A pair of octopi jet by, pause to study their work, and then jet off again. The Changer watches them go, fully aware, even if Vera is not, that the multiarmed creatures are making jokes about the limitations of the human-formed upper torsos. He does not comment, knowing that all shapes have their limitations, and that most have their strengths.

"Arthur didn't ask," Vera continues, "if you would go by."

The Changer nods. "True."

"And the Ocean Monarchs are, of course, beyond such solicitation. What just struck me is that Arthur didn't ask about *any* of the seafolk. Do you know if they do magic?"

"Many do," comes the mild reply. "Perhaps more than on land, since many are my brother's children."

"But they couldn't come on land to be tested." Vera's grey eyes grow thoughtful. "Of course, Lovern could come here!"

"Would he?" the Changer says. "He has long been on bad terms with my brother."

"True. Still, it's worth asking about. Magic . . ." Vera shakes her head. "For the last couple of centuries, technology has made abilities we once needed magic for so easy: long-distance travel and communication especially. Now, all at once, we need magic for everything."

"Especially to overcome that same technology," the Changer comments. "And once where there were mountains, now there is ocean, and where once there was ocean, there is land. Such shiftings are the way of the world."

Vera looks at the shapeshifter, realizing he is not using a metaphor. Suddenly, she feels very shy. Remembering the changes through which he has lived, the ancient working alongside her seems far more alien than the fish that dart and glide around her in the water. For him, geologic ages must have been like the shifting of the seasons.

She shivers.

"How do you bear it?" Her voice is a whisper, yet she can hardly believe that she has spoken aloud.

"Change is the way of the world," he replies, "the one great constant, and I am the Changer."

The difference between genius and stupidity is that genius has its limits.

—AUTHOR UNKNOWN

IT IS A GAME, PLAYING HIDE-AND-SEEK ABOUT THE STABLE yard, a game given spice because Frank has told her in no uncertain terms to make herself scarce whenever he has visitors.

Still, Shahrazad cannot help herself—or more accurately, she does not want to help herself. Yesterday she had been so clever, tagging right at the heels of both the cow man and Frank. Neither had known she was there. At least she's pretty certain they hadn't known.

She places the blame for her scolding that evening squarely on Stinky Joe. She had seen the big golden tomcat watching her from a hayloft, the broken tip of his tail twitching back and forth, just like Arthur drumming on a table with a pencil eraser. He must have told on her, him or one of the unicorns. Her friends would not have, having grown philosophical—or perhaps merely inured—to her risk-taking.

Now she skulks along, the difficulty of her game increased in that there are three men today, not just two: Frank, the cow man, and the cow man's man. Coyotes are not the sticklers for hierarchy that wolves are, but she understands well enough the difference between alpha and beta.

Wayne is alpha, Jesus beta. Frank is not part of their hierarchy, but, judging from his behavior, Wayne wants to dominate Frank. He speaks in short, barking bursts, waves his hands about, pushes through doorways.

Jesus is clearly accustomed to Wayne's need to assert himself, and with dips of his head or lowerings of his gaze he constantly signals his submission. Frank doesn't appear to notice, though Shahrazad is certain that he knows perfectly well what Wayne wants.

In the little dominance games that almost all animals play, Frank is a master. He can face down a dog or wolf, put a restive stallion into line with a single word, and even convince a cat that he's worth listening to. If he chooses not to dominate Wayne, there must be a reason.

Instead, Frank smiles and nods, soft as water and as hard to push against. Wayne becomes frustrated and pushes harder. Shahrazad is reminded of the time she waded into a pond and suddenly the bottom dropped out from under her feet, leaving her paddling furiously. This time Wayne is doing the paddling.

Eventually, the three humans go into the house. Using one of the dog doors, Shahrazad slips in after. Her route takes her past the ever-closed door. Remembering her nightmares, she walks faster, slowing only when the click of her toenails against an uncarpeted section of the wooden floor threatens to give her away.

When she hears footsteps coming closer, she slips under a small table set in a corner. She curls into a ball, pretending to be a sleeping dog. Her ruse is for nothing. The man walking past doesn't see her.

"Where'd you say the john is?" Wayne calls to Frank.

Frank calls concise directions.

Peeking over her flank, Shahrazad watches. According to her unwritten rules for the game, she has just won a point. She'll win another if she changes position and Wayne still doesn't notice her.

The clouded leopard, asleep on a high shelf bordering the living room, winks a green eye, silent scorekeeper. When Wayne has gone into the bathroom, Shahrazad listens, marks the rise and fall of Jesus's voice in the kitchen, Frank's soft reply, the clatter of plates.

Having placed them and knowing by the continual stream of urine hitting water that Wayne is still occupied, she uncoils and comes out from under the table. A few feet away, there is an overstuffed chair—a very daring hiding place, since Wayne will pass within a few inches of it on his way back to the kitchen and dining room. Wanting the points this will win her in the clouded leopard's estimation, Shahrazad ducks under the chair and resumes her sleeping-dog pose.

She settles just as the stream of urine stops. Wayne emerges, buckling his belt. Reaching behind him, he closes the bathroom door. Shahrazad is tensing for the moment he will pass her hiding place, when, to her surprise, the man glances around the living room then walks briskly down the hallway leading toward Frank's bedroom, office, and several unused bedrooms.

He stays there only a moment, then emerges, glances again toward the kitchen. Listens to the rise and fall of conversation, and then heads down the other corridor. Here his snooping is baffled, for all the doors are kept closed. Most lead to storerooms or unused bedrooms, a thing Wayne learns with a quick opening of the door and peek inside. One door, however, is the locked one.

Wayne tests the knob, finds the door locked, tests it again, and then, with a curious expression on his face heads back up the corridor toward the living room. Pausing again to listen to the conversation in the kitchen, he is apparently satisfied that he has been unobserved.

Returning to the bathroom, he flushes the toilet, then makes a much less stealthy exit. He passes the hiding coyote without noticing her, even though in her puzzlement she has raised her head to watch him go by.

"Sorry to be so long," Wayne says in his loud, aggressive, alpha-male voice. "Had to take a crap."

Shahrazad doesn't listen to Frank's reply. Coming out of her hiding place, she glances up at the clouded leopard. The wild cat blinks at her.

"Humans!" the look says.

Shahrazad can only agree.

¤▣¤

Once again the computerized voice of the international operator informs Chris that all lines into the city of Monamona are busy now.

He groans softly. The lines have been busy for the past twenty-four hours. Yesterday evening, before he left work, he told Arthur he had been unable to get through and had promised to continue trying from his home until he went to bed. Arthur had actually been pretty calm about it.

"I don't need to reach Anson to inform him of any crisis," he had said, "so don't stay up late on my account. Phone service to these third-world countries often goes out."

Chris had taken the King at face value, making his last attempt at eleven before climbing into bed. He'd been certain that he'd get through this morning, and the recorded message is beginning to sound like a personal insult.

Bill wouldn't be in for a while, having an early class or something. Chris debates whether or not to report his latest failure to the King, decides against it—the situation is unchanged since his last report—and tries to get ahead of some of his other duties.

After three more encounters with the recorded message, pushing the redial button on the phone begins to seem like a Sisyphean task. Arthur will be certain to ask questions when they have their usual informal lunch meeting. Chris realizes that he doesn't want to admit that all the effort he has made in his assignment is to punch a single button on the phone.

He starts his new investigation by calling the number of the hotel in Lagos where Eddie and Anson had stayed. That call goes through. Heartened, he asks the clerk for the number of their branch hotel in Monamona, thinking that maybe there has been some change in the number or the area code. The number he is given, however, is the same as the one scrawled in his notebook.

"Can you transfer me somehow?" Chris asks, willing to grasp at straws.

"Sorry, sir," the clerk says, his accent very strong but subtly different than that which Eddie had demonstrated when showing off his Nigerian persona. "All lines to dere is out."

"Out?"

"Weatha conditions, sir."

"Weather conditions?" Chris repeats the phrase distinctly, positive that he could not have heard correctly.

"That's right. All phone is out."

"Thank you for your help," Chris says, and hangs up.

He tugs at his nose as if that will help him think.

"Weather conditions. Right."

Turning away from his telephone, he logs on to the Internet. In a few moments, he has found a site dedicated to worldwide weather, complete with constantly updated satellite maps. Zeroing in first on Africa, then on Nigeria, then on the southern portion of the country, he finally locates Monamona. The city is completely occluded by a reddish brown mass that the web site's key politely informs him indicates the presence of high winds.

Going for more detail, Chris learns that the wind resembles a cyclone or tornado, but is stationary.

"Curiouser and curiouser," he mutters.

There is nothing more he can learn here, so he tries hot links to various sites, hoping for a more detailed discussion of the phenomenon. He learns little, but the little that he learns is quite interesting. He sums it up for Arthur when, about a half hour later, he goes to report.

"Monamona has, to all intents and purposes, become the roosting place for an anomalous windstorm. Most of the meteorologists who are studying it agree that it is not merely an intensification of the usual *harmattan* wind pattern."

He pauses in case Arthur needs (as he himself had) a definition of this term. Arthur, however, has experienced the *harmattan* and simply nods for Chris to go on.

"The dominant theory is that the Monamona windstorm is caused by the *harmattan* encountering some other factor that has made the wind cycle back onto itself. The two most common guesses as to what this other factor might be are increased temperatures generated by the city itself or the height of the city's buildings creating something like an artificial mountain range."

"Bosh," Arthur says, rather rudely.

"I agree, sir," Chris says. "The meteorologists are somewhat hampered in their investigations since the Nigerian government is not permitting any travel at all into Monamona. In fact, they have cordoned off a five-mile-wide area surrounding the city."

Arthur cocks a brow at this. "They're worried about it, then. Note the advantages of a totalitarian government."

Chris, who now knows something of Arthur's frustration with his own inability to govern the fractious and strong-willed athanor, chooses not to take this last too seriously.

"The Nigerian government *is* worried, sir. I decided to find out—just for academic interest—how much trouble I would have getting a tourist visa. I was refused flat out."

"Oh? Any evidence that they are deporting tourists?"

"The opposite, sir." Chris frowns. Both Anson and Eddie have been among the humans' strongest supporters. "I can't swear to this, but, judging from various factors, the government is preventing people from departing."

"What factors?" Arthur snaps, not in temper, but as a battlefield commander would request information.

"Nigeria has always had an active tradition of news reporting," Chris says, "something I remembered from one of my journalism classes. I've hunted up on-line news from the area and learned that Lagos airport is temporarily closed to international flights. The official story is that something is out in one of the control towers. As of now, no one is reporting differently, but I thought it rather odd.

"I checked further and learned that hotels in Lagos are filling up. When I asked why, I was told that the borders with Benin, Niger, and Cameroon are closed. Again, the official word is that troops are being diverted from their usual posts in order to maintain the cordon around Monamona. Therefore, they aren't available to provide routine customs on the border. However . . ."

Chris licks his lips and flips a page on his notes. "However, the news services in those border countries report an intensified Nigerian military presence on the borders."

"Oh, my!" Arthur says. "And all because of a windstorm?"

Chris shrugs. "That's all I could find out. I've sent a copy of all my notes directly to your computer."

"Thank you." Despite his evident worry, the King smiles graciously. "You have done a fine job. There are certainly advantages to having a reporter on staff. Keep trying to get through to Monamona. This storm may disperse, and it will all be a tempest in a teapot."

"Right."

As Chris leaves, he hears Arthur pick up the telephone.

"Lovern . . ."

He closes the door behind him. Arthur doesn't think this a tempest in a teapot. Neither does he. The question is, what is it and, perhaps more importantly, what does this mean for their friends?

¤▣¤

Aduke has overcome the feeling that she is going to slip into undignified hysteria, but she admits to herself that she is quite confused. That response seems safe, far safer than acting as if everything is normal.

Still, she wishes that she understood more of what Oya and her new associates intend to do. When she does learn, she realizes that there are times when ignorance *is* bliss.

They have gathered once more in Oya's conference room, all three of the newcomers, herself, and Oya.

"I've spoken with Katsuhiro," says Anson, the one Oya had first addressed as Eshu, "and he is comfortable for now. Regis has taken his sword, and he wishes to reclaim it before he leaves."

"Not *Kusanagi*!" Oya says. "I am surprised that he permitted such an insult!"

Eddie, the only one of the three newcomers who had not been associated with the name of one of the *orisha*, and so the one with whom Aduke paradoxically feels both most and least at ease, shrugs, his expression wry.

"I suspect that Katsuhiro was not given an opportunity to protest the loss. That says our opponents did their homework."

Dakar, who rather frightens Aduke with his mountainous size and tendency to bellow, thumps the tabletop with his fist.

"How much homework would it take?" he grumbles. "Katsuhiro teaches both *kendo* and *kenjitsu*—as well as other martial arts."

Aduke has already noted that sometimes Dakar speaks of this Katsuhiro with a grudging respect and sometimes as if he hates him. She wonders at the relationship between these three men—and theirs with Oya. Certainly it is more complicated than mere tribal affiliation or nationality, yet she senses that it is something like that, too.

She wonders, too, why Oya has included her in these meetings. Certainly she has nothing to contribute, and she can tell that her presence makes all of them, but especially Eddie, guard what they say.

"Very well," Oya says, "if your friend will not leave without his sword, his sword must be found. Did you have any luck in that direction, Eshu?"

" 'Anson,' " the thin man corrects gently. "Here and now I am 'Anson.' Eshu does not have the most savory of reputations in these civilized days."

Dakar chuckles. "Satan. That's who the Christians and the Moslems think Eshu is. What stupidity! They would have been better to think of him as the angel Gabriel."

Anson shakes his head. "Eshu's skin is too black for them to see him as an angel, though he has been a messenger between gods and men. However, I am Anson A. Kridd, and that will be ample trouble for our enemies. Now, we have decided that Katsuhiro will seek his sword, and I will attempt to visit him again tonight. What can we do in the meantime?"

"Our problems," Eddie says, "are like the Worm Ouroborus, biting on its own tail. The city faces famine and riot unless the wind wall is dropped. However, if the wall is dropped, the smallpox may spread."

"Will spread," Oya says firmly.

"Will spread," Eddie corrects himself. "However, if we do not do something about the smallpox, it will spread anyhow. This city is not Lagos in population, but it is not small. Most of the younger members of the population will not have been vaccinated."

He looks at Aduke. "Have you been vaccinated?"

She nods.

"When my baby . . ." Her voice falters, but she swallows and goes on, "was ill the doctor gave me something."

"And your family?"

"Yes. All the members of our household."

"That's something," Eddie says. "What a thoughtful doctor. I wonder how he knew what he was looking at? In its early stages, smallpox is often confused with chicken pox—a disease most children get."

"He was a very old man," Aduke says, almost defensively. "I think he had seen the like when he was younger."

Oya leans forward. "Leave her alone, Eddie. She's a victim, not a criminal. Remember, too, that smallpox was rampant in Nigeria until the late 1960s. Many doctors will recognize it."

Eddie doesn't apologize. "One more question, Aduke. Did your baby contract smallpox here or in Lagos? You did say you lived in Lagos with your husband before coming here, didn't you?"

Aduke nods. She can see what he is trying to learn.

"I'm not certain, sir. We visited here frequently, but I first noticed that he was ill when we were at home in Lagos. Baby was so fussy that we came here where I would have family to help me tend him. My sister Yetunde is married to one of my husband's brothers, so I am doubly related to them. When after several days Baby grew no stronger, Taiwo's mother consulted a *babalawo* and his verses directed her to the old doctor."

Proud that she has managed this recitation without breaking down, she stops before she must relive the tremendous hope she had felt when the old doctor had come. He'd seemed so wise, with his white hair and sparse beard, a worn leather doctor's bag clasped firmly in his gnarled hand. She doesn't want to remember the despair that had followed when, despite the doctor's best efforts, Baby had grown worse.

Mercifully, Eddie does not ask more, perhaps because Oya is glowering at him, her eyes holding all the lightning that she had stolen from Shango.

"Thank you, Aduke," Eddie says. He looks at the others, his expression bleak. "So, despite whatever we do here, Lagos may already be infected. If it is, the infection will spread outward."

Oya shakes her head, causing the cloth of her head wrap to snap as if in a high wind. "If we accept that train of thought, we are defeated before we begin. Our battlefield is this city. Let us concentrate on what we can do here."

"And *do* something," Dakar agrees.

"We have electricity again," Eddie says, "but no telephone. That means we cannot rely on help from outside."

Anson nods. "I am the only one of us who can get inside Regis's compound without being detected. Therefore, I must be our scout."

He looks at Oya, "Unless you, lady, have some other magical tricks?"

The very matter-of-fact way that he speaks of magic makes Aduke feel once again that her reality, a reality bolstered by the knowledge so carefully learned in school and at university, is as fragile as a soap bubble.

"Oya controls the winds," says Oya, "and can be quite fierce as well, but I do not think that she has any gift suited for reconnaissance."

Anson shrugs. "Then if there is to be scouting, the scout is to be me."

Dakar grumbles. "I cannot wait longer. I will go join one of the police patrols. Perhaps I will hear something that we can use. I, for one, do not think that this quick mobilization of the militia is coincidence. Someone was prepared for a crisis, whether this one or another."

"A coup?" Oya asks.

"Why not?" Dakar answers, eyes narrow with distrust. "It is practically the traditional way for the Nigerian government to change hands."

"Go then," Anson says. "I think you are wise."

"That's a first," Dakar says.

Eddie says, "That leaves me as backup for Anson. Oya?"

"I will speak with the wind," she says, "and learn what I can. When the time comes for us to move against Regis, perhaps Oya can prove once more that she is the wife more dangerous than the husband."

"Which," Anson says, "brings us to the matter we have been skating around."

"Shango," Dakar says.

"Like you," Anson says, "I have wondered at this quick readiness of the local military. The electricity is back on. Perhaps that is enough to ask of him."

"Then you don't trust him," Eddie says.

"Do you?"

Eddie shrugs. "I don't know. We don't need him yet, so why take more risks? We're taking enough as it is."

He looks at Oya as he says this, and Aduke feels anger on her friend's behalf. Oya's expression, though, remains as expressionless as windswept sand, so Aduke holds her peace, still wondering if they have been wise to put so much trust in these three strange men.

Oya has another surprise for her.

"Why don't you three move into this part of the factory? I have spoken with the old Malomo Fadaka and she is willing, especially since I have hinted that you will bring food with you and everyone is worrying about the possibility of famine."

Aduke has already noted that Anson eats constantly, so she is not at all surprised when he chuckles.

"I might have a sack or two of something laid by against a midnight snack." He turns to his associates. "What do you think?"

Dakar shrugs. "I go for a soldier. Whether I report here or there means nothing."

Eddie is more cautious. "We could bring harm to these people."

To her astonishment, Aduke hears herself answering: "The *babalawo* predicted that my family would face many evils. Perhaps *we* will bring harm to *you*!"

Eddie looks at her with respect. "I can risk that. In any case, Anson's comings and goings have caused some comment from our landlady."

"There may be other advantages as well," Oya says mysteriously. "Do you need help with your baggage? Aduke's brother drives a lorry."

"Yes. That's a good idea," Anson says. "No one will think

anything of the lorry coming, and so our arrival will be unnoticed by your few neighbors."

"Then it is settled," Oya says. Standing, she dusts off her hands like any housewife in all the world. "Come, choose what rooms you want for yourselves."

Trailing after, Aduke wonders why, since everyone else is treating this as routine, she feels as if something terribly momentous has just occurred.

¤◘¤

Georgios is proud of himself, really proud, of the way he'd handled this affair. The last time he'd been out on his own he hadn't been out on his own, not actually. He'd been shepherded here and there, by Demetrios, by Monk, by members of Arthur's staff.

Oh, it had been fun, had shown him what he was missing, but what they wanted to do he hadn't really wanted to do, or at least not much. Looking at girls can be fun, especially when your looking has been restricted to gazing from a distance for so long. It doesn't compare to touching girls, though, and that had been ruled right off-limits.

Georgios had agreed then (well, except for some discreet fanny pinching and a couple of gropes in the fun house at the Fair), because he'd been as nervous as the rest of them about the consequences. But now the rules have been changed. Humanity is going to learn about the athanor sooner rather than later. He figures he'll be in the vanguard.

First step had been checking the local directories for limo services—no need to worry about finding taxis or driving yourself in a strange city that way. Like most theriomorphs, he has credit cards. He also has an excellent credit rating. Computer programming is one of those jobs where you can telecommute. It had been a good new career option when video porn had supplanted most of the written stuff.

After the limo had been arranged, Georgios had bribed the concierge to recommend a good place to pick up hookers. Escort services were out, as were houses. He wanted girls who had no support system, except maybe the kind of pimp who wouldn't care who took the girls for a ride as long as the pay was good.

And would he and his buddies ever take those girls for a ride! He gets hard just thinking about it.

The other three satyrs agreed to cover for him, Hunk, and Stud in return for a promise that they'd get nights out of their own. Georgios had rented them some top-grade porno flicks as thanks—and because no one in his right mind would try to roust them from their viewing, thus providing yet another level of cover.

Waiting until most of the tuckered-out *Pan* crew has retired to their rooms, Georgios leads his stalwart pals down a fire stair to a back door that lets out into a parking area.

The limo driver is a jaded-looking fellow, a balding white guy with freckles and jug-handle ears. Even his neat chauffeur's uniform can't make him look like anything but the kind of guy who is stuck driving cars for other people. He's affable enough, though, even more affable when Georgios presses a couple of crisp twenties in his hand.

Directed to keep his eyes forward, the driver pulls down a privacy screen of some sort. Their first stop is a liquor store, where they send the chauffeur in for some bottles of jug wine. Unlike the fauns, who are often connoisseurs, most satyrs just like to get drunk.

A bottle in his hand, Georgios grabs the ceiling mike and tells the chauffeur to take them cruising along the Strip, then to where they could find some action. He'd been a bit worried about their fancy stretch limo being noticeable, but it isn't particularly so. Most of the type who hang out here have seen it all before—or at least like to act like they have. The late hour probably helps.

"Whoo-hoo!" Hunk enthuses, his gaze firmly fastened where a candy-apple red vinyl miniskirt stretches across a pert behind. "Baby, baby, baby!"

"There! There!" shouts Stud, pointing to a pair of tits, bouncing high and round in a fluorescent green tank top. "I'm gonna lose it just looking!"

Georgios hears himself moaning and panting at the parade of pulchritude. At first he doesn't see individual women, just fantastic parts barely concealed by low-cut blouses, tight skirts, and tighter pants. His hand is busy, automatically working to ease a tension that doesn't often have another outlet. He pulls it away with an effort.

"Do some looking, boys!" he says. "Here's the candy shop, and you get to stick it in the jars!"

After a few passes up and down—passes that mark them out as serious shoppers to the women on the stroll—they each choose. Hunk remains faithful to the candy-apple red skirt, but Stud can't decide whether he wants a voluptuous black girl in a tight leopard-print jumpsuit or a sloe-eyed blonde wearing denim cutoffs that would have made Daisy Mae blush.

"Take 'em both," Georgios suggests. "You can afford it. We can pass them around for everyone to sample, like at a Chinese restaurant."

Inspired by his own imagery, he chooses one Asian beauty and a redhead whose legs won't stop. Hunk then insists that he needs another girl, and the fluorescent green halter joins the order. The chauffeur helps with the negotiations in return for another tip, and the girls pile into the back.

"Stop for more wine, then take us to a no-tell motel," Georgios orders, his hand up the redhead's skirt and his fingers squeezing the Asian's small breast. "Clean room, big beds, maybe something to get wet in."

"Right! About fifteen minutes, maybe twenty."

Georgios manages something vaguely articulate around the large peach-colored nipple he has in his mouth before letting go of the microphone. The limo starts to move. He barely feels the motion, getting ready for a ride of his own.

¤▣¤

Demetrios is uneasy. He can't say why. Rationally, it is because this is one of the few nights in recent centuries that he has spent away from the protection of his home. True, home has changed several times over those years, but it has been a long time since he has voluntarily left that safety.

The trip to Albuquerque had been the first time and then he had laid the groundwork with great care. Also, he had known that Arthur and the Accord—the same Accord whose validity Demetrios was challenging—would protect him from discovery. Odd, now that he thinks back, how eager he had been to change things when the change had seemed unlikely to happen. The closer they had come to confrontation, the more he had wanted to back off. Only momentum and dear Rebecca's constant reminders of how much they had to gain had kept him going at the end. This trip is different. He feels as if he has been drafted—literally pushed before a powerful elemental force over which he has no control. Maybe when he has the fairy dust that Lovern has promised he will feel safe.

For now, though, he is uneasy.

Demetrios swings his goat legs out of the hotel bed, moving quietly so as not to disturb Phoebus, his roommate, who had gone to bed exhausted from rehearsal. When Tommy works with them, the power of his music buoys them all up. The recording is a pale imitation, like caffeine replacing honest sleep.

He does not bother with his disguise before stepping out into the hallway—this floor is restricted to only the theriomorphs, Tommy, and Lil. Not even Mary Malone can get up here, a thing that keeps her safer then she might realize, since in an ideal universe she would begin their day with a round of calisthenics and aerobics before breakfast.

The satyrs would probably rape her, Demetrios thinks dryly. For them the line between enthusiastic sex and a bit of genial roughness isn't that well marked. Not that fauns are particular angels, but goaty as they are, they have a bit more self-restraint.

As he trots down the hallway, long brown hair pushed back from his rather pointed ears so that he can hear more easily, Demetrios focuses on one of the things that had bothered him, even in the comparative quiet of his room. The satyrs aren't noisy enough.

He's heard the ruckus they can raise often enough. During auditions they made some small effort at self-control, each eager to be chosen for this great opportunity. However, since then, they've been so rambunctious that Lil finally rented the rooms both above and beneath their suite to halt the complaints.

Demetrios sometimes pities the roadies who have those rooms.

Pausing outside of the satyrs' suite, he presses an ear to the door. Dominant is the repetitious sound track of a porno film underscored by simulated cries of passion from several women and probably a couple of men. Then there are the raucous comments of the observers, rude and anatomically graphic.

But as he sorts through these, wincing occasionally as they suggest things obscene even to his experienced hearing, Demetrios becomes more and more certain that something is missing.

Where is Georgios's voice? The herd stallion normally leads such commentary, but his distinctive turns of phrase, showing ample evidence of the years he spent writing pornography, are missing from the mix. So are the voices of Stud and Hunk, his two greatest disciples.

Demetrios frowns. One of them might have fallen asleep, but all three? He can't believe it. It would be a point of macho pride for Georgios, at least, to stay awake as long as the others.

He tries the door. It is unlocked and he enters.

The room is lit only by the light from the big-screen television on which two women and a man perform some erotic maneuvers involving a blue-velvet sofa and an astonishing array of sex toys. Beer cans are scattered on the floor, and pizza boxes are piled on the end tables.

Two satyrs lounge on the beds. A third leans with his back against the footboard, one hand in his lap, the other around a can. The room smells of semen and beer and onions.

There is no sign of the missing three, but the door into the other bedroom is closed. Without speaking to the satyrs, Demetrios crosses to it. His hand is on the knob when the satyr on the floor, one Mikos, notices him

"Hey!" he says, loudly if not very intelligently. "You!"

Demetrios turns the doorknob. It is locked. He takes the passkey from the thong around his neck.

"You can't go in there!" Mikos says. He sounds like Sylvester Stallone as Rocky after he'd been hit in the mouth a couple too many times, but he is an excellent dancer.

"I can," Demetrios says, sliding the key into the lock. "And I am."

The room is dark. There is no sound of breathing, no smell of food or drink. He feels for the light switch, aware that the three satyrs have risen and are sputtering at him. He ignores them, flips the switch.

The room is empty.

"Where are they?"

Mikos glances at the bathroom door as if searching for an excuse, but the door is open, and there is no way three beefy satyrs are hiding in there.

"Out," he says sullenly.

"Out? Out as in off this floor or out of the hotel?" Demetrios looks suddenly wild and fearsome. Something in his attitude reminds the satyrs that the word "panic" has its root in chance encounters with a faun.

"Out of the hotel," Mikos mutters. "Don't know nothing more."

Demetrios believes him and feels his heart begin to pound. Fauns are not immune to panic.

"What am I going to do?" he wails.

"They'll be back," Mikos says. "They just went to get laid. They'll be back pretty soon."

"I hope so," Demetrios says, wringing his hands as he imagines the consequences if they should not return. "I don't know what I'll do if they don't!"

If you cannot get rid of the family skeleton, you may as well make it dance.

—GEORGE BERNARD SHAW

LOUHI HADN'T EXPECTED TO BE SO LUCKY. OF COURSE, AS she reminds herself, running endless loops in her little aluminum wheel, it hadn't been all luck. She's been working hard, very hard, reaching out with what little power and concentration remains to her. Sometimes, it's hard to be a mouse.

Actually, it's almost always hard to be a mouse.

The coyote pup, her sister, had disappointed her by showing far more resistance to Louhi's probing than Louhi had thought possible. When Shahrazad had taken to sleeping with the rest of the furballs on Frank MacDonald's bed, the cats had effectively shielded her. Damn furballs!

Louhi had experienced a bad time then, seeing her hopes for escape sinking to nothing. In her rage and frustration, she had sunk down into the mouse mind, gnawing at her wooden chew stick, eating seeds, digging burrows in the fluffy pine shavings of her bedding. She'd recovered, though, not like that stupid Head, who, to the best of her knowledge, has sunk into the ground-squirrel mind and remained there.

Maybe the Head thinks it's imprisoned beneath the sea again and is again biding its time, waiting like some fairy-tale princess for a knight to rescue her. Frankly, Louhi doesn't care. She's not waiting for some prince. She's questing for the key to open her cell, and now she knows that key has a name and the name is Wayne Watkins.

She caresses the name in her mind, reciting it over and over again until it becomes a mantra for freedom. Wayne has fingers. Wayne has hands. Wayne has a voice to speak, a car to drive, and money. Best of all, Wayne has powerful aggressions, aggressions she can touch, tap, channel. Like many powerful men, Wayne has superstitions, superstitions she can twist to her advantage.

When Wayne had first visited Frank's house Louhi had touched him with the light sensory web she had managed to maintain despite the eroding force of passive cat magic. The rancher's true purpose for being there had been so obvious that she had been certain that Frank would read it as she did.

But Frank's gifts are not shaped that way and, with the Cats of Egypt and several of the other athanor cats away, there is no one to warn him.

With a fresh understanding, Louhi realizes that the absence of the cats has let her magic grow stronger. Never before had she realized how powerful the felines' passive protections could be. Unlike iron, which dampens magic without discrimination, cat magic seems to enhance what that cat desires and to diminish that which the cat does not.

Even if Louhi hadn't been a mouse, at that moment she would have loathed cats.

But her spirit is buoyed by the memory of Wayne. Before he had departed, she had sunk a hook deep into him—a slender magical harpoon with a barbed head sunk deep into the human's dura mater. A silver cord plays out and connects to her.

Now, running hard on the wheel so that the tiny runes she has scratched into its surface vanish in a blur, Louhi sends pulses down the silver cord. She likes what Wayne plans to do next, for it will bring him closer to her. Then she can convince him that there is a charm in Frank's house that will make him a success.

That charm, of course, will be a pink-nosed female mouse with silvery white fur and eyes the unforgiving blue of ice.

¤◘¤

In a house built into a hillside in the forests of Oregon two creatures are asleep on a custom-built bed, for even a king-size bed would be far too small for them. Big feet poke out from under the quilt. There is the sound of deep breathing, restfulness, peace, all interrupted by the ringing of the telephone.

Bronson Trapper comes awake at once, brought alert by reactions honed when mastodons and giant sloths still shambled across the plains of North America. His wife, Rebecca, wakes a little more slowly, but she is the one who recognizes the source of the disturbance and reaches for the phone.

"Hello?"

"Becky? This is Demetrios."

The faun's voice still sounds strange to Rebecca. Despite the fact that they do talk on the phone and have met in person, to her, Demetrios is still best represented by little lines of type marching across her computer screen. However, even if they had talked daily, Rebecca might not have recognized Demetrios's voice tonight. His normally cultured diction is broken, his voice pitched higher with tension.

"Demi?" The lady sasquatch gets out of bed, not bothering with a wrapper or robe since her fur will keep her warm. "What's wrong?"

Bronson also looks concerned. He knows that his wife's best friend would not call at—he glances at the bedside clock—five in the morning without good reason. Padding to the kitchen, silent despite his bulk and the size of his feet, the sasquatch puts a kettle on the stove.

"I learned just a couple of hours ago," Demetrios says, "Georgios and two of his buddies. They've gone out!"

"Out? As in they're not in their rooms?"

"They're not even in the hotel," Demetrios moans. Rebecca can imagine him nervously rubbing his short goat's horns. "I've checked—discreetly, of course. They're not here."

"Where did the satyrs go?"

"All the remaining three satyrs will admit is that the others went out to find women."

"Oh!"

"And we're in Las Vegas."

"Oh?"

Demetrios clarifies. "You know how this city makes its living?"

"Gambling, right?"

"Yes. And conventions. That means lots of males with money away from their families, temporarily cut loose without the usual social restraints."

Rebecca nods, intellectually but not instinctively understanding. Sasquatch are naturally monogamous, something which, combined with their low birthrate, has contributed to the small size of the population.

She replies, "So there are lots of easy women?"

"Lots!" Demetrios's laugh is humorless. "You walk down the Strip here—that's what they call the main street—and men hand you flyers advertising call girls, girlie shows, strip clubs, nude dancers. This in broad daylight, at night . . ."

His voice trails off, desperation and despair warring for prominence.

"So you don't know where to look for them."

"I don't have the first idea where to start! I can't call the police. The satyrs have been gone only a few hours. Even if I could call the police, I can't call the police. They can't learn what the satyrs really are!"

"Maybe the satyrs will be back soon." Rebecca doesn't sound hopeful. "The night isn't over yet."

"It's five in the morning!" Demetrios wails. "Rehearsal starts at nine. The choreographer wants everyone to turn out for warm-up exercises at eight-thirty. I can make excuses then, but at nine . . . The cat's out of the bag."

"So you have three hours," Rebecca says, her mind whirling through possibilities, discarding most of them. "If they aren't back by then . . ."

"I'm in big trouble! Lil will skin me and make my hide into a handbag! She's terrible when she's angry."

"Nonsense," Rebecca says sternly. "You aren't to blame. It's the satyrs who are in big trouble."

"So," interrupts Bronson, who has listened to Rebecca's side of the conversation, "are the rest of us if the satyrs are revealed for what they are: nonhumans, theriomorphs, creatures that shouldn't be."

Rebecca nods agreement, but she doesn't repeat it. Why add to her friend's worries?

"Demetrios," she says calmly, "let's assume that Georgios and his buddies went out to party and that in the course of doing whatever they were doing, they lost track of time."

"That's fair," Demetrios says. "The others said they meant to sneak back so no one would ever know they'd been gone."

"Good. Now, you've known them a long time . . ."

"Too long!"

"How would they react if they woke up and discovered that they'd stayed out too late? Would they come back and hope not to get caught or what?"

Demetrios, presented with a concrete problem, calms somewhat. "Georgios is in charge, and I don't think he would sneak back. One of the things that has been bugging him has been being ordered around. He didn't expect that. He thought that being in a rock and roll show would be like what you see in the movies—wild parties, late nights, lots of sex and drugs and women. He didn't realize that a show like Tommy's is big business."

"So you don't think he'll sneak back," Rebecca prompts. "I think you're right. The next question is will he stay where he is or will he hide?"

"Stay," Demetrios says promptly. "Georgios isn't dumb—not brilliant, but not dumb. He has a gift for calculation, at least when he's sober."

"We can't count on his being sober," Rebecca reminds.

"True, but he would have been when he made his initial plans for a party night out. That means he would have gone someplace where the satyrs with less than human features would be fairly safe from discovery."

"By anyone but the girls they picked up," Rebecca corrects.

"True. My guess is that he decided to keep the women drunk or stoned." Demetrios sounds embarrassed. "That's an old trick, dating way back even before the Accord."

"Okay." Rebecca blushes. "So Georgios is fairly safe from discovery wherever he is—and you don't think he'll run and hide?"

"No, that would mean admitting that he's done something wrong. Georgios is defiant. Remember, satyrs are half stallion. They're very hard to push when it's a matter of territory."

"Right." Rebecca thinks. "So they won't come back, but they won't move on. That means they could be tracked down."

"Not by me!" Demetrios says. "Boots hurt my hooves after a while. I can't possibly tramp up and down the Strip—and there are hundred of thousands of hotel rooms in this city."

"Not by you," Rebecca agrees, "but maybe by Lil and Tommy."

"Lil will kill me!"

"Not if you take action to protect yourself," Rebecca says, well aware that Lil Prima, also called Lilith, can be ruthless. "If the satyrs aren't back by the time Bill and Chris are at work, I think you've got to call them. You're going to need help. It'll be easier to talk with one of them rather than going directly to Arthur."

"Arthur . . ." Demetrios moans again.

"He asked you to take this job," Rebecca reminds the faun sternly. "It's his responsibility to help you. He didn't get you the magic you requested, did he?"

"Not yet."

"Then it's his fault. He let the satyrs out without properly preparing you."

"It's not the King's fault that the Blind Lion tour had to be delayed, and we got started sooner than planned!"

"True. That's no one's fault, I guess." Rebecca suppresses a passing thought that Lil or Tommy could have refused to take the new slot.

"Yeah." Demetrios sounds repentant. "Sorry I got excited there. I've been in a panic for hours."

"I'm sure. I wish I could be there to help, but I expect I'd just add to your troubles."

Demetrios chuckles. "Even in Las Vegas you'd stand out, Rebecca."

"True enough. Now, get something to eat. You've got another hour or so before you can call Pendragon Productions. Spend the time drafting an e-mail with all the details, including our deductions as to what Georgios is likely to do and not to do. If Arthur recruits reinforcements, Phoebus can send the e-mail from another line so you don't need to waste time repeating yourself."

"Good thought." Demetrios sighs. "Thanks, Becky. I'll do just what you say. And apologize to Bronson for my waking you up early. I just couldn't wait any longer. The other fauns are as nervous as I am, and the satyrs are alternately arrogant and defiant. I finally locked them in their suite, disconnected the phone, and set guards on the door."

"You're welcome. Bronson understands. Promise to call me when you know more?"

"Promise."

"Now, call room service and order some breakfast. You don't need to face this on an empty stomach."

"Yes, ma'am."

"Good luck."

"Thanks."

Bronson turns and hands her a cup of golden brown tea, sweet with honey.

"I didn't think," he says in his gruff, low voice, "that you'd want to go back to sleep."

"No," she says, taking the tea and leaning forward to kiss the bare section of his cheek above his reddish brown fur. "I don't think I could sleep. If you want to, I'll go feed the animals."

"I couldn't sleep either," Bronson admits. "I'm frightened. It's all I can do not to grab you and run for one of our safe havens deeper in the forest."

"Thanks," she says. "But I'll start packing—just in case."

¤◙¤

Never one to wait when action would serve, Katsuhiro Oba begins the morning by opening the door to his prison apartment and stepping into the corridor.

Anansi had visited him the night before, bringing with him

a small, comparatively lightweight handgun and a box of ammunition. The Spider had been visibly wearied by the effort, grateful for the honey-coated dates and cold *moi-moi* that Katsuhiro had saved for him. He had promised to return again, bringing more ammunition and more news.

The former would be welcome. The latter was certain to be disturbing, as all news from Monamona had been thus far. More than ever, Katsuhiro looks forward to taking action against those who would use disease as a weapon against defenseless civilians.

This step into the corridor is the first part of his campaign. The four guards, accustomed to his passive acceptance of captivity, are slow to reach for their weapons. Katsuhiro has no wish to take them on with his comparatively small gun and bare hands. He doesn't doubt his ability to win such a combat, but he is not willing to reveal the gun just yet.

He has taken two steps down the corridor, heading in the general direction of Regis's office, when one of the guards orders him to halt.

Katsuhiro doesn't even pause, continuing his unhurried departure. Behind him is a muttered conference, then the same guard yells:

"Stop where you are or we'll shoot!"

The sound of automatic weapons being readied punctuates this statement.

Katsuhiro had been prepared for this. He turns slightly, not cringing, but as a shogun would have turned to stare down some courtier whose manners were less than perfect. After subjecting them to a stare from eyes fully as dark as the guards' own, but made hidden and mysterious by their slant and the concealing fold of the eyelid, Katsuhiro frowns.

"Will you?" he asks. "Are you certain that Chief General Doctor Regis would be pleased? I am the key to an important business deal. If I die, you may make apologies for him to his honored guests."

Uncertain, the frontmost guard lowers the barrel of his rifle slightly, the tip wavering. Katsuhiro swallows a snort of disgust, maintaining instead stiff arrogance.

"I am bored with my rooms," he continues. "With patience

I have waited there three full days with hardly any company. I shall not wait a fourth."

Turning his back on them, he continues to walk forward. After the first three steps, he knows that his bluff has worked. They fear Regis's anger and, as of yet, Katsuhiro is showing no inclination to escape.

From Anson, Katsuhiro knows that the telephone system is out and that the wind is cutting off all but limited radio communication. Therefore, he is not surprised to hear the head of the guard detail designate one of his men as a runner to go inform Regis or the Balogun of this new development. Of course they speak Yoruban, which they do not realize he understands.

The runner does not go by Katsuhiro, but takes a stairway at the other end of the corridor. The Japanese files this information against future need.

"Permit us," says the chief guard, coming up beside him, "to act as your escort, Mr. Oba."

"I shall," Katsuhiro agrees haughtily. "I wish to stretch my legs, then to speak with someone. Perhaps Taiwo Fadaka."

The guard nods, smiling the broad, insincere smile of one who is very nervous.

"This way." He barks orders in Yoruban to another guard, telling him to learn if Taiwo is in the compound.

Katsuhiro finds this interesting. He had thought the younger man privileged. Now it seems that he may also be trusted.

Escorted by his remaining two guards, both nervous enough to shoot him if he does the least thing that strikes them as peculiar, Katsuhiro takes a leisurely stroll about the compound. Much of this he has seen and noted before, but he will not pass up the opportunity to refresh his memory. The walk also gives him his first clear glimpse of the wall of wind enclosing the city.

The upper regions, though fairly clear of dust and debris, are still visible to the naked eye, swirling currents distorting and filtering the sunlight. It looks quite formidable, and Katsuhiro, who is a pilot, ventures to guess that any aircraft attempting to penetrate the wall would be badly battered, if not completely ruined.

Complaining of the heat, Katsuhiro insists on being permitted to continue his stroll indoors. The guards, relieved that he has not yet made any effort to escape, agree with alacrity. They are completing their tour of the ground floor of the main building when the first runner returns. He reports that both Regis and the Balogun are absent but that the next in command has agreed to let Katsuhiro continue his walk as long as he makes no effort to escape.

They have walked through the second and third floors when the other runner returns. In language lewd and bawdy, he explains that finding Taiwo had taken some time as the young businessman had been taking advantage of Regis's absence to avail himself of Teresa's body.

Another walking dead man, Katsuhiro thinks. *Or perhaps Teresa has shown him mercy as well.*

Somehow, remembering the fury he had glimpsed in the beautiful woman's eyes, he doesn't think she will have done so.

By now he has seen as much as he can easily commit to immediate memory. Several areas provide promising places to hold his sword, including an armory, a vault, and Regis's own quarters. His guards, of course, believe him ignorant of the area's significance, hurrying him away with the curt explanation "Restricted area." They don't know he understands Yoruban, however, and their conversations with each other told him all he needed to know.

Katsuhiro is willing to bet his life that Kusanagi is in one of these three places. Indeed, when the time comes to retrieve the sword, betting his life is precisely what he will be doing. Raising the odds for success seems prudent so he snaps at his escort:

"I desire companionship. Have you located anyone—Taiwo or one of Regis's other business associates, perhaps? I would even settle for speaking with that woman Regis sent to me."

The tone of command works the trick, that and the fact that his guards have decided that he is not interested in escape. They confer and decide that they had better not give the Japanese access to Teresa, as she is Regis's own property, but that Taiwo can do no harm.

Katsuhiro is somewhat disappointed, but hides it well. Striding along, he draws maps in his head, maps that he will pass on to the Spider when the other calls on him tonight.

¤◘¤

"I must admit, I see no way around it, but I dislike doing it. I am already in his debt. I have no desire to be in anyone's debt, but in his, perhaps, least of all. It is impossible to know what he will want in return."

Arthur sighs. He had called Chris into his office as soon as the human had arrived, even before the other had reached his office, needing desperately to talk out this problem before the day grows any older.

Now the King toys with the pot of hot tea set on his desk, adds a minuscule amount more to his cup, sighs again, rubs his beard, and continues:

"But I see no way around it. I must ask the Changer for a favor. I cannot risk that our people are waiting for me to send them aid."

Chris Kristofer, seated in what has become "his" chair in Arthur's office, nods. He has spent the last day or so garnering every scrap of information he could about the windstorm surrounding Monamona, Nigeria. He now knows the force of the storm winds, their patterns of dispersement, and their basic characteristics. That all the meteorologists who have offered their opinions—officially or otherwise—have admitted to being stumped has been no great comfort.

"An airplane," Chris says, "even if we had one flown in illegally from Benin, the border country closest to Monamona, could not penetrate the wind. Nigeria is not permitting tourists, and most other requests for entry are being closely scrutinized. As you have said, you need someone who can enter the country illegally and unnoticed."

"And," Arthur sighs, "someone who can blend into the population once inside."

"And," Chris prompts helpfully, "work completely outside the human population if necessary. That severely narrows your options. Are there other shapeshifters who might suit the bill?"

"There are others," Arthur admits, "but none who I could be certain would do the job as well. The Changer is unique among us in the range and variety of his forms. He is very . . . old."

Chris wonders at the awe in Arthur's voice when he says that single word. Old. What is "old" to a person who once ruled in ancient Egypt, whose deeds are recorded in the oldest written epic known to humanity?

Intellectually, Chris knows that the Changer has been around a lot longer than Arthur, but his frame of reference gets shaky when asked to accept a man who was old when dinosaurs walked the Earth. Maybe Arthur's frame of reference gets shaky, too.

"Call Duppy Jonah's palace," Arthur says, "and see if you can get the Changer to the phone. I'm going to call Lovern and tell him what I intend."

Chris places the call and when he signals that the Changer is waiting Arthur switches lines. Demonstrating a trust that Chris had not expected, the King motions for him to remain and switches the call onto intercom.

"Changer," Arthur says, his measured tones showing nothing of his anxiety, "this is Arthur Pendragon."

"Arthur," acknowledges the Changer's deep, gravelly voice.

He offers nothing more, and after a polite pause the King continues:

"I am calling to beg a favor of you."

"Blunt. Ask."

Chris thinks it rather courteous of the Changer to substitute "ask" for Arthur's "beg."

"Something has arisen in Nigeria . . ." Concisely but completely, Arthur reports the situation. "I am concerned about those of our people who are there: Anson, Eddie, Dakar, Katsuhiro, and, if last reports remain correct, Shango. Would you locate them, tender them aid if needed, and help them to depart if required?"

The Changer doesn't pause. "What are you offering?"

"Favors."

Chris can see the effort Arthur is making not to sigh. He understands why. What the King is offering is, within the athanor economy, the equivalent of a blank check with at least six zeros drawn in and room for more.

"If you ask a favor of me," the King continues, "I will grant it as quickly as possible. I can intercede for you with another member of the Accord. In such cases, I cannot promise alacrity, but I can endeavor to achieve it."

"Fair," the Changer replies, "but you have always been fair with me, Arthur."

"Then you will go?"

"On one condition."

"Ask."

"If I die while undertaking this job for you or as a direct result of it, you will transfer whatever credit I have earned with you to my daughter, Shahrazad."

"Done." Arthur nods crisply, though of course the Changer cannot see him. "Would you have me send a copy of a contract? I believe Vera has effected some computer access in your brother's palace."

"No. Your word is enough for me. Besides, I want to get going as soon as possible. Tell Frank MacDonald that I will be out of touch for some days. Shahrazad is with him."

"I shall. Thank you."

"Anson is my friend. I respect the others in varying degrees. Besides, I have not seen anything like this windstorm you describe for a long, long time."

"You've seen!" Arthur begins excitedly, but the Changer has hung up the phone.

"Do you want me to try and get him again?" Chris asks, his finger on the redial button.

Arthur looks thoughtful. "Yes, but the Changer would have told me what he suspects if he wanted to. There is no bullying him. He's tossed me that crumb, whether as comfort or clue I don't know. If Lovern wasn't so blessed busy, I'd have him look into it, but I suppose it's academic.

"Speaking of Lovern's problems," the King continues, dismissing the Changer's cryptic statement with visible effort, "have you or Bill had any luck tracking down possible candidates for the Academy?"

Chris shakes his head. "Bill keeps coming up blank on

Alice Chun. My time has completely focused on the windstorm. Now that that's settled . . ."

"As best as it can be for now," Arthur interrupts.

"Yes, sir. Now that that's taken care of, I can help either you or Bill with your recruitment efforts."

"Help Bill first. I'll send you a part of my list."

"Yes, sir." Chris rises, knowing from Arthur's tone that he is dismissed.

"And Chris?"

"Sir?"

"Don't mention my conversation with the Changer to anyone, please. Tell Bill, but no one else. If anyone calls asking about the windstorm, direct them to me."

"Sire?"

Arthur acknowledges the question in Chris's tone and posture, though the human does not articulate it further.

"The Changer may have been hinting that the storm is being caused by one of our own. If he was giving me a warning, I do not wish to ignore it."

"Thank you, sir. I understand."

"And Chris?"

"Yes, sir?"

" 'Arthur' is fine. You're doing a very good job."

"Thank you . . . Arthur."

¤◙¤

When the Changer tells Duppy Jonah that he is leaving and why, the Sea King nods and wishes him well, but he cannot resist a parting cut.

"Are you certain you have not become Arthur's lackey?"

"Positive," the Changer says. "I have my reasons for going. Had I learned of this independently and all things were equal, I still would have gone. To have Arthur owe me favors for assuaging my curiosity pleases me."

Duppy Jonah laughs. "A safe journey to you then, brother."

Amphitrite embraces him, her expression serious. "And do be careful. We have enjoyed your company. Shall I say farewell to Vera for you?"

"I'll do it myself," the Changer says, his tone a bit brusque. "My route carries me that way."

He doesn't know if they believe him, but at least they are wise enough not to tease him. With great strokes of his triton tail, he arrives at the site of Atlantis. Vera is in counsel with a rather extraordinary electric eel but excuses herself when the Changer asks for a moment of her time.

"I'm going to Africa," he says, "at once. Arthur's business."

"Africa!" She makes the connection immediately. "Has something happened to Eddie?"

"I don't know. Neither does Arthur. That's why I'm going."

Vera, part of Arthur's privy council, doesn't ask for details. Either the King will give them to her or not.

"I wanted to say good-bye," the Changer says, "since I don't know when I'll be back this way, and I have enjoyed our visits."

"Thank you." Vera's cheeks color slightly. "I have, too."

"Good."

The Changer starts to move away, preparatory to shifting into something that can cover the distance to the west coast of Africa as quickly as possible. He pauses and returns.

"And you should know something."

"Yes?"

"You are beautiful."

Vera, who has been called wise, saintly, valiant, and brave, but rarely beautiful, stares at the ancient athanor. He isn't mocking her.

"Beautiful? Me?" She gestures at her mermaid form. "This is just Lovern's art."

"Do you think I look at shape, Vera?" The Changer laughs softly. "Me? You have not always been beautiful, but you have become so. You should know this, because I may be the first to notice, but I will not be the last. Take care."

He is gone then, a surge of his tail, a blur of motion, and then a lean, aquadynamic shape perfectly made for tirelessly covering distance beneath the water. Never mind that the creature it belonged to has been extinct these ten thousand years or more. No one but a few fish will note the anomaly, and they cannot tell anyone who will be troubled.

Vera hardly notices the Changer's new shape, though once she would have shaken her head with disapproval at anyone taking such risks. Now her mind is on other things, other types of changes.

"Take care," she calls after the departing form. Then, ever practical, she returns to her conference with the eel.

¤▣¤

Bill Irish is waiting in the office he shares with Chris Kristofer when the other returns. Bill's expression is somber and, despite its warm brown color, his face is definitely pale. Without a word, he hands a printout to Chris. The compact paragraphs spell out a problem both of them had dreaded, but had never really believed would happen.

Chris falls back into his chair, his eyes never leaving Demetrios's report. When he finishes, he looks at Bill.

"I just got off the phone with Demi," Bill says. "The satyrs have not returned. Demi's exhausted and frantic, but is steeling himself to go tell Lil and Tommy what has happened. He asked that we tell Arthur."

"Right." Chris stares at the paper. "Can they handle the problem on their own? Isn't Lil supposed to be some sort of witch?"

"She is," Bill agrees, "but I think Demi's more afraid of her reaction than he is of Arthur's. Besides, this is a serious matter for the Accord. Demi's too honest to want it swept under the rug. Even if it's resolved without a crisis, Arthur should know what has happened."

"Right." Chris thinks of the King, whom he had left in relative peace. "I'd better get onto this right away."

He squares his shoulders and heads back to Arthur's office. He hopes that the Changer is swimming as fast as he can. Now, more than ever, he wishes that Eddie were here. He suspects that Arthur is going to wish it even more.

He's mad that trusts in the tameness of a wolf, a horse's health, a boy's love, or a whore's oath.

—WILLIAM SHAKESPEARE

THIS TIME THE MEETING IS HELD NOT IN AN EMPTY HOUSE but in a deserted office building. Eddie and Anson have just given Shango a much-edited version of what they have learned. Since Shango might hear of Oya himself, they reluctantly have told him something about her, lest he learn of her or of their relocation and wonder.

"I can hardly believe," Shango says, shaking his head so vigorously that the heavy gold hoops in his earlobes swing, "that one person could have raised this wind and maintained it for five days. Do you believe her?"

Anson shrugs. "We have no reason not to do so, but I admit, I don't know her. None of us do, eh? That's why we have moved our dwelling so we can keep a better eye on her."

Eddie feels only slightly unhappy about misleading an ally. Shango's report had been less than satisfactory, especially to someone who has spent millennia giving and taking reports. There were lacunae, bits of vagueness, and other times when Eddie had been certain that Shango was lying.

Maybe those lies were meant only to protect an informant

or human ally, but they make him uncomfortable and less inclined to trust the other.

¤◘¤

Eddie is not the only one with concerns. After he leaves the meeting, Shango goes to his office and summons his three key henchmen to him. One of these is Paul Aafin, the mayor of Monamona. One is Otun Maluu, the chief of police. The third is Regis.

"We must move soon and quickly," Shango tells them, "if we are to see our plan come to anything."

After the other three have acknowledged his statement, Shango continues, modifying the truth to fit their knowledge of the situation.

"This windstorm must be bringing Monamona to the government's attention more quickly than we had hoped. When the wind falls, we must be in full control of the city."

"We are," answers Police Chief Maluu. "The wind has been a great help in that. Most of the citizens now rely on us for food and fresh water. Communication has been limited to word of mouth. We have suspended internal postal delivery for the duration of the crisis."

"Good." Shango nods approvingly. "This is important, but more importantly we must be prepared to move on the national government as soon as the wind falls."

"My contact with our allies has been limited," Mayor Aafin protests. "I cannot reestablish it until the wind falls."

Shango deliberately says nothing reassuring—although truly Paul Aafin is not at fault. To him the Mayor has always seemed the weakest member of their group, the one with the most to lose and so the most inclined to vacillate.

Paul Aafin's political connections are vital, however, so Shango has worked with him. If all goes according to schedule, Mayor Aafin will last long enough to become President Aafin and to name Shango his vice president. Then he will become ill and Shango will be president, first in fact and later in name as well.

The succession will be completely legal and will be the means by which Nigeria publicizes its newest tragedy to the world—the epidemic of smallpox, an epidemic that should bring in foreign funding, sympathy for the new government, and a reluctance to interfere with local politics.

Shango rubs his hands together gently as he studies Regis. Technically, the Chief General is no longer as vital as he once was. The smallpox virus is prepared, as is a good supply of vaccine. The knowledge on how to make more is available.

But Regis is like a pawn that, having plodded its way across the chessboard is suddenly transformed into a second queen. Although Shango has made his own arrangements for dealing with Regis, he cannot ignore how the men have come to identify Regis with Shopona, an identification that gives Regis an intangible power more difficult to deal with.

Even those gone to's, as local dialect names those who have been educated abroad, who know intellectually that smallpox is only a virus—albeit a deadly one—fear the curse of the King of Hot Water. Regis can threaten the curse without the need to follow up with the illness, and with his laboratory skills he can cultivate other viruses to serve Shango's needs.

No. Peculiar though he is, Regis is still useful.

The mayor's protests penetrate Shango's musings.

"... but I cannot contact any of them, even those I am certain will support us. Who knows what has gone on in almost a week? If only we knew when this wind will fall!"

Shango smiles urbanely, thinking of the woman Oya who claims to have raised the wind. When he had told his allies about her, one and all had dismissed her as a local crank—although Chief Maluu had looked rather nervous. Shango, who knows that magic does work and that lightning and wind can be summoned by one who knows the art, had encouraged them to mock the woman. Better that they not worry about a goddess in their city.

Now, however, in response to Mayor Aafin's unhappiness, he thinks of Oya and his urbane smile broadens into something fierce and warlike.

"The wind will fall," Shango says to the mayor. "When it does, speak with your contacts and report to us. We must be ready to adapt our plans, then to act almost at once."

Mayor Aafin continues to protest. "How do you know the wind will fall?"

"I know," says Shango, for once letting the other see the commanding force of his personality, a brilliance he normally veils lest they realize the level of his ambition. "Be ready."

The mayor nods stiffly, remembering that if he is to be president, he must act like a president.

"I will expect you to deliver," Aafin says sternly.

"I shall," Shango purrs, mock-humble. "I shall."

When his fellow conspirators have departed, Shango rubs his hands together.

Tonight, he thinks, *I shall extract this Oya from her stronghold, and when I have her, the wind will fall and she will either join me or fall with it.*

¤◘¤

Creeping through the barbed-wire fence to do some more scouting on MacDonald's land is the work of a moment for Wayne Watkins. He'd come up here right after finishing their business lunch, and he'd come back today as soon as he could, drawn there by the image of the wolves he would hunt, the kill he would make.

The land he's running his cattle on is to the east of the OTQ. He figures that if he's going to find wolves, they've got to be farther west, on the far side of where the two pieces border. That's only good sense speaking, since if the wolves were denning closer, there would be more evidence of them bothering his herds.

So Wayne has worked his way west, staying in the cover of the rocks and trees whenever possible, though Wayne figures that if MacDonald sees him, he'll say that one of his dogs had strayed and he's looking for it. How's MacDonald to know the difference?

The November air is cool, crisp, just enough to make every blood cell in his veins feel alive, as if they've nipped a bit of extra oxygen and are feeding it directly to his brain. Moving with a stealthy grace of which he is extraordinarily proud, Wayne glides like a ghost across the land. Not even the blue jays or the crows comment on his passing.

A rabbit grazing on a patch of browning grass seems not to see him at all. Wayne is tempted to creep up to it, to wring its neck with his bare hands like some Indian in an old Western, but he opts to be prudent. He's after bigger game than rabbits.

As the rancher turned hunter glides over the land, his eyes alert for any sign of his prey, he reviews possible ways to get MacDonald away from the OTQ. He has to be gone. Otherwise, there is too great a risk that he will interfere.

Wayne pauses, sniffing the air, realizing that he's never seen a ranch hand about the OTQ. There must be some, since there's no way that MacDonald could maintain the place single-handedly, but maybe they're on vacation or only come in a couple times a week. He makes a mental note to check that there's no one else on the OTQ when he opens hunting season.

Coming up on a dense copse of trees, Wayne inspects the duff for wolf sign. No tracks, no convenient tufts of fur hanging on low-lying tree limbs. Searching with that preternatural alertness that has been with him ever since he crossed onto the OTQ today, Wayne finds the partially eaten carcass of an elk.

Leaves and branches have been dragged over it. Wayne isn't such a tyro as to touch them with his hands. Using the toe of his boot, he lifts enough to get a good look at the tooth marks.

Triumph surges in him. Here are his wolves. He's certain. He doesn't bother to ask himself why there are no foot marks, why the carcass is so well concealed. Joy that he knows where to find his prey fills him.

Next step: Get MacDonald clear of the place.

Smiling, Wayne trots east, eager to get back to his own land, his mind busy making and discarding plans to deal with the human element of his problem. In the end, the plan he comes up with is so simple, so elegant, that Wayne can hardly believe his own cleverness.

After meeting Jesus, MacDonald had agreed to sell Wayne three of his quarter horses and two other horses that, while good enough cow horses in themselves, lacked the pedigree of the other three. That provided both mounts and remounts, since much of the work would still be done in the pickup trucks.

One of those horses would be the bait. On the day Wayne chose to go hunting, Jesus would phone MacDonald from the farthest of Wayne's holdings in the area. He'd tell MacDonald that one of the horses was acting strange, like it was sick. Then Jesus would beg MacDonald to come and look at the horse.

MacDonald would go, of that Wayne had no doubt. The trip to the holding would take an hour, probably more. Then he'd have to look at the horse. Jesus would have orders to keep MacDonald for as long as possible.

Meanwhile, Wayne would be hunting wolf with no one to interfere with his fun. With what he'd learned on his scouting trips, he should be in, out, and gone before MacDonald returned.

The one weakness in the plan was that the horse, of course, wouldn't be ill. Wayne toys with the idea of giving the horse something to make it sick, then decides against it. Even the two nonpurebreds hadn't been cheap. He doesn't care to risk wasting his money.

Besides, so what if the horse wasn't sick when MacDonald arrived? Jesus wouldn't dare say anything, neither would the other greasers. They had their legal situation to consider. That just left the horse and, hell, the horse wouldn't be talking!

¤◘¤

"This first day's search has been a bust, baby," says Tommy Thunderburst in his calm, laconic way.

Though Demetrios would have been more tactful, especially with Lil Prima scowling as she stares into a bowl of water, the faun essentially agrees. Morning had turned into afternoon and afternoon is fading into early evening. A hotel suite has been transformed into command central, and the athanor members of the *Pan* tour have been working overtime, but the satyrs remain missing.

Demetrios would never have believed this would be the

case when, after hearing his nervous report at nine that morning, Lil Prima had made a queenly gesture and ordered her scrying bowl brought to her.

Scrying might seem like a foolproof way to locate someone. All the scryer needs is a bowl of water or some other reflective surface. Mirrors work; so do crystal balls. Depending on the talent of the person doing the scrying, additives can help. Lil puts oil into her scrying bowl. Since she is trying to locate someone specific, she has also put in a fine powder made by grinding some of the missing satyrs' hair (there had been ample in their currycombs) in a mortar and pestle.

But scrying just shows a picture of the person or people being sought. In this case, what Lil sees is a nice hotel or motel suite equipped with two queen-size beds and a bathroom with a Jacuzzi tub. That is it.

The window curtain has been drawn, so they can't guess where the hotel is from the landmarks outside. No hotel stationery is visible on the bedside tables, at least not under the litter of wine bottles, pizza boxes, and discarded clothing.

The telephone shows only an extension number on its base, no phone number. If the hotel provides guidebooks to the hotel or the surrounding area, these are also buried in the considerable litter created by three rutting satyrs and their molls.

Conversation between the three satyrs and their six girlfriends has been limited to three categories: sex, drugs, and food. Where the first is coming from there is no doubt. None of the girls looks at all interested in leaving. Some of the combinations the three satyrs come up with would fascinate the makers of blue movies, but none of the participants protest.

A supply of drugs, mostly marijuana and cocaine, had apparently been laid in before someone Georgios referred to as "the driver" had been dismissed. Food is delivered by room-service waiters who leave the cart outside of the door. Given the size of the orders, doubtless their tip is added automatically to the bill. Booze (mostly wine, though Stud shows a lamentable taste for cheap beer) is acquired this way as well.

Quite possibly, one of the nine inhabitants of that suite has said something that would have pinpointed their location at some time or another, but even Lilith cannot maintain a constant scrying. The best she can do is to check in periodically and hope for a change in location or some newly revealed clue. Thus far, there has been nothing.

Following Demetrios's initial report, rehearsal had been canceled for the day. The three remaining satyrs refuse—even under threat of being fired—to help in the search for their buddies. Doubtless Lil would have had no qualms about resorting to torture if she thought it would help, but, like Demetrios, she believes them when they insist they know nothing beyond the most general elements of Georgios's plan—getting laid and getting laid again.

Therefore, the three remaining satyrs are locked in their suite with a rotating shift of fauns guarding them—and some of Lil's magic added in just in case one of the fauns feels a pang of sympathy for his fellow theriomorphs.

With Phoebus's help, Demetrios has spent hours on the phone, trying to learn anything that would limit their search. He has just finished calling all the taxi and limousine services, asking if anyone had picked up a fare at their hotel who answered the description of Georgios and his pals. Thus far, he's learned nothing. The suspicion that many of the transportation companies would routinely lie rather than risk annoying a former customer keeps him from believing that negative information is information at all.

"Doubtless," he sighs, hanging up the phone and rubbing his pointed ear, "the satyrs are using a credit card to pay for their debauchery, but the credit-card company is not going to tell us where those charges are being made."

"No. We'd need to be the police or FBI to get that kind of cooperation," Phoebus agrees.

"And we're not," Demetrios says. "Nor is any athanor listed in the Accord's files."

Tommy Thunderburst, comparatively sober and very, very mellow, shambles over and drapes his long-limbed frame over one of the desk chairs.

"What athanor'd be a Fibbie?" he asks. "Man, they print you, blood type you, piss test you, and check your background from here back to conception. You'd need to be a wizard to pass all of that and what for? Any athanor with that much power can get what they want without being a cop."

"True." Demetrios sighs. "But it sure would be useful now."

"What we need," Phoebus says, "is a diviner. A really good one who could use Lil's image as a start and then divine where the satyrs have gone."

"Good idea!" Demetrios says. "Tommy, can Lil divine?"

"Lil," Tommy says with is broad grin, "is divine. But it's beyond me if she can divine."

He leans back, laughing at his own joke, then calls to where the elegant witch is once again leaning over her scrying bowl.

"Hey, baby. Furry-legs here has a good idea. Can you divine?"

Lil is seated in a corner of the room, bent over a bowl set on one of the hotel's writing tables. With her golden hair falling like a straight, solid curtain between her face and the rest of the company gathered in the room, Lil seems so isolated that it is something of a shock when she lifts her head and turns to Tommy.

"Divine, *mon chèr*?" She frowns, a cupid bow pout that clears. "I had considered that, *certainement*, but there are too many people in this city for me to isolate three. There are too many hotels, even."

"Oh," Phoebus slumps, and Demetrios reaches and pats his arm. "Darn."

"But divining may be our best course," Lil says, showing uncharacteristic kindness. "Demetrios, we must limit our search."

"Yes'm."

"Call hotels. Ask if they have rooms with jacuzzi tubs. Then ask if they have rooms with two queen-size-beds."

Demetrios smiles. "Done, my lady, done."

"*Bon*." She sighs. "I am tired, but this cannot wait. I shall go and refresh myself, then I shall have one of the roadies drive me from hotel to hotel, seeking our lost stallions. Demetrios, can you prioritize that list a bit?"

"I'll do my best," he answers, nervous about the responsibility.

"And Tommy"—Lil turns those emerald eyes on her sometime lover, sometime charge—"you shall call Lovern. Tell him we are so angry that he has not sent to us the promised amulets. Tell him to come here at once."

"Baby!" Tommy protests. "It's late afternoon—hell, it's evening! Lovern lives in the boonies now. He might not be able to get a plane until morning, and you gotta have found them by then!"

Lil Prima shakes her head. "I do not 'gotta.' I am tired. I have been doing this scrying all day. Now I divine all night? I do not think so. Get Lovern here. There are many flights between Albuquerque and Las Vegas. He may even be able to get one this evening."

"I'll try," Tommy says, "but I don't promise."

"Get him," Lil repeats fiercely, and strides from the room.

Tommy looks after her, his expression rueful. "I guess I'd better get him. I know that look. It means 'or else.' Sure hope Lovern doesn't have any plans for the evening."

¤▣¤

Shahrazad is puzzled. All morning she has kept coming across human scent, as faint and wispy as if it is very old, but her memory tells her that it was not here when she hunted in this area in the hills above the ranch house a day or so before.

Sitting on her haunches, the young coyote vigorously scratches her right ear and tries to think. It isn't easy. Even with cold weather prompting many of the rodents that are her usual prey into hibernation (or at least torpid retreat), the air is alive with interesting scents. She wants to track them, to dash around, to feel the winter thickening of her coat push back the cold, but she can't stop worrying about those scents that shouldn't be there. It's rather frustrating.

Far down below, she can see Frank's tiny figure coming out of the ranch house. He's shrugging into the quilted jacket he wears when he plans to be outside for a long stretch and is carrying a large pack slung from one hand. A couple of the dogs bounce at his heels, getting more excited as Frank turns toward the garage. In another minute, one of the pickup trucks pulls out of the garage, two dogs in the bed, another in the cab.

When the truck has vanished down the driveway, Shahrazad no longer has the excuse of watching it as a distraction. Hip and Hop balance on their back legs, browsing idly on the dried leaves still clinging to a sapling. They have confirmed that Shahrazad's scenting is not just her imagination, but that is where their interest ends.

For the first time, Shahrazad realizes that her mind works differently than theirs. It is not just the difference between jackalope and coyote, nor even that of older and younger. Just yet she cannot place what the difference is, but it both scares her and fills her with elation.

Dangerously close to revelation, the coyote distracts herself by taking another sniff at the old scent trail. Concentrating, she sorts it out from all the surrounding scents, including a strange impulse to believe that it is not there. She struggles against this last, frustrated by the conflict between her nose and her mind, until something in her mind snaps. The scent trail is no longer occluded.

A human passed here the day before. A male. A male known to her. Wayne, the human who smelled of cows and who had prowled around the ranch house. She lowers her head and begins coursing the trail.

Wayne had passed here, walking with confidence yet keeping behind rocks and big trees whenever he could. For a time he had stopped and studied the ranch house, then moved on. Shahrazad picks up her pace, wondering that she should have had any trouble finding this trail, wondering, too, why the corvids who normally would warn Frank of any intruder on his land had not spoken. Could it be that Wayne's trail had been hidden from them as well?

That thought so shocks her that she halts, flopping down to consider how this could be so. Like most wild things, she depends on the corvids. Nosy scavengers that they are, their caws and jeers provide the audible newspaper of the animal world.

Even now Shahrazad hears a couple of jays harassing a

bobcat as it slinks through the undergrowth with a rabbit hanging loose in its jaws. More distantly, a small flock of crows are commenting on the remnants of a dead deer. When she had hunted at dawn, she had saved a portion of her kill for a couple of juvenile ravens who, though not athanor, had reminded her of her father. Probably they are in the general vicinity, wondering if she is going to do any more hunting this morning.

With a sudden sense of urgency, Shahrazad follows Wayne's day-old trail again. He had shown some skill, for a human, but there are times she can lope along swiftly, tracking by eye rather than by nose, dipping her muzzle now and then to confirm that she is still on his freshest trail.

When she comes to the fringes of the territory claimed by the wolves she halts, her back paws actually digging small furrows in the soil. The signpost urine is strong and rank. It reminds her of her lesson several days ago, reminds her that wolves are far bigger than coyotes and that the pack does not suffer trespassers lightly.

Even though she has become acquainted with those werewolves who help Frank with various chores, this does not mitigate Shahrazad's fear. Wayne's track goes on, but here is a line that she will not cross. She backs away to the nearest cover, hearing relieved chirps and whistles from Hip and Hop.

Trotting downhill and back toward the ranch house, she considers what she has learned. If Frank were here, she would try to explain things to him. His comprehension of coyote concerns is almost canine. Since he is human as well, he might be able to explain to her what Wayne was doing—or he might tell her that Wayne had permission to come onto OTQ land.

The last thought gives her some relief. Frank had entertained Wayne, had even given him food. Perhaps like the Wanderer or the Changer, Wayne is become a friend and as a friend he can cross into Frank's territory. She is still thinking about this when she hears the corvids call out to the western fringe of the ranch, a call that means intruder.

Abruptly heading that way, Shahrazad sees a flash of raven-dark feathers. Quorking hoarsely one of her young ravens lands on a branch of a nearby evergreen, putting himself between her and the west.

Shahrazad may not speak to animals as Frank does, nor is there any romantic *ur*-language that enables animals to speak with each other, but she is coyote enough to know that the bird is warning her. She appreciates this, takes it as tribute for the numerous kills she has shared.

West, though, is the direction in which she heads.

A coyote's lope covers distance far more rapidly than one might assume from such a small canine. It must. In sparsely populated areas, a coyote's hunting territory may be twenty-five or thirty square miles.

"Her" juvenile ravens fly with her, darting ahead to check the lay of the land, coursing back to keep her company. The two jackalopes follow more reluctantly. They have not stayed alive as long as they have by tempting human observation. For the first time since Frank assigned them to chaperon Shahrazad they show real reluctance to follow where she leads. Even when she had tempted the wolf pack they had not been this edgy.

But Shahrazad is too interested in learning who has crossed into Frank's land to back off now. She has her suspicions, but oddly enough the errant darting of the wind does nothing to confirm them. If Wayne once again prowls the OTQ, he has found a way to conceal—not merely to mask—his scent.

Now the cries of the corvids are growing more erratic, more confused, as if the crows, ravens, and jays are losing sight of the invader. One by one, the voices drop into silence until only the determined quorking of one athanor raven, a son of the Raven of Enderby who inherited his father's long life without his father's tendency toward magic, sounds the alarm.

There is a single barking shot, as from a hunting rifle, and the Son's voice also grows still. There is an indignant clamor of corvid call, then silence.

Shahrazad knows where she is going now. More importantly, for it antidotes to the force that is attempting to cloud her senses, she has her suspicions. This morning she had laboriously tracked Wayne's old trail as he headed toward the wolf wood. Now she makes the assumption—a great deductive leap—that Wayne is going that way once more.

She stops searching the wind for sign, stops listening for birdcalls. Instead she moves stealthily, that rifle shot warning her to keep to cover, heading to intercept Wayne's trail.

About a half mile shy of the wolf wood, she finds him. Dressed in the mottled clothing she has been taught to associate with hunters, a cap pulled snugly down almost to his brows, Wayne strides along a deer trail. From her hiding place beneath a low growing evergreen, her belly fur pressed into the duff, Shahrazad studies him.

The cow man knows how to handle himself in the forest. The coyote recognizes the difference between how he moves and how she has seen other humans move. Yet he is making no great effort to hide himself, opting instead for a balance between speed and efficiency. A rifle is slung at his back. He carries another loosely in one hand. The Changer has taught her to recognize an armed human, so Shahrazad also sees that Wayne carries knives and a small handgun on his belt.

All these weapons make her edgy, but what truly frightens her is that to other eyes, Wayne seems to be invisible. A small bird bouncing on a branch lets him pass so close that he could have stroked her feathers. A fox sniffing about for rabbits doesn't even look up when Wayne tromps by. Even a deer mouse, normally among the edgiest of the woodland animals, lets him pass without fleeing.

Creeping after the human, Shahrazad checks to see if Hip and Hop are aware of him. She is reassured to find that they do see him. Soon after she realizes that if the jackalopes lose direct sight of the man, they tend to dismiss the threat he offers. It is less that he is invisible then that he radiates an aura signaling that he is unimportant and unthreatening.

Sincerely afraid now, Shahrazad considers whether it might be best if she, too, tried to forget that Wayne is a threat. The concept is so tempting that she can feel it sliding clouds around her thoughts even as she considers it.

After all, Wayne's evident prey is the wolves. Wolves do not like coyotes. Coyotes do not like wolves. These wolves in particular have threatened her. It would be easy to let

Wayne hunt them. A wolf or two less would make the OTQ a friendlier place for coyotes. True, Frank likes the wolves, but that is his shortcoming. He can do with a wolf or two less.

The idea has almost gotten its teeth into her when Shahrazad notices a flicker of white in the forest north of Wayne. She focuses on it and realizes that she is not the only one who is tracking the human. One of the unicorns, the white mare Pearl, is stalking him as well.

Shahrazad has never gotten over her feeling that it is unfair that an herbivore be as well armed as a unicorn. Now, beneath her automatic flash of resentment, there is relief. Someone else knows that Wayne is there. The responsibility for dealing with him is not hers alone.

Pearl, Shahrazad sees, is by herself. She wonders where Sun, the golden unicorn is, as the two seem to graze together. A distant jay's call, deeper in the mountains, gives her an answer. Doubtless Sun has led the rest of the unicorns into the hidden valley that is their ultimate refuge. His size and strength, which would not help him track the invader, would make him an ideal defender if Wayne heads that way.

Shahrazad has never been to that valley, though she knows of its existence from things Frank has told her. It is on the other side of the wolves' territory. For the first time, Shahrazad realizes that the wolves defend the unicorns. The peculiarity of this concept vanishes almost as soon as she thinks about it.

Her mind is performing one of those uncomfortable stretches it has from time to time in her life. Almost painfully, Shahrazad recategorizes the creatures who live under Frank's aegis on the OTQ.

They are not divided, as she had thought, into carnivores and herbivores or even into hunters and prey. She thinks about the eagle-puma, the Eyes. She considers the jackalopes and the Cats of Egypt, the unicorns and the wolves. She remembers the gatherings at Arthur's Pendragon Estates and the different shapes, sizes, scents, and sounds of the creatures who had gathered there as equals. For the first time, she realizes that she is more like one of them than like any other coyote she has ever met.

A surge of fellow feeling, of kinship similar to what she feels for her father, connects her to these creatures. She remembers how she had felt on that dark night when she had danced a complicated design with the other guests at the estate, prancing a measure with a cat, another with a king, another with a great brown-furred creature that was neither human nor bear. Without words, without discussion, Shahrazad finally understands that she is athanor.

She wants to sit, to rub her head in the dirt like she might against a rotting bit of carrion, to luxuriate in this new concept, but she realizes with a start that she cannot. The wolves deserve her help, even those wolves who are not part of the Dance, for they are the kin of those who are her kin.

Glancing back at the nervous jackalopes, Shahrazad feels real fondness for them, a fondness that goes beyond the games they have shared, beyond an awareness of how patient they have been with her puppy foolishness. Opening her mouth, she pants a smile and a reassurance that she is not going to do anything impulsive. With a wrinkling of her muzzle, she directs their attention to where Pearl stalks Wayne.

Will the unicorn attack the human? Certainly the herbivore is capable of stopping him. Pearl might be small and slight for a unicorn, but if she ran forward and drove her horn deep into that unsuspecting human's back, the man would have no chance.

Shahrazad, although close to her full growth, would have more difficulty successfully attacking the man. He is too big to grasp in her jaws and shake as she does a rabbit or a mouse. Also, something in her shrinks away from killing when she is not personally threatened. There must be something else she can do.

Meanwhile, Wayne walks forward, crossing the invisible line into the wolves' territory. Shahrazad balks, then follows.

Il lupo cangia il pelo, ma non il vizio.
(*The wolf changes his fur but not his nature.*)

—Italian proverb

Almost certainly, Katsuhiro Oba would have waited to break the peace within Regis's stronghold until he had located his sword and had laid the tactical groundwork for his escape if he had not come upon four of the Chief General's guests passing Teresa from man to man like a party favor.

Regis's pretty secretary is naked to the waist. Rat-faced Mr. Ekute holds her arms pinned behind her back while his assistant reaches up under her skirt to peel off her panty hose. Judging from the items of clothing held like prizes by the other men in the room—a blouse, a bra, and a pair of high-heeled shoes—this game has been going on for a while.

Teresa is taking the abuse with a dangerous patience, a small, ugly smile on her lips. Katsuhiro knows why. When the game evolves into rape—as it most certainly will—she will have her revenge.

For a moment, Katsuhiro considers letting the game go on. He has seen worse—has taken part in worse—at various points in his life. He is not called the Swift Impetuous Male without cause. However, two things force him to act. One is a feeling of responsibility toward Teresa. He has vowed to rescue her from this place—though she knows nothing of this vow. Therefore, his honor is entangled with how she is treated in his presence.

The second is a rational awareness of the sexual habits of the African male. Even those who are technically Christian often have, in effect, multiple wives. Those wives may also have multiple partners, depending on tribal customs and the strictness of their husbands. AIDS has spread rapidly in this hospitable climate, and many victims are children who were never given a choice.

Still, in all personal honesty, the challenge to Katsuhiro's honor is what moves his hands, what raises a battle cry to his lips, what causes him to leap forward and into the crowded room.

His guards, dulled by the previous day's slow tour of the facility, fail to stop him. Once Katsuhiro is in the midst of the throng of honored guests, they dare not shoot. One guard runs to find Regis. The others cluster in the doorway, shouting at him to stop.

Katsuhiro is enjoying himself far too much to take heed. A flying kick of the sort he would never condone in any *dojo* he supervised knocks Supreme General Agutan onto his round, fat ass. He wheels smoothly, forearm raised to block an unskilled punch from young Taiwo Fadaka. Gently, then, for Katsuhiro rather likes the young scoundrel, he knocks the man unconscious.

The other three men drop back, blustering but not moving out from the relative security of their position. Teresa, half-sobbing, half-laughing, quite close to hysteria, has moved behind Katsuhiro. Only he can hear what she hisses between her clamped teeth.

"You shouldn't have stopped them. I could have killed them all! The filthy bastards!"

Katsuhiro wonders that the venom in her gaze alone is not enough to kill. However it will not, and he should not kill Regis's guests, no matter what he thinks of their behavior. The guards, having learned long ago that knowing too much is the fastest way out of a job, have turned their attention to the corridor, preventing escape but nothing more.

Striking a pose straight from a Bruce Lee film, Katsuhiro sets himself between the violated woman and her attackers.

"So," he says, studying them, narrow-eyed over hands raised to attack or defend, "is this how you treat our host's hospitality when he does not have you under his eye?"

The men who are conscious glance at each other. Now that their testosterone-fueled camaraderie has been interrupted they seem less like important men and more like schoolboys caught stealing candy.

"We were just messing around a bit," says Agutan. "The woman didn't seem to mind."

Katsuhiro snorts, raising his eyebrows slightly, deigning to respond to such a juvenile response.

"Fadaka started it," Ekute adds. "When we came in here for a meeting, he was feeling up the girl and kissing her. We protested, and he said that there was plenty of her to go around."

Katsuhiro sneers. "So instead of stopping an impetuous youth at his dishonorable game, you joined him. Now, one at a time, toss her back her clothing. If you move before I give the word, I will attack!"

They are so cowed, no one questions the apparent bravado of this statement, or perhaps some deep instinct tells them that it is not bravado at all. To Katsuhiro's vague disappointment, the would-be rapists politely return first the bra, then the blouse, and lastly the shoes.

Teresa is buttoning her blouse when Regis pushes in past his guards. The mulatto does not look at all pleased. Indeed, the urbane manner that had marked him at their first meeting has all but vanished. His eyes are wild, and the true cruelty of his nature is close to the surface. For a moment, Katsuhiro wonders if he will have to fight him here and now.

Regis glowers at the three men against the wall, at Taiwo, who is moaning softly on the floor, and lastly at the Japanese standing before the trembling, disheveled woman. Careful to keep his own expression neutral, Katsuhiro wonders if anyone other than himself realizes that Teresa's trembling is not from fear and shame, but from hatred and rage.

Determined to shelter her from her own impulses, Katsuhiro steps forward, bows shortly, and speaks in the clipped manner of a soldier giving a report. "These men were disgracing you with your secretary. I took the liberty of interfering before they could do more than frighten her."

After studying him for a long, tense moment, Regis returns Katsuhiro's bow.

"Men do strange things in times of crisis," he says, his tone that of a scholar discussing an abstract point. "Psychologists say that when a man is confronted with death, oddly his thoughts often turn to a woman. I could forgive these fools if I believed that they acted merely from fear because our city is besieged by a strange wind."

Regis does not invite the others to speak in their own defense but continues to look at Katsuhiro. "What are your thoughts on this matter, Oba-san?"

Katsuhiro recognizes a trap when it is laid for him. Agreement is dangerous, for if he excuses the men on the grounds that they were afraid, he is saying that abuse of Regis's rights is permissible. However, if he says that they were wrong and acted out of bounds, then he is implying that Regis's control of his household is less than absolute.

"It is true," Katsuhiro replies, "that frightened men often act like children or animals. However, even a child knows that his father has a strong whip hand. Therefore, frightened or not, these men were fools, for they forgot that your rights are paramount."

Regis nods, permits a tiny smile showing a line of white teeth, and then faces the three men. Taiwo still lies with his eyes closed tightly. Katsuhiro wonders if he is truly unconscious or shamming.

"Take them to the lower rooms," Regis says, "where they can think about my whip hand."

The guards comply, herding three and preparing to drag Taiwo. Regis raises a hand to stop this last.

"Put him in his rooms. He at least had permission to visit with Teresa and has given me no explanation for his actions."

Musing privately over this new evidence of Taiwo's privileged position, Katsuhiro waits. Regis's condemnation of the others does not automatically mean praise for himself.

"I understand that you have taken it upon yourself to leave your apartments," Regis says.

"I was bored," Katsuhiro counters, "and there was no reason to keep me prisoner. Certainly my manners are far better than those oafs'."

"True. Perhaps I did not mean to imprison you. Perhaps I meant to protect you from fools such as these."

Katsuhiro acknowledges this possibility with a short bow.

"I would prefer if you returned to your apartments and stayed there," Regis says. "I have much to consider. However, lest you grow bored, I will send Teresa to you after she has washed and changed her clothing. She may keep you company for as long as you wish."

"Thank you, Chief General Doctor," Katsuhiro replies. "That would be pleasant."

After a few more banal exchanges, they part, Regis leaving with slightly more haste than is becoming.

Something is about to happen, Katsuhiro thinks, *and he wants me where he can find me. Therefore, Teresa and I must leave here tonight.*

¤◘¤

During his taxi ride in from the airport, Lovern feels mocked even by the skyline. The cabby's route takes him within sight of the Excalibur Hotel and Casino. The tall white towers, capped in red and blue and gold, are spotlighted against the night sky, inspired by the memory of a dream that had ended in a dismal failure.

As if to remind him of his own role in that failure, the lowest of the red-capped towers houses a dramatic figure of Merlin robed in purple, dignified white beard spilling across his chest, a golden wand in his hand. He is the only member of all of Arthur's court to be so dramatically depicted, a guardian who was lured off guard, a wizard whose enchantments were not strong enough to stave off the end.

"That's right," Lovern mutters, not caring if the cabby thinks him crazy, "make me feel really good about myself."

Arriving at the hotel housing the *Pan* tour, Lovern finds no grand welcome, no stalwart knights to be directed into battle. When Lovern bangs on the indicated door the faun

Demetrios, looking as if he has spent the last few hours shredding his normally tidy goatee, opens it.

"Lil is resting," Demetrios explains, logging off his laptop computer. "Tommy is with her, playing music so that she will sleep. The other fauns are either asleep or on guard duty."

"So you are to brief me?" Lovern says, not terribly pleased. He holds nothing against the faun. Demetrios is a nice creature in his frivolous way, but Lovern's status as a member of Arthur's inner circle demands more. Belatedly, the wizard recalls that Demetrios had been named to Arthur's council soon after the events in September. He decides that puts a better face on it and tries to be gracious.

"Thank you for staying up."

"You're welcome." Demetrios crosses to a table where some maps are spread. "Have something to eat and drink while I fill you in."

Fatigued, Lovern agrees. At the end of the faun's report, Lovern puts his hand out for the list of possible hotels.

"Show me which hotels Lil has already checked," Lovern says, trying not to sound perfunctory. "The sooner we find those three satyrs, the sooner I can skin them alive."

"Surely," Demetrios replies, although he must have been entertaining similar thoughts, "that is a bit extreme."

Lovern grumbles, "I'm not sure about that. Do they have any idea how frantic Arthur is? He and his staff have been phoning everyone who might be vulnerable, warning them to get ready to flee, though where they'll go is anyone's business. We have only dreaded exposure on this scale—not planned for it."

"What about the underwater refuge?" Demetrios asks, earning a scornful snort from the wizard.

"Atlantis isn't ready to take refugees—it won't be for quite a while yet."

Demetrios nods. "I forgot. It seems like centuries since I left my peaceful orchards to join this rock and roll show, but it has only been about a week."

Lovern has no patience for the other's complaints. He continues griping as he scans the list and matches locations to a map spread on a table.

"If I'm here, I can't be there advising the King. Vera isn't answering her phone. Amphitrite says she went off for a long swim. Anson and Eddie have gone missing in Africa, and Jonathan Wong is teaching a law course at Harvard and won't quit so close to the end of the term unless the King declares a full-blown crisis."

"Hopefully," Demetrios says, his tone more forceful than Lovern had thought possible, "you or Lil will find the satyrs and there will be no crisis. Certainly standing here and complaining isn't getting us any closer to a solution."

Lovern opens his mouth to reply, snaps it shut, and then says with what he hopes is becoming humility:

"You are right, Demetrios. I'll keep you posted as I check each place. That way Lil won't duplicate my efforts when she wakes up."

Demetrios smiles and extends a hand. "Good luck."

Even with two talented sorcerers on the project, they don't find the satyrs until late afternoon. Part of the difficulty is the sheer number of places to look, part is that magic is dampened when the practitioner is in contact with iron or steel. Lil and Lovern can avoid direct contact, but they cannot avoid indirect.

Steel girders hold up the buildings around them. Metal mesh strengthens the concrete. Rebar provides the internal structure for apparently stone walls. Nothing is as it seems, and only the prevalence of plastic and plastic by-products save them from being completely overwhelmed by static.

As it is, Lovern can hardly believe that his reading is correct when, standing in the men's room of a hotel a few blocks off the Strip, the divining rod in his hand jerks and twitches, pointing deeper into the building.

Lovern tries the reading again, aware that he is very hungry, aware, too, that he has forgotten to eat since a midmorning snack. The divining rod jerks again, seeming impatient with his doubt.

Bypassing the desk, Lovern strolls toward the elevator. Around him, slot machines chime and jingle. He cannot influence them, so he takes it as a good omen that one pays off when the hem of his jacket brushes against it. The round-faced woman happily sweeping quarters into a plastic bucket smiles at him.

He nods to her. "Your lucky day. I hope it's mine, too!"

She beams at him. "Me too!"

Lovern's luck holds. He gets an elevator to himself and presses the UP button. Priming the divining rod, he gives it a gentle jog at each floor. Nothing. Frowning, he checks again as the elevator goes back down. Still nothing. On the ground floor, it jerks again, toward the heart of the casino.

Lovern follows the tug, working his way around roulette wheels and slot machines, glancing wistfully toward the quieter areas where card games are being played. He likes poker. Maybe once this is over, he'll stay overnight and play a few hands. It seems like ages since he's had a break.

The divining rod pulls the wizard entirely through the casino, out a back door, across an area where an outdoor swimming pool has been drained for the winter, and to another gate. This is locked, but Lovern bollixes the electronics with an impatient tap of his staff.

Once through the privacy gate, he finds himself amid a collection of semidetached bungalows arrayed in groups of four around a central traffic circle. Most seem empty, but outside of one several room-service carts await pickup. From the litter of wine bottles piled onto them, he knows that he has found the satyrs.

All Lovern's exhaustion threatens to catch up to him at that moment, but he pushes it aside. Unbidden, he thinks of Purrarr and the Cats of Egypt, of how they can lend a bit of strength when needed.

Maybe, he thinks, surprising himself, *I* do *need a familiar*.

For now, however, he must draw on his own depleted resources. Fortunately, the time for magic should be over. Locating a pay phone over by the swimming pool, he dials the number where Demetrios should still be waiting.

"I have them," he says as soon as the faun answers, "or I believe I do. I wanted to let you know before I actually braced them."

"That was wise," Demetrios says, and such is the joy in his voice that Lovern actually feels complimented rather than vaguely miffed that he could be expected to do any but the wisest thing.

There is a momentary pause while Demetrios tells whoever is in the room with him that the satyrs have been located. From the sudden burst of syrinx music and ebullient cheers, at least one or more of the fauns must be there.

"Where are you?" Demetrios asks. When Lovern has given him the address Demetrios continues, "Lil and Tommy left here just a few minutes ago, heading in that general direction. I can call their limousine and send them to you. Can you wait and watch until they arrive?"

"I can," Lovern says. "Let me give you directions for how to find this part of the resort."

When he has rung off, Lovern returns to where he can watch the satyrs' bungalow from the porch of an untenanted unit. After a moment, he scrounges a partial bottle of wine and an untouched half sandwich from the room-service cart.

Thus he is somewhat refreshed when the electronic gate at the far end of the bungalow complex slides open to admit a sleek silver limousine. Tommy Thunderburst is driving, his lips moving as he sings along with the radio. Lil, tense as a cat stalking a bird, sits beside him in the front seat. She gets out even before Tommy finishes parking the car. Lovern intercepts her.

"In there?" the witch says.

"Yes. I think that the other three bungalows in this quadrant are empty, but remember, we're not alone."

"I cannot care," she says. "I will eat their balls for them, the stupid horses' asses!"

Tommy, a guitar now slung by a strap around his neck, pads up and puts an arm around her.

"Lunch later, baby," he says. "You and Mr. Wizard do something to keep the neighbors"—the toss of his leonine mane of hair includes the high-rises around them—"from seeing what will trouble their mortal minds. I'll handle the party animals and their friends."

Lovern nods, not liking being called "Mr. Wizard" but resigned to Tommy's casual flippancy.

"Tommy has a good point," he says. "The Cats of Egypt

have taught me a new variation on the charm for unnoticeability."

"That I know already," Lil snaps. "I have been a cat, from time to time."

Her smile is as cruel as a cat's might be, and Lovern does not press the point. Assuming her agreement, he walks to the oval of ornamental grass and flowers at the center of the traffic circle. Lil's high heels clicking on the pavement tell him that she is following.

Joining hands, they sit together on the little bench provided. To a casual observer, they might seem honeymooners, enjoying the pleasant late-afternoon weather.

Tommy chuckles. "That's sweet. Give me the cue, and I'm gone to do what I can do."

"Count four measures," Lil says. "That is all I need."

Lovern nods. Her fingers in his hand feel as fragile as blown glass straws. She has been pushed even harder than he has been, for she has been searching for the satyrs for over twenty-four hours. Yes, she has slept and he has not, but he doubts that even with Tommy's magic she is very well rested.

Together they build the spell far more quickly than either of them could have alone. Yet, only the fact that both of them are tremendously talented and that both are draining power from reserves normally left untapped establishes the spell in the promised four measures. Lovern would have preferred to take longer, but he is not about to argue with Lilith, not here, at least, and not over this.

Tommy announces his arrival with a crescendo of Spanish-sounding guitar chords. He drums on the door with his boot toe.

"Hey, guys. Let me come in."

A strained voice, male, but otherwise most unlike the boisterous tones of Georgios the satyr, replies:

"And if we don't what'll you do? Huff and puff and blow the door down?"

Tommy waves his hand and vines sprout from the mouths of the wine bottles on the room-service carts. They grow rapidly, thick green cables unfolding leaves, and dragging bunches of grapes behind them.

"I don't think I need to do that," Tommy says mildly. "Do you know who I am?"

The door opens and a satyr tumbles out, flinging himself prostrate before the young man with the guitar.

"You are the Great God Dionysus," Georgios gasps. "And I am your slave."

"Not mine," Tommy laughs, turning the satyr over with the toe of his boot. He does so effortlessly, as if the bulky theriomorph is a child. "His, perhaps." The boot toe indicates the satyr's limp penis, "but not mine. A slave of mine would be better behaved. He would know that I give both joy and sorrow, both pleasure and pain."

The other two satyrs have joined in the groveling. The six whores, all in various states of undress, are huddled against a back wall of the room. Vine leaves invade here as well, and heavy bunches of grapes spill from the vine-covered ceiling.

"It's Tommy Thunderburst!" shrieks a black woman dressed in nothing but a single fishnet stocking. "I got his album."

"I hope you like it," Tommy says.

"I do," the woman says. "I gotta get the new one."

"I'll give you one," he promises, "but first you must do me a favor."

"Anything!" she says. "I won't even charge."

Tommy reaches up and plucks a bunch of grapes. He presses them between his fingers and the juice runs free.

"This is my blood, the mark of my covenant with you," he says, his voice a caress, "drink it and all will be well between us."

The black woman looks shocked for a moment, but doubtless dallying with satyrs has expanded her idea of what is and is not possible. Extending her tongue, she licks the juice from his long musician's fingers.

Tommy crushes other grapes, extends his hands to the other women. Already under his spell, they move forward, lick the juice where it drips from his fingers, down his wrists, where it spots his trousers.

Lovern, watching from where he sits with Lil, mutters softly, "That's the most erotic thing I've ever seen."

"He is," Lil agrees, her tone both proprietary and sad. "My Tommy. They will remember nothing now, nothing but a wonder, like maenads, though without the madness. It is the gift of the vine. One he can rarely give."

When he has finished with the women, Tommy smiles sadly. "Now, my dearest ones, have you been paid?"

The black woman who had spoken first nods. A smile has transformed her face, making its tired charms radiant.

"Georgie-boy gave us lots of cash from a cash machine. We're set there."

"Dress then and go forth."

"Master, what shall we do?" asks the little Asian girl, pulling on her blouse. "How shall we follow your way?"

Tommy shakes his head. "I have no way, not even for myself. If you would honor me, try to give more joy than pain. Sing more than you weep and when you must weep, weep well."

This seems to satisfy them. Tommy gives them time to redon their tatty finery, to brush their hair, to reapply the cosmetics that are their pride of office. To each he gives a copy of the *Pan* album and a kiss on the brow. Then he directs them out by the back gate. Twilight is falling now and seems to embrace them as they walk back toward the glow of the Strip and the lives they have made there.

Through all of this, the satyrs have crouched naked and unmoving on the stoop outside of the bungalow. Tommy studies them before raising each onto his hooves.

"Personally," Tommy says, his voice still mild, "I feel more sorrow than anger, but I don't think everyone feels that way. Do you, Lilith?"

Lil merely smiles, but the satyrs blanch beneath their olive complexions at that smile.

"Get your belongings," Tommy orders. He waves his hand, and the vines begin to wither, the grapes—all but one bunch he gathers in his hand—to shrivel and dry. "I will check you out of the hotel over the telephone."

"Master," Georgios whimpers. "Protect us!"

"From Lil?" Tommy laughs. "Why? I cannot protect myself from her! How should I protect you? Still, ready yourselves, and I will do what I can to sweeten her."

As the satyrs hurry to oblige him, Tommy saunters from the bungalow to where the wizards sit, still clasping hands.

"That room smells like a stable and a winery crossed with a brothel and a . . ." Tommy shrugs, smiles his gentle, infectious smile. "Man, I can't tell you how it smells. Stay here, and I'll handle them."

When Lil starts to protest, he presses a grape, round, blue-black, and ripe between her lips. She sighs with pure happiness.

"Tommy . . ."

"Hush, my love, my destroyer," he purrs. "Take of me and eat. That's what you always want, isn't it?"

He breaks off a cluster of about six grapes and gives them to Lovern. "You have exhausted yourself in my service, wizard. Take and eat this small token of my esteem. It will restore your lost energies and prepare you for what lies ahead."

Lovern accepts mutely, overwhelmed by the honor. The first grape tastes like all the best wines he has ever drunk, sweet but not too sweet, dry without the least trace of acid.

Beside him, Tommy feeds the remaining grapes one at a time to Lil. Visibly she regains her strength, and some of her anger ebbs from her. As Lovern meditates upon the taste of those grapes, the wizard thinks that the satyrs may keep their balls after all.

Checkout completed, grapevines vanished into thin lines of grey powder that the wind sweeps away, the group departs. The prodigal three cower in the backseat of the limousine, casting anxious glances at Lil.

For her part, she contents herself with darting the occasional smoldering glare back at them from where she sits in the front seat. Only Lovern knows how much sham there is in her fury. Her fingers are entwined with Tommy's, and she hums along when the great god sings.

¤◘¤

Shahrazad can't make herself go past the wolves' scent mark. Certainly she had done so once, but that was nearly two weeks ago, when she was young, callow, and unsophisticated. Now she understands about wolves and has the wisdom to fear them.

A whimper, low and pathetic, escapes Shahrazad's throat. Across the deer trail, the unicorn Pearl lifts her head, ears pricked and listening. The young coyote cringes to the ground, bad enough to fear—worse to be detected in that fear.

Pearl looks toward her, those china blue eyes seeming to see the coyote through the brush and bracken in which she hides. There is humor in that pale gaze, humor and a sense of purpose.

Don't worry little pup, the gaze says, *When your elders are present, they deal with problems.*

Shahrazad acknowledges this. Isn't that the way of things? The Changer may not be here, but Pearl is, and she will stop Wayne. The wolves will not harm the unicorn. They hadn't harmed her on the day that Shahrazad had first encountered them. They won't harm her now.

Why then, does she feel so shamed?

Dreading what will happen if she crosses the wolf line, but unable to remain in safe territory, especially with her new awareness of the Dance binding her to the wolves, Shahrazad drags herself forward. The first steps are the hardest. By the time she has advanced to where she can smell dead elk cached beneath some bracken, some of her normal cockiness is returning.

Then from the forest steps a stranger.

Everything about him is big and aggressive, from his bristling hair and beard to shoulders and thighs like tree trunks. He wears a flannel shirt, jeans, and boots. A double-bladed axe is slung across his shoulders. The wind that crosses his trail tastes of wolf.

"Who th' hell are you!" she hears Wayne blurt, the rifle in his hands now swinging up to point at the big man's chest.

"Lupé will do," the man answers in a wolf-growl voice. "This is private land. Get off."

"You work for MacDonald?" Wayne asks casually, not lowering his weapon.

"I help him out," Lupé says.

Wayne laughs. "You look like Paul Bunyan in that getup."

"I am not Paul Bunyan."

"No," Wayne says, sounding puzzled. "I never said you were."

Something is happening to his eyes.

He had been talking to a man, but the man has vanished. Where he had stood is an enormous wolf, growling menace. With vision suddenly gone panoramic, Wayne now notices other wolves hiding in the underbrush around him.

Cunning steals into his soul. First, he must kill the one directly in front of him, then swing and shoot the white one just in back of him. He no longer wonders why he had sat up late last night, dipping bullets in molten silver.

Shahrazad listens to the alpha male challenge Wayne. Why doesn't he just tear out Wayne's throat? Why doesn't the unicorn run Wayne through his back?

She is trying to gather the courage to spring when, without the slightest warning, Wayne pulls the trigger of his rifle. Almost as if caused by the rife's report, rather than by any physical agent, two bright red spots blossom on the werewolf's chest, neatly clustered over his heart.

Even ears stunned by the loudness of the gunfire hear the wolf pack scattering into deeper cover. Only Shahrazad, paralyzed by shock, does not move. Only Shahrazad sees Wayne wheel to his right and fire two more shots into the unicorn.

Keening in pain, Pearl falls. The shots had been low, but one at least has shattered her left foreleg. Her belly is streaked with red, though from a wound or from splattering Shahrazad cannot tell.

Something rips in Shahrazad's brain, a searing pain similar to one she had felt once before, a pain she associates with a few terrible chords of music.

This time she is not knocked unconscious by the shock. Instead it focuses her, leaving no room for fear. Fur bristled out like a porcupine's spikes and lips peeled back from her fangs, Shahrazad leaps.

Compared to a wolf, or even to a full-grown male coyote, she isn't much, but even so twenty-five pounds of solid, growling coyote is enough to knock Wayne flat on his face.

The bullet he had been aiming to finish Pearl plows into a tree trunk.

Shahrazad's jaws clamp on the back of his neck. The man is not a mouse or rabbit, but surely she can bite hard enough that she won't need to shake. His blood is leaking down her teeth, pooling against her tongue when something like a series of sharp-pointed sticks knocks her away from her prey.

Hip and Hop have launched themselves from the underbrush, pushing her from the human. Now they sit on him, weighing him down, guarding him, preventing Shahrazad from killing him.

Her confused and furious barks do not move the jackalopes, and she is reluctant to attack them—not from fear of their antlers, but because they are her friends.

A wind stirs above, and the eagle-puma lands. It screeches warning at her, refusing to let her kill the man. Shahrazad yaps her frustration, but knows this is an impasse. If she were the Changer, she might be able to challenge these three, but she is just a little coyote.

Behind her, a branch breaks, and she starts, jumping straight into the air as she might when mousing. Then a familiar voice soothes her.

"Easy, Shahrazad. I'm here now, and everything is going to be all right."

Frank MacDonald's hand brushes the top of her head as he moves past her to where Wayne lies prone in the dirt.

"Unconscious. You bit him pretty hard." Gentle Frank raises his hand and hits Wayne solidly on the back of his head. "That will make certain that he stays unconscious."

Moving more quickly now, he goes to where Pearl snuffles with pain, her soft cries closer to those of a deer than a horse.

Hands steady, Frank checks her over, ending by inspecting her foreleg.

"The rest of the wounds are superficial, but this is a very bad break," he tells the unicorn. Shahrazad, creeping up beside him, realizes that he is speaking less for the benefit of the nearly unconscious unicorn than for the rest of them. "But we should be able to treat it, though you're in for a long spell of recovery. I'll need more than what I could bring in my little black bag. Is anyone else hurt?"

A wolf bitch has emerged from the wood. Shahrazad recognizes her as the alpha female. In answer to her whine, Frank shakes his head.

"Lupé is dead. Somehow Wayne knew to load with silver. I've been careful, but he must have seen something. Who knows how much time he has spent spying on us?"

The bitch whines again, less imploring this time than heartbroken. Shahrazad forgets her fear and, going to her, licks the widow's ear with a compassionate tongue. The wolf permits the liberty, but her gaze never leaves Frank.

"Revenge is a complicated matter," he answers, his hands busy beginning to treat Pearl's injuries. "And will be more rapidly addressed once the wounded are treated. If you want to speed things along, go to the house and bring me back . . ."

Shahrazad cannot follow the list of medical supplies he rattles off, but the alpha bitch apparently understands. With a defiant howl that turns into a very human wail, she shifts shape, becoming a diminutive, though singularly scruffy, human female.

"Let the griffin carry you," Frank suggests. "It will be faster. Right now speed could save Pearl's leg."

Grunting acquiescence, the alpha female does so. Hip the jackalope sings a short protest.

"I know we're taking risks," Frank answers, "but that can't be helped. I've lost one friend today. I won't let another be crippled."

Shahrazad bumps her head against Frank's arm, then takes a tentative lick at the drying blood on Pearl's flank. The unicorn shivers, and Frank quiets her with a hand to her head.

"The little coyote just saved your life," he tells her. "She isn't going to hurt you now. Better get those cuts cleaned before they fester."

Glad to be able to do something, Shahrazad continues licking, but she does spare a moment to stare accusingly at Frank and then at the still-unconscious Wayne.

"You wonder why the jackalopes didn't let you kill him, don't you?" Frank answers. "Because Wayne's death couldn't be hidden or easily explained. That would raise trouble—human law officers investigating, perhaps learning more than I want them ever to know. Moreover, with your bite marks on him, some canine would have to pay.

"Accord policy, which in this case is just common sense, is never to cause a death that cannot be hidden or explained by normal means. For Wayne to die here, on my land, killed by a coyote—or a unicorn's horn, a griffin's talon, a werewolf's hand—would cause problems. If Wayne hadn't shot Lupé, Lupé would have subdued him, and I would have 'discovered' him later."

Shahrazad whines a question.

"No, Lupé wouldn't have killed him. At least, he would have tried not to. He was a very old werewolf and very wise in avoiding trouble with humans. I'll miss him."

For the first time, Shahrazad hears the tears that thicken Frank's speech.

The griffin's return ends conversation. Shahrazad slinks back as Frank begins to straighten Pearl's shattered leg, cringing each time the unicorn screams. After an interminable period, the broken leg is set. Sun, the gold unicorn, arrives to tend his mate, and Frank can turn his attention to Wayne.

Earlier, when the human had started to come around, Frank had given him a mild tranquilizer. Now the human lies drowsy and muttering on the ground.

"I can't let you carry him," Frank says to the griffin, "not in this condition, and getting a horse up here would be a waste of time, not to mention difficult."

Sun snorts a question.

"No, you stay with Pearl. She's going to need you. I can carry him if the werewolves will help me load."

To Shahrazad's surprise (and she had truly thought she was beyond surprise), Frank begins removing his clothing. The action is so matter of fact that she instantly recognizes what he is about to do. The Changer had done the same thing whenever he had left human form.

She yips laughter and Frank grins in return.

"I have a small gift," he says. "In fact, I wasn't born a human. About two thousand years ago, in the Middle East, I was born a camel, and as a camel I attended the birth of a child in a stable. Later, as an auxiliary to the Romans, I watched his short, but brilliant career. It changed my life."

Saint Francis shifts then, becoming a brown quadruped with a humped back, flat feet, and broad lips. Only his brown eyes with their long lashes look familiar. Shahrazad thumps her tail in approval and applause.

Back at the ranch house, Frank tests Wayne's reflexes, decides he can handle another dose of sedative, and puts him in one of the spare bedrooms. Then he heads for the telephone.

Although the door is locked and the windows shuttered, Shahrazad leaves nothing to chance. Exhausted, she drapes herself across the doorway before collapsing into sleep.

Caput gerat lupinum.
(*Let his be a wolf's head.*)
—OLD ENGLISH LAW

EDDIE SPOKE SOFTLY TO HER IN THE CHINESE OF A COURT that had vanished long before Jesus Christ was an item, when well-spoken men and women wearing silk practiced politics as subtle and intricate as the designs embroidered on their clothing.

"So the Celestial One has again graced Earth's poor soil with the caress of her dainty slipper."

Oya, large of breast and hip, wrapped in layers of brightly patterned cotton print, turns to meet his gaze and smiles.

"You've found me out, have you, Eddie?" She speaks the same ancient language, her voice different than the one he had known, reshaped by a broader chest, a flatter nose. "What gave me away? I thought I was doing quite well."

Eddie shrugs. "Little things. The way you cradle a cup. How you lightly blot your lips when wiping your mouth. A turn of phrase so subtle that even now I cannot place it. I'm not certain that anyone who had not been as intimately associated with you as I once was would have seen the likeness. And, of course, I have been trying to figure out who you were since you admitted to raising the wind. That narrowed the field quite a bit, but still, it was the semblance of my Tin Hau, the Queen of Heaven, that told me who you are."

"Sometimes," Oya says, "I wonder why we separated. You may be my favorite love over all the long years of my life. I think you are still fond of me, too."

"I am," Eddie says, "but Arthur needs me—without me he blunders, and people get hurt. You could not bear my loyalty to him."

"No," she says bluntly. "I could not. He is a born ruler, true, but you are too good to be stuck with the role of first follower."

Eddie shrugs again. They have had this discussion before. It never ends differently. Better to remember the closeness, the delight that they have felt in each other's company, the friendship they have maintained despite Arthur's influence.

Oya must have come to the same conclusion, for she changes the subject without surrendering her point.

"Were you surprised to find me here?"

"Very. I thought that you were quite happy with the role of Alice Chun, novelist. What are you doing in Nigeria?"

"It's a long story, but one I have been looking for an opportunity to tell, since part of it sheds light on our current difficulties. Come into the kitchen with me. I have some Chinese oolong that I have forborne from making lest you remember my fondness for that particular blend."

"I'd enjoy that," Eddie replies. "Will we be left alone? Or have you told your Aduke about your past history?"

"Aduke is writing a letter to her absent husband." A line forms between Oya's brows. "Then she is taking her turn caring for the little ones. Besides, if we talk Chinese, she will not understand us, even if she runs up here for something."

"Very well," Eddie answers. Having dealt with this routine matter of security, he is prepared to listen. "I would love to join you for tea and a tale."

Oya begins speaking even as she moves around the kitchen, graceful despite her generous figure, putting water on to boil, rinsing the dust from a delicate porcelain teapot, and performing other little domestic tasks.

"Last June at the Lustrum Review," she says, "I found

myself in conversation—argument at times—with Dakar and Anson on the future of Africa. As you well know, they both are devoted to this continent, Dakar particularly to Nigeria, since he was born here. I learned a great deal both about its problems and its potential. I agreed with them that Nigeria, properly handled, could do much for the continent at large.

"The details of our conversation are neither here nor there, but I decided to make a visit. As you know, I am quite skilled in magic. Through various ways and means that I will not bother explaining now, I provided myself with a new shape, a command of several local languages, and identity documents."

Eddie interrupts. "Pendragon Productions could have handled some of that. That's part of what you get for your dues."

Oya dismisses this with a wave of her hand and pours water carefully over the tea leaves.

"I didn't need your help. In any case, as I recall, you were having troubles of your own at that time. Now, where was I?

"Ah, yes. I came here," she continues, "illegally and blended into the population without a great deal of difficulty. Although Nigeria does have its shortcomings, I began to seriously consider relocating here. Alice Chun is becoming too noticeable, and I have written all the books I want to write—at least for now. Nigeria is rather like America was in the beginning."

Eddie takes the cup of tea she offers him. "I don't quite follow you there."

Oya smiles. "When Europe became so stratified that the local athanor could no longer blend in at the higher levels of society (where so many of us prefer to be) without causing difficulties or having to memorize long genealogies, many came to the Americas, where fortune and reputation was there for the making."

"True," Eddie nods.

"Well, Nigeria is like that. It also has the advantage of not being effectively computerized."

"I've learned that it's rather hard," Eddie comments, "to maintain computer records when the electricity keeps going out. And with the insects, the humidity, and the constant social and political upheaval. I understand that no one believes the results of the last census."

"That's right," Oya agrees. "Too many groups have too much to gain from declaring that a specific tribe or religion is dominant. Names are a problem, too. Many people maintain different names for different situations. My little Aduke, for example. Do you remember how I introduced her?"

"Aduke Idowu," Eddie replies promptly.

"And you took that to mean that her first name is 'Aduke' and her surname is 'Idowu.' "

"Isn't it?" Eddie asks, searching his artificially created memory of Yoruban to find a contradiction.

"It is and it isn't," Oya replies maddeningly. " 'Aduke' is a pet name meaning roughly 'She whom one competes to cherish.' "

"Nice."

"I think so. 'Idowu' is a name given to a child who is born after twins. The Yoruba believe that such children have great personal power, meant to help society deal with the twins, who also have personal power."

"But what's her real name?" Eddie asks.

"You mean the one given on her official records?" Oya teases.

"That will do."

"Joan Idowu Fadaka, or in some cases Mrs. Taiwo Fadaka. Her grammar school records, of course, will give her father's family surname—if he used one."

"I get the picture," Eddie says thoughtfully. "This would be an ideal country for an athanor to set up in, especially if he or she didn't mind settling, at least for a time, in one of the cities where people wouldn't expect to know their relatives."

"Exactly!" Oya says. "And Nigeria alone has 250 different ethnic groups, though the Ibo, Yoruba, and Hausa dominate. It has a thriving literary tradition, tremendous natural resources, and, since English remains the official language, there is no barrier to international trade."

"You begin to sound like Anson," Eddie comments dryly.

"So I like the place. Even before that mess in September, I had decided to set up at least a dual identity here, to give it a trial run, so to speak. Alice Chun could continue producing a book every couple of years, so I didn't need to burn my bridges all at once.

"I started looking for a place to live. Dakar had not relocated to Nigeria yet. Apparently, he and Katsuhiro were up to one of their silly games."

Eddie corrects gently, "Actually, they were looking for Sven Trout at Arthur's request."

"A silly game if I've ever heard of one," Oya persists. "What is more foolish than seeking Loki? He shows up when you want him the least.

"In any case, Dakar wasn't here, but when he was, he'd probably settle in Ire, which traditionally is Ogun's city. Anson was doing the international-businessman routine, so I didn't need to worry about him. I'd gotten to like Monamona in the course of my tours. It's big, but not too big, old, but not so old that the social structure has calcified. Moreover, it already had an athanor presence, and that can be useful."

"Shango," Eddie says.

"Yes. I decided to call on him, let him know what I was planning, and learn if he had any difficulties with my coming here. If he did, I probably would have settled in Oyo. I learned where Shango's office is located. It wasn't hard, since he's the minister in charge of the electrical utilities. Then, wearing my new persona, I went to call on him.

"I thought I'd picked a quiet time, since most billing inquiries come around the middle of the month, and this was near the end. Certainly, there were few supplicants in the waiting room. I gave a false name and a bit of dash to the receptionist and settled down to wait.

"It was a long wait, long enough that I excused myself, found a private corner, and changed into a dove. In that form, I flew to where Shango's window should be. The day was warm—as they all are here, one of my few complaints—and the window was open. Shango was in conference with a couple of men."

Oya frowns, pours more tea, sips, and then continues:

"I couldn't stay listening for long, but what I overheard didn't seem related to keeping the flow of electricity going. I also was impressed by how these men acted toward Shango.

Although at least one of them—the mayor of Monamona—should not have deferred to him, in many subtle ways, he did so.

"I did not survive in the courts of China without developing prudence in matters political. Telling Shango of my intentions no longer seemed a good idea. If he was playing politics, as it seemed he was, he might not like my being there. Instead, I decided to keep my own counsel and watch Shango for a while.

"With this in mind, I cultivated the acquaintance of the family who now lives in this factory. Taiwo, Aduke's husband, acts as liaison between someone in Lagos and Shango. Shango himself proved more difficult to follow than I had imagined possible. Since he does not know I am here—or didn't until you told him . . ."

Eddie shrugs. "You didn't tell us any of this."

"No, I didn't. I wasn't certain you weren't working with him yourselves. You've been very closemouthed."

"So have you until this afternoon."

They glare at each other for a moment, then, almost as one, shrug. That breaks the tension. Laughing and shaking her head, Oya says:

"Well, he doesn't know *who* I am, nor is he certain that I am athanor and not just a braggart or local eccentric."

"And I certainly won't tell him. Besides," Eddie continues, "we don't know that he's up to anything other than playing local political games."

"No, we don't." Oya tugs at her earlobe. "But like you, I have been snooping around this Regis's compound, and yesterday I saw something that troubled me greatly. Taiwo, the same young man who is Aduke's husband and has been working with Shango, came out of the compound."

"Are you certain?"

"Positive. I thought he was Kehinde, his twin brother, and called out to him to come help me carry some groceries. He looked at me as if I was insane. Then very formal and stiff, he told me that I must have mistaken him for another."

"You are certain it was him?"

"Kehinde is not triplets, and this man looked exactly like Kehinde, though he wore European clothing and Kehinde very self-consciously dresses in the traditional style."

"Interesting."

"Yes. Very. Regis styles himself after Shopona, the God of Smallpox. Shango claims that he cannot move against him because Regis has threatened him with infecting the city. I suppose that Taiwo could be Regis's representative to Shango, but what if he is not, what if Shango and Regis are working together?"

"An uncomfortable thought," Eddie muses, "but one that explains a lot of little things that have been bothering me."

"Moreover," Oya continues, "and this may be stretching the point—but Shango was ever one to appreciate a flamboyant touch—do you know who some myths say is Shopona's father?"

"Not Shango?"

"Yes, Shango. Regis may not be Shango's biological son, but the mythological connection is certainly a bit of poetry."

"If Regis is athanor"—Eddie recalls their earliest discussions of the problem—"and, like you, under the Accord's protection though working under another name, we dare not act too precipitously."

Oya stares at him. "You sound like a politician yourself, Eddie. This man uses disease to fight for him. I don't care who he is or whose son he is: Nothing is going to protect him. The only reason Regis has lived this long is that I need to know where he has cached his supplies and what time bombs might be set to go off if he dies. Once they are defused . . ."

She makes a swift slice, finger across her throat.

"Do you understand?"

Eddie bows his head. "I do. And I agree."

¤◙¤

By swimming steadily and hitching a ride on one of his brother's subjects when he grows tired, the Changer arrives at the west coast of Africa less than forty-eight hours after granting Arthur's request.

Rising to the surface of the water in the Bight of Benin, he can see the ugly sprawl of Lagos before him. The air is hot and muggy, even though the sun is beginning to set. Well fed and rested, since he had ridden most of the last section of his journey, the Changer sees no reason to delay.

Normally, the Changer is no different from any other traveler in that he needs to know where he is going. Although his conversations with Anson have given him a general idea of where Monamona is in relation to the other major cities in Yorubaland, the Changer has never been there. However, he trusts that the windstorm of which Arthur had told him will provide landmark enough. Shifting into a fish eagle, he leaves the water for the sky and flies inland.

He bypasses Lagos entirely and once away from the city's heat and pollution, he gets his first sense of the windstorm. It is faint, nothing more than a slight hum in counterpoint to the steady thrum of the *harmattan* wind. When darkness falls and he must navigate by the stars alone, the Changer becomes more aware of the windstorm's song as it plays against the magnetic compass within his avian breast.

With each major population center the Changer passes, the hum of the windstorm becomes more and more apparent. By the time he arrives on the outskirts of Monamona, wing-weary and hungry, he has a suspicion as to what might be causing the wind.

Finding something to eat is not difficult. Vehicles surround the perimeter of the city, safely outside of the outermost limits of the storm. There are tanks and all-terrain vehicles, jeeps and vans, cars and trucks, some civilian as well as military. The Changer lands on top of a van rigged out as a chuck wagon. Goaded by hunger, he finds the strength to shift into a monkey and slip inside. There he eats his fill of *gari foto* and black-eyed peas, finishing his meal with a large yam or two, eaten raw.

This urge satisfied, he considers whether or not to sleep. The hour is late but not yet midnight, so he decides he can risk at least a short nap before trying to penetrate the windstorm, which should be done under the cover of darkness owing to the number of potential observers.

Shortly after one in the morning, the Changer awakens, eats again, and, so refreshed, emerges into the night.

The air is curiously still here. Even the *harmattan* winds, which had made his flight inland less than pleasant, have ceased. Directly above, the stars shine hard and bright, a sight that makes those locals who are awake distinctly nervous. At this time of year, the sky should be decently veiled with dust. Even in the clear seasons, there is a faint haze of humidity. Directly above the windstorm, however, the sky is as clear as at the top of the Alps.

This small phenomena adds a piece of information to the Changer's list. Before heading through the storm, he shifts into an owl and makes a slow circuit of the vehicles, noting a few insignia with surprise. He wonders if those imprisoned within the storm realize how much attention it has attracted.

With another small shrug, he changes into another bird, choosing this time an eagle accustomed to dealing with high mountain winds. Then, like a surfer riding a wave, the Changer enters the whirlwind.

The airplanes that he had seen wrecked outside had made the mistake of trying to go *through* the wind. However, even the lightest and most flexible of them lacked the dexterity to ride with the wind's shifting force, so the matter is moot.

The Changer does have the dexterity. Indeed, he has a dexterity beyond that of any bird, for he can reshape his wings, lengthening and shortening individual feathers as needed in order to keep in balance with the air current around him.

It becomes a game between him and the swirling air, a dip here, a rush there, banking, then catching a thermal current so that he can rise to where he can coast, catch his breath, reorient himself, and swirl inward once more.

When the Changer spills inside of the whirlwind, above a quiet section of road at the verge of the Monamona, he is exhilarated rather than exhausted. Still, he does not abandon common sense and go for another ride. Bowing his eagle's head slightly as in salute, he shifts again into an owl and soars up silently, startling a solitary sentry who wonders if he has disturbed a witch going about its business.

Achieving altitude, the Changer wonders where to begin searching for the missing athanor. A burst of gunfire and the sound of shouting nearby seem an answer. Beating his wings faster, he flies in that direction.

¤◘¤

Shahrazad's nightmares return that night as she sleeps outside the door to Wayne's room. She had not joined her usual companions on Frank's bed, but had stoutly held to her post, even though Frank had told her all was well.

"Wayne's absence may cause some problems, but no one will come looking here. And on the off chance anyone does, I'm prepared."

Shahrazad had just raised her head and stared from steady yellow eyes, so he had bent and patted her on the head.

"You remind me of your father when you look like that. Sleep well."

She doesn't, though. Her dreams are full of ice storms and fields filled with orange flowers with black centers that smell of sleep. Ice covers her, imprisoning her in glassy walls so thick that neither sound nor scent can penetrate them, and the little light that does refracts crazily among the crystals.

In her dream, she tries to dig her way out, but the ice is tight around her limbs, encasing not just legs and paws, but each hair in an unbreakable insinuating hold.

If Wayne had not stumbled across her when he opened the door, Shahrazad doubts that she would have heard him leave.

When she feels the thud of his foot against her flank, her eyes fly open. Vision momentarily confuses her, for she had thought her eyes already open. By the time she has resolved this, Wayne has recovered his balance, stepped over her, and turned down the corridor toward the central wing of the house.

Shahrazad's muscles do not seem to know that they are no longer asleep. Though she struggles to rise, she cannot get her legs to obey. Only by concentrating on one limb at a time, raising her hindquarters first, then her front legs, then her head and neck, and finally her tail does she come free of the dream's hold.

The ranch house is unnaturally silent. Normally there are many small sounds, the snores, wheezes, snorts, and snuffles of dozens of sleeping animals. Gone, too, are the sounds of those animals who do not sleep through the night but instead come and go about their business through windows and door flaps left open for that purpose.

Tonight, the only sound is the faint jingle of keys and a single set of footsteps padding down the carpeted hall.

Shahrazad moves toward those sounds, carefully keeping to the carpet so her toenails won't click against the wood or tile. If she can sneak up on Wayne, she can knock him down again. She doesn't care if she leaves teeth marks on his neck.

Somehow, she knows she cannot awaken Frank quickly enough for him to help her. By the time he peels the ice from his limbs, Wayne would be gone.

Shahrazad arrives in the central portion of the house in time to see Wayne emerging from the room whose door is normally kept locked. There is a small white creature in his left hand: pale white with a pink nose that wiggles nervously as the mouse sniffs the air.

Moving as if asleep himself, Wayne goes to the end of the hallway and opens the door to the outside that Frank locks at night. Frustrated, Shahrazad barks sharply, knowing that Wayne has too great a head start for her to catch him by stealth alone.

The air around her swallows the sound, chasing it back upon itself, deadening it, as a blanket or pillow does. The mouse hears, however, and Shahrazad cringes nearly to the floor when a translucent figure manifests around it.

It is a woman, slim and fair, with hair like ice and blue eyes like winter cold. The delicate lines of her features hold no mirth, no merriment. A human would recognize her as beautiful. To Shahrazad, who has known only pain and cruelty from that woman, she is more terrible than any monster.

"You," Louhi says, and her voice is like a whisper of a memory of a voice, heard inside the mind, not with the ears. "You, little bitch. I'm leaving now. You can do nothing to stop me. If I could keep my hold on this man and get you . . . but, by the time you rouse anyone, I will be gone."

Wayne appears to have seen the woman, for his sleepy expression turns to one of appreciation and awe.

"Come along, dear," he says. "Let me take you home."

The woman vanishes, and there is only a mouse, but

Wayne doesn't seem to know this. He carries her outside. A few minutes later, while Shahrazad is still trying to escape the fear that had crippled her at the sight of Louhi, she hears the sound of an automobile engine.

That mundane sound breaks the fear and she runs down the corridor, barking warning and threat, but, as Louhi had promised, she is too late. The red glow of taillights receding down the driveway is Shahrazad's only reward.

The young coyote is still wondering what to do when a large shape, dark against the dark sky, lands nearly soundlessly beside her. From the curious mixed scent of bird and cat, Shahrazad knows the griffin. The eagle-puma screeches inquiry at her and Shahrazad barks that everyone is asleep, though no one should sleep.

Surprisingly, the griffin understands her, miming sleep by tucking her head beneath her wing and pulling it out again, then shaking her head after the fashion of humans. Relieved to have someone understand her, Shahrazad indicates the open door of the ranch house, Wayne's scent trail on the cold ground, the missing pickup truck.

The griffin becomes greatly agitated. Apparently she dislikes Louhi as much as Shahrazad does. Then she does something very strange. As she had when she carried the female werewolf to the ranch house, the griffin hunkers low to the ground. Looking at Shahrazad, she makes soft crooning sounds in her throat.

Shahrazad has watched humans ride horses and unicorns, but has never contemplated a similar mode of travel for herself. The idea entices her. They could chase down the truck with Louhi and Wayne, learn where they are going, perhaps stop them. The griffin is quite formidable, and Shahrazad has a fine belief in her own abilities. After all, didn't Louhi get in the state she is in because of Shahrazad?

Nothing loath, the coyote leaps onto the griffin's back. Immediately, she slides to the ground.

"Go without me," she whines.

"No. I can't let anyone see me," the griffin replies in perfect but accented (mostly because of the shape of its ears) dog sounds. "Hold on with your teeth."

Shahrazad tries, but the eagle feathers tickle her nose and

make her sneeze. The lion hindquarters are not sufficiently long for her to straddle.

If only I had hands! she thinks in desperation. As once before in her life, she feels the anger, fear, and frustration within her flow into a part of her she had nearly forgotten existed until this moment.

When Shahrazad looks down at herself, she sees that while her head and torso are still those of a coyote, her arms and legs have shifted to something closer to those of a human. Her feet remain like coyote feet, though somewhat longer, and her front paws have become hairy, but fully usable hands.

Gleefully, she spins before the griffin, displaying her new form.

"Come, Changer's Daughter," the other screeches. "We must fly before they go too far, before light comes and I must hide or fly very high indeed."

Shahrazad climbs onto the griffin's back, straddling as she had seen the werewolf do. She is even smaller, hardly larger than a toddling human child, and the griffin makes a satisfied noise as she launches into the air.

"Sharp eyes below, little one," she screeches. "We shall have them yet."

Shahrazad grins a coyote grin and, lifting her muzzle to the thin sliver of the moon, howls.

¤◙¤

"Those of us on the inside," Anson had reminded them just moments before, "must do four things. We must get Katsuhiro. We must get Teresa. We must get Taiwo. Finally, if we can, we must get Katsuhiro's sword. Your job on the outside is to give us time to do these things."

Their plan for entry had been cast with the simplicity born of desperation. When Anson had returned hours earlier from his nightly trip to Regis's compound, he had brought news of the Japanese's defense of Teresa and what it meant for his situation.

Since Katsuhiro was presumably no longer able to roam

at liberty, and since Teresa was with him in his room, that very night seems the best time to act.

Thus, in the postmidnight hours, when the guards on the midnight-to-seven shift should be growing bored and tired, Anson would cross into the compound in monkey form. He would bring another gun, ammunition, and a knife for Teresa. It had been decided, given what Katsuhiro reported of her state of mind, not to trust her with a gun.

Meanwhile, Eddie, Dakar, and Oya would be waiting below. There was no way that even such a talented duo as Anson and Katsuhiro could expect to simply walk out of the compound. Therefore, the strike team outside was prepared to create distractions and, if necessary, to break into the compound to get them out.

Neat. Tidy. Full of room for improvisation.

It is amazing how quickly this simple plan goes to hell.

Teresa starts the problems. She recognizes Anson when he swings in through the open window, only raises an eyebrow at his nudity and hands him, without being asked, a pair of Katsuhiro's undershorts.

"A good thing he wears boxers," she says. "When Mr. Oba warned me that we were breaking out tonight and that there would be help from the outside, I thought he might mean you."

Anson, stepping into the shorts, bows acknowledgment. "I am sorry about Adam's death. Had I known what had happened to you both, I would have tried to rescue you sooner."

Teresa shrugs. "What is is. There is no changing it. Now, tie me to that chair, good and tight. I will say I was overwhelmed. Since we have refocused the security camera—not that I think Regis has time for watching tonight—there will be no one to gainsay me."

She sits in the indicated chair and the two men exchange helpless glances.

"Teresa," Anson says sternly, "you are leaving with us. There is nothing further you can do here. If you stay, you may be killed."

"I am already dead," she says, frighteningly matter-of-fact, "and so do not fear death. I will not leave until I am certain that Regis's heart no longer beats and the good air is no longer fouled in his lungs. I cannot say 'until he is dead' for as I have told Mr. Oba, Regis is already as dead as I am."

"Others have already sworn to kill him," Anson says soothingly. "There is no need for you to be further sullied. Come!"

Her reply is to lean back against the chair and close her eyes. Katsuhiro tears a strip from his bed linen.

"A gag is a good first step," he says, "then her hands."

In ancient Mycenaean, he adds, "We could leave her, but I prefer not to do so. Since she will not cooperate, she can be our hostage. At least some of the guards will hesitate before shooting Regis's woman."

Anson nods agreement and begins belting Katsuhiro's boxers around his own much smaller waist.

"These don't have pockets," he says in English, "but I'll use my fanny pack to carry ammunition."

"Good," Katsuhiro replies. "I'll need to leave most of my luggage. Regis's minions have taken my money and identification, but the latter can be replaced." To Teresa he adds, "Open your mouth, you stubborn woman."

She does so, placid but fierce, and he stuffs in a gag and ties it firmly into place. Anson twists her hands behind her and holds them while Katsuhiro binds her wrists. Only when the samurai hobbles her ankles, then wrenches her to her feet, does Teresa realize that they are not leaving her behind.

Immediately, she begins to struggle. Anson, who is far stronger than his skinny body would seem to indicate, holds her easily with one arm.

"Keep struggling, my friend," he tells her cheerfully. "It will make our charade seem all the better."

She cannot curse him as the low growls in her throat seem to indicate she would wish, but her eyes are hot with hate.

Katsuhiro appropriates the knife meant for Teresa, checks his gun for readiness, and grins at Anson.

"I am so looking forward to a fight," he says.

"Then let me brief you," Anson says. "Our reinforcements are prepared to cause a distraction when needed. Moreover, the door nearest to the garage will be open and covered. Our job is to get out after finishing our scavenger hunt."

Katsuhiro's grin does not fade. "We have Teresa. Taiwo

is being held in his own quarters one floor below this one. The staircase at the right end of the corridor outside will take us almost to his door."

In Mycenaean, Anson says, "I had planned to shift again and go down to his room so we would have someone with him, but Teresa's behavior makes that impossible."

"We will adapt," Katsuhiro answers in the same language. "By the way, I saved you some candy. It's disgustingly sweet, but should help you keep your strength up."

Anson takes the offered candy with the hand that is not gripping Teresa.

"Cloying," he says, switching to English, "but not disgusting. And a great help. Are you ready to go?"

"Ready," Katsuhiro says. "You first with Teresa. I'll slip out behind and take out the guard on the right. From there . . ."

"We improvise, eh?"

"*Hai!*"

Anson takes a deep breath, then opens the door. Even before it swings fully open, he is jabbering nonsense in rapid-fire English.

"Mary had a little lamb, her fleece was black as night . . ."

He's in the corridor now, kicking out almost as if performing a dance step. His bare foot hits the guard on the left of the door solidly in a khaki-trousered knee.

"And everywhere that Mary goes, tha' lamb, she take a fright!"

Anson grins, making certain the two guards closest to him (there are four in all, one on either side of the door, two leaning against the wall across the corridor) see that he holds a gun in addition to Teresa. Behind him, he hears an "ooff" and thud as Katsuhiro takes out the guard to the right of the door.

Dragging the struggling Teresa with him, Anson takes a giant step into the newly opened space.

"Hey diddle diddle, that cat has a fiddle, the cow jumps over the moon."

Katsuhiro is a blur of motion, launching across the woman and knocking the guard out with a blow to the side of his neck.

One of the two remaining guards is struggling onto his feet, swearing at the pain in his knee. The other decides to shoot.

His shot, aimed professionally for Katsuhiro's torso, is upset when Katsuhiro leaps for him, but even so, it plows a furrow in the other's right side.

"Plague song!" Anson announces, then sings, "Ring around the rosy, a pocket full of posies. Ha-choo! Ha-choo! We all fall down!"

Despite Teresa's resistance, he's gotten to the top of the stair. Footsteps are tramping up, rapid and controlled, soldiers responding to a situation, not civilians.

Holding Teresa in front of him like a shield, Anson whispers in her ear. "Don't give me trouble, eh? Then maybe they no shoot you, too."

She leans back, so limp and heavy he wonders if she has fainted. When the first man peers around the stairwell, Anson shoots him quite neatly in the middle of the forehead.

Katsuhiro, coming up beside him, growls. "You should have let him step out first! Now the others will be more cautious."

"Are we clear behind?"

"Those four are out of it." The dripping red knife blade in the Japanese's hand explains how and how permanently. Without saying more, Katsuhiro creeps on his belly until he is alongside the stairwell doorway. Listening, he holds up his fingers: two or more on the other side.

Anson nods and fires a couple of shots through the windowpane in the stairwell door. As he had hoped, the whine of the bullet ricocheting from the concrete walls flushes the men in the stairwell. When they charge out, half-panicked, half-furious, Katsuhiro coolly picks them off.

As he's reloading, Katsuhiro motions to Anson. "Go ahead. I'll follow and lock this door. If we're lucky, they were watching Taiwo, and his door will be temporarily unguarded."

Anson nods, griping playfully as he carries Teresa over the bloody corpses in the doorway. "You could have let them get a few steps farther . . ."

Katsuhiro barks laughter and follows. "The gunfire will

have alerted the guards on the wall. You say we have people outside?"

"Three," Anson grunts. Teresa is being very difficult, struggling, then going limp. Frustrated, he thumps her on the head, but all that does is make her angrier. "Crazy woman," he mutters.

Leaving seven dead behind them, the athanor hurry down the stairs. The corridor outside of Taiwo's room, as they had hoped, is temporarily empty, but shouting both outside and in the building indicates that it will not be so for long.

Belinda: Ay, but you know we must return good for evil.
Lady Brute: That may be a mistake in the translation.

—JOHN VANBRUGH

OUTSIDE THE WALLS OF THE COMPOUND, THREE LISTENING athanor tense at the first sound of gunfire. Then Dakar Agadez lifts a high-powered rifle to his shoulder, takes aim through a nightscope and fires. There is a sound rather like a cat spitting, and one of the men on the wall falls.

For a moment, Eddie considers protesting, then his older training comes forward. There are no innocents on a battlefield, and anyone trusted enough to stand on that wall holding a weapon is willing and able to kill them.

Oya, as he must now think of Alice Chun, is frowning slightly, but in concentration, not consternation. They have been watching from across the street the dual entrances into Regis's compound, one large enough to admit vehicles, another, smaller, meant for human traffic alone.

During a break in the gunfire, Oya slips across the street to the smaller door. Before she begins work on the lock, she stretches a trip wire across the opening. Anson knows to look out for it, but anyone not with him will not. A small trick, but time could be precious. When she unlocks the door, she moves to the vehicle door. In this case, her job is to jam it, not open it.

While Oya works, Eddie keeps up a steady exchange of shots with the guards on the compound wall. Dakar has trotted away. By firing other shots from random points along the rest of the wall, he can create the illusion that their force is much larger than it is.

In a sense, Regis's sinister compound has helped them. The tenants in the nearest houses and shops have long since moved away. The darkened buildings, many with boarded-up doors and windows, provide ample shadows and alleys in which the athanor can hide. They have a short grace period during which no neighbors will interfere, and all the official military—police and militia alike—are posted at the edges of the city, patrolling lest Oya's wind fall and leave them unprepared for whatever waits outside.

Yes, for now, everything is going according to plan. Eddie hopes that things are going as well for Anson and Katsuhiro.

¤◙¤

Picking the lock to Taiwo's room is laughably easy for the Spider, but that doesn't make him careless when he opens the door. Teresa is slumped in a sullen heap on the floor, and Katsuhiro is watching the corridor for any trouble.

Anson kicks in the door, rolling in low to the ground and hoping that Taiwo isn't still so trusted as to be armed. When Anson comes to his feet, his gun in his right hand, he counts his blessings to find himself whole. Taiwo is sitting on the edge of the bed, his eyes round with astonishment.

"You look a lot like your brother," Anson says conversationally.

Instantly, he realizes that he has said the wrong thing. Taiwo tenses, reaches for something to throw. Since the nearest thing to hand is a pillow, Anson isn't terribly worried, but he mentally kicks himself for forgetting that, since Taiwo hasn't been visiting his wife, he probably is not on the best of terms with his twin either.

"On your feet," the Spider orders. "We're taking you out with us. I don't really care how much you're bleeding when we do."

He does care, actually, since the idea of dragging both Teresa and Taiwo is highly unpleasant—not to mention how much it would reduce the odds of a successful escape.

Taiwo, however, is convinced, perhaps because anyone who is crazy enough to take on a fortress with nothing more than a baggy pair of underwear and a gun is a someone not to be treated lightly. He gets to his feet and takes a hesitant step in the direction of the open door.

"Through there," Anson says. "And while you're walking, tell me. Where did Regis put the sword he took from the Japanese?"

"In his quarters," Taiwo says promptly. "I've seen it there, hanging on the wall."

Anson nods. "Hear that?" he calls to Katsuhiro.

"*Hai!*" comes the reply, punctuated by several neatly spaced shots. "Stop jabbering!"

When Anson and his captive emerge into the corridor, there are two more bodies lying at the far end.

"There may be more coming up in the stairwell behind us," Katsuhiro comments, "but they'll be delayed by the door I just locked. I think this corridor is clean. No one has emerged from the other doors."

Taiwo volunteers in the tight voice of someone trying very hard to sound nonchalant, "Regis's other guests had these rooms, but since he moved them to the dungeon below, they are probably empty."

"Then we go this way," Katsuhiro orders. "That stairwell is marginally closer to the door Oya should have open for us. We have the two most valuable pieces in our scavenger hunt. They must be gotten out first."

Anson nods. "But your sword?"

"Can wait. There's a lot of talk about a samurai's sword being his soul," Katsuhiro says, taking point, pausing only to scavenge weapons and ammunition from the man he has just killed, "but I've never seen the use of a soul without a breathing body to house it."

"A practical," Anson says, relieving the same corpse of a

roll of hard candy from its breast pocket, "but less elegant philosophy."

Teresa walks with them now, shuffling rapidly within the limits of her hobbles. Perhaps the trail of corpses that Katsuhiro has left behind him has left her less certain about crossing him. Perhaps the presence of immediate death has made her treasure what life is left to her. Whatever the reason, Anson senses the change and cuts her gag.

"With us now, little sister?" he asks kindly.

"Yes," she croaks, her throat sucked dry by the gag.

"Good," he bends and cuts her hobbles, but leaves her hands bound. Taiwo watches in some puzzlement.

"All will become clear," Anson promises, pushing a candy between Teresa's lips, "if you live long enough to get out of here. Now move!"

Taiwo does, trotting a few feet behind Katsuhiro as the other leads the way down the stair. Teresa comes next. Anson brings up the rear, guarding both against anyone coming up from behind and from treachery in the middle.

He knows from his scouting and Katsuhiro's report that they have one more flight to go. Then they must cross the ground floor before making a short hop through open ground within the compound. From the sound of gunfire outside, Dakar and Eddie are doing their part, but he feels far from certain that he and Katsuhiro will get both themselves and their charges out safely.

¤▣¤

Eddie has just shot the latest guard in the shoulder and is cursing himself for his lack of accuracy—too much paperwork and too little practice on the range has made him slow—when a bird flutters to the ground at his feet and resolves into a man.

"Eddie," says the gravelly voice of the Changer, "Arthur sent me to find you."

Eddie appreciates the economical way that the Changer anticipates what should be his first questions (Why are you here? How did you find me?) almost as much as he appreciates the shapeshifter's timing. He raises his rifle, shoots a roundness that might be a head, but might be another shoulder.

"We're waiting for Katsuhiro and Anson. They're inside. Should be heading for that door. I don't suppose . . ."

"I'm gone," is the reply, and the Changer resolves into something with wings. Eddie sets up a wild burst of gunfire to cover its vanishing over the wall. Then, having done all he can, he reloads and continues his methodical coverage.

¤▣¤

The Changer finds Katsuhiro and Anson outside the guardroom on the ground floor, unable to get beyond the half dozen armed men who have built a semifortified position by overturning furniture and the like.

Anson is watching the corridor at their back while Katsuhiro trades shots with the guards. Two Nigerians he doesn't know watch each other warily. The woman holds a knife.

Perhaps Anson's own gift for shapeshifting makes him hold his fire when the owl flies into the corridor from an empty room. Perhaps he just figures an owl can't do much harm, but he does smile when the owl resolves into the human-form Changer.

"Naked as a jaybird," Anson says, "and twice as welcome, eh? Eddie or Dakar send you?"

"Eddie," comes the laconic reply. "He's getting tired of shooting shadows and wants to know when you'll finish messing around in here."

"We have a problem," Anson says. "Six problems. We can't get around them, and all the other ways out of the building take us across an awful lot of open ground."

"Six?" the Changer asks. Then to Katsuhiro, "Susano, do you have an extra gun?"

Katsuhiro never looks away from the room he is watching, but he nods. The Changer, ignoring the Nigerians, who are staring at him with astonishment close to terror, walks over to Katsuhiro and accepts a handgun.

"It's loaded already," Katsuhiro says, squeezing off a shot. "Be quick. I've ammo enough, scavenged from the dead, but

I cannot shoot forever without something jamming."

"Of course."

The Changer walks back the way he had come, pausing only to stare at Teresa and Taiwo. "See you later," he says in soft menace. They don't see him wink at Anson as he passes.

Returning to the empty room through which he had entered, the Changer contemplates shapes. He's getting tired, but there are still floodlights operating inside the compound, so he prefers to travel quickly and in a shape smaller than a human.

Shifting back into an owl, he grasps the handgun in his talons. When he is outside the guardroom, he finds a sheltered spot cast into deep shadow by the spotlights glaring on the open area around the building. Then he shifts back into a human and crouches low.

Creeping around to the door, the Changer thuds his shoulder against it, making a loud noise. A shrill scream from within tells him that Katsuhiro has taken advantage of someone's momentary inattention. No one on the wall has noticed him, so the Changer checks the doorknob. It turns easily.

Someone must have seen the turning, because the metal-jacketed door is shot at from within. That was stupid; the door is bulletproof, and the resulting ricochet wounds someone else.

Listening to the anguished sobbing, the Changer hazards another thump, gambling that nerves within are beginning to fray. It's easy enough to be valiant holding your own against one man. It's not so easy when suddenly there is an enemy at your back.

Again there is a shot, and this time Katsuhiro calls out—in Yoruban so the guards within are meant to understand his words—"Throw the grenade now! I've got this side covered!"

Grinning sardonically, the Changer heaves a rock through the already cracked pane of glass set high in the guardroom door. The sound of shattering glass is completely drowned out by screams and gunfire. He waits patiently. After a moment, Katsuhiro calls in Japanese:

"I think I have them all. Mind checking?"

The Changer, still watchful of his back and of the men patrolling the wall (though most of their attention seems to be for the darkness without, from which death comes with uncanny ease) obliges by opening the door, standing back, and then, when no further gunfire ensues, dropping low and peering through. He sees six men, dead or dying.

"All clear," he says, "but hurry."

The two Nigerians, herded by Anson, come quickly, but Katsuhiro hangs back.

"I thought I might get my sword while we have the upper hand," the Japanese explains.

Anson sighs and mutters something about Katsuhiro's change in philosophy being too good to be true, but he doesn't protest. The Changer studies Susano.

"Or, knowing that I am here," he says, "you hope that I will get your sword."

Katsuhiro shrugs, not at all embarrassed. "It's in the master suite," he says, and gives directions. "I would owe you much if you would help me."

The Changer nods. "Yes, you would."

When Katsuhiro bows, accepting the debt, the Changer shrugs his shoulders preparatory to shifting shape one more time.

"See you outside," he says, and is gone.

¤▣¤

Stinky Joe is the first to push out from under the spell with which Louhi has ensorceled the Other Three Quarters Ranch. From his favorite perch in Tugger's hay rack, he drops onto the horse's broad back. The athanor horse does not open his eyes, does not even shudder his skin, just stands there splay-legged, so deeply asleep that his nose brushes against the sawdust bedding in his stall.

Stinky Joe takes a few worried licks at his shoulder. He might not be one of the Cats of Egypt, steeped in magic, but he is cunning, streetwise, and very, very old. Within the time it takes to shake the last persistent cobwebs of sleep from his brain, he has resolved to find Frank.

Entering the ranch house, the cat finds the same unnatural

stillness that had reigned in both stables and barnyard. The clouded leopard sleeps before the cold fireplace, looking like an exotic rug. A pair of ferrets coil on an ottoman. Birds that should have awakened with first light continue to drowse with their heads beneath their wings.

Worried now, Stinky Joe streaks toward Frank's room. He leaps over the menagerie sprawled around the sleeping saint and lands squarely on Frank's chest. But for a slight "oomph" of exhaled breath, Frank sleeps on.

Joe butts his head against Frank's cheek and is rewarded by a stirring. He butts again, hard enough to bruise, and Frank mutters a string of nonsense syllables. Reluctantly, for he views Frank as one of his many charges, Stinky Joe unsheathes the claws on his right paw and whacks Frank soundly on his rather prominent nose. This time, Frank's eyelids fly open, and he sits up so rapidly that Joe must jump to one side.

"What the heck!" Frank expostulates. "Joe? What's wrong?"

Even as the cat explains, Frank notices the light streaming in through the gaps in the window curtains, feels the stiffness in his muscles, and realizes that he has slept far later than he had intended. Usually the animals will not let him oversleep—being far too aware that he is the one who feeds them—so Frank realizes that Stinky Joe is telling the truth. Something has bollixed both him and his many-headed organic alarm clock.

Pushing a still-sleeping jackalope to one side, Frank swings his feet to the floor. Shuffling into his slippers, Frank hurries to the room where Wayne should be sleeping. The door is open, the room empty, and the young coyote who was guarding the door gone.

"Damn!" Frank curses. He's about to hurry outside to see if there is any sign of Wayne, when Stinky Joe yowls, drawing his attention to the door that is always kept closed. It is ajar now, and when Frank hurries inside he sees that the mouse cage is empty. The ground squirrel remains in his cage, staring up at Frank from mismatched eyes that are empty of anything but vague curiosity about the lateness of breakfast.

Moving automatically, Frank fills the rodent's food dish and checks that it has sufficient water. Then, closing and locking the door behind him, he heads outside. The haste is gone from his pace. He no longer expects to find either Wayne or the mouse. He just hopes he won't find Shahrazad a crumpled heap of lifeless fur in some corner.

"Wake the others," he tells Stinky Joe. "Start with the dogs. I need them for tracking. I'll need a raven or jay to do some scouting."

Stinky Joe blinks at him, catlike, considering whether or not to take orders, then flicks the broken tip of his tail in acknowledgment. After all, breakfast will be further delayed if Frank doesn't have help. He does ignore Frank's priorities, waking the felines first and delegating them to help him wake the others. It is far below his dignity *ever* to deal with dogs.

Meanwhile, Frank has gone outside, ignoring the cold November winds that whip through his pajamas and chill his feet through his slippers. One of the trucks is gone. That's simple enough. He also finds the marks of the griffin's talons and hind paws in the snow, side by side with the marks of small coyote paws. The snow coverage is scattered, so he cannot read the full story; however, he sees enough to draw some uncomfortable conclusions.

Sending a jay to warn the werewolves and unicorns, he goes inside. Tugger can feed the horses. It's long since that Frank rigged something to that purpose. The other animals can wait a bit longer. He needs to phone Arthur.

"Pendragon Productions, Chris Kristofer speaking."

"Chris, Frank MacDonald. I need to speak with Arthur."

"Arthur Pendragon," the King's ringing baritone says a moment later. "How's the situation?"

"Bad," Frank says bluntly. "You might want to leave Chris on the line to save you from having to brief him later."

"That bad," Arthur says. There's a click, and the sound takes on the slightly hollow sound of a speaker setting. "I'm ready. Both Chris and Bill are with me."

Succinctly, Frank sums up his discoveries. The long silence on the other end tells him that his auditors fully understand the seriousness of his report.

"How," Arthur says, and it is evident that he is struggling to sound mild, "did Louhi manage to accumulate so much power without your noticing?"

"I'm not a wizard," Frank says. "She is. I fed her and cleaned her, but otherwise had little contact with her once she seemed settled into being a mouse. If she was hiding something from me, I'd never know."

"But what about . . ." The King pauses. "Wait. I think I understand. The Cats of Egypt and the Raven of Enderby, all of whom are magically inclined, have been away from the ranch for over a month now."

"And the less magical cats for at least ten days," Frank adds. "She may have grown bolder without them present."

Bill Irish chimes in. "Can you check her cage, find out if there's anything to indicate how she did this?"

"I can and will," Frank answers. "I can take this phone with me to that room. Meanwhile, I'm worried about Shahrazad. Can you contact the Changer?"

Arthur clears his throat awkwardly. "I'm afraid I can't. He's gone to Africa on some business for me. I've been meaning to tell you, but the last time we talked, the werewolf's murder drove everything else out of my mind."

"Africa?" Frank asks.

"Nigeria. Several of our people, including Eddie, have been out of touch, and there's been some strange windstorm. The government's denying visas, so I needed someone who could . . ."

"Right." Frank sighs. "Damn. I was hoping we could get him here in time to track her down. As I said before, my guess is that she went after Louhi with the griffin. If we could find her, we should find them."

"If this Wayne stole Frank's truck," Bill reminds, "you can report it to the police. They might find it—especially if you say that the thieves are dangerous, y'know, make up something about them assaulting you when they took the truck. You should be able to fake it."

"That's an idea," Arthur says slowly, "but we don't want to attract the police's attention. Who knows what Louhi might do? In the past, she's been capable of turning men into pigs when they annoy her. I'd hate to add another anomaly."

Frank agrees. "The police might also spot Shahrazad and the griffin. Also, if Louhi is aware that she is being followed, she might alert the police."

Bill clears his throat. "I hadn't thought of that. Still, she isn't going to say a mythological beast and a coyote are chasing her, is she?"

"No," Arthur says, "but she might weave a glamour so that the police would see them as something else—dangerous animals or something. I don't know what she can do, but she has been capable of malice in the past."

"Right," Bill says. "I'm new to this."

"Frank, I'll get Lovern to try to find them," Arthur promises. "Louhi may have some sort of shield up against scrying, but Shahrazad and the griffin won't."

Chris cuts in. "Your Majesty, Lovern is in Las Vegas. When Lilith called to say they'd found the satyrs, she said that he was exhausted and staying on."

"Locate him right away," Arthur commands. "Tell him to get back here and why. Bill will brief you later if there is anything more."

"Right."

"Is there anything more, Frank?" Arthur sounds hopeful.

"Well, I've been studying Louhi's cage. On the side of her wheel that faced the wall there are some complicated runes scratched into the plastic."

Arthur gives a low whistle. "A wheel with runes. That sounds like what we're looking for. Can you copy what it looks like or photo . . ."

Bill interrupts. "Why doesn't he just express mail the whole thing? That way Lovern can check it out personally."

"Great! The voice of the twentieth century speaks. Can you get it to us overnight, Frank?"

"Consider it done."

"I'll have you kept posted as things develop."

"Thanks. I'll do the same, though, to be honest, I hope there aren't any more developments."

"Me too, but I expect that that's too much to hope for. Thanks again, Frank. Keep a weather eye on the Head."

"Stinky Joe just showed up, and he's settling in to watch the Head. I think he's offended by the chaos in his kingdom."

"Him and me both," sighs King Arthur. "Him and me both."

¤◙¤

The air crackles around Shango as he looks down at the mess on his office floor. He is as full of barely restrained electricity as he is of barely restrained temper. Last night had been a cascade of bad news.

First, he had gone by the old Belgian factory where Anson had told him this Oya resided. He had planned to enter via the door on the roof, then kidnap this Oya and at least one of her human associates as hostage against her good behavior and cooperation.

He had the situation choreographed in his imagination and was looking forward to seeing the wind drop, to his armies moving forward shouting, "*Kabiesi!*", proclaiming him, not that fool of a mayor as ruler. It had been too long since he had been so hailed, but with the mayor's death—a thing he intended to arrange as soon as he had Oya securely in his keeping—he would be the natural successor.

But his plans had become ashes, for when he had made the laborious climb to the top of the factory and had eased open the rooftop door he found the place uninhabited. Sneaking down the stairs, he ghosted through the sleeping family who occupied the second floor, but though he looked down onto many sleeping faces, he did not find Oya, nor did he find any of the athanor.

He did find something that creased his brow with worry. One of the men had the same features as Taiwo, one of his tools, and thus must be Kehinde, Taiwo's twin. One of the women looked to be Aduke Idowu, Taiwo's wife. It troubled him that Oya had taken up residence with people so closely related to one of his tools. What did she know? What did she suspect?

Forgoing a hostage, for he had no idea who was dear to Oya and who was not, Shango went up to the roof again. He was preparing to climb down when he saw the white flash of gunfire and heard its fainter report, both coming from the direction of Regis's compound.

Cursing under his breath, he clambered to the ground, running so that he would be at home when the report of the disturbance was brought to him. He arrived only moments before the messenger and covered for his being up and fully dressed at a time when a respectable minister would be asleep by hollering at the messenger.

"See! You are so slow that I am awakened and have time to ready myself before you even drag your loathsome feet across my doorstep. Take a message to the chief of police!"

He scribbled the message, demanding that an elite squad be prepared for his use and that the off-duty men be awakened and ready for combat. The exhausted runner hurried off, and Shango took a few minutes to gather his favorite weapons, including a set of thunderstones. These he would use only as a last resort—for like any athanor he has learned to dread anomalies—but a burst of lightning from the sky had turned the battle for him more than once.

But when he met his elite squad and raced to Regis's compound, he was too late. Over half of Regis's guard was dead, both the night squad who had been on duty and those who had been awakened by the first shots and hurried to back up their fellows. Katsuhiro Oba was gone, as were Taiwo, Teresa, and Regis.

Shango spent a bloody hour searching building by building, room by room, turning over corpses to confirm for himself who was present and who was not. The Balogun did not have time either to mourn or to meditate on the ramifications of the night's activity. He barely managed to choke out appropriate responses to Shango's questions and to check off each of the dead on a roster he carried on his clipboard.

At last, leaving the Balogun in command, Shango returns to his house. Only after he has dealt with the host of panicked requests and reports that await him can he escape to his private office and consider what to do next. He can't decide whether to scream or rejoice when Regis steps from concealment behind a door and bows before him in insolent humility.

The Chief General Doctor is smeared with sewer filth, explaining how he had escaped the compound where so many had died in his defense.

"Hello, boss man," he says in broad pidgin accents. "And what for we doing now?"

"You fool!" Shango bellows. He forgets himself, forgets his plans, forgets how useful Regis could be in the future—both as a control on those superstitious Nigerians who will be ready to tremble before the God of Smallpox and as a researcher into new and more terrible biological weapons.

Forgetting all of this, Shango strikes his hands together. A bolt of lightning jolts out from where his hands meet and it hits on the carpet just in front of where Regis stands. The proximity of the electricity wipes the insolent grin from the human's face.

"*Kabiesi!*" Regis cries, falling flat to the floor, heedless of the burned spot in front of him. "I never knew! Forgive me!"

"That's better," Shango replies, but the air still crackles around him.

When the sun rises high, Shahrazad is ready enough to agree to the griffin's demand that they get to cover. Before this, she had hoped that any moment they would see the truck on the road ahead of them. She had envisioned how they would land on the bed of the truck, how she would break the little window in the back of the cab and reach in to stop Wayne from driving any farther.

She doesn't fear the mouse, for it is small and she has eaten many mice. It doesn't particularly bother her that this mouse might well be her half sister. She'd never liked Louhi.

However, they never catch up to the truck, and the griffin, though quite powerful, has grown tired. She has flown several hundred miles, carrying some twenty-five pounds of not-quite coyote. Moreover, she has not flown where people might see her for what she is in a long, long time. Although brighter than either eagle or lion, the griffin is still animal in her adherence to pattern and habit. The higher the sun rises, the slower she flies, until by midmorning she takes them down into the shelter of a copse of trees.

Once Shahrazad has stretched kinks out of muscles unaccustomed to the cramped posture she had maintained on the griffin's back, she shifts back into her familiar coyote form. The griffin can get plenty of water from the snow, but she cannot leave to hunt without risking detection.

Remembering how once, long, long ago, her father had hunted for her, Shahrazad assumes the responsibility for feeding her companion. It takes a lot of rabbits to satisfy the griffin, but there are plenty here, and, since there are no predators to speak of this near to a highway, Shahrazad finds them easier hunting than the canny creatures she had pursued on the Other Three Quarter's Ranch.

Gnawing on a leg bone from her own, much smaller, meal, Shahrazad tries to think where Louhi and Wayne might have gone. Respecting the griffin's greater age and experience, she whines a query. The griffin answers promptly:

"To Lovern. He is the only one who might be able to give her back her body."

"Lovern?" Shahrazad does not have an inordinate respect for the scrawny wizard. Her father had treated him as if he were some sort of joke, and she herself had encountered Lovern during a rather bad time for the wizard. However, the griffin is adamant.

"Lovern."

"Lovern belongs to Arthur," Shahrazad says, "but he has his own den, too. I've never been there, but it has been spoken of."

The griffin nods. "We cannot chase the truck. Let us go to Arthur when darkness falls. The way will be shorter if we do not need to follow these human roads."

"Do you know where Arthur lives?"

The griffin hunches her feathered shoulders in something like a shrug. "South. In a big city. You lived there. You will find it for us."

Shahrazad isn't certain that she can, but as she cannot think of a better plan, she agrees. They sleep side by side then, letting the short November day wheel past.

When twilight comes Shahrazad shifts herself into her hybrid form and climbs onto the griffin's back. This time when the eagle-puma rises into the air, she takes them south, toward the distant city of Albuquerque.

Man kann, was man will, wenn man nur will, was man kann.
(*We can do what we will if we only will to do what we can.*)

—GERMAN PROVERB

ADUKE STARES IN HORROR AT THE MAN SEATED IN ONE OF the chairs around Oya's conference table. At first she had thought it was Kehinde, that he had trespassed on the borders of Oya's territory, perhaps in eagerness to learn something of the folklore to which the elder often alluded. Kehinde's greed in such matters is enough to overcome common courtesy toward a hostess, and he has hinted once or twice that their strange landlady must know more than she is telling.

That Kehinde would trespass on their benefactrix shocks her enough, but when Oya gently explains to her that it is Taiwo, not Kehinde, who sits so slumped in the chair before her, Aduke feels her knees grow weak.

"It cannot be my husband," she protests. "He is in Lagos. No one has come into Monamona since Oya brought the wind, so this cannot be Taiwo."

"It is Taiwo," the man says, and raises his head for the first time. He looks terrible. Dressed only in once-stylish pajamas now sullied by his night's travel, he seems a boy dragged out of bed, not a grown man, and certainly not the confident young businessman who had courted her, winning her consent and even her love.

"Taiwo?" she echoes. "But how? If you have been in Monamona since the wind rose, why didn't you come to see me? Why haven't you answered my letters? Your mother," she says, aware even as she speaks that she is bordering on hysteria, "has wished to see her son!"

He sighs, a great shuddering thing, and meets her gaze.

"I was in Monamona on business, business that my boss did not wish to be known. There was no hope of secrecy if I came to see you. Even if you didn't talk, Mother would, or one of the sisters or husbands or children. So I stayed away."

Oya, seated at one end of the table, makes a tut-tutting sound. "Haven't you had enough of lying, Taiwo?"

He looks sharply at the older woman. Clearly, in his focus on Aduke, he had forgotten that she and his strange captors are present as well. With this realization, he shrivels further, but tries to maintain his bravado.

"It is the truth," he maintains.

"But only the smallest part of that truth," Oya persists. There is no kindness in the gaze she turns on him. "You have been playing with dangerous people, thinking yourself the great man while your wife misses you."

Anson pauses in his meal. Since their return he has been eating steadily, matched in his voraciousness by the strange white man with the long black hair they call "Changer." Aduke notes that no one explains his presence, any more than they explain the presence of the wild-eyed woman who sleeps now in Oya's own bed. With what she is learning, Aduke isn't certain she wants to know.

"And, Taiwo," Anson says, "those games are ending. We want help from you, help that will finish your masters' reign of terror as swiftly as possible."

From him, the words do not sound melodramatic, but merely a statement of facts. Aduke sees Taiwo cringe, and with a sinking heart realizes that the accusations are true.

"What have you been doing?" she says softly.

He turns to look at her, speaking as if they are alone, not with a half dozen other people.

"I thought I was building a place for us in this new Nigeria of ours," Taiwo answers. "I thought I was making connections that might someday see me a national minister and you one of the first ladies in the land. By the time I realized that my employers were dirtier, more dangerous people than I had ever suspected, I was in so deep there was no getting out."

Oya pushes a glass of cold lemonade to him. "You're telling the truth now, Taiwo. Keep telling. There may be salvation for you in helping fix what you have broken."

Taiwo doesn't even look at her. "I killed our baby, Aduke."

She gasps, staring at him, gone beyond horror into dull shock. Oya's hand on her shoulder is no comfort. She feels so desolate she cannot even manage a single word, but Taiwo continues unprompted.

"Did you ever wonder how Baby caught the smallpox—especially in Lagos, where you kept so much to yourself?" Taiwo says. Despite the lemonade he has sipped, his voice is rusty. "I gave it to him. Remember how you and I had a series of vaccinations—the ones I told you were a fringe benefit of my new position?"

Aduke nods.

"Actually, they were to preserve us from the smallpox. I demanded shots for all my family, and my request was granted, but they wouldn't give me anything for the baby," Taiwo shrugs, "so I went into Regis's lab and I stole a vaccination. There were two cabinets in his lab, one labeled 'Live' and the other labeled 'Killed.' Of course, I took my vial from the one labeled 'Live,' for I wanted the baby to live.

"As I learned later, I was a fool. What I had taken was no vaccine. It was the live virus itself. By the time I had learned this, I knew why Baby had caught the smallpox. When he died, I could not bear to face you, so even when business brought me to Monamona I stayed away."

Aduke wants to hate Taiwo for this, and finds that she feels only pity. She can see him as he must have been, arrogant and confident, stealing the vaccine, administering it to Baby. When Baby had fallen ill, Taiwo must have thought at first that he had incurred the curse of the King of Hot Water. Only later had he realized that the only curse had been his own pride.

No, she does not hate him, but when she searches for the love she had known for her husband it is gone as if it had never been. She realizes that the man she had thought was Taiwo had been an illusion as insubstantial as one of the bush ghosts in Kehinde's tales.

When Aduke still does not speak, Taiwo labors on, "In my grief and shame, I behaved like a man who didn't care what his ancestors thought of him. I connived at murder and kidnapping. I indulged in rape and petty bullying. I became as great a monster as those who have been called my 'masters'—but they did not make me evil. When I was drawn to them, I was merely ambitious. It was the shame of killing my own firstborn son that made me evil."

Aduke scrubs tears she had not realized she was weeping from her cheeks and straightens beneath Oya's hand. Grief will only drown her. There is redemption in action, and Oya has shown her that she is not without resources of her own.

"Taiwo," Aduke says to her husband, "Oya and I are going to finish your masters, whatever it takes. Will you tell us what you know of them and their plans? Consider it an offering to our dead son's ghost, then maybe his spirit will trust enough in the living to be born again."

Taiwo's answer is a quiet "Yes," but the pain in his dark eyes shows her that only now has he realized that they are finished. Aduke is appalled to realize that he had believed that somehow he would still hold her to him. She shakes her head in dismay, and says one word:

"Idowu."

As if her reminder that she was born with power greater than even that of twins is a command, slowly Taiwo begins to speak. Soon Oya and her allies are gathered round the council table, taking notes, asking questions, planning a kidnapping—and perhaps a murder or two—of their own.

¤◙¤

Louhi has never been to the Academy, indeed she barely knows of its existence, but she has been to Pendragon Estates. Even if Lovern is not there already, there he will come, for in crisis the wizard will be at his king's side. And wasn't she a crisis?

If a mouse could smile, she would have smiled then, but the twitching of her whiskers that substitutes vanishes almost as quickly as it occurs. She and Wayne have not traveled as quickly as she could have wished. Indeed, the five-hundred-or-so-mile drive could have been accomplished in a night, bringing them to Arthur's doorstep before Frank would have awakened from the binding ice of sleep.

However, her tool is weak, muddled both by Frank's drugs and by wounds inflicted by her bitch half sister. She does not believe that her control of him is sufficient to guide him through driving at night. Therefore, once they are well away from the Other Three Quarter's Ranch and the roads show some traffic, she has him park at a rest stop.

While Wayne snores, dreaming of her, Louhi meditates, trying to restore her power. She would have liked to have her wheel, but that would have meant bringing her cage as well, and she is finished with cages.

They arrive in Albuquerque after nightfall the next evening. To Louhi's ire, the journey has taken almost a full turning of the clock. Once upon a time, she would have thought this good journeying for such a distance over such terrain—after all the Rocky Mountains had been in her way. Now, though, she has been spoiled by modern conveniences and feels only impatient.

"So we change as the world changes around us," she thinks, and is amused by the thought, for she has always considered herself the Changer's daughter though he has done little enough for her.

At her prompting, Wayne presses the intercom button alongside the gate to Pendragon Estates. A male voice, but not one Louhi knows, emanates through the speaker:

"Yes?"

"Wayne Watkins. Let me come in."

There is a pause. Doubtless the man answering the door has gone to report to King and wizard. Reply comes in the form of the gate swinging open—like magic, though what moves it is nothing more than electronics.

Wayne follows a driveway whose twistings, like the landscaping that fringes them, are meant to conceal the hacienda from the road. In late autumn, following the first hard frost, this is less effective than it had been in September, when Louhi made her last visit. Still, all even the most nosy could see are the solid two-story walls of the inward-looking house.

Louhi suspects that Arthur will be waiting for her in his office. Inside the house is more secure than outside, both from prying eyes and from other forces. So confident is she that the confrontation will take place inside that she is completely unprepared when something very large and very solid rocks the back of the pickup truck.

Had she been so equipped, she might even have screamed, but mice squeak, they do not scream. Wayne is reacting to the new stimulus by driving erratically, weaving so that the front end of the truck scrapes against the chamisa and sagebrush planted along the driveway.

"Stop!" Louhi snaps, and the man hears a word, not a mouse sound. "Drive slowly. Keep to the middle of the road."

Barely has she finished giving her orders when there is a thump against the small window at the back of the pickup truck's cab. Scurrying around, her tail raised for balance, Louhi sees something rather like a fist hit the window. It bounces off, but when it returns it holds a rock, and the window shatters.

Louhi curses the limitations of her mouse sight. Everything is so large that she has trouble gaining perspective, and she is so panicked by this attack that she cannot sort out the smells suddenly flooding through the broken window. Unlike the Changer, she prefers to change others rather than change herself. Even her enforced tenure in mouse form has not taught her much about the language of scent.

A long hairy arm shoves through the broken window, groping after her. Louhi leaps from Wayne's shoulder to the seat, bouncing uncomfortably when she hits the vinyl cover. Finding it difficult to get a grasp on the smooth surface, Louhi slides, then manages to recover. She is climbing up

Wayne's coat to the safety of his pocket when there is another crash of breaking glass, this time followed by a frustrated bark.

Instantly, Louhi realizes who is after her. But how had the little bitch gotten here so quickly? A dozen possibilities flood the witch's mind, and she dismisses them all. How does not matter. Why Shahrazad had pursued her is obvious. What the coyote will do when she has caught Louhi is also terrifyingly plain.

Mechanically, Wayne has continued driving. Louhi senses his confusion when he comes to the top of the driveway. She frantically orders him to park the truck, then to get them both out of it. He is following her orders when Shahrazad finishes breaking the window. A triumphant howl precedes her as she dives through the opening, all white fangs and terrible, grasping claws.

Louhi discovers mice *can* scream.

¤▣¤

"Shahrazad, no!"

Arthur feels like an absolute idiot, yelling at the thing in the back of the truck as if she is still a puppy chewing on his carpet, but he doesn't have time to think of anything clever. The Changer's daughter has thrust herself through the back window of Frank's pickup truck and is scrabbling with long-fingered, hairy hands after something small and white that darts back and forth on the seat.

The man standing by the open driver's side door of the truck looks dazed. Arthur has too often seen people suffering from sorcerous control to give him more than a passing glance. He barrels past the man, still shouting, the scene before him lit like a stage by the truck's dome light.

He hears a shrill shriek as Shahrazad's hand closes on the white mouse without undue gentleness.

"Shahrazad, no!" the King shouts again, reaching for the mouse.

The coyote head snaps at him and snarls, lips peeling back from young, white teeth, every hair on her hackles bristling out, stiff and angry.

Gods, she's grown! Arthur thinks inanely even as he is grasping for the wrist above the hand holding the terrified mouse. *She's as big as a wolf now! Where the hell is my backup?*

Shahrazad growls in defiant fury, her jaws snapping just inches from the King's face, close enough that he feels her saliva splash his skin. Lucky for him, she seems to have forgotten her free hand, for she could rake him with her claws.

"Down, Shahrazad!" he yells. "Down!"

Shahrazad doesn't seem inclined to give way, and Arthur is resigning himself to getting bitten when several things happen almost simultaneously.

A shrill eagle's scream cuts through the night and Shahrazad yelps in pain, dropping the mouse. At almost the same moment, a globe of pale green light encircles the mouse. Recognizing it as a warding spell, Arthur doesn't hesitate to grab the fleeing rodent, getting a firm grip on her long, pink tail.

When he backs out of the pickup truck, the King glowers at his wizard. "What took you so long?"

Lovern, who looks distinctly the worse for wear, glowers back. "Your big backside was in my way. I had to run around the truck to take aim from the other side. I also paused long enough to convince the griffin that stopping Shahrazad was a good idea—and you could thank me for that. You almost ended up on the punishing end of the griffin's talons, not the damn coyote!"

Arthur nods, covering his slight embarrassment by getting a better grip on the mouse. Anticipating his need, Chris Kristofer trots up, a coffee tin with holes punched in the plastic lid in his hand.

"Drop her in here, Your Majesty," he says. "I got this ready when Frank called to tell us what we were up against. The metal should dampen her magic at least somewhat."

The King complies. "Good show, Chris."

Out of the corner of his eye, Arthur notes that Bill Irish has taken custody of the dazed Wayne—and is leading him toward the hacienda. Useful men, these two humans, full of initiative.

Most of his attention, however, is on the back of the pickup truck, where Shahrazad crouches, watching them from beneath the shelter of the griffin's arched neck.

She is much smaller than she had seemed when snapping and snarling within the confines of the truck's cab, hardly larger than a toddling child. The yellow eyes that study him are angry, not abashed, and her hackles are still raised. Arthur looks at the hands she rests on the edge of the truck bed for a long moment before turning to Lovern.

"I guess this answers one question, at least. She *can* shift shape. How long until Frank gets here?"

"Probably not until morning," Lovern replies. "He had to convince the werewolves it was safe for a couple of them to come down and guard the ranch."

"Great." Arthur shrugs and moves cautiously toward the truck. "Hi, Shahrazad. Want to come inside with us?"

She growls and snaps at him, but the griffin purls something deep in her throat. Arthur waits, fascinated, as the two creatures talk. At last, her hackles receding to just a faint accent of her ruff, Shahrazad gives a very human shrug. The transformation is so swift that Arthur almost misses it, but when she jumps from the truck, she is a coyote once more.

"There's room for you, too," Arthur says to the griffin. "You can either fly over the roof and into the courtyard or come in the front door."

This time Shahrazad seems to be doing the convincing and after a few more interchanges of bark, growl, and shrill, the griffin flaps to the ground and follows their small procession into the hacienda.

¤◘¤

Finding Shango takes over twenty-four hours, but early in the evening of the day following that on which Taiwo had made his confession, the Changer pads silently into Oya's conference room.

Eddie notes that, despite continuing as a "white man," the Changer looks rather good in the loose traditional robes that Oya had procured for him. He wonders if the Changer might have made some subtle adaptations to his build to accommodate the clothing. He grins at the idea. Certainly someone as ancient as the Changer is immune to such human vanity. But then is vanity merely a human trait?

Further speculation on this matter is stalled when the Changer, reaching across the table for the pitcher of heavily sugared iced tea, says economically:

"I've found him."

Eddie blinks. "Shango?"

"And someone who should be Regis."

"Where?" Eddie holds up his hand. "No, wait. Let me call the others. There's no need for you to report twice."

The Changer nods, settles down at one end of the table, and methodically begins consuming slices of baked yam. That's the only indication Eddie gets of how hard and how long the Changer had been searching.

Recalling the others takes several hours since the Changer isn't the only one who has been out collecting data, but arrangements had been made for them to check in at various points. Aduke's nieces and nephews are all too happy to earn a *naira* for running errands.

"Didn't you ever consider," Eddie teases Oya when she returns, "that taking out the phones would inconvenience us as well as Shango?"

She smiles back at him. "I had no control over what happened to the telephones. The wind has her own ideas."

The Changer, who has said nothing since his brief report to Eddie, nods. "Naturals do have wills of their own, a thing too many forget."

Eddie looks at the other, expecting to see one of his faint grins, but the Changer looks serious. He is remembering how very old the Changer is when the ancient continues, speaking to Oya:

"Have you considered that the wind may not wish to release the city? You have given her recognition that has not been hers since men stopped worshiping the elements."

Oya seems calm, but Eddie, who has known her in many lives, notices that she is gently scraping the edge of the table with one fingernail and realizes that she is anxious.

"I summoned the wind," Oya answers the Changer, "and I expect my power should be enough to disperse it."

"That may be too much to expect," is all he replies.

By common consent, the subject is dropped when Aduke arrives, followed thereafter by Anson, Dakar, and Katsuhiro. The latter two take seats at opposite ends of the table. Dakar is arrogantly smug, Katsuhiro aggravated. He hasn't much liked the fact that his appearance keeps him from doing any scouting, but has steadily refused to allow himself to be disguised as anything but Japanese.

"The Changer," Eddie says, calling the meeting to order with nothing more than a glance, "has located Shango. Changer?"

"I would have found him more quickly," the Changer says apologetically, "if I had realized sooner that he had reverted to 'type."

The athanor knows that the Changer means "to archetype," but Aduke looks vaguely confused.

"When that thought occurred to me," the Changer continues, "I started checking power plants. I found him at a secondary electricity-generating facility on the edge of town. A man who matches the description of Regis is with him. Moreover, the facility is heavily guarded."

Dakar nods, his voice a deep rumble. "Scuttlebutt among the militia and police is that the mayor expects an internal coup. Therefore, all the sensitive points within the city are being guarded."

"A good excuse," Anson says, appreciative of cleverness even from an opponent, "since we know from Taiwo that there *is* a coup planned, only the mayor is one of those planning the coup and that it is to be against the central government, not within Monamona."

"Plans can change," Dakar says, "and I do not think that Shango ever meant the mayor to last long as president of Nigeria. The troops are quite captivated by him. I have heard his salute *Kabiesi!* on their lips. Rumors circulate freely that he is indeed Shango reborn, not merely the minister of electricity."

Dakar seems torn between disgust and admiration at this last, and no wonder. Like Shango, he had once been hailed as a god by these people, but unlike Shango, he had not attempted to regain his deific stature once European influence made it dangerous to retain.

Again Eddie reflects on the strange psychology of the athanor, so many of whom crave both power and privacy. Arthur has managed both by setting himself up as king of the athanor, but there can only be one such king. He doubts that Shango will be the last to interpret the Accord's more permissive view on interacting with humanity as an invitation to set up as gods.

"Many guards?" Katsuhiro asks.

"At least forty," the Changer says. "As I scouted, I wondered at the number of troops I saw."

Dakar rumbles, "Many are 'reserve,' not regulars. That's why I had no trouble inserting myself into conversations. The regular Monamona police force is about what you would expect in a city of this size. The reserves, though . . . By my estimate, they are at least triple the size of the police force and among them is where I found the greatest concentration of those who wear Shango's badge."

"Shango's," Eddie says, checking to make certain he understands. "Not Minister Omomomo's?"

"That's right," Dakar agrees. "I had not thought clearly about it before . . ."

"You wouldn't," Katsuhiro mutters, but he does softly enough that Dakar can choose to ignore it. To Eddie's pleasant surprise Dakar does, continuing as if there had been no interruption.

"It confirms Taiwo's story that a coup had been being planned before Oya raised the wind. The wind has just moved up the timetable."

Oya looks relieved until the Changer adds:

"The wind may have done more than move up the timetable. I circled the city before I entered, and there is quite a force out there. Among the encampments, I saw a heavily guarded sector. No one guards against a bird, so I flew in and took a closer look. There are several national ministers present—and the president himself. If Shango is not stopped and his forces dispersed before the wind falls, then a coup attempt is inevitable."

Anson shakes his head in mock dismay. "And you didn't think to mention who waits outside for us?"

"Until now," the Changer replies levelly, "it didn't seem important." Then he grins.

Eddie shakes his head and refocuses the meeting. "Now that we know where Shango is we can plan how to go after him."

"*Him*," Anson stresses softly. "I have no desire to kill men whose only crime is that they defend someone they believe is at least a great leader, if not a great god."

Nods around the table answer this. Eddie notices that Aduke has full control of herself now, amazing in a woman who has suffered so many shocks so close together. Oya has chosen well.

"Our choices then," he continues, "are sending in an assassin or luring Shango out. Let me add," he says, raising his hand for silence, "that the Accord's policy against assassination has not changed."

He stares hard at Anson and the Changer as he says this, but the first merely gives him an innocent smile and the second his usual unreadable calm.

"So we don't send in an assassin," Katsuhiro prompts. "Then we need to get him out and, presumably, subdue him sufficiently that he can be assessed before the Accord."

Eddie nods. "That would be ideal."

Aduke raises her hand. "Eddie, should I be present for this? I am not unaware of the glances people have been giving me. If I am restraining your ability to speak plainly, then I should leave."

Oya frowns, but before she can speak Eddie says, "Aduke, someone providing a little restraint is not a bad idea, believe me. The question is, do you want to hear things that you must realize by now will need to be kept secret?"

Aduke looks so serious that his heart aches for her. She is little more than a child herself, just a college girl, really, who has been forced to confront death, betrayal, and political intrigue within the span of a few weeks. Why should she choose to face more? Her answer surprises him, for he had expected her to gracefully retreat.

"I have helped raise Oya's wind," she says proudly. "I

have heard the names of old gods used in familiar speech. My place is with you people, if you will have me."

Eddie looks around the table. "Any objections?"

No one even looks doubtful. Anson appoints himself spokesman for the rest.

"No objections. Let the woman stay. She has already proven her wisdom in offering to depart."

"Then," Eddie says, "Aduke, we appreciate your concern, but we welcome your help and advice. We must ask, however, that you never speak of the more fantastic elements we raise."

Aduke nods solemnly. "I promise. May I ask one question?"

"Yes."

"What is this 'Accord' you have mentioned?"

"It is the set of laws that governs the group to which all six of us belong." He glances at the Changer, but the Changer gives a slight nod indicating that he does not mind being mentioned as if he is a signatory, though he is not. "One of its cardinal tenets is that we will not—unless there is no other choice—kill a member of our own company."

"And Shango is also one of you?"

"He is. Nothing he has done, thus far, has broken the Accord, although he has stretched certain new provisions rather farther than many will like."

Aduke nods. "I'm glad to learn that this Accord of yours does not condone mass murder."

Eddie forbears from mentioning that it doesn't precisely forbid it. Aduke will be more comfortable if she doesn't know just how little restraint the Accord puts on its members' interactions with humanity.

Katsuhiro says impatiently. "Now that we've settled this, can we move on? The night grows no younger."

Anson pokes him. "Stop fussing. I tink it no becoming in a samurai, eh?"

Glad that he didn't need to chide the Japanese, especially when he's in a bad mood, Eddie rubs his five o'clock shadow.

"Now, kidnapping Shango will not be easy if he stays inside that electrical plant. It can be done, but there will most certainly be casualties. Therefore, we need to lure him out."

"Send Kehinde in," Aduke suggests. "He looks just like Taiwo, and Taiwo is trusted by the minister."

Eddie nods. "That's not a bad idea. However, it would mean taking Kehinde into our confidence. I'm not prepared to do that."

"Oh." Aduke looks abashed. "I hadn't thought of that. He would be easy enough to bribe. I know he longs to hear some of the stories he is certain Oya has. He would do anything for that."

"Still," Eddie says kindly, "I would not like to put an innocent scholar at risk. However, at least two of our company are masters of disguise. Anson? Changer?"

He notes Aduke's surprise when he names the white man, and admires her restraint when she does not question.

"My Yoruban," the Changer says, "is adequate but somewhat archaic."

"I could do it," Anson says. "I'd enjoy it, actually. If Taiwo remains repentant, I should be able to get him to tell me enough for me to pass as him."

Aduke is obviously bursting with a desire to ask how Anson can disguise himself as a man far shorter and with a heavier build. Twinkling at her, Anson waggles a finger.

"Eddie did say that I am a master of disguise, did he not? Have faith."

Aduke smiles. "I do, Eshu."

"Where would be the best place for you to lure him?" Eddie continues. "Changer?"

"The electrical plant is at the edge of the city," the Changer replies. "Normally, it would be somewhat isolated, since there are only factories and such around it. However, with the military cordon around the city, the area is swarming with men."

"Even at night?" Katsuhiro asks.

"I suspect so," the Changer says. "I can check when we are further along in our planning. Dakar, do you have any idea what guard shifts are?"

"I don't know for the electrical plant in particular," Dakar replies.

He has not touched anything alcoholic since the promise

of military action began, and Eddie is astonished by the difference in him. He makes a mental note to tell Arthur that the best way to keep from having trouble with Dakar would be to give him more steady work of this kind, rather than the occasional troubleshooting/punishment mission.

"However," Dakar continues, "they are using six-hour shifts right now: six to noon, noon to six, six to midnight, midnight to six."

"Sounds like a charm of some sort," Katsuhiro mutters.

"What time is it now?" Eddie says, ignoring him.

"Eight," Oya supplies.

"Then we could move in after the midnight shift is on," Eddie says. "That gives us the cover of darkness and a potentially tired group of guards."

"It worked last night," Dakar protests, "and for that reason, I don't think it will work today. Shango must know who made that attack on Regis's compound. He's going to be shitting bricks tonight. We won't catch him asleep, neither him nor his guards. They'll be waiting for trouble."

"Good point." Anson shrugs. "So when then?"

Aduke raises her hand. "In the morning, when the streets are filled with people going to market. Soldiers won't want to fire weapons, and civilians will not want to get involved in other people's business."

"Clever girl," Anson says admiringly. "She's right. Moreover, a visit from 'Taiwo' will seem more normal then. We could even send a note tonight indicating that Taiwo hopes to sneak to Shango later. He'll spend all night asking himself questions and when Taiwo arrives, Shango won't be able to refuse to see him."

The Changer nods. "I'll carry the note when I go scout out the best place for us to take Shango so that we can restrain him."

Dakar gets up from his seat. "And I will go learn if the guard shifts at the electrical plant are the same. Perhaps Obasan can work out how to restrain someone who can throw lightning. I believe he and Shango share some talents in that area."

Katsuhiro brightens at the prospect of making a useful contribution. "I will do that. Tell me, how do we get Shango out of the country without drawing unwelcome attention to ourselves?"

The Changer smiles. "If everything else is under control, I can send a message to my brother. He can certainly arrange for transportation that will not be questioned."

Eddie bangs an imaginary gavel on the table. "Then this meeting is adjourned until we have more data." He turns to Oya, who has been far too silent, and speaks to her in a lowered voice. "Oya, are you going to be able to lower the wind when we need to get out of here?"

She frowns. "Aduke and I will look into that. The Changer has raised some interesting points."

Eddie sighs, noting from the others' expressions that they have overheard, but that since he did not make the issue public, they will hold their questions for now. That won't last, but he's grateful for it now.

"I was afraid of that," he says.

For a fleeting moment, he wishes he were back in Albuquerque, where the problems are little things, like wondering if sasquatches can go to rock concerts or satyrs sing and dance. Then he pushes that lovely thought aside and goes to make certain that Anson is not outclevering himself in the note he is composing under the Changer's indifferent eye.

Love your enemies. It makes them so damn mad.

—P.D. EAST

THE MORNING FOLLOWING SHAHRAZAD AND LOUHI'S arrival in Albuquerque, Chris Kristofer watches Ian Lovern pace back and forth in front of the King's desk. Chris, sitting discreetly in a corner, his laptop open, ready to take notes or send messages at the King's command, thinks the wizard looks much more invigorated than he had when he had arrived at the Albuquerque airport.

Just as Chris had been the one to locate him, calling casino after casino, then bullying a staff member to check the card tables, so he had been the one to meet the wizard, to brief him on the situation, to run a few errands for him.

When he had arrived, Lovern had looked so tired that Chris doubted he could be any help. A meal or two and time away from the debilitating metal frame of the aircraft had helped, but when Wayne and Louhi had arrived, he had still been worn—so worn that he had not detected the lurking presence of Shahrazad and the griffin.

The estate's wards only cover the buildings, not the sprawling acreage surrounding them, but from what Chris had learned, if Lovern had been at his best, he would have been able to sense the newcomers.

All of which makes his transformation into vigor all the more astonishing. Tense and excited, the wizard badgers the King.

"What has Louhi done wrong?" he asks for the third or fourth time. "That's all I want to know."

Arthur sighs. "As we have discussed before, her controlling the human Wayne Watkins is against the policies of the Accord. I know, I know"—he holds up his hand to forestall Lovern's interruption—"Louhi is not a member of the Accord. We ourselves ruled her out of Accord as punishment for her role as Sven Trout's accomplice in the doings last September. However, her manipulation of the human has led to the death of two athanor: the werewolf, Lupé, and the son of the Raven of Enderby."

"Dark-Feather," Chris provides helpfully.

Arthur nods. "Those two deaths are on her head—and after the losses we suffered in September, Lupé's death is one that Harmony can ill afford."

With undiminished enthusiasm, Lovern surges back into the argument.

"But we don't know for certain that Louhi was responsible for the deaths. Yes, she may have drawn this Wayne Watkins to her, but we have no proof that she commanded him to kill."

"However," Arthur says, "if she had not drawn him to her, had not provided the protection under which he moved onto the OTQ land, he could not have gotten past Frank's guardians to do his damage."

"We don't know that!" Lovern protests.

"None of Frank's charges has died on his own land from anything other than natural causes," Arthur counters, "in all the time he has owned the OTQ. I think that statistics are in Frank's favor."

Lovern remains defiant. "I'd say he was due for some bad luck."

"The 'bad luck,' " Arthur replies coolly, "was that he was kind enough to take Louhi into his house."

Lovern changes tactics. "He wouldn't have had to take her into his house if she hadn't been transformed into a mouse."

"True."

"And that transformation was unauthorized by the Accord."

"True again."

"And even then," Lovern persists, "no one made him take her in. She could have been set free."

"From the earliest reports that Frank sent me," Arthur says, his patience wearing thin at last, "Louhi and the Head both were little better than automata for the first several weeks of their transformation. Without his protection, they would have been eaten by the first cat who found them."

Chris is startled by a rough-edged feminine voice coming from one of the other chairs.

"Most certainly, they would have," agrees Purrarr, queen of the Cats of Egypt. "We hunted most enthusiastically after Sven Trout, and many a rat was eaten in the days that followed his escape. A mouse is even easier prey."

Lovern glowers at the cat. "Who invited you in here?"

"No one," Purrarr says equably around licks to her tail tip. "They say a cat may look at a king. I wanted to look."

"And listen!"

"And listen," she agrees, sitting up to paw at her whiskers. "Why did you ask for us to be brought here if you didn't want our input?"

"Your magic is useful," Lovern replies shortly. "I wanted you here in case I needed to draw on your support."

Purrarr stares at him from unblinking eyes. "We are not amulets to be drawn on at your will, Ian Lovern. We will have our say in how our magic is used."

"Everything," Lovern mutters, "is a goddamned democracy these days!"

Chris swallows a laugh. The more he sees of athanor government, the more it seems like poorly controlled anarchy to him. Remembering Demetrios's e-mail report of the satyrs' adventure, he has to swallow another chuckle. Then he feels a sudden chill. What had happened in Las Vegas is only funny because Lovern located the satyrs before, say, the hotel had grown unhappy with their antics and called in the local police. What if they hadn't been found?

Arthur is saying, "Lovern, you have tried long enough to convince me that Louhi is guiltless. Accept that I will not agree. However, you have raised a question in my mind. Why did she come here? Why did she break out of Frank's keeping rather than merely inform him that she was unhappy being a mouse?"

"I"—Lovern hesitates—"I haven't asked her. I wanted to straighten this out with you before I did."

"Then," Arthur replies, rising from his desk and stretching, "I think we should ask her. Purrarr . . ."

"Yes, Arrthurrr."

"Will you and your vanity provide security against Louhi's escape if we take her out of her coffee tin?"

"Delighted."

"Then let us convene in . . ." Arthur frowns, considering. Chris takes the hint.

"Bill and I could have one of the larger conference rooms set up in time for a meeting right after lunch."

"Good. We need a big room if the griffin and Swansdown are to be present, and I'd prefer that everyone who wishes to do so be present. Otherwise, we run the risk of being accused of passing secret judgments."

"Consider it done, sir."

Lovern tries to speak, but Arthur waves his hand. "Enough, my wizard, enough. I need time to clear my head. Chris?"

"Yes, Arthur?"

"Any word from Eddie or the Changer?"

"None yet. I'll stop to check the e-mail on my way to get Bill."

"Thank you." Arthur stands, dismissing the meeting. As they file out, the King saves a gracious nod for Chris. "You're doing very well, you know."

Chris grins. "Someday, I'll even get used to talking cats and to griffins arriving out of nowhere."

"I doubt it," Arthur says ruefully. "I don't think I've ever grown accustomed to it, and I've had a lot longer to try."

Anson A. Kridd is feeling very good.

This trip has not been as much fun as he had hoped it

would be. He'd been looking forward to taking dear Eddie out of himself, to get him back to those irresponsible days when he'd been just Enki-dinki-dinki-du, wildman of the Sumerian plains. Of course, Anson hadn't known Eddie then, but that was part of his reason for wanting to get to know him that way now.

But he doesn't want to think about that at this moment. He's cool and clean in one of Taiwo's suits. (The Changer, bless his furry little hide, had defied anomaly and gone to get him one from Taiwo's room at Regis's compound). His mind is full of information he'd gotten from a long interview or two with Taiwo. Slipping from sunbeam to shadow on the street behind him are Dakar and Katsuhiro. They're so busy watching him and not being seen themselves that they don't notice the fourth member of their little parade.

Funny, those two, always looking for a fight, always needing a fight, and deep down inside as good as gold and far, far nicer than he himself is. He has seen too much to be really nice.

Eshu, the woman Oya had called him, and while this is not the time for that name, Anson really does identify with Eshu, trickster god, messenger god, bringer of what they got coming to those who got it coming. The people of Monamona have been sacrificing to the old gods of Yorubaland, and every sacrifice sets aside a portion for Eshu.

Anson figures they've got a big return coming to them.

Arriving at the electrical plant, Anson glances toward the roof. A dove sitting up on the edge bobs a few times and makes a soft, purling noise. Anson doesn't speak dove, but he doesn't need a translation to know that the Changer is saying: "Shango's here. Regis is here. Have fun."

Anson likes the idea of the Changer saying that last. Most of the athanor see the ancient as dour, but Anson suspects that the Changer has a sense of humor, one shaped and molded by all the centuries he has spent as various animals, but Anson doesn't doubt that it is there. The Changer loves, and love is impossible without a little sense of humor.

Swaggering to a side door, Anson motions aside the two big Yorubans who frame the entrance. They're dressed in khaki trousers, khaki shirts, khaki socks, black boots and belts. Shango's lightning bolt is drawn on an armband with red marker.

The slightly broader of the two blocks Anson by the simple expedient of stepping directly in front of the door.

"Who are you?" he demands.

"My name is my own business," Anson says haughtily. "I am here to see the minister."

"We have been told to let no one in," the soldier replies.

"Then I am no one," Anson answers, before he realizes that this would be out of character for self-important young Taiwo. "I am an intimate associate of the minister. My name is Taiwo Fadaka."

The two soldiers exchange glances. Anson presses his point. "And the minister is waiting for me."

"One moment," the spokesman says reluctantly.

Anson expects him to depart, leaving his fellow on guard, but all he does is knock slowly four times. A voice, slightly muffled by the thickness of the door, calls, "Yes?"

"A guest for the minister. On the list."

"Let him pass then."

Inside, Anson is hustled along utilitarian corridors to an equally utilitarian office. Probably, he thinks, the plant manager's office on quieter days. Shango sits at a metal desk, Regis stands in a corner to his left and slightly, but only slightly, behind.

Anson does not waste time. As soon as the door has closed behind him, he widens his eyes and lowers his voice.

"Minister," he begins, then he glances at Regis, stops, looks uncertain. This should be convincing. Taiwo had told him freely about his recent problems with Regis. "I need to speak with you—privately."

Shango hesitates.

"I have a message only for your ears."

Shango still remains silent, and Regis stirs, looking cocky, certain of his high place in Shango's esteem.

"I was told to tell you one word if you were unwilling to hear me," Anson presses, glad that Taiwo is such a conniver.

"One word?" Shango cocks an eyebrow, and Regis sniggers. "One word?"

Anson nods solemnly.

"Then say your magic word," Shango orders, breaking down as Anson had known he would. Shango has many virtues, but like most storm gods, patience is not one of them.

"Athanor," Anson replies, speaking it carefully as if it is a newly learned, meaningless sound.

"Who gave you this word!" Shango demands.

"That is part of the message."

"Tell me the rest!"

"Only if we are alone."

Shango glances at Regis. "Leave us."

Regis's smugness melts from him. He looks hurt and offended. Anson is pleased. The word had been chosen to serve two purposes. The first was to prompt Shango to hold a private conference. The second was to test whether or not Regis was an athanor. Had he been so, doubtless Shango would have insisted that he stay, perhaps even revealed who he was. Regis's dismissal confirms what Anson had already suspected. Regis is not athanor and, therefore, unprotected.

"Leave you?" Regis bleats.

"Step outside until I hear what this stubborn puppy has to say," Shango says, his tone barely conciliatory. "I'll summon you back immediately."

Regis scowls but does as he is told. Then Anson makes a great production of sidling close to Shango and speaking his message in a whisper.

"The Japanese gave me that word. He demands that you meet with him at the Grove of the Gods. Otherwise, although he will still reserve his revenge on you . . ."

Anson pauses, as if temporarily forgetting a memorized message. He waits until he has the pleasure of seeing Shango fidget, then he goes on, "I mean, he will personally take his revenge on you but he will also report your doings to something he called an Accord. He said to remind you that this Accord is rather sour about kidnapping these days."

"Is that all?" Shango demands.

"Basically. If you go, he's willing to deal with you personally. If you don't, he's going to ruin your reputation as well."

"He won't kill me," Shango says, as if speaking to himself, "not if he wants the Accord's favor."

"The Japanese said nothing about killing you," Anson replies, "but he insists that you come to him."

"But the Grove of the Gods is such a public place!" Shango protests.

"All the more reason," Anson coaxes smoothly, "to believe that he does not plan to kill you."

Shango spends the better part of the next five minutes considering his options, muttering to himself, and finally removing from a cabinet in one corner of the office an ornate double-bladed axe and a beaded-leather pouch.

Anson recognizes the axe as Shango's personal weapon, the equivalent of Katsuhiro's sword Kusanagi, but he imagines that Taiwo would be a bit confused.

"You're not bringing that, are you?" he asks, carefully phrasing his words so that if Taiwo has been shown the axe sometime in the past Anson's imposture will not be revealed.

"I am," Shango says shortly. "Tell Regis to be prepared to attend on me, then fetch one of the long raincoats from the locker in the front room."

Anson nods and does as he is bade, carefully masking his elation beneath an expression of polite confusion. Only when they have left the protection of the electrical plant does he say to the dove who has been fluttering behind them:

"We're coming. Tell the warriors to be ready."

The dove coos and flutters off. Shango looks at him in astonishment.

"You're not Taiwo!"

"No. They made offerings to Eshu," Anson replies. "Eshu has heard them."

Regis starts at this, then slinks closer to his master's side. Shango snorts in disgust.

"So it is not just Katsuhiro who awaits."

"No, several of the Accord are gathered."

Anson does not bother to mention the extra shadow who has followed them to this point. Let her flitter after if she wishes. By his way of seeing things, it is her right.

Shahrazad sits on a chair between the griffin and Frank. She has been listening to babbling voices for so long that her head aches. First Arthur talks, then Lovern, then a cat, then a yeti, and then Frank. Then Arthur starts talking again. When he finishes, Chris brings forth a coffee can and gently takes the white mouse, Louhi, from it.

The sorceress does as Shahrazad has seen her do before, making a ghost of herself around the mouse. And then the ghost talks!

Shahrazad grumbles to herself and chews the edge of her chair. She is angry, frustrated, and impatient. As far as she can tell, the gist of the argument is whether or not Louhi did anything wrong in enchanting Wayne and, if she did wrong, what can be done to punish her.

Louhi, of course, sees the matter differently. To her, the wrong is that she was transformed into a mouse and forced to live in a cage. She dismisses Frank's protest that he would have set her free if she had asked by furiously asking what good would her freedom do her if she was just a mouse.

The talk goes round in circles this way for a long time, and Shahrazad grows angrier as she chews on the chair seat. The only interesting development, to her way of seeing things, is that someone—probably one of the cats—has figured out Shahrazad's role in changing Louhi into a mouse. Shahrazad is pleased to have this recognized. By her way of thinking, it was a good day's work, better only if she'd been permitted to eat mouse, ground squirrel, and rat as she had planned.

So the talking goes on. When the meeting breaks, Shahrazad hopes that the others are as tired of talking as she is of listening, but the athanor troop back into the conference room. Shahrazad wants to go run on the grounds, but the griffin and Frank convince her to stay: the one because daylight is not a safe time for coyotes, the other because he actually thinks she is learning something from all this chatter!

Something more than eating must have gone on during the break, however, for even Shahrazad, prepared to chew her chair some more, is aware of an altered tone.

"So we are prepared," Arthur says, "to offer a compromise. Louhi will be given what she wants most—she will be unlocked from her mouse form. In return for that service, she will grant Lovern a year of her time, during which she will work at the Academy as both teacher and enchanter."

Shahrazad is appalled. They can't undo her mousing! She likes things the way they are! As before, when anger fills her, she becomes aware of that odd channel to the part of her mind she has used twice before: once to transform others, once to transform herself. The power is there, rich like the smell of something rotting, full of potential. She need but reach out, and Louhi will be locked even more firmly into mouse form.

Perhaps she should sidle up there, as if drawing close to watch. Then her jaws can snap, and Louhi will cease to be a problem for anyone but Shahrazad's stomach.

Liking this coyote plan, she is slipping to the floor to carry it out when a terrible bitter taste floods mouth and her mind. It is somewhat like the fear she had felt when she had seen Louhi first arise from the mouse but stronger, so strong that it chokes her.

Shahrazad tries to swallow the bitterness, to fight it back, to tell which of the magical creatures gathered here is responsible for inflicting this upon her. Then she realizes the flavor is not completely unfamiliar.

It is the taste of the power that flows within her, but now that power is seasoned and spiced by the emotion that roused it.

The first time Shahrazad had raised the power, she had been furious, but her anger had been righteous in that she was angry that those who had harmed ones she loved should go free with so little penalty.

The second time, her anger had been anger not only that Louhi should escape, but that Shahrazad herself could do so little. Then her power had shown her how she could do something, how she could change herself and pursue the fugitive.

This time, however, the anger is spiced with pride. Shahrazad is angry not that Louhi should go unpunished—for certainly spending time as a mouse is punishment—but that any but she should dare alleviate that punishment.

Shahrazad's haunches hit the floor with an ungraceful thump as she recognizes that the bitterness that chokes her is loathing for herself . . . no, not precisely for herself, but for what she is becoming. Each time she has grown angry, her power has been easier to tap. Soon she will only be able to tap it through anger. Therefore, she will find more excuses to be angry.

Yet, the temptation to learn to use the power easily, to have no more barriers . . . Even as Shahrazad contemplates this, the bitterness in her mouth becomes somehow succulent.

In her mind's eye she sees herself, free of fear, free of weakness, free to use her great potential. She is as big as a wolf or griffin, sparks fly from her fur, and when others speak to her their voices drop in deference and respect.

But does she want this? Shahrazad isn't at all certain. She remembers those she has best loved, most admired. Anson the Spider, with his ready laugh and tickling hands. Gentle Frank, who speaks to rabbit and wolf as if both are worthy of his attention. The Changer, who, though powerful, is like a great pool of water, sustaining as well as potentially annihilating. Hip and Hop, who romp with her.

Were she to become the anger-power she envisions, all of these would be cut off from her. She would be more like those she does not admire. Lovern, so confident in his power yet so occupied with making everyone know he is important. Lilith, who can only love as she destroys. Cold Louhi. All of these have power and all of these have traded something of their souls to gain it.

Shahrazad crouches on the floor, thinking harder than she has ever thought in the many months of her life. Coming to a decision, she raises her nose to the ceiling and howls.

The talking stops (and a small part of her mind views this as a great improvement). Eyes in many faces turn to look at her. Wagging her bushy tail, Shahrazad trots to the front of the room. When she faces the audience, she is smiling.

¤▣¤

Aduke is amazed at how efficiently Oya and Eddie have arranged to have the Grove of the Gods cleared in anticipation of Shango's meeting with his fellow athanor. A few words to the Grove's keepers, a liberal distribution of *naira*, and both inner and outer groves are emptied of those who had come to worship, sacrifice, or consult the diviners.

The keepers lock the gates around the inner grove and promise to patrol the unfenced perimeter of the outer grove, letting through only those who are on the short list that Oya recites for them.

There will be those who slip past the keepers, of course, drawn by rumors that something odd is happening in the sacred precincts, but this has been anticipated. One reason the Grove has been chosen as a meeting place is because several of the athanor fear what they evasively refer to as "anomalies." Within the Grove, anomaly will be translated to "miracle" on the lips of any unwanted observers.

Looking high to where she can see the swirling curtain of the wind, Aduke wonders what would seem anomalous to her any longer. So much has changed these last weeks. Once again, she touches inside herself, probing the place in her soul where Taiwo should be. There is nothing, not even the dull throbbing sensation of loss that has replaced her sharpest grief over Baby's death. She doesn't even feel betrayed.

Oya's voice interrupts Aduke's reverie just as the human is trying to decide whether her numbness is a sign of shock or not.

"The Changer!" the wisewoman says, hastening to unlock the gate. "Are they coming?"

The strange white man pulls his long black hair out of his robe as if he had just donned the garment a moment before coming to the Grove. Aduke wonders if he just might have.

"Anson says they are," the deep gravelly voice answers. "I have told Katsuhiro and Dakar that it's unlikely they will need to break the Spider out of Shango's keeping, and so they should arrive here shortly."

"Good. Did you study Shango?"

"I didn't even try."

"Ah." Oya shrugs. "I was wondering how far he is going to have to be pushed."

The Changer mirrors her shrug. "Anson was in there some time. Either Shango is very confident or very nervous."

Eddie comes to join them, giving Aduke a faint smile by way of greeting. "We are set then?"

"As set as we can be," Oya answers. "I hate leaving this to Katsuhiro's best judgment—he is known neither for diplomacy nor balance."

"But he is clever," Eddie reminds her, "and if we did not give him this opportunity to gain some redress for the wrongs Shango has done him, there would most certainly be a vendetta, if not a full blood feud."

"They are here," the Changer says quietly.

Aduke hastens over to unlock the gate for Katsuhiro and Dakar. (How had she not seen the Changer arrive? The surrounding bush offers only slight cover). Excitement ripples from the two warriors as they enter the Grove. Aduke feels it like the pull of static electricity. Katsuhiro even seems to shed sparks.

"At last!" he says. "Did you bring my *hakama* and *gi*?"

"They're in the keeper's office," Eddie answers. "Don't yell at me if I didn't set the stuff out in the right order. It's been a long time since I worried about the formalities of *kenjitsu*."

Another of those small mysteries, Aduke thinks. Oya's associates are revealing more and more of themselves now that they trust her.

Last night the Changer had gone out, returning late with a sizable portion of both Taiwo's and Katsuhiro's luggage. Aduke had helped carry the bundles down from the roof, determinedly not asking either how the Changer had gotten into Regis's guarded compound to obtain it or why had he brought it to the roof instead of through the door on the ground floor.

Doubtless another one of those "anomalies."

Katsuhiro is emerging from the diviner's shelter dressed in a black-and-white outfit like something out of a kung-fu movie when Aduke hears the crunch of footsteps on the gravel path leading into the Grove's main entrance.

"Oya," she calls softly, "they are here."

"Let them in, child," Oya replies, then she crosses to

where she can speak to Aduke in a whisper. "And you may wish to take this opportunity to depart yourself."

Aduke, working the great key in the iron lock, makes a puzzled sound. "Now?"

"This will be more than summoning the wind," Oya says. "After this, moving backwards into innocence may only be done at a great sacrifice."

"I have no innocence," Aduke replies, "no longer. He"—she indicates Katsuhiro with a toss of her head—"challenges the one you call Shango, right?"

"Yes."

"And Shango is among those who tempted Taiwo, so in a sense Katsuhiro fights to avenge me. I wish to see that fight."

"It will not be what you expect."

"How do you know?" Aduke grins at her strange mentor, suddenly feeling light-headed, as if she has drunk too much palm wine. "I have great expectations, for both of them."

Oya chuckles and shakes her head. "Stay, then. You have helped summon the wind, after all."

Aduke nods firmly. "I have indeed. Now, I think I shall see the lightning flash and hear the thunder's complaint."

As she is swinging the gate shut and refastening the lock, Aduke thinks she sees motion off to one side of the path between the inner garden and the outer. She watches carefully for a long moment, but sees nothing and the byplay unfolding in the central plaza is far more interesting than nothing.

There beneath the gazes of the long-headed stone carvings of the great Yoruba gods, Katsuhiro is confronting Shango. The Minister for Electricity of the city of Monamona looks so very tired, so very vulnerable that Aduke thinks that these athanor must be mistaken, he cannot be one of their own.

"You have taken liberties with me, Shango," Katsuhiro says, apparently not at all uncertain who he faces, "and my honor demands satisfaction."

"If you want an apology," Shango says meekly, "you have it. I'm sorry I had you kidnapped, terribly sorry. Look what it has brought me!"

He gestures, and his gesture encompasses not only himself

but the situation around them, even the wind wall surrounding the city, and the troops dispersed around the perimeter.

"I am very sorry," Shango repeats. "I had been convinced"—he glowers at Regis—"that I had the means to coerce you, and that coercion was the best way to get you to understand my way of thinking."

He shrugs. "I was wrong. I should have waited until you would have had no choice but to do things my way, but I grew impatient, and the money from the oil sales would have made things easier."

As Shango speaks, he grows cockier, until he flings off the last—and all the deaths and sorrows attendant upon it—as if everything had been nothing more than a prank.

Aduke, who had to that point been rather awed by his titles—both governmental and deific—now begins to rather dislike him. Katsuhiro seems equally unimpressed.

"That isn't much of an apology," he observes dryly.

Shango spreads his hands. "It's the best I have."

"You have bent—if not broken—the laws of our Accord."

"How?"

"You have involved yourself in the lives of nonathanor in a fashion that endangered our secret."

"I'd enjoy a chance to discuss that in front of a jury of *our* peers," Shango says, with the air of one who has already considered this point. "With some of the recent adjustments to the Accord I think I could make some persuasive arguments." He looks falsely modest. "Like our Vera, I have been known for my sense of justice."

"Don't," rumbles Dakar, "get confused with your own myth. Oaths are sworn on iron."

Shango raises a brow. "Now who is getting confused with his own myth, brother?"

To Aduke's surprise, Dakar, does not lose his temper or bellow. All he does is glance first at Anson, then at Shango.

They have something in mind they're not talking about, she thinks and a glance at Oya confirms this guess, for Oya looks expectant, not concerned.

Katsuhiro steps forward a pace as a reminder that he, not Dakar, is the one Shango needs to be concerned with.

"Shango, don't fool yourself. Whatever the recent modification to the Accord, your releasing smallpox to fight for you will disgust most of our kin."

"I," Shango says haughtily, "was not the one to first release smallpox. In fact, you should be grateful to me. When I initially encountered Regis, he planned to seed the disease in all the major cities—starting with Lagos. I convinced him to restrict his base of operations to Monamona."

"You could," Katsuhiro says hotly, "have stopped him."

"I had the greater good of my people in mind," Shango answers. "A few deaths here would have meant great benefits for the survivors throughout the country. Generals throughout history have been praised for similar decisions."

"With the fires of Nagasaki and Hiroshima in my eyes," Katsuhiro answers, his level tone more furious than his outspoken anger of a moment before, "I am the wrong person to offer that argument."

Shango smiles nastily. "But all athanor are not Japanese."

Katsuhiro glowers. "I have no wish to wait for my satisfaction until we can drag you before Arthur."

"That dragging might be a bit difficult, wouldn't it?" Shango replies with a toss of his curls. "Given that Arthur is in New Mexico and we are here."

"Details have been worked out," Katsuhiro answers with a glance toward the Changer. "But I have an alternative for you."

"I'll listen," Shango says, suddenly serious. Apparently he, too, respects the Changer.

"Since, like you, I am a member of the Accord," Katsuhiro continues, "if you appeal to its justice, I must permit you to go before its tribunal or be in violation myself."

"True."

"And, as I have said, we have made arrangements to get you to Arthur, far more rapidly than you might imagine."

"There's also," Eddie adds, "the possibility that a panel of judges could be sent here. Then you must come before them or invalidate your own request. So don't think that escaping from us would relieve you from your responsibility."

Shango nods stiffly. "I am not newborn."

"Ah," Eddie says, rubbing the stubble of his beard, "but as you yourself said, there have been recent alterations to the

Accord. I didn't want you to think this had also been changed."

Shango nods, but his gaze has already drifted from Eddie back to where Katsuhiro stands.

"And your alternate offer?"

"A duel, not to the death, simply to my satisfaction. The Accord does not smile upon athanor who deprive Harmony of one of our kind, and we have taken losses enough of late."

"I would take a terrible risk if I dueled with you," Shango says, but Aduke notes that he glances toward a raincoat-wrapped bundle on the ground.

"Would you?" Katsuhiro replies. "We have ample witnesses. They could make certain that my just wrath does not rob you of your life."

"But you are a warrior; you have always been a warrior. I"—Shango affects humility—"have lately been naught but an administrator and politician."

Aduke is not at all surprised to hear Anson chuckle. The rest of them look quite serious, especially Regis, who is in the uncomfortable position of finding that his protector is quite prepared to reject him.

"You have the advantage in that we are on your land," Katsuhiro says calmly. "Other than what weapons we use, our talents are similar."

Shango shakes his head in self-deprecation, but Aduke is certain that no one misses the light that flashes in his eyes as he nonchalantly fingers the earrings in his right ear.

"What would be to your satisfaction?" Shango asks.

"Hold your own against me for five minutes," Katsuhiro replies promptly. "If I win, you agree to take part in a proposal that will be put to you. If you serve us well, I will consider myself recompensed for my suffering. If you win, you are released from any obligation to me for the kidnapping. You may still listen to the proposal, but you are not obligated."

"That's it?" Shango sounds surprised.

"I," Katsuhiro says smugly, "do not expect to lose, and I firmly expect to make you suffer greatly during those five minutes. Just because I do not plan to kill you doesn't mean that I will not hurt you."

"I have heard legends," Shango frowns, "that wounds caused by Kusanagi's blade cannot be healed other than by magic."

"That isn't true," Katsuhiro replies, "but since you raise the question, why don't we agree to live with our scars as a reminder for fifty years or so?"

Shango looks genuinely nervous yet strangely tempted. Aduke wonders at the source of this temptation until she realizes that he is envisioning half a century of bragging rights for scarring the Japanese warrior.

"Let me consider," Shango says slowly. "A proposal is one thing, but you've just raised the stakes."

"So you expect to lose?" Katsuhiro taunts. "Then let us appeal to the Accord. Somehow, I don't expect you to escape with just a few scratches when they are done with you."

"Let me consider," Shango repeats.

"You have five minutes, no more."

After three minutes, during which he speaks to no one, not even to Regis, who seems rather put out at this slight, Shango turns to his accuser.

"Can I name the master of the lists?"

"Yes."

"Dakar then."

Aduke, recalling the apparent rivalry between Dakar and Katsuhiro, suspects that Shango seeks to annoy Katsuhiro, but the Japanese only nods and says:

"Just the man I would have chosen myself. Let Eddie be the timekeeper."

"I agree—to Eddie as timekeeper and to your offered duel. Let the other Accord members stand witness."

There are muttered agreements from all but the Changer. Once again, Aduke fleetingly wonders just what his relationship is to the others. Then Oya summons her to help mark the lists.

As they do so, Katsuhiro recites the terms of the duel: "There are to be no seconds. We may use any weapon that we can lay hands on. The purpose is to defeat the other without killing him. If the master of the lists thinks that either duelist has lost control, he may halt the duel for the purpose of permitting that one to regain his balance."

"If the duel is halted," Shango asks, "will it recommence from that point or from the start of the five minutes?"

"From that point," Katsuhiro says, "but don't think of this as a way to chop the duel into small segments with rests in between. We will swear on Dakar's iron, thus he will have no trouble telling feigned fury from genuine."

"Very well," Shango says.

"Wait!" Regis steps from where he has been standing to the side, growing increasingly nervous. "What about me?"

"You?" Katsuhiro glances at him, then at Shango. "You are just Shango's tool."

"But I was the one who kidnapped you. I was the one who held you prisoner." Regis seems frantic for recognition, or perhaps he is simply terrified about his fate if his protector loses the duel. "What happens to me? Will you challenge me next?"

"You," Katsuhiro says, narrowing his eyes into slits, "are beneath me. Kill you, yes. The world should be rid of scum like you, but duel with you? Never!"

"Minister Omomomo!" Regis turns imploringly to Shango. "Aren't you going to defend me?"

"It depends," Shango replies honestly, "on how this duel is resolved. You see, until it is over, I myself am in a rather ticklish position. If I win, I certainly will deal with you."

Regis does not seem comforted. "Remember my securities," he threatens. "Things will happen if I die or am imprisoned!"

Shango looks at him scornfully. "I learned weeks ago where your 'securities' are kept and can defuse them when I wish. Did you think that *I* would suffer to let a madman blackmail me?"

"No," Eddie says so softly that Aduke hardly hears him, "only let him spread disease and terror for your glory."

No one else hears his words, but Aduke finds herself strangely comforted to realize that at least one among these peculiar folk has not forgotten how normal people have been used in Shango's bid for power.

"Do you have your weapons with you?" Katsuhiro interrupts impatiently.

"I do," Shango says. He unwraps the bundle in the raincoat. "I would like a minute to stretch before we begin."

"Take it."

Shango unwraps a beautiful double-headed axe and strikes at the air with it as if to accustom himself to its weight. Katsuhiro also stretches, but Aduke notes that he does not draw his sword.

Oya, now standing beside her, says: "To draw the sword is to commit himself to its use. He will wait until the duel begins, even if that gives Shango the advantage."

After sixty seconds, they stop and take oath at the shrine of Ogun to abide by the terms of the duel. Then Eddie calls them to order:

"Take your places gentlemen. The clock will begin to run when I say: 'Begin.' I will call a halt after three hundred seconds. Continuing after that point will be subject the duelist to a penalty from the master of the lists. Failing to halt when the master of the lists so demands will also subject the duelist to a penalty. The master may lay hands on either duelist.

"This duel is to defeat, not death, not blood. If death occurs, the witnesses will vote on whether death was accidental or deliberate and will testify before a senior tribunal of the Accord to that effect. Are there any questions?"

Two terse negatives come in reply. Aduke feels the Grove grow tight with tension as if the gods whose images encircle the perimeter are now watching. Eddie pushes a button on his watch.

"Begin."

A bolt of lightning crackles from the clear sky, heading directly toward Katsuhiro. Faster than Aduke had imagined possible, the samurai draws his sword and parries the lightning. Part forks out toward Shango, the rest breaks into electric blue lines that course over Katsuhiro, spitting sparks from the jutting black hairs of his beard.

Shango dodges one of the lightning forks, shunts the other aside with one of the heads of his axe. Beneath the tremendous clap of thunder that follows, Aduke murmurs to Oya:

"Are they gods then, to fight with lightning?"

Oya replies, her gaze never leaving the field where Katsuhiro, white lightning outlining his sword blade, is striking at Shango: "You summoned the wind. Are you then a goddess?"

"No!"

The fine hairs on the back of Aduke's neck and arms are standing on end and, though the college-trained part of her knows that this is merely a reaction to all the electricity in the air, the "bush" part of her feels as if the gods are preparing to punish her for blasphemy.

"No!" she repeats. "But you and I had to make sacrifices and dance for most of a night to get Oya to summon the wind. These two"—she gestures to where Shango and Katsuhiro are sending a gradually reducing lightning bolt back and forth between the wide metal edges of their respective weapons—"call the lightning without pause or consideration."

"They have had," Oya says, "a long, long time to practice. When they began, I suspect they, too, needed to focus their powers through ritual and appeal to the naturals through sacrifice."

"Oh." Aduke says, wondering just how long a "long, long" time might be. Remembering penalties exacted for fifty-year spans, she suspects it is far longer than one human lifetime.

Ignoring the conversations around them, the two warriors concentrate on their duel, double-bladed axe against katana. Each is a master of his weapon, each can fight with lightning and thunder as well as by more mundane means. Neither yet has so much as scratched his opponent. Aduke, who had been certain that Katsuhiro Oba would win, now has her doubts.

She watches as if the very intensity of her gaze might affect the battle, dodging as if the double-bladed axe is coming at her, flinching when lightning crackles from the sky or from Shango's hand, feeling the pump of adrenaline fill her blood with uncontrollable energy.

Then, through the crackle of the lightning, almost drowned out by the rumbles of thunder, comes a sound so mundane, so regular, that Aduke nearly dismisses it. Even when her brain registers the gunfire for what it is, she first looks to the combatants, certain that one of them must be the source.

Neither of them have so much as paused in their trading of blows electrical and otherwise, yet over to one side Regis is falling, his body shaken as if by kicks from an invisible giant.

Aduke's mind, open now to the wonder of gods fighting with lightning a few paces away, seems to have difficulty grasping the very mundane realization that Regis has been—is being—shot.

Even so, she is the first to cry: "There's someone out there with a gun!" She hears her voice, high and shrill with panic, the words tumbling over each other in their haste to carry the news to the ears of someone who can do something about it.

The duelists do not pause. Dakar does not move from his place as marshal of the lists, nor does Eddie spare more than a worried glance, but Oya and Anson run over. The Changer merely nods as if Aduke's announcement is expected.

In mid-stride, Anson tosses something in the direction Aduke still points, her arm as rigid as a signpost. Nothing leaves his hand—nothing that Aduke can see—but when she looks at the fence a portion is covered by a heavy white veiling, like a spiderweb.

"Damn!" Anson says. "Missed whoever it was."

"Teresa," says the Changer calmly, his gaze now returned to the duel. "I thought you knew that she had been following you."

Anson hesitates, then a smile lights his face. It seems incongruously happy given the man bleeding to death on the ground before him, the fevered heat of the duel behind him.

"I did," he admits, "but I didn't know what she planned to do. Did you?"

"No."

Anson kneels next to Oya. "How is he?"

"Dead or dying," she replies. There is no sorrow or shock in her voice, only a calm relating of information. "A quicker death than he deserved."

"So now we don't need to trouble ourselves with him."

Oya glances at Anson. "Is that why you let Teresa follow you, ancient? Did you put her up to it?"

Aduke finds herself holding her breath, waiting for Anson's reply. Somehow, she doesn't want to learn that the cheery Spider could be so calculating.

"No," Anson replies to her infinite relief, "but I think it all to the best. Teresa has been driven mad with grief and rage. This death by her hand may free her to return to sanity."

Oya nods, and Aduke finds herself nodding as well. The Spider rises to his feet, dusting off his trouser legs—Taiwo's trouser legs—with quick, businesslike motions.

"I'd best go after her," he says, "before she does more harm to herself or to others."

Then, though Aduke had believed herself immune to wonder, she feels her heartbeat quicken as Anson's arms grow longer, or is it that he himself has grown smaller? All she knows for certain is that within two clashes of the sword and axe, where a man who had looked like her husband had stood there is now a brown monkey. The monkey slips out of the heap of clothing, swarms up the fence, and jumps over into the nearest tree before vanishing into the bush.

Aduke watches him out of sight. When she turns Oya is studying her, concern on her broad features.

"Aduke?"

"He turned into a monkey," Aduke says, bending to pick up the clothing from the ground. "Like something from an old market woman's tale. Amazing!"

Oya hugs her around the shoulders, wordlessly congratulating the human for her calm. Then as one, they return their attention to the duel.

And if your friend does evil to you, say to him, "I forgive you for what you did to me, but how can I forgive you for what you did—to yourself?"

—FRIEDRICH NIETZSCHE

KATSUHIRO HEARS THE GUNSHOTS FROM ONE CORNER OF his mind, but he cannot spare any attention. Fighting for his honor—and quite possibly for his life—Shango is giving the Japanese the best battle he has had in several centuries.

At least two minutes remain, and Katsuhiro is having a wonderful time.

He chases a fresh lightning bolt down Kusanagi's blade, but Shango catches it with the broad part of his axe, dispersing the electricity into the elaborate runes etched in the middle. They sizzle and fizz blue-white, and Katsuhiro fully expects his own power to be sent back at him.

Shango, however, absorbs it into himself, growing stronger and perhaps a bit larger, then dances back a few steps out of the range of Katsuhiro's sword.

Expecting another lightning bolt, Katsuhiro is taken aback when his opponent breathes fire. He drops and rolls to avoid being burnt. True to his samurai training, though, Katsuhiro rolls toward Shango rather than away. Shango's next blast passes over him. When Katsuhiro come out of his roll, he is nearly touching Shango's legs.

About a minute left, Katsuhiro thinks. *Time to end this.*

He surges to his feet and back a step or two. Again Shango breathes fire, this time directly into Katsuhiro's face. Ready now, Katsuhiro beats back the fire with a blast of his own storm wind. There is a smell of burning hair as the fire gutters out, and Shango belches like a boy who has swallowed air.

Now!

Katsuhiro makes a quick slice, and Kusanagi lays open the left side of Shango's face—not a pretty cut like a dueling scar, but an ugly thing that exposes the bone, leaving meat and skin hanging in a palm-wide swatch.

Shango screams and Katsuhiro feels blood patter like warm raindrops against his skin. Without pausing, he brings Kusanagi down in a hard, sweeping cut. All the power of his formidable strength is behind the sword as its blade shears through skin, muscle, bone, and tendon, severing Shango's leg cleanly through the middle of the right thigh.

Katsuhiro freezes, breathing in smoke and a fine mist of blood, sword poised to defend.

For the merest instant, Shango stands balanced upon the severed member. Then, greased by the blood that gushes from severed veins and arteries, the thigh beneath the sword cut slips loose and the lower leg tumbles, knee bending in grotesque parody of homage, falling slow motion to the sodden ground.

Shango wails. Lightning crackles from the sky, a single white-hot bolt that cauterizes the wound. Then, reeking of cooked meat, the defeated athanor collapses to the blood-soaked earth.

¤◙¤

Louhi cringes as she sees the tawny red coyote trotting down the aisle toward the front of the room. Gods! After everything they've discussed, don't these people realize that the little beast is dangerous? Why are they letting her run free? Why doesn't someone stop her!

She squeaks despite herself, trembling where she sits on the table in front of Arthur. Her bowels release, leaving a little puddle of urine and a few brown flecks on the towel they have set her on. Embarrassed, Louhi flicks her tail nervously, but still they let the coyote approach. She takes little comfort in the fact that the gathered Cats of Egypt are watching closely. Who can trust a cat to guard a mouse?

But Shahrazad stops a few feet away from the table where Louhi trembles and gradually Louhi realizes that the lolling jaws are not a sign of her imminent demise, but a canine smile. Everything looks so different from this perspective.

When Shahrazad turns her amber gaze on Louhi, her eyes are as big as those of a dragon. Then, to Louhi's surprise, she hears a voice in her head. It is feminine but not female, the inflections of one quite unaccustomed to speech involving words—even thought words—rather than scents and ear flips and little noises. It is, she realizes, Shahrazad's voice.

"*So, do you like being pissed off all the time?*" Shahrazad asks.

Louhi bristles at the importunity of such a query, then realizes that the coyote is not being insulting. She's just calling the shots as she sees them.

"*I didn't know I was,*" Louhi counters, also using thought speech. "*Right now, I'm just scared.*"

"*You're not,*" the coyote says confidently, "*not deep inside. You're angry. Angry you're a mouse, angry you're little, angry you have to ask for favors. Angry. Do you like it?*"

Louhi considers. No one else can hear this conversation, and if she keeps the little beast talking, maybe someone will grab her and lock her up.

"*I never thought about it,*" she offers.

"*You should try,*" Shahrazad returns. "*I did. I don't like it. I don't want to be angry at you, even though you scared me, even though you hurt the Changer.*"

"*He hurt me!*" Louhi's reply rises too quickly, always a problem with mental conversations.

"*How? He's a good parent, even when he bites.*"

"*He bites?*"

"Of course, how else is he going to tell me when I'm wrong?"

"He could explain."

"To a pup?" The coyote's voice fills with merriment. *"Pups don't think. I still don't think, much . . ."*

"The Changer bites you." The thought is a new one. Louhi had always known that the Changer bit, that he was dangerous, but somehow she'd always imagined Shahrazad's upbringing as an idyll.

"Yep. Bites, thumps. When I wouldn't hunt, he let me get hungry until I learned stillness."

"So he gets angry," Louhi says, steering the conversation back to Shahrazad's original gambit.

"No. Not at me."

"But he hurts you."

"That's not the same."

"He left you when you were bad."

"That's right," Shahrazad sounds abashed. *"You know about that. Yeah, he left me. I think it was a new type of biting. I kept waiting for him to pull me out of trouble, like he always did before, even when you hurt him for it. I had to learn to be careful. Did hurting him make you feel better?"*

"No." Louhi is surprised by her own honesty. It doesn't make her feel any better, either. In truth, it makes her feel rather sick. *"No, it didn't, but he never cared for me like he cared for you. I wanted him to."*

"So you bit out his eye and made him bleed."

"Yeah."

"I guess that makes sense," Shahrazad says, memories of many times that coyote love made her bleed, *"or would if you weren't angry when you did it."*

"You know. I almost get your point."

"They're going to turn you back into a human. Did you know that?"

"Yes."

"And you're going to work with Lovern for a year. You used to be angry with Lovern a lot, too. Are you going to like working with him?"

"Not really, but it's the best deal I could get."

"So you'll stay angry."

"I never said I was angry!"

"Then why are you shouting?"

"Okay. I'm angry. I've been angry for a long time. Why shouldn't I be? My father abandoned me. I don't remember my mother. I've had power, but men only use me for it and go their way. So I learned to make deals, to gather more power, to make enchantments. I had the Head for a while, then even he *enchanted me and I still want to vomit when I think how he used me."*

"Vomiting is good when it gets the bad stuff out. You just keep it inside. No wonder you're always angry."

Louhi twitches her whiskers. *"It must be great being what—six months old? Everything must seem very simple. I don't think I ever remember being six months old."*

"I'm seven months old."

"I'm more than seven thousand times seven months old."

"That's more than I can count," Shahrazad responds, awed. *"And you've been angry all that time?"*

"Leave off the anger, would you?"

"I was just wondering."

"Why should you care?"

"Because," says the coyote with a happy wag of her tail, *"I'm going to turn you back. I think you have a point about not wanting to be a mouse, and if you don't want to work with Lovern for a year, I don't see why you should have to."*

"You're going to turn me back?"

"That's right. Get ready to grab that towel, okay? I can't do clothes and humans are funny about these things."

"But I'm your enemy!"

"Why?"

The simple question floors Louhi, leaving her mentally silent, not just speechless.

"Because you turned me into a mouse!" she answers at last.

"No, you were angry before then. I remember how you glowered at me in the yard of that place where you tied me to a tree. You were angry at me before you met me."

"I suppose I was angry at the Changer."

"For not biting you when you were small."

"I . . ." Louhi frowns. *"I still think he is my father."*

"Then I'm your sister. You can't be the Changer's daughter unless you're Shahrazad's sister." The coyote tail wags. *"My sisters are dead now. I think I'd like to have one."*

Stubbornly, Louhi persists in what Shahrazad must be made to recognize is deep and abiding anger. *"I still think a father owes his children something."*

"Do they?" Shahrazad twitches an ear. *"Depends on the animal, I think. The Changer cared for me because coyotes do, but if I had been born a fish or something, he might have tried to eat me. What were you born?"*

Louhi starts. "Human, I think."

"Then someone must have cared for you because human babies are even more useless than mice. Do you know he didn't?"

"No."

"And why aren't you angry at your mother?"

"I don't know who she is!"

Shahrazad wags her tail. *"You have more knots in your thinking than I have in my coat. Be angry if you want. All I can do is make you not a mouse."*

And, as simple as that, Louhi isn't a mouse. She's standing on the table, a slightly soiled towel in one hand. Quickly, she drapes herself, grateful that it's a big towel. Shahrazad looks up at her and wags her tail in a satisfied fashion.

Louhi gets off the table, and, as she does so, she catches her reflection in one of the windows. She looks as she usually does, a slender, pale blond woman of stark Nordic beauty, but there is one change.

Where Louhi usually deliberately evokes ice, in the form that Shahrazad has given her, the clean, straight sheet of her almost-white hair is embellished with pink and yellow five-petaled flowers, rather like a child's drawing of a daisy. The flowers are printed directly onto her hair. Amazed, Louhi examines one lock. The color goes through the depth of her hair.

"Pretty," comes a parting thought from Shahrazad. *"I like flowers. Don't you?"*

Shango crawls out of the unconscious darkness, feeling pain humming like a hive of bees: present but dulled so that he can almost ignore it. Someone must have given him a painkiller. With a conscious effort he forces his eyes open and finds Katsuhiro staring down at him. The Japanese's eyebrows have been burnt away, as have the outer edges of his beard and hair, but otherwise he seems unharmed.

"That was a good fight, Shango," Katsuhiro says. "You have been keeping in practice."

"I have," Shango admits, barely moving his mouth. The left side of his face has been bound up and is suspiciously numb. "There was no advantage to telling you."

"Here," says a soft, female voice with just the faintest quavering in it. "Sip this."

Shango looks and sees Taiwo's wife offering him a bottle of water. She props him up against a heap of something soft—probably pillows taken from the shelters. As he cautiously swallows a mouthful, he forces himself to look into the human face of the misery he has caused and feels ashamed.

Yoruban myth says that the god-king Shango committed suicide once when he could not face having slain his own followers in a fit of righteous anger. When he rose from the dead, he realized he was one of the *orisha*. Only Shango himself knows how true that story is. He feels tears hot in his eyes at the thought that he could ever have forgotten a lesson learned at such a price.

"Thank you," he says, clumsily wiping away the tears. "Thank you."

Aduke withdraws, and Shango says huskily to Katsuhiro Oba, "I have lost and am prepared to listen to your proposal, Oba-san."

Katsuhiro nods. "You know you have lost your right leg?"

"Through the thigh," Shango replies. "And I must live with that and with the scarring of my face for fifty years before I can seek help from a 'plastic surgeon.' "

"We have cleaned and treated your wounds," Katsuhiro says, "but even when it is healed your face will be quite hideous. Your leg . . ."

Shango nods, the painkiller in his blood making him feel

distant enough from his own suffering that he can appreciate the cleverness of Katsuhiro's choice of target. If the leg had been amputated at a joint, an artificial leg would have been much easier to fit. This way, either further trimming must be done—slowing any possible regeneration—or he must live with the deadweight dangling from his hip, a constant reminder of his folly.

Shango suspects he will be quite angry later, but for now he takes refuge in the numbing drug.

"You had a proposal," he persists.

Katsuhiro looks approving. "Dakar, this is more your business than mine. Would you begin?"

"I could use Anson," Dakar says, looking around.

"He went to seek Teresa," Oya explains from where she sits near the gate, "after she shot Regis."

Shango turns his throbbing head in the direction she had glanced and sees Regis's corpse crumpled on the ground off to one side of the dueling field. Flies already swarm around the drying blood on the Chief General Doctor's shirt.

Upon seeing his onetime ally dead, Shango is filled with a weird joy and a sense of being set free. Using disease both to blackmail his opponents and as a means of gaining sympathy and relief money from the first-world nations had seemed a good idea when it had first come to him. When Shango had begun to have second thoughts, he could not withdraw lest Regis see his weakness. By then, too, Regis had gathered power and influence of his own.

"Tell me, Dakar," Shango croaks, "what you propose. I will attend to Anson's part as well."

"You know why Anson came to Monamona," Dakar begins, uneasy in the unaccustomed role of spokesman.

Shango nods painfully and resolves thereafter to lie perfectly still. "To meddle. He always does."

"Yes, to meddle," Dakar starts growing angry and instantly is more relaxed. "To meddle for the good of people you and I claim for our own. He wanted to see oil revenues administered for the good of the people rather than being siphoned off by corrupt ministers or used for showy projects."

"I am, of course," Shango sadly, "one of those corrupt administrators."

"You don't have to be," Dakar growls. He gestures widely toward the statue of Shango off to one side of the Grove. Presents of gowns, chickens, bitter kola nuts, and yam porridge are heaped at its base. "Join us."

"What?"

"That's our proposal," Dakar says impatiently. "Join us. Give up your ambitions to be president of Nigeria or whatever it is that you want and join us."

Shango hears a thump. Anson, back in his own typical form and wearing nothing but a pair of briefs (probably stolen from someone's wash), has jumped down from the fence.

"You don't even need to give up your ambition," Anson adds, accepting the pair of trousers that Aduke hands him, "just postpone it for a while."

Shango frowns. This sounds far too good.

"Why do you want me?" he asks.

"For the same reasons we wanted you before," Anson says. "You have political connections, followers, influence. You can help us decide who must be bribed, who can be ignored, who must be gently encouraged out of office."

"I do," Shango muses, "have something to offer, don't I?"

"*I* think so," Anson says. "Dakar may need convincing."

"I will," Dakar agrees.

"And I will be watching," Katsuhiro adds, "to see that my business associates are not cheated."

Shango nods slowly. "I expected nothing less. And Eddie, what does he want?"

"Nothing," Eddie replies. "I'll be working on this project with Anson—if Arthur can spare me—but I want nothing additional."

"My intentions," Oya adds, "are much like Eddie's."

"And the Changer?" Shango glances at the ancient who stands leaning back against the statue of Olodumare.

"This is not my business," the Changer says, "but I have a personal dislike of those who use disease as weapons. If I learn you have returned to such things, I will come after you, and, I promise, there is very little that can infect me."

Shango turns to Aduke. "And you, lady?"

"Who am I," she says, "to dictate to those with the powers of gods?"

Shango thinks of the heap of sacrifices at the base of his statue. "A person without those powers," he says, "is the very person who reminds those with them of our responsibilities."

"That," Aduke replies in complete seriousness, "I am fully prepared to do."

"Shall we return then," Anson says, "to Oya's place and discuss this further?"

"What do we do about that?" Katsuhiro gestures toward Regis's corpse.

In reply, Dakar scoops up the body, then drops it at the base of the makeshift clay statue to Shopona, the King of the World, the King of Hot Water.

"Leave it there," he says, "as a reminder that none of us, no matter what powers we wield, are gods."

¤▣¤

Forty-eight hours are needed before various loose ends are tied up, ends that must be resolved before the wind wall can be dispelled.

Shango is carried on a litter to his allies. With Dakar ever at his side, he tells them that now is not the time for revolution. He hints that great things are yet to come, that promises made will be fulfilled. Despite his wounds—or perhaps because of them—he succeeds in convincing them.

Regis's compound must be dismantled and every trace of the deadly viruses that the Chief General Doctor played with eliminated. The Changer demands a role in this, his yellow eyes lighting with a passion few have seen in him before. Anson welcomes his help. Wearing Taiwo's form and bearing a letter from Shango that tells of Regis's disgrace, the Spider disbands the private army, paying them off with *naira* from Regis's enormous hoard. If later some of the cruelest of the survivors are found dead in mysterious circumstances, no one asks questions.

Most of the sufferers in Regis's "hospital" have died from neglect or from the smallpox. Those who survive are taken to a clean, well-lighted place where a handful of medical professionals—all vaccinated against the disease—tend to them. There is hope that when the athanor doctor, Garrett Kocchui, can be brought in that he will have some means to repair the scarring, blindness, and other side effects of the virus.

Then there are problems that can be contained, but cannot be so easily resolved.

There is Teresa who, after killing Regis, fled into the tangled streets of Monamona. There Anson found her, brought her to Oya's floor of the factory, and locked her in a room.

The first time Teresa is let out she sneaks downstairs and nearly kills Kehinde, believing him Taiwo. Currently, she sleeps a dreamless sleep in Oya's own bedroom, comforted by sweet music and Oya's gentle singing. Plans are for Garrett Kocchui to tend her as well: to learn if she indeed has contracted AIDS and then to do what he can for her damaged body.

Teresa's damaged mind is something for which no one may have a cure.

Taiwo is another problem. Unlike Shango, he believes himself irreparably evil and does not trust himself ever to do good. The consensus among the athanor is that the only thing that might get him to reconsider is forgiveness from Aduke, but Aduke will have nothing to do with him. Therefore, he must be kept locked in a room. Given his past intimacy with Teresa, he, too, must be tested for AIDS.

Aduke is aware of all of this, but she determinedly doesn't think about anything except for the specific project she is assisting with—and especially she doesn't think about Taiwo.

That part of her soul is still numb, still empty, and she doesn't care to have it reawakened. So, though it embarrasses her, she looks the other way when Oya tries to persuade her, even going so far as to flee to the lower reaches of the factory, where Oya will not dare broach the subject in front of the family.

The Fadaka family is taking the comings and goings from Oya's floor with a mixture of curiosity and complacency. They, Aduke thinks, have not had to learn uncomfortable truths in return for their new home. The knowledge that she is, in a sense, paying the rent gives her the strength to defy Oya.

And so when the athanor gather to lower the wind wall, Aduke is with them, ready to do anything but speak with the man who sits alone in a room down the hall, staring at the wall.

She wears her dancing clothes of scarlet and purple and brown. Oya has told her that the wind will need to be dispersed much as it was called, with songs, sacrifices, and entreaties. Oya had looked worried, Aduke had noted, but she had not thought about it overmuch. Oya is a colleague of those who throw lightning and change shape at will. Certainly, there will be no problem with a wind.

"The wind is always weakest after sunset," Oya explains, "just as it rises with the day's heat. It should listen to us then."

"Don't you mean," Aduke says, "that Oya should listen?"

"I mean what I say," Oya says. "The wind, like Oya, can have a mind of its own."

The Changer speaks, startling Aduke a little. That one can go for an entire day not saying anything at all.

"When I crossed the wind," he says, "it seemed to me that she did have a mind of her own and that she was very much enjoying having a city looking up at her with wonder and awe."

"Do you think she will refuse to release the city?" Dakar asks, looking concerned at the prospect of an opponent that he cannot hit.

"I do," the Changer says. "We must be ready for the prospect."

And so it is a solemn, intense group who mounts the ladder to the roof and sets their offerings on Oya's altar. These are much the same as before, though Shango has added some pretty trinkets of his own. He has also brought a *bata* drum with him and, since he cannot dance, plans to beat accompaniment.

"It is Shango's drum," he explains, "and I need to remember Shango's responsibilities."

Aduke, herself, is rather nervous, for her place will be with Oya at the center of the dance. The men, including Katsuhiro but excepting the Changer, will dance around the edges.

Despite the large meal Anson had insisted on preparing earlier in the evening, Aduke feels empty and afraid. As on the day of the duel, she feels as if the gods are looking down on her, watching and judging. She shivers.

"Cold?" Oya asks, coming to hug her. "You'll warm up when we start dancing. Are you ready?"

"Yes."

And so, to the steady beat of the *bata* drum, they begin as they did before. In raised voices they sing Oya's praise names, thanking her for her generosity, telling her that the crisis has ended, asking her to lower the wall of wind and let her people go out into the world and spread the news of her greatness.

They dance for hours, never relenting, never ceasing in their praise. This time the deeper voices of the men join them, husky and rich, making the women's voices seem lighter and sweeter by comparison.

The stars wheel above. The moon, her light distorted by the wind shroud about the city, slowly rises. Even when Aduke has long since forgotten that her feet could feel anything but swollen and sore, that there is any motion outside of the shuffling bounce of the dance, still the wind continues to hold the city in her arms.

Then a new voice joins the ones already raised, a voice speaking Yoruban that is vaguely archaic, but still understandable, a male voice whose intonation is one of command, not entreaty. It is the Changer.

"Enough of this nonsense! We have been polite to you. Be polite to us. We have humored your vanity. We have thanked you for your assistance. Now release your hold on these people, people who will slowly starve, who will cease to feel wonder but will instead feel hate, people who will no longer view you as a protecting mother, but who will come to fear you as the cruelest of jailers. Release this city. Drop your wall, or you shall deal with me!"

Aduke turns her head, moving it slowly on a neck grown sore and tired, and sees that the Changer has risen to his feet. She wonders what he is that he should speak so to the wind. Then her attention is drawn by something else, a miniature cyclone above the altar, a form that has no mouth but nevertheless speaks.

"Why should I grant this?" it howls. "I would be no less kind to these people than they are to each other. Let all within my hold acknowledge me, call me goddess and patron, then I will bring them food. I will shower them with rain. Within my loving hold they will build a paradise, knowing that the divine is not far and uncaring, but near and nurturing."

One by one, the athanors' voices fall silent. Aduke stops singing aloud, but her lips still move through the praises, afraid what might happen to her if she stops.

"You are not divine," the Changer replies, "any more than I am."

"Brother of the Sea, Ancient, Changer," the wind retorts. "If they knew you, they would call you divine."

"Would that make me so?"

The wind howls in fury. "I am the wind!"

"You are one wind."

"I can hold these people for my own!"

"I can stop you, and I will."

"Try it!"

"Wait!"

Aduke hardly realizes that she has spoken until the word escapes her lips. The Changer looks at her, and she is certain that there is a faint smile on his lips.

"Yes?"

"Must you? I'm so very tired of fighting, of watching fighting, of all of this. What is that?" she points to the swirling cyclone. "Is that Oya, or is it another creature like you?"

"It is not Oya," the Changer replies. "It is an athanor, a rare but powerful type. When your mentor called up a wind, she thought it was her own sorcery that shaped the wall, but because she drew upon your latent powers, she used charms that spoke to the listening winds."

Oya nods. "What he says is true. I did not suspect that I had done more than use our powers to create a sorcerous wind until the Changer warned me otherwise."

"Innocent!" hisses the wind. "I am far older than you, older than the human-form who think themselves so wise."

"Not older than me," the Changer says, "or so I believe."

"Wait!" Eddie says, unconsciously echoing Aduke even in intonation. "Is this a natural? I thought wind elementals were just legend!"

"I am the wind!" the cyclone whispers. Then when the Changer glowers at it, it rephrases the statement. "I am a wind!"

"It is a natural," the Changer says. "In the old days sorcerers would sometimes bind them, giving birth to the legends of Aeolus and his bag of winds, and of weather workers. Many were slain in those days, and those who remained became wild and shy. Don't you recall?"

"I have never been a wizard," Eddie says, "and such claims seemed exaggeration to me."

"They are not," the wind protests. "I am a wind. I have sisters in waters, in trees, in great old rocks. Only the fauns and satyrs have maintained our memories green."

Eddie shakes his head in disbelief. "I knew—had heard of—the dryads. I thought that even that was an exaggeration."

"And you are old," the Changer says, "for a human-form, but not old compared to the Earth."

"Surely you don't want a city!" Katsuhiro protests, his beard blown askew by the swirling wind. "I have some small wind magic of my own. I am sure that winds don't want cities."

"Small magics you have," the wind agrees. "Farts."

Aduke giggles nervously and feels the wind's attention drawn to her. She stiffens, falls silent, but it is too late.

"Give this one to me," the wind says. "She sings well and with conviction. Give her to me, and she shall be my chief priestess."

Oya steps forward. "We do not give people away!"

"I hadn't noticed," the wind whistles snidely. "What else is war but the giving of people to death?"

Aduke puts a restraining hand on Oya's arm. "Wind? Do you really want to be worshiped?"

"I want to be," the voice agrees. Something like a hand tickles Aduke's face.

"Why?"

"I am the . . . a wind!"

"But what good will worship do you?"

"I . . ."

Aduke takes advantage of the hesitation to charge forward. "My husband wanted power and lost everything for it. This man called Shango wanted power and was crippled for it. What is worship if not a form of power? You don't need it to sustain yourself, do you?"

"No! I am a wind!"

"What good does power do anyone—especially power for no reason but for having power?" Aduke demands.

"I am a wind."

"Would you be less a wind if you were not worshiped?"

"Everyone would forget I am a wind!"

"I would know, the Changer has never forgotten, these gathered here can tell their fellows. You are known now. How will worship change that?"

"I am . . . a . . . I have always been a . . . I have always been wind. I have so long been a-lone. These days many eyes have looked at me. I have not been alone, invisible, breathed but unacknowledged. I am a-lone."

"So am I," Aduke whispers. "My baby is gone. My husband is mad. I cannot tell my sisters what I now know to be true. I am a-lone, too. You spoke of your sisters. Can I be your sister?"

"You are a-lone?"

Aduke realizes she is crying, but she can't stop.

"I am terribly alone, wind. I have no son, no husband, no father or mother. Knowledge sets me apart from my kinfolk. I am the one mortal among those who are almost gods. You are rich in un-aloneness compared to me."

Aduke notices Oya looking at her, big eyes both sorrowful and proud, but there is no time to wonder what Oya thinks now.

"Poor child," the wind whispers. "Be my priestess, and I will make you ruler of this city and many others. You will be first among mortals and honored by athanor."

"No!" Aduke chokes around a sob. "That is a madness and a special kind of a-loneness. Do you really pity me?"

"Yes."

"Then be my friend. Walk with me in the market. Touch my cheek, pat my hand, carry my laughter, dry my tears. Then I won't be alone and neither"—she pauses, looks where the eyes would be if a cyclone had eyes—"neither would you."

"I would not be a-lone. I would be a wind. I am a wind." The soft words rush over each other as if spoken by three sets of lips with one mind behind them. "My sisters are far away. Most flit through distant crags, over lonely ocean, afraid of the bags. You would not let a wizard bag me?"

"Never!" Aduke says fiercely, not knowing how she could keep such a promise, but knowing that she would.

"Should we let the city go?"

"I think so. Many of these people are separated from those they love. Many are afraid. Let them go. You can walk with me instead of being worshiped by those who fear you."

The wind sighs. "I could be a goddess. You could be honored."

"If I was your friend," Aduke says firmly, "that would be honor enough. Nothing can make you a goddess—ask Shango."

"A friend," the wind whistles. "Why not? Maybe later, we will be goddesses together."

And felt as a popping of ears, the wind wall about the city of Monamona falls. There is a tremendous stillness, then the westward beating of the *harmattan* resumes.

Aduke raises her hand to shield her eyes from the dust and feels a gentle breeze coasting over her body, driving away the dirt and heat, leaving her deliciously comfortable.

"Let me, sister," the wind says softly. "I will protect you who are my friend."

Aduke nods thanks and only then does she find the courage to face the six athanor who have been listening to this strange conversation. The Changer is the first to break the silence.

"I'm very pleased," he says. "I've never found it productive to fight against the wind."

EPILOGUE

I can govern the United States or I can govern my daughter Alice, but I can't do both.

—THEODORE ROOSEVELT

THE GLOSSY PROGRAM IN ARTHUR'S HANDS READS: "PAN: A Musical Experience." The fancy titles are printed over a photograph of Tommy Thunderburst playing the lyre. He is wearing nothing but a leopard skin and a vine wreath. Adoring females with wild hair, clad only in strategically placed vine leaves, cling to his legs or bite into huge, dark purple grapes. In the background, fauns play accompaniment on their syrinxes and satyrs dance or drink or leer at the girls.

"I can't believe I'm here," Arthur mutters to Chris.

The human just grins at him. "My friends can't believe I have front-row tickets to this show. It's the hottest concert going right now. Those who don't want to hear Tommy want to get a look at the fauns and satyrs so they can brag that they saw through the stage makeup."

Arthur moans softly. "I can't believe that Lil and Tommy insisted on using them after all the trouble Georgios and his buddies caused."

Chris's grin doesn't fade. "From what little I know about both Lil and Tommy, the risk would be irresistible."

"That's true enough."

Arthur looks over his shoulder, back around the Pit, Albuquerque's premier sport's arena and concert facility. Every one of the seats is packed, the place aswarm with moving bodies, reeking with the odors of marijuana, alcohol, and human sweat. Idly, he wonders just how many ordinances are being violated here tonight.

"I do wish," he continues, "that the theriomorphs had accepted Tommy and Lil's offer of a box. We would have been safer there."

Chris shakes his head. "This"—he gestures to the front row seats—"is exactly what they wanted—a chance to experience a concert up close and personal. In a box, you might as well be at home watching on the video screen. That's what lots of the folks in the back are going to be doing anyhow."

"I just hope that Lovern and his team can maintain their illusions," Arthur says, glancing over to where Lovern, seated beside Louhi, is deep in conversation with Bronson and Rebecca Trapper. The sasquatches had driven down with Monk and Hiero, two of the *tengu*. They are disguised, courtesy of a temporary illusion—the trouble with the satyrs had left no time to make permanent amulets—to look like two very tall African-American humans.

Louhi, for her part, is visiting quite socially with a young woman—not one of their own party, Arthur notes nervously. Since the women must shout to be heard over the general hubbub, he is able to eavesdrop on their conversation.

"I just love your hair," the young woman is saying. "It's so cool! Where did you get it done?"

"My sister did it," Louhi answers.

"Wow! Does she have a salon?"

"No. She's still . . . in school."

"Around here?"

"No, she lives on a ranch in Colorado."

Shahrazad's sister, Arthur thinks, shaking his head slightly. No one knows what passed between the young coyote and the sorceress, but whatever it was, Louhi no longer hates Shahrazad—as her maintaining the outlandish hair coloring demonstrates. Louhi still may not be acknowledged as the Changer's daughter, but apparently being Shahrazad's sister means something special.

Maybe, he thinks cynically, *this is simply Louhi's newest attempt to get a hook into the Changer, just like maybe her agreeing to work with Lovern is merely a way to get an inside track on athanor politics and to win her way back into the Accord. She must know that there are those of us who aren't as ready as Lovern to forget the werewolf Lupé's death. Flowers in her hair or not, I'm not ready to trust Louhi quite yet.*

Louhi's apparent change of heart is hardly the biggest revelation of the past few days. Arthur has spent hours on the phone or writing e-mail, bringing Eddie up-to-date on events in the U.S. and learning what had happened in Nigeria. Shango's ambitions hadn't surprised him—athanor are far from immune to ambition—but the confirmation that there are indeed wind naturals has shaken him deeply.

Arthur has always had trouble acknowledging the existence of the dryads, but the fauns' devotion to their charges had forced him to consider that there might be something there. But trees, like cats and coyotes, have bodies that stay in one place. The concept of a wind with a mind of its own bothers him.

In light of that, learning that yet another human—the woman Aduke Idowu—has been taken into the secret of the athanor's existence seems a minor thing indeed.

He looks over where Bill Irish is showing Swansdown the yeti (who will be returning to Alaska after the concert) some dance steps, to where Chris is ordering ice-cream bars for Purrarr, Tuxedo Ar, and several other cats. These, disguised as small children, are there to provide support to the wizards' illusions.

Human allies *have* proved to be a pleasant surprise. Arthur will continue to worry about the breach in security—that's his job—but Bill, Chris and, hopefully, Aduke Idowu should expand the athanor's ability to merge into the modern world.

The opening act, Coyotes Howling, comes on stage and begins to play something that makes Arthur very glad that he'd brought earplugs. Pressing them firmly into place diminishes the din to a dull roar.

The band members, probably in imitation of the "fake" satyrs and fauns who are so eagerly anticipated later in the show, have done their stage makeup so that they look like a hybrid between a human and an animal. Arthur guesses from the large, furry ears they mean to resemble coyotes.

The theriomorphs seem to think the whole thing is very funny, but Louhi looks quite thoughtful. No wonder.

Arthur knows that it will be a long time before he forgets his own shock at first seeing Shahrazad changed into a monster possessing all of a wild animal's fierceness but a human's hands. Shahrazad had seemed quite content to stay a coyote after that encounter, but one of the reasons that Frank brought her back to Colorado as soon as possible was to remove her from further temptation to display anomalous shapes to the public.

His other reason had been to get the newly amnesiac Wayne back to Colorado before too much worry could erupt over his disappearance. Wayne will be found in an arroyo on his property, a sizable bump on his head to explain his loss of memory. As he gets better, he will hazily "remember" going for a hike and slipping. That should end the problem.

The Changer, to no one's surprise (but to Arthur's considerable annoyance), had refused to hurry home to teach his daughter prudence and manners.

Pointing out that Frank is as capable of teaching such lessons as he is, the Changer had added that if Shahrazad only behaves when her father is around to beat sense into her brain, she is learning nothing at all. To make it nearly impossible for Arthur to reach him, the Changer has chosen to go to Atlantis, where Amphitrite coyly reports that he is spending a great deal of time with Vera.

An elbow digs into Arthur's side. He notes that Coyotes Howling has left the stage.

The Wanderer (who had arrived driving a vanload of East Coast fauns) mimes pulling out the earplugs, and Arthur reluctantly obeys. Immediately, he notices that the audience noise has diminished to an expectant hum.

"Show's starting," Chris says, as the lights dim, leaving the stage dark.

Purrarr jumps into Arthur's lap, settling on one knee. "Perrfect," she rumbles. Other cats have taken seats on Chris's lap and the Wanderer's.

Over the loud speakers, Lil's voice, impossibly sexy even with electronic distortion, says:

"Welcome."

There is a single plucked lyre note.

"To mystery . . ."

Syrinx piping joins further lyre notes.

"To enchantment . . ."

A faint tapping of drums joins pipe and lyre. Arthur starts to relax, idly stroking Purrarr. Perhaps this will be easier on his ears than he had imagined.

"To magic . . ."

The stage glows with pale pink and lavender light: pastel, like the first gentle hints of dawn. Figures can be just glimpsed beneath dark shadows that look like trees and rocks. The music remains soft, teasing, tempting, but increases in tempo.

"To mystery, enchantment, magic!" Lil suddenly screams. There is a thunder of guitars and drums, an electric wail. "Welcome to *Pan*!"

The lights come on full, bright, illuminating a Grecian grove out of a madman's drug dream. Pulsing strobes break the dancing figures of Tommy Thunderburst and Lil into staccato snapshots.

Tommy wears skintight leopard-print spandex pants and a vine wreath in his hair. His chest is bare. Lil is clad in vine leaves that seem in imminent danger of falling off.

When the strobes abruptly stop, the fauns and satyrs prance on stage. Glaring white lights reveal every inch of their hairy bodies, their horned brows, their hoofed feet, their eager, lascivious eyes.

"Welcome," Lil purrs, her voice coaxing once more, "to reality!"

The audience shrieks in appreciation as Tommy merges into his latest radio hit: "Reality Is What I See."

Arthur feels Tommy's music stir him. In the seats closest

to the King, sasquatch dances with human, faun spins with yeti, *tengu* bop with *pooka*, cats smile and look smug.

A wind tickles his ear.

"Welcome to reality," it whispers.

AUTHOR'S NOTE

IN WRITING THIS STORY, I TOOK SEVERAL LIBERTIES WITH the Yoruba language. Yoruban is a tonal language. If I were to be completely accurate in transcribing it, the tones should be marked.

However, as most readers of English (myself included) find a plethora of accent and pronunciation marks intrusive, I have eliminated them on the most commonly used words (such as Adùké or Mònàmóná). I have retained them in infrequently used words to give some sense of the language's rise and fall.

Readers familiar with Yoruban material may have encountered words such as "Shango" and "orisha" spelled without the "h." As the "h" sound is very soft, it is often omitted or indicated by a dot placed under the "s." I followed the convention used by many of the English writers and included the "h," feeling that it more closely represented the pronunciation of the word.

Monamona is a fictional city.